TO EACH THIS WORLD

The Finest in DAW Science Fiction and Fantasy
by JULIE E. CZERNEDA:

THE CLAN CHRONICLES

Stratification
REAP THE WILD WIND (#1)
RIDERS OF THE STORM (#2)
RIFT IN THE SKY (#3)

The Trade Pact
A THOUSAND WORDS FOR STRANGER (#1)
TIES OF POWER (#2)
TO TRADE THE STARS (#3)

Reunification
THIS GULF OF TIME AND STARS (#1)
THE GATE TO FUTURES PAST (#2)
TO GUARD AGAINST THE DARK (#3)

TALES FROM PLEXIS

* * *

NIGHT'S EDGE
A TURN OF LIGHT (#1)
A PLAY OF SHADOW (#2)
A CHANGE OF PLACE (#3)*

* * *

SPECIES IMPERATIVE
Omnibus Edition
SURVIVAL | MIGRATION | REGENERATION

* * *

WEB SHIFTERS
BEHOLDER'S EYE (#1)
CHANGING VISION (#2)
HIDDEN IN SIGHT (#3)

* * *

WEB SHIFTER'S LIBRARY
SEARCH IMAGE (#1)
MIRAGE (#2)
SPECTRUM (#3)

* * *

IN THE COMPANY OF OTHERS

THE GOSSAMER MAGE

TO EACH THIS WORLD

*Coming soon from DAW

TO EACH THIS WORLD

Julie E. Czerneda

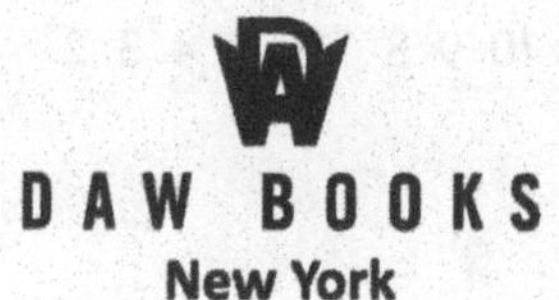

DAW BOOKS
New York

Cover art and design by Faceout Studio / Jeff Miller

Interior ornaments courtesy of Shutterstock

Edited by Sheila E. Gilbert

DAW Book Collectors No. 1932

DAW Books
An imprint of Astra Publishing House
dawbooks.com
DAW Books and its logo are registered trademarks of
Astra Publishing House

Printed in the United States of America

ISBN 9780756415426 (trade paperback) | ISBN 9780756415433 (ebook)

First printing: November 2022

10 9 8 7 6 5 4 3 2

For
Leo and Luke,
each our world.

Acknowledgments

Stories like this take a while to grow, at least for me. The seed for it arrived as I wrote "Down on the Farm," my short story for *Far Frontiers,* edited by Martin H. Greenberg and Larry Segriff. The story was about the future of farming, among other things, but key to it was how we might bring our biology to another world while protecting what already lived there. I envisioned a barrier—in my story created by Earth's settlers—to divide the world in two, separating their biota as long as possible. It seemed prudent and polite.

And utterly fascinating. The idea grew on me, being fascinated by life and its tendency to flout rules. How might such a barrier function? More interestingly, what would happen if it were breached? The notion branched. What if we found a world already divided? Who'd done it and why would they?

How did I tell a story about any and all of this?

Years passed. I kept what was now a folder of notes going but didn't mention it to anyone for the usual reasons. Mostly because I wasn't ready. Fortunately, I'd the kick in the authorly pants I needed from the wonderful Sara Megibow. To establish our author-agent relationship, Sara needed a book proposal from me. I grabbed the folder, wrote it up, Sara sold it to Sheila E. Gilbert (WHOO!), and *To Each This World* became real. For that, Sara, and so much more I thank you. You're a treasure.

Of Sheila, my editor-dear and dear friend these many years—because oh, yes, 2022 is my 25th anniversary of my first book with DAW—I can't say enough. The pandemic kept us apart, but you're always in our hearts, being family. To the next DAW Dinner (TM), quiet moments on the deck, and being together!

My thanks to all at DAW Books, and Penguin Random House Publicity, for their work on this book (and its predecessors), in particular to Jessica Plummer for her wonderful celebratory graphics and Leah Spann for taking over the Internet. Jeff Miller of Faceout Studios, you captured the essence of this book with your spectacular cover and I couldn't be happier. My thanks to Robin Cook for an excellent and helpful copyedit.

This story leans on its share of cutting-edge science and I needed help. My sincere thanks to Brian Cousens (Professor, Igneous Petrology and Geochemistry, Chair, Department of Earth Sciences, Carleton University) for a memorable Zoom call brainstorming plausible alien technology with which to divide a planet. Brian led me to the wondrous possibilities of volcanism and magma. Eric Choi (engineer and space/satellite expert) gave me real world constraints for my satellites. I rewrote three chapters to take full advantage of his knowledge, improving the story immensely. Science rocks! Thank you also to Mark Robinson, stormhunter extraordinaire, who kindly read my weather passages, and David DeGraff, astronomer and writer (and professor at Alfred University), for your insights into the mistakes we might make when leaping into the void. Colleagues and friends. I look forward to thanking you in person, over beer. Any content errors or misinterpretations are, of course, mine.

This book is very personal. The names in it are either part of me or from people part of me. Thank you Bryan, Carol, Chris, Colin, Erin, Frank, Jacqueline, James (plus tritone!), Jeff (captain prof), Jennifer, Maureen, Misty, Philip (Flip), Scott (plus dissonance!), and Tony. Thank you, Roger, for discussions of space and time. All hail my first readers, dear friends Janet Chase and Shannan Palma, who saved my brain and deepened this story, and Ika Koeck, who helped me solidify the derived culture of World III.

The pandemic raged on but fandom—and booksellers—found a way. I did several virtual events and must acknowledge with gratitude not only the organizers and those who attended, but my knight in tech armor, Roger, who'd rush to save the day every time my tech faltered. (The best had to be the time he showed up with a cable from the first floor to hardwire my computer to the Internet.) I participated in SciFiChat, joined Gerald Brandt at his McNally Robinson launch, did workshops and panels at Flights of Foundry, was guest speaker for HAALSA, panelled at When Words Collide, and gave another workshop for the Wordsmith Institute. Bakka-Phoenix Books and Becca hosted the best-ever virtual launch, with real books I signed in front of their owners. Such a joy! I know I've missed many of you. I apologize and have but one excuse. The other event in 2021 was the self-destruction of my laptop in early November, taking with it emails and contacts.

We made it to one in-person event before Omicron arrived. World Fantasy in Montreal. It felt as weird as it did wonderful to be in the company of others again. Our heartfelt thanks to the concom and volunteers and hotel staff for keeping us safe.

By November, when this book comes out, I sincerely hope we'll have stayed the course, cared for one another, and that I'll be able to sign a copy for you in person. There could be hugging. (There'll be hugging. I've been pent. Be forewarned. Run if you must.)

Thank you all.

. . . start a conversation.

Doublet

BETH Seeker cupped her hands to shade her eyes. Seared brown desert stretched to wavering distant lines that might have been hills, but you didn't use Human words for things in the Split.

Human words didn't belong here.

Technically, neither did she. The thought made Beth chuckle as she resumed her task, pulling close another piece of ropy purple vine, careful not to lose any leaves as she wove it around the others she'd selected from her stash.

Wasn't a vine. Weren't leaves. Did have little mouths along the rib you didn't touch if you were fond of your fingers and because it didn't belong here either?

Well, nothing fooled what divided the world better than putting its halves back together. Good thing, because those weren't hills in the distance, north and to the south, dividing the land, but huge round pots filled with melted rock pulled from deep below and kept boiling. How was a mystery. Why, not as much. Try to cross using a machine and lightning shot from the nearest magma pots to toast you in place.

Ancestors named the phenomenon a Sweep, maybe to lessen the terror. Name stuck. So did the fear of it.

Walking was allowed, if you did it smart, moving fast and alone, picking time and place to suit. Problem was, without something from Away, you couldn't stop walking, or make a sound, or drop a thing—

Doublet, they'd called their new home, being old Earth for a pair of words that started the same but came to be different; the meaning suited a planet with its sole land mass split in two. Giving it a name helped some, Beth's forebears confused not to wake where they'd been aimed to go.

A nip warned Beth to shift her thumb.

The Split wasn't natural. Was tech, no doubt of it, alien and potent. At the beginning, there'd been relief. If this world was already inhabited, they'd neighbors over there. Maybe help. All they'd need do was reach the aliens and introduce themselves, a heady dream that crashed against the stark reality of the Split, where nothing lived above ground and whatever was beneath?

Wasn't the talking kind.

Doublet's oceans treacherous and the next generation with the trick to crossing the Split alive, most times, the halves became Home and Away. Home was good to the settlers. Doublet's Humans chose surnames for their children and children's children from where they were born, names like Blueridge and Firstfall, it being important to maximize outcrosses in those first generations. Down through five or so to Beth's, now it was custom to pick a partner from as unfamiliar a place to you and yours as was, and a particularly free stage of life when one traveled in search, hosted by any.

After that, your name might change, if you'd a thing you were better at than others. Then you were named for it, rest of your days. Beth Redriver, she'd been born and raised; partnered, loved, and raised children of her own to independence.

Having her own, she'd become Beth Seeker, that being the job she did better than others—better than most, truth be—and roamed the Split as few dared, crossing into Away in search of neighbors who didn't want to be found, if they still existed at all, and to bring back needful things.

She'd have gone for curiosity's sake, like a kid drawn to what wasn't known, over what was.

Landed her this job, not that she'd a complaint.

To start a conversation.

New Earth

Preface

A shipwrecked sailor drinks the last from a bottle. Rum, maybe, or laudanum. He's sitting on a beach, perhaps, or a rock—where it's cold or warm, sheltered by pine or palm trees. Wherever he is, he stares without blinking at the horizon-spanning ocean that lies between him and his family, his past, all he's known; a separation not only of space, but time. By now, the toddler he kissed goodbye on the dock will be talking. Before he's found—if ever he's found—she might be grown, warning her babes of the sea, for it swallowed her father whole and broke her mother's heart.

He makes sure the bottle's dry inside. His message is ready. A strip of his shirt, stretched between rocks. Soot from a cooled ember for slow, careful lettering. He rolls the strip tightly and pushes it inside the bottle, replacing the cork with slow twists until it sets in place.

Before he can doubt, the sailor walks into the water, perhaps, or climbs a rock. He's marked the current with knowing eyes or guesses. Practiced the throw with rocks or wood or not at all.

Stretches one arm to point at home. Whips the other around and releases the bottle—

He watches or turns away. Spots the glint of floating glass or doesn't. The message is what counts.

"I'M ALIVE. JOEY LACE."

"See you on the other side."

ON the day the message probe reached New Earth—more precisely was intercepted on approach and began its passage through the hands of consecutively more alarmed individuals on the surface—Arbiter Henry m'Yama t'Nowak was on the other side of the planet, weeding his grandfather's vegetables.

A peaceful, long-anticipated afternoon's task, weeding, punctuated by occasional visits from his grandfather, who leaned elbows on the porch rail to survey Henry's progress from beneath bushy, wild eyebrows.

Majick Nowak was the sum of his grandfather's name, which said a great deal, Henry believed, about the man who'd raised him. A first name was a family gift. The *type'* or *t'* prefix to the last meant the individual's genome had been added to the Human Diversity Expansion Database. Majick wasn't interested, having the family genealogy in a box in the attic, with little bags of baby teeth donated by successive Tooth Elves dating back, he claimed, to Arrival—when the Sleeper Ship *Adamant* landed and woke her passengers.

Majick had also refused, when finished school, to pick the aspirational *mark'* or *m'* signifying an historical figure from the Origin Earth's Archive to emulate in his life. Farmers on any world aspired not to starve, he'd say, half joking.

Half not, Henry thought, smiling to himself as he stretched. The produce from this garden went straight to his grandfather's kitchen, anything extra to the roadside stand. He did his best to help whenever here.

And didn't mention the unplanted fields and rusting machinery. Like its neighbors, the farm was fading, starved for new blood. As Arbiter, he saw the figures. Birthrates. Demographics. On reaching ten and half million, New Earth had opened the next new region. The Southern Plains would siphon away the young and adventurous for the foreseeable future and there was no preventing it.

Things were, his grandfather would say, what they were. Abandoned farms would be consolidated and put under the care of Alt-Intels, once their work preparing the plains was done. The sentient constructs were efficient and careful of the land, but it wouldn't be part of them. A lifestyle would become history.

They weren't there yet. Henry eased himself down the row, ignoring the complaints from the knees and back he hadn't asked to bend in weeks.

Settled, he drew his fingers along the line of cowering blue-green sprouts. Grass he was sure of—the rest, not so much, but the low, fat plants he'd plucked out had to be weeds. *Weren't they?*

He focused with renewed confidence. Pluck. Pluck—

"Henry." A hand fell on his shoulder. "Time you took a break."

Henry glanced up at his grandfather, haloed by the sun. He hadn't far to look, Majick being stocky and short. *Shorter than his last visit.* "Almost done." This row. Twenty more stretched behind him.

"They'll be here tomorrow. Come sit with me." A gnarled hand gripped two bottles by the neck, glass dewed with tempting condensation.

Henry suddenly realized he wasn't only overheated but parched. He gave a grateful nod as he got to his feet.

Staggered a step, and his grandfather reached out to steady him. "Hat," he scolded.

"Forgot," Henry confessed sheepishly, feeling a boy again. He'd been eager to be out in the sun.

Majick shook his head.

They sat on the porch stairs, in welcome shade and comfortable silence, sipping beer. Watched the chickens hunt and pounce between the rows. "Look how hard I worked today. I've callouses," Henry boasted, showing the palm of his right hand.

His grandfather showed his, the skin thick and furrowed. "These are callouses, lad. Those are blisters." A grin. "Another beer?"

"I'll get it."

When Henry returned to the porch, lofty white clouds showed along the horizon. "Thunderstorm tonight?"

"What, no meteorological report to consult? No fancy experts?"

He tipped his bottle to his grandfather's. "I've you." A relief, to shed the tech normally surrounding him, to silence the constant data stream and demands of others. It had been a long three weeks, arbitrating the dispute between Earth Station Niablo and the Kmet.

The Kmet not being Human and Niablo's comptroller choosing to ignore that simple fact had complicated the situation in every possible way.

Fortunately, humanity and the Kmet had achieved a remarkable level of mutual understanding since the Kmet Portal first appeared in orbit, when Henry had been a boy living on this farm with his grandparents. Necessarily so, as the Kmet hadn't left, seeming content to have found company in a universe kmeth described as barren and lonely and dull.

At least, that was the conclusion of the linguists who'd scrambled to interpret an alien's use of Human words, picked up from New Earth broadcasts. That the Kmet came prepared for peaceful conversation calmed a startled Human population and certainly made things easier.

A succession of Arbiters, the Kmet having insisted on a single Human authority, negotiated orbital safety regulations and protocols, crafting the Duality that today governed everything from pilot rotations to communication equipment. The Kmet needed partners to obtain the minerals kmeth required and cleverly gave Humans technology requiring them as well. To obtain those, the Kmet sent Human ships across space through kmeths' Portals; kmeth did not share how those worked.

Beyond that? The Kmet valued certain Human foods, if not art or history, and, while Earth scientists continued to obsessively ponder everything about the Kmet, the aliens seemed disinterested in learning more about Humans or their planet. The Kmet stayed in space, Humans on their world, and the sole interface remained whomever Earth's governments designated as the Arbiter.

Henry'd held the post now for seven years, would—barring calamity—until retirement, and was doing, he hoped, a decent job of it. He'd settled the Niablo dispute—with a great deal of help, freely admitted. The Arbiter's Office had authorization to second any and all expertise, planet-wide, and he hadn't hesitated to use it. As a result, the newly built station would gradually expand its orbit so as to no longer impede the Kmet's view of Earth, a less economical location, according to Niablo. In recognition—or as a gift or possibly retribution, even experts unsure on the finer points—the Kmet offered kmeth's Portal to transit three Niablo freighters to Rogue 58 and back at no charge to deliver spare parts to the mines there and bring back refined metals.

There'd been the usual Kmet clause insisting Humans not loiter, whatever that meant to the aliens. Nothing that breathed willingly lingered on one of the sunless, hostile worlds the Kmet favored for mining.

His grandfather pushed back his hat and squinted at the bright lilac sky. He licked a finger and poked it up, considering a moment. "Yup," he declared. "We'll need to bring in the chickens."

Henry nodded, content to have his universe encompassed by poultry and rain.

After saying goodnight to his grandfather, Henry went out on the porch to enjoy the play of lightning as the storm rolled closer across the plain. He cradled a glass of the fine whiskey he'd brought, feeling the last tension melt from his bones, replaced by the satisfying, if painful, twinge of newly used muscle. The blisters on his palm had responded to cream. He put a hand to the nape of his neck, felt the heat of sunburn, and grinned ruefully. *Hat tomorrow or he'd not hear the end of it.*

Involuntarily, his fingers swept up through his hair, the tips feeling his scalp for lumps, proving to himself there were none. The neural lace lay beneath bone, riding his brain within its protective meniscus. He should be used to it by now—*was,* Henry thought, dragging his betraying hand down.

Truth be told, he no longer liked hats and let his hair grow shaggy between trims, having to wind up his nerve to endure anything on his head or anyone touching it; a not uncommon reaction, he'd been assured, the longer he spent away.

That's what they called it, *being away,* when Henry m'Yama t'Nowak, Majick Nowak's grandson, sunburned and achy, was popped into a can and his mind went—

ARBITER, PLEASE RESPOND.

The summons was subvocal, a vibration against his inner ear he heard despite the rumble of thunder, and entirely unwelcome.

Even if it did originate from his Facultative Linked Intelligent Polymorph, the latest Human iteration of Kmet technology, placed within the Arbiter's Office by the other Alt-Intels of New Earth as being the most likely employer to consider weird as wonderful.

And Flip was. A companion, colleague, and friend. *Who knew better.*

"No," Henry said firmly, closing his eyes. "I told you I wasn't to be bothered, Flip. I'm on vacation." *Doctors' orders—*

WHILE I REGRET THE NECESSITY TO DISOBEY YOUR INSTRUCTIONS, HENRY, I HAVE AN IMPERATIVE NEWS BRIEF TO DELIVER. A PROBE HAS ARRIVED FROM THE HALCYON CLASS STARSHIP *HENDERSON.*

Henry found himself on his feet, whiskey dripping from his fingers; somehow he kept hold of the glass. "A sleeper ship?!"

CORRECT, HENRY. ONE OF SIX SUCH STARSHIPS TO DEPART THE SYSTEM IN THE YEAR—

"Yes, yes. I know." *Everyone knew.* You learned about the sleeper ship program in school, with its high drama and Human sacrifice. New Earth's first and only attempt to set foot on other worlds, to fulfill the vow made a millennia ago to keep the Human species spreading outward.

A vow grown more compelling with the loss of their original home, for Origin Earth fell silent during their ancestors' journey here; her final messages passed beyond New Earth before the *Adamant* landed and woke her passengers to listen. No way to know what happened within the preceding 120 years to end the civilization that sent them forth. No way to know if other ships had launched after theirs.

No way to know they weren't alone.

Using the ship's Archive, determined to treat their world better, the descendants' first focus was to improve manufacturing and agriculture methods. Only when confident they'd thrive on New Earth without harming it did they reach for space once more; the Halcyon Project became a shining beacon of how far humanity had come. Would now go—

Fate intervened. A forecast solar storm had rushed the launch from the orbital space dock, overshadowing what was to have been a planet-wide celebration. No time for speeches or vid coverage. Worse, no farewells to loved ones about to be parted forever.

Then the ships were lost—

Apparently not all. "How sure is it?" Henry asked numbly.

THE PROBE HAS BEEN AUTHENTICATED AS BEING MANUFACTURED BY THE *HIGHER THAN SKY SHIPYARDS,* TWO HUNDRED AND SIX YEARS AGO, AND THE TIMING OF ITS ARRIVAL DOES ALIGN WITH PREDICTION. THE NUMBER OF AMATEUR ASTRONOMERS DEDICATED TO WATCHING FOR SUCH PROBES IS IMPRESSIVE, HENRY. SEVERAL HAVE CLAIMED TO BE THE FIRST TO SPOT THIS ONE.

His grandfather had set up a telescope in the barn loft; Henry's younger self had been politely disinterested. The sleeper ships, if they'd survived the storm, had a maximum sustained velocity of one fifth light speed. Six message probes were to be accelerated to that speed as the final act of each mighty engine, pre-descent to the surface of a new world. One to New Earth, to confirm humanity had its foothold in the stars. Five flung at their sister ships' destinations in a bold, oh-so-Human effort to maintain connection between impossibly far-flung settlements.

Henry remembered wondering what those settlers hoped to gain. It wouldn't be company and couldn't be help.

"*A century out, a century home,*" he murmured. "*If any ship made it, that's when we'll know.* Damn."

PARDON, HENRY?

"A children's—I learned it—doesn't matter." He had to wrap his head around the fact, and quickly, that the effort might have succeeded.

Hail arrived as Henry hurried across the porch, kicking up gouts of dust and rattling the old metal roof his grandfather refused to replace. "Flip. The message—was there a message?" For all he knew, the *Henderson* might have spat her probes if about to collide with an asteroid.

THERE ARE FORTY-SEVEN MESSAGES WAITING FOR YOU, HENRY, MARKED URGENT.

He was through the door, running barefoot through the dark kitchen. Curtains billowed in the wind, an open window letting in rain. Henry changed direction. "Ignore my incoming mail. The *probe,* Flip." Setting his glass on the counter, he leaned over the sink to close and latch the window. "Did it contain a message from the *Henderson*?"

YES, HENRY. A pause as Flip consulted. A SHEET OF LAMINATED FOIL WAS FOUND IN THE PROBE, INSCRIBED WITH STELLAR COORDINATES DATED, IN EARTH TERMS, NINETY-NINE YEARS AGO.

A message in a bottle. "They made it," Henry whispered to himself, stunned.

THERE ARE NOW EIGHTY-EIGHT, CORRECTION, ONE HUNDRED AND THIRTY-TWO MESSAGES WAITING FOR YOUR ATTENTION, HENRY, AND EVERY ONE CONCERNS THE SIGNIFICANCE OF THE PROBE.

He gripped the edge of the sink. Coruscating raindrops obscured the yard, the porch. There'd be little streams racing between rows in the garden, a torrent in the roadside ditch, and the Arbiter had to gather badly scattered wits before touching that mail queue.

His first thought, clear and chilling: *This isn't the world the sleeper ships left: humanity's then-furthest-known outpost, bold and curious.*

The probe returned to the Duality, the carefully orchestrated partnership of Human and Kmet. To a Human population who'd spent the past two centuries down a very different path. As for curiosity?

Since the instant of first contact, the defining trait of their species had refocused through that lens, every research project, school subject, and proposed regulation rethought within the context of shared Kmet technology and, yes, kmeth's potential reaction. New Earth prospered, presumably Kmet had by kmeth's own inscrutable measure, and—

The next and crucial thought: *No Human on this Earth would board a starship for any reason, let alone agree to sleep for a hundred years on the vague promise of a new world.*

Why should they? A Kmet Portal could send them anywhere in an instant.

Including, now, a planet Humans *had* reached, possibly thrived upon for a century, and of the growing list of voices waiting for the Arbiter's undivided attention, Henry had the sinking feeling most, if not all, were demanding he ask the Kmet to do just that.

The *no loitering* clause in the Niablo agreement came to mind.

Along with the absolute inability of his predecessors to convince the Kmet that New Earth, lacking starships, had once sent forth a veritable fleet of them.

According to Kmet, Humans were *here*, not there, as any Kmet was *here*, not there, and not a single Human had been able to parse a deeper meaning than the obvious. Kmet weren't, in fact, visiting. Though yet to touch the planet's surface, the Kmet considered Earth in some fashion home. *Here.*

Now, in one battered little spacecraft—if his memory of a museum trip served, the size of the kettle beside him—came proof of Humans *there*.

What became of the Duality then?

A question for the Arbiter of any species-critical dispute to have answered before contacting the news services. "Flip, are the Kmet aware?"

THE PRESUMPTION IS KMETH WOULDN'T HAVE NOTICED, HENRY, AS SIMILAR SPACE DEBRIS IS INTERCEPTED ON A DAILY BASIS. THE REVELATION OF THIS INFORMATION IS, OF COURSE, THE ARBITER'S DECISION.

The rain would soften the soil and make weeding easier tomorrow, if muddy. He'd boots.

No longer remotely his concern. "How soon can you get here?"

I *AM* HERE, HENRY. With amusement.

A huge disc eased down through the rain to fill the view out the window, hovering just above the garden plants. Henry threw an arm over his eyes as it stopped rotating and gaudy landing lights snapped on around its outer rim, blazing through the kitchen and unmissable in any direction, storm or no storm.

"Turn those off!" he ordered.

Flying Saucer Flip obeyed, plunging him back into the dark, save for lingering spots of afterglow he couldn't blink away.

Under the circumstances, Henry was *not* going to acknowledge the accuracy of the rendering, however much he shared the polymorph's fascination with anachronistic science fiction television.

"Give me ten minutes to pack."

Vacation over.

A small plaque by the door dated the farmhouse as part of the infamous Second Spread, 450 S.A., Since Arrival. A surge in population had rushed the expansion into the fertile central plains of the continent, the draft relocating five percent of families from their coastal homes to the new land. Tragedy followed. A blizzard, the worst yet recorded on New Earth, struck while they were sheltered only by tents; less than half survived. The planetary government resigned. The draft was abandoned and subsequent spreads were done as originally intended, cautious and careful of a world they were learning, regardless how dire the need.

The farmhouse's age showed in its narrow, steep staircase centered between kitchen and the large room with its stone fireplace. The room had been his grandmother's studio, Henry's playroom, the family party room, and, its most recent iteration, his grandfather's library, with a pair of big shabbily comfy chairs waiting.

Still half-blind, Henry felt his way up the worn uneven stairs. Before he reached the top, a soft light came on to reveal slippered feet and striped pajama legs. "Hens all right?"

Somehow Henry wrenched his brain from interstellar space to chickens. "I coaxed the last two in before the storm hit." Unable to see his grandfather's shadowed face, he hesitated.

"You're off, then." The beam of light rose and flickered off. Finding the switch—a house with switches, no less—his grandfather turned on the overhead fixture. His expression was a mix of solemn and resigned. "C'mon, Henry. I'll keep you company while you pack up."

Most of Henry's vacations were cut short, but this would be the first where he hadn't a chance to sleep in his own bed at least once. He touched the other man's shoulder in passing. "Sorry for the rush. You know how it is."

"The garden will survive." Eyebrows waggled dramatically. "What you've left of it."

"Hey—" Henry mock-protested.

"Might be some beans you missed."

Those were the beans? Shaking his head, Henry led the way into his bedroom, where he went straight to the corner wardrobe. He hadn't brought much, this trip. Hadn't needed to, the wardrobe containing an assortment of his about-the-farm clothing, so it was mainly a matter of retrieving toiletries and what to wear.

His grandfather sat on the window bench, watching him change, hands on his knees. "Straight to the office, is it?"

Or to a waiting crowd of reporters. Henry shrugged on his jacket. "Probably."

"Don't let them push you back into that can. You're still pale from the last stint." A frown. "Where you aren't bright red. That's gonna peel."

Henry touched the back of his neck. Hot and getting sore. *As for the rest?* He grimaced. "I won't know till I get into my messages, but don't worry. They take good care of me." He picked up his bag and turned, abruptly ready.

Far from it, inside.

"See they do." His grandfather stood, gripping Henry's shoulders. "What you do's important, I know. Settling folks, finding a way to get things done. Though why that brain of yours can't tell a bean sprout from a dandeburr—?" With a gentle shake. "Proud of you." Gruffly. "Always have been. Always will be."

His grandfather smelled of clean laundry and hand soap, with a whiff of the whiskey they'd shared earlier on his breath. His eyes, this close, were misted by cataracts he couldn't be bothered to have fixed during the growing season.

The house wasn't alone in being old and worn and precious.

Not a thought to leave on. Henry found a smile. "I've had a good teacher. See you on the other side," he promised, as he did every trip, and gathered his grandfather close.

***

Flip lowered a short ladder, the hatch raised overtop to make it less likely Henry would slip on a wet rung, though wind gusts swirled the rain in every direction, including under the porch roof. His grandfather, whose reaction to the flying saucer had been a reassuring snicker, would wave from the open kitchen door.

Henry tossed his bag inside and started up, careful of his footing. Stopped suddenly, blinking raindrops from his eyes. "Flip! I forgot to call Ralph."

Flip's voice came from inside the shuttle. "I took care of it, Henry. See?"

He turned and squinted, shielding his eyes with his free hand, buffeted by wind and rain.

There. His grandfather was waving, his grin catching the porchlight. Next to him, waist-high, stood the companion Henry'd arranged when his visits became less frequent and more interrupted. Pre-polymorph tech, Ralph resembled his namesake, an oversized, hairy blend of authenticized Great Dane and possibly spaniel, with limpid brown eyes, remembered by the family as a Very Good Dog, which he'd been, most of the time.

The alternate-intelligence, or Alt-Intel, edition of Ralph guarded the chickens and barked at strangers. Alt was also a full citizen of New Earth who played a mean game of chess, conversed—or argued—with Majick as needed, and came fully equipped with sensors to monitor alts charge's health and a list of emergency contacts if Henry couldn't be reached.

His grandfather conveyed his displeasure at being monitored by insisting this Ralph shed more than the original. And that alt stay in the basement while Henry was home, a flagrant abuse of a sentient construct had Ralph, knowing alts charge well, not agreed to the arrangement. After all, alt needed downtime to compose, alts music quite popular among alts kind, if not Humans.

Among Kmet? Impossible to say. Kmeth used machines to operate the Portals and assist in mining, but these were autonomous, not sentient. Having noted the inconvenient confusion when the aliens faced different individual Humans, the Alt-Intels of New Earth had proposed the existence of non-biological intelligence be kept off the negotiating table until the Kmet expressed an interest in the possibility. To date, kmeth had not. Perhaps could not.

Humans didn't mind keeping something back, especially something as precious and important as humanity's partners on New Earth. Including the one shouting at Henry. "Henry, you now have five hundred and thirty-two communications. Correction. Six hundred and—"

"Coming, Flip." Henry waved once more at his grandfather before turning to climb the ladder into the shuttle.

Inside was round, as he'd expected. Bare, he hadn't, and Henry hesitated, bag in hand.

"Here, Henry." Flip opened a hidden cupboard door to the accompaniment of dramatic and unnecessary beeps. Repeated the sounds after Henry stowed his bag and the door closed, then asked hopefully, "Wasn't that fun?"

Henry half-smiled. "It was, Flip. Ah, where do I sit?"

With another series of beeps, these higher in tone, a seat folded out from the wall, a harness attached. A small, round table rose from the floor next to it without sound effects.

When Henry sat down, the tabletop began to glow an eerie yellow. He pulled on the harness, noticing it was unusually substantial. "Flip. No spinning with me inside, please."

Silence.

"Flip?"

"Understood, Henry." With disappointment. "You now have—"

"Good. Auto-reply to all incoming messages with my ETA at the—" He shouldn't assume. Other orders might have arrived. "We're heading to the Arbiter's Tower, aren't we?"

"Yes, unless you have another destination in mind, Henry."

"No. A summary of the messages, Flip."

"Preparing."

Henry leaned his head back, careful of his sunburnt neck, to find himself gazing at a featureless gray ceiling. "A view, Flip, please."

The ceiling became transparent.

Rain. Rain. A flash of lightning lit the clouds around them. *As if inside a bag of giant marshmallows.*

Then they rose above the storm. He began to make out stars.

"I have the summary, Henry. The majority express a firm belief there will be descendants of the *Henderson*'s complement, regardless of the lack of any evidence to suggest this is the case."

Flip sounded perplexed. Henry smiled at the sky. "What do they want me to do about it?"

"Requests are split between urgent demands for you to expedite the reunion of such descendants with Earth's inhabitants and those urging you to conceal the probe's arrival. The latter category is divided between those who express anxiety over Kmet reaction to the news and those concerned for its impact on New Earth."

Covered the options. "I have to get ahead of this. Forget the flight plan. Clear the road, Flip." In an emergency, the Arbiter could claim right of way, a privilege Henry hadn't invoked in his term of office.

"Yes, Henry! Broadcasting now." A pause, then, with slightly disturbing anticipation, "Please tighten your harness."

Flip didn't get many chances to show off in Earth's atmosphere. *There'd be saucer sightings.* At the cringeworthy notion, Henry almost changed his mind.

Planet-wide consternation over the probe's significance was, if not an emergency, the signal one might be approaching faster than Flip—especially once the Kmet were involved.

He needed information before that happened. "Put me in contact with an expert on sleeper ships, Flip."

To talk with the Kmet—his hand strayed to his scalp. He needed to be more than this. Needed the hardwiring of that other body, his copy, his epitome. It meant climbing into the can—*again.* Meant letting go of his real self to operate inside what wasn't—*again.*

An epitome was always prepared and waiting for the Arbiter. If the Arbiter wasn't the least ready—*didn't matter.*

"Have the second floor get ready."

"Henry, you have not spent the recommended time as—"

Himself? "I'll recoup on the other side. Do it, Flip."

"When will we be brave again?"

WHEN Henry arrived on the second floor, he found his medical team sitting around a table, playing cards amid stacks of emptied fish and chips boxes. Behind them, through closed double doors with frosted glass and multiple locks, lay the Arbiter's Repository. On the wall above the doors, in stark black lettering, was the mission statement of the Public Safety Commission, Epitome Division, otherwise known as the Print House.

No More Heartbreak.

The words always caught his eye; today, they shook him to the core.

Two hundred years ago, Henry's predecessor had authorized the emergency launch of the sleeper ships ahead of a burst of highly energized particles from the Sun. Saving them, it now appeared, New Earth's last space farers.

The irony stung. Unable to flee, the thousands living in orbit and in colonies elsewhere in the system rushed to their shelters to wait.

By the time the massive CME intersected Earth's orbit, the planet's population was as ready as possible, snug beneath atmosphere. Warned, far from fearful, people around the world had looked forward to an astonishing once-in-a-lifetime light show as the magnetosphere above them danced.

What came was catastrophe.

When the stream of highly energized plasma intersected Earth's orbit, as predicted, it slammed through her layers of satellites and space stations. Communications were temporarily disrupted, as expected.

Charges collected. Released as tiny bolts of lightning shooting through control systems. Predicted. Expected. Nothing beyond repair—until something on a manufacturing station exploded.

Panels and modules kesslered like scythes across the orbits of two other stations, shattering those. The debris fields began their inevitable, unstoppable decline into the atmosphere. Most burned harmlessly on re-entry.

Some didn't.

Thousands fled projected impact sites; not all made it. Whole cities were lost, New Earth's launch capability with them, stranding those in space.

After the final piece struck, every effort was made to rebuild, to get supplies up to the survivors before theirs ran out, to get medical help to those sickened by radiation before they died, but there wasn't time, there was too much damage, there were mistakes of haste and desperation, there was—

Never any hope. All of New Earth listened as the cries of those beyond reach failed, one by one. It took one hundred and fifty-seven days for the last to fall silent, a time known from then on as the Heartbreak, and it changed everything.

The inhabitants of New Earth had come to accept their aloneness, to take responsibility. With Origin Earth gone, theirs was *the* Earth, home of humanity.

A home now damaged and fragile. To lose anyone else to space was unthinkable. Rebuilding the space program, other than essential satellites, paused until a safe way could be found. Research into artificial intelligence and machine servants accelerated. The Public Safety Commission was tasked with removing any risk to the living.

No More Heartbreak. The same goal lay behind every act of the Arbiter's Office since, if not as bluntly stated. As for how?

The answer waited behind those frosted doors.

Spotting Henry, Neurologist Aadila m'Bath t'Fascione folded her cards and set them down. "Long time no see."

A joke—and not, Henry knew. He'd walked out of this room the day before yesterday; he shouldn't have been back for weeks, even months. "Hello again."

Ben m'Nabulsi t'Humppi had turned in his seat, an arm along its back. His eyebrows shot up. "You forget something, Henry?" Ben was from the Print House, assigned to this repository with its single client to monitor the time spent in and out of self—and prevent exactly what Flip had fussed about: returning before he'd fully recovered.

"My epitome," Henry said firmly. "I need it. Immediately."

The rest abandoned the game to stare at him. Aadila's head began to swing in a negative; Ben opened his mouth.

Henry raised his hand. "I've a meeting with Kmet-Here." Meaning he'd need his xenologist and linguist, specialists in the Kmet, consulting in real time. "And if that goes well?" He pointed upwards.

Meaning a trip into space.

They got up without argument. The two assistants went to the doors, uncoding the various locks in sequence.

Waiting his turn, Ben beckoned Henry over, then bent to his ear. "Delegate. It's not a bad word."

Henry chuckled. "I'm working on it."

The office did have three arbiter-secondaries, presently negotiating a dispute between the suboceanic cities of the northern pole and surface shipping interests; a property claim impacting lupin migration; and a recurring spot of trouble over water use in the Central Marshlands he might have to take over after dealing with the probe. None could take over for him in this; by law and the practical constraints of an uncertain language interface, relations between Human and Kmet had to be negotiated via a single point of authority.

The Kmet knew *him*.

"I gardened," Henry added, louder so they'd all hear. *Counted as exercise.* "Outside."

Refraining from comment, though a heavy eyebrow twitched, Ben pressed his palm on the second-last lock, granting the official approval of the Print House. He stepped aside for Henry to open the final one. Consent and, with the prickle of subdermal needles taking samples, confirmation of identity.

The doors slipped into the walls. The room beyond was full of white mist, clearing from the floor up as suction drew it aside. As the team entered with Henry, lights brightened to full, sparkling on metal and ceramic, dispelling shadows. A surgical table waited in the middle, overhung by a polymorphic array, quiescent as yet. To either side were the long, low encapsulation chambers known as cans, connected to the wall and floor by myriad pipes and cables. Their domed lids were down and opaque, but Henry knew the can on the left had an occupant: an epitome, a living copy meticulously grown and maintained by the Print House, lacking only a mind.

The can on the right was his.

His heart began to pound.

It felt like death every time, climbing into the can, watching the lid come down. Didn't matter how many times he'd been through this, it did.

Having accessed the repository's schematics, Flip kept trying to show Henry vintage horror films with similar rooms ready for their unsuspecting victims; he'd yet to be sure if the polymorph thought to help or had developed a disturbingly macabre sense of humor.

A hand brushed his neck. Henry started.

"Sorry." It was only Fetu, checking his skin. "Will you want the sunburn, Henry? It'll only take a minute," he informed him, gesturing to the array that was his pride and joy. Epitome Technician Fetu m'Biggiogera t'Moules was in charge of matching Henry's epitome to his self's current appearance, from hair length to any conspicuous changes such as a new scar or tattoo, whatever his mind would require to settle into another body and believe it hadn't left.

"I'll manage without, thanks."

Fetu nodded, trusting his judgment, well aware of his rating. To function through an epitome required an ability to focus as well as an inner stability regardless of outer stress; Henry'd tested at the high end of those scales.

Existent Technician Astrid m'Tisherman t'Rizzo tsked. "That'll peel." Astrid watched over his real self, his *existent* in their parlance; she and Fetu maintained a friendly competition over his iterations that Henry found faintly disturbing. "With your permission, I'll leave a note for the maintenance crew to add skin cream to your regime."

He gave it with a nod. Astrid was the best the Print House had to offer, as was the always-focused Capsule Mechanic Elea m'Wilcox t'Buwalda, currently on the floor under one of the two cans in her charge. Henry's, as it happened.

Team Nurse Norman m'de Lellis t'Hatoski handed him a robe and slippers, along with an opinionated grunt echoed by the neurologist and a piercing head-to-toe look. As usual. Henry had yet to learn if the former surgical room nurse disapproved of epitomes in general or habitually stored his current state in memory, Norman abjuring machine scans. He did know the nurse had come out of retirement for the neurologist, and Aadila would work with no one else.

Aadila and the other five were the face of the process to Henry, reassuringly familiar by now. In the beginning, he'd thought to introduce himself to maintenance as well, but Ben dissuaded him. *How had he put it?* Those who cared for the mindless preferred it when their subjects didn't start a conversation.

The rest got busy at the cans and table, doing whatever was necessary to put him in and bring out his copy, created by the Print House to be ready the day of Henry's promotion to arbiter-primary, maintained here under their auspices.

Preferring not to watch, Henry went into the prep room. He stripped to his skin, putting his clothes, sandals, and effects into the cupboard provided for them. When he closed its door, a second would open, allowing the techs to retrieve his things for his epitome to wear.

Henry stepped in the shower and dutifully cleaned himself. Hot water stung the sunburn, a reminder of weeding in the sunshine. *Better study bean sprouts before he went back.* It was important to have thoughts like that, about being himself, this self. A normal rotation, say, for a spacer going up to an orbital station, was five weeks as an epitome, fifteen back on New Earth as yourself. Ben had Henry's latest list, as did Flip, and likely his grandfather. Six and a half weeks away, then two days.

Now—*However long it took.* Henry shut off the water, letting the air jets blow him dry, bending to get his hair. He combed the mass back with a swipe of his fingers as he came out, sitting on the bench beside the pale yellow jumpsuit provided for his use. The paper-thin garment featured a wealth of concealed openings he'd rather not think about at the moment.

He leaned his head back, closing his eyes. "Flip."

YES, HENRY, the voice in his skull answered immediately, warm with concern. HOW ARE YOU FEELING?

Naked, damp, and terrified.

He let it all go. "Ready for my verification." Proof he was the person who went into the can. Proof he hadn't been replaced or forced or drugged—Henry had his own list of extravagant what-ifs. Poor Ben would be scandalized to think the Arbiter, of all people, held such archaic superstitions. "When will we be brave again? Repeat it, please, Flip."

'WHEN WILL WE BE BRAVE AGAIN?' In his voice, Flip literal by default. I WILL REQUEST VERIFICATION WHEN YOU ARE IN YOUR EPITOME, HENRY.

If he failed to say it correctly, Flip had standing orders to refuse to obey what only *looked* like the Arbiter and to send an alarm screaming along emergency channels. It wasn't much and hardly foolproof. The consequences, should he happen to forget his own phrase and Flip send the alarm, would be messy, to say the least.

The team in the next room would probably never talk to him again.

He might lose his job.

Didn't matter. "Thank you, Flip."

Henry opened his eyes and picked up the suit.

Time to enter another skin.

". . . a convenient nuisance."

SUNBEAMS poured through the windows of the Arbiter's Office, situated atop the tallest tower in Greater Maritime City. Upper floors and penthouses had lost their appeal after the Kmet Portal arrived to hang overhead, making the rent reasonable enough for governments and nonprofits.

Henry doubted the people who'd fled this real estate market comprehended the atavistic nature of the impulse to keep their collective heads low. *Just as well.* It wasn't as if six floors nearer the ground was significantly further from space—or the Kmet.

He'd urge them not to worry, if they ever asked. Space wasn't coming any closer and if the aliens had come to invade their planet like the monsters of Flip's movies, Henry wouldn't be standing here waiting for the uplink to Kmet-Here, the individual in the Portal orbiting Earth, who was apparently finishing kmeth's lunch.

The wait had its benefit. He used the time to reacquaint himself with his epitome, a minor adjustment to a body abruptly alert, well-fed and rested; easier, in that sense, than the return to self, with its disconcerting weakness. The can took over his self's autonomic functions and stimulated his muscle and bone to the extent possible without affecting the link, but immobility cost.

On the bright side, before he came back, his sunburn might heal.

The body was fine. Was *his*.

Something wasn't quite right, though. His fingers strayed to the base of his skull, worked up into his hair, hunting—*what?*

He dropped his hand, stared at the palm. *No blisters.* That had to be it. "Flip, status check?"

In his office, Flip's smooth comforting tones emerged from unseen speakers. "Unchanged from four point three minutes ago, Henry, when you last asked. I'm on the roof, ready to take you to the Portal. The weather is fair." A pause. "Needless repetition is unlike you. Would you care to repeat the verification phrase?"

When will we be brave again . . .

"We both know I'm me," Henry said tersely. "I just—" *What?* "—wanted to hear your voice," he finished, despite knowing that wasn't it at all.

"If so, Henry, I would be happy to read to you. I recently acquired a complete set of antique mysteries from the Archive, by Louise Penny, which I believe you would enjoy. Or I could—"

"Not right now, thanks." He leaned a shoulder against the wall, staring out the window without seeing the view. "Maybe it's coming back so soon that feels different. It's nothing to worry about," he added to forestall the polymorph alerting the repository team. *Flip could be a little too helpful at times.*

"At your request, none of the additional connections within your neural lace have been filled, Henry. Is it possible this is what you feel? It was—" with, yes, disapproval "—a change from routine not recommended by the repository personnel."

Was that it? His grandfather'd teased him about the experts in his head. During his vacation, he'd relished being free of them, but that had been as himself. It was disturbing to think his epitomeself somehow needed them. Yet, now that Henry examined it, the *different* feeling might almost be . . . hunger.

Individuals able to form a solid neural connection with an epitome were called oneirics. The Arbiter's Office kept a list of qualified volunteers, sorted by knowledge or backgrounds of use in a negotiation, and normally, before Henry moved into his epitome, those oneirics were connected for him, ready to be summoned at his command. Entering the dream state, they'd be guests within a space created by his mind, or passengers to ride along, seeing as he did. With additional technology at each interface, an oneiric could even be projected, experiencing his surroundings for themselves.

As an epitome, unlike those lost in the Heartbreak, he was never alone. The epitome-oneiric connection was immune to solar storms and unaffected by distance, being an entanglement at the quantum level Henry gladly left to the physicists.

Yet alone he was. This being anything but a normal negotiation, he'd insisted on interviewing his potential oneirics first. In person. To be sure they were willing to come with him on this extraordinary journey, while staying on New Earth.

If the delay gave his epitome cravings, so be it.

"Henry?"

"I made the right decision, Flip." He smiled to himself. "Stand by. And hope Kmet-Here is in a good mood."

A dutiful, "Yes, Henry." A more hopeful, "I look forward to our trip."

Flip's first through a Portal, if not to space, and Henry smiled. "Cross your fingers. Figuratively speaking."

Henry gave his attention to the view out the window, gazing at the sparkling water of the harbor below, with its clutter of slow ships and busy ferries, and felt a stir of curiosity. Were there harbors and ships on the world the *Henderson* had seeded?

If Kmet-Here accepted the probe as proof—*no guarantee*—and was willing to put the Portal at the Arbiter's disposal, he might see for himself this afternoon.

Appalling speed for an adventure on that scale. He'd gone up to the Portal in Earth orbit a grand total of five times in his career, each for a brief, essential in-person ceremony, and twice the Kmet had refused to leave kmeth's den. Henry hadn't experienced transit.

Yet.

Others had. Did, routinely. Would, tomorrow. The first epitome in the first shuttle to transit through a Portal had found herself above a rocky planet orbiting a red dwarf distant from New Earth's Sun, her oneiric with her as if she'd never left the room. It was a triumph of budding interspecies relations and a first for all humankind—if you didn't count the sleeper ships, as the Kmet most certainly did not.

And if you counted an epitome as an ordinary Human, which the Kmet most certainly believed, the early language interface not up to the task of explaining the difference. A lie of omission grown into self-serving policy. Kmeth didn't come down to New Earth, only epitomes went up, so why confuse the situation?

As for how a transit bypassed space instantaneously—Henry stopped right there. It worked. People did it. Kmet did it.

He would.

He'd skydived once, as himself. Before becoming Arbiter and harder to replace, but a spate of reckless youth had to count.

He'd manage, whatever it took.

One more time, Henry went over what he'd learned on the flight here, putting thoughts in order for his meeting with Kmet-Here. The historian's hasty briefing had given weight to those believing in Humans on another world. The sleepers had been outfitted with more advantages than publicly released. She'd a list.

Difficult, two hundred years later, for someone on New Earth to imagine living without the aid of Alt-Intels like Ralph—or Flip, for that matter.

Harder still to relate to a mindset bold enough to strike out into the unknown.

Still, what the settlers had taken with them was impressive. Better than state-of-the-art fabricators. Then-classified human-augmentation suits, mass-effective substitutes for heavy machinery. A plethora of still-experimental communications gear and miniature satellites, should they obtain fuel for rockets to launch them.

Forget any thought of launching themselves; the sleepers woke to starships reassembled as shelters, their engines so much slag.

Another not-for-the-public fact. The historian blithely presumed the brave souls who boarded the ships knew it was a one-way trip.

Given the hasty departure of the sleeper ships, the confusion of the moment? Rather than assume, Henry added *did you know* to his growing list of questions—if and when he found the right moment and person to ask.

They'd taken stores of seeds and livestock, asleep and frozen embryos, a slice of the Human ecosystem pre-adapted to cope with what was known, albeit via remotes, of their new environment.

Assuming he'd correctly interpreted the historian's circuitous hints around what was an edgy, ethics-fraught topic, the Humans asleep on the ships might have undergone some genetic modification of their own.

Would the Kmet notice if they had? Common knowledge: kmeth had extreme difficulty telling Humans apart. The experts were divided on whether kmeth could and refused to admit it, or if the startling reality of upright bipedal organisms to a species that dragged itself along the ground precluded kmeth noticing individual Human characteristics.

To be fair, Humans struggled to tell which Kmet they were dealing with at a given time, the proximity of kmeth's Portal apparently the key signifier. Kmet-Here. Kmet-There. He'd yet to hear of any other name in use—

"Henry?"

He smiled at the reflection in the window before turning. Simmons m'Hammarskjöld t'McAlistair was all bony elbows and knees, with a tendency to drop his blond-haired head over his chest to disguise a remarkable height. *Not done growing—and so earnest.* It had taken the better part of a month for Henry to convince his new personal assistant to call him by name, at least away from the public. They'd come a long way since.

"Let me guess, Simmons. Kmet-Here is having dessert."

The younger man's eyebrows rose. "I've received no notification—oh." Seeing Henry continue to smile, he relaxed and grinned. "Dessert, yes. Quite possibly." More seriously, "The probe's hit the news."

Flip's amateur astronomers. "The Kmet?"

"There's been no response. Maybe kmeth haven't seen the coverage?"

"Or being late is the response."

Simmons's face fell. "What can we do, Henry?"

Hope the uplink went through and fast. Not a helpful answer. Henry tapped a knuckle against his teeth, gazing at his assistant.

A Human served as pilot on each Portal, an arrangement suggested by the first Arbiter and willingly seized upon by the Kmet. Whether kmeth, lacking hands, admired the dexterity of those with them or simply wanted a sample to study had never been clear. The advantage to New Earth was: access, however limited, to Portal technology.

Pilots were epitomes, of course, however persistently the System Coalition lobbied to allow spacers up as themselves, part of its expansionist goal. To date, no government would risk public opinion to allow it and it was outside the auspices of the Arbiter's Office to promote.

However much the present Arbiter agreed. *When will we be brave . . .*

While Portal pilots were under kmeth's command, a request from the Arbiter's Office took precedence. Something along the lines of *What's Kmet-Here's reaction to today's news?* would do nicely.

Henry let his hand drop. "Where are we in the rotation?" While Kmet might not recognize individual Humans, kmeth were profoundly disturbed by comings and goings. Rotating pilots in and out caused a period of functional mistrust during which a pilot couldn't touch any controls. It might last an hour or go on for days.

Simmons tapped the air, calling up the display from his operations board. A swipe later and he sighed. "The new pilot just swapped in, Henry. Killian m'Lamarr t'Brown."

Her epitome, Killian's self in its can at the Spacer Repository. Where her partner oneiric, typically a senior pilot, would reside until the next rotation. The oneiric, when awake, was a point of access. *Not one to use lightly.* There were rules strongly discouraging interference with an epitome-oneiric connection; Henry relied on them himself. "What do we know about Killian?"

Simmons grimaced at what he read on his board; closing his fist dispelled the interface. "Qualified but—first time on a Portal."

Meaning first time with the Kmet. With an inward shake, Henry dismissed the media, the unresponsiveness of Kmet-Here, and heartily wished this Killian luck. "Then we wait."

"That's actually why I'm here, Henry." Simmons brightened. "Your oneirics have arrived. I left them in the meeting room."

"Potential oneirics," Henry qualified, hiding a surge of relief. *At last.* "I trust they've been informed of the risks?" He relaxed further as Simmons nodded. "Good. It's important they feel able to refuse my offer." *Much as he hoped not.*

"But they can't!" At Henry's lifted eyebrow, Simmons swallowed but persisted. "I mean you—the Arbiter needs them. That's what matters."

"Not to me," Henry said patiently. "To be at my disposal perhaps indefinitely, with what that means. The time stolen from their own lives. It's no light thing."

A flash of worshipful eyes. "I'd do in a heartbeat, sir. If—if I could help."

What did he say to that? "You're already indispensable, Simmons," Henry replied sincerely, gesturing to the door. "While we wait for Kmet-Here, let's greet our guests."

***

Across the hall from Henry's office, the meeting room had windows overlooking the mountain range that cupped the city and harbor in its massive arms. The view was breathtaking.

The four waiting for him had their backs to it, seated to face the door.

Henry nodded, unsurprised. "Hello," he greeted, moving to stand at the round table. Simmons went to his station at the side of the room. There were documents to be signed.

By those willing. On the table, in front of each, rested a slim white ring sized to fit their thumb, its outer surface patterned with close-fitting black lines. The ring contained an oneiric link: once cued to the corresponding wristband—presently hidden by his jacket sleeve—at his summons the link would drop the wearer into a dream state, able to communicate with him within his consciousness.

If willing. He didn't allow himself confidence.

"I'm Arbiter Henry m'Yama t'Nowak, present as my epitome." *No point wasting their time or his.* "Thank you for coming on such short notice. Please introduce yourselves for the record." A nod at Simmons, whose hand moved to briefly illuminate his recorder, floating in midair.

"Professor Ousmane m'Sima t'Garcia, ah, chair of pre-CME history and archives at the Museum of Science and Technology." She inhaled in abrupt gasps, like punctuation, an artifact of implanted lungs. "We spoke last night. Late, ah, last night." Ousmane was slim, black, and wore a well-tailored navy suit. A pair of silver rockets dangled from her earlobes and she'd a silver brooch of a sleeper ship on one lapel. Black hair framed her head in a dense cap, with a single twisted curl on her high forehead, above crisp eyebrows and sharp brown eyes. She wasn't smiling.

The tall woman to Ousmane's left was, warmly, and Henry smiled back, acknowledging his old friend. For the occasion, Rena'd coiled her thick black hair, holding it neatly in place with gem-studded insect pins, but predictably kept on her worn lab coat. She valued the pockets. At a guess, she had on her sensible boots as well, as if at any moment she'd be asked to walk an alien world and wouldn't risk the delay to get them. "Rena m'Attenborough t'Wang, xenologist. I'm a consultant to the Arbiter's Office on the Kmet."

"As am I," announced the heavyset older man seated to Ousmane's right. "Shomchai m'Chomsky t'Deng, sociolinguist with a specialty in the Kmet interface, seconded from the University of the Lesser Maritimes. Though we've not yet met in person, a colleague." A nod to Rena. "Arbiter. An honor and a pleasure, sir." Shomchai stood and reached his hand over the table.

"Henry, please." Rena and Shomchai had helped him during the Niablo negotiation. He met the linguist's hand with his own, repeating the welcoming gesture with Rena and Ousmane, then offered his hand to the final member of the group, seated beside Shomchai. "Sofia, welcome. My apologies for pulling you from an emergency." A volcanic eruption in the Deepen Island Chain, if he recalled correctly.

"The evacuation's complete or I wouldn't be here, Arbiter's request or not." Logistics Expert and Crisis Intervention Specialist Sofia m'Rogers t'Patel withdrew her cool brown fingers from his grip and sat back, sweeping her gray braid over a shoulder. Her features were narrow except for wide-set brown eyes, eyes filled with a daunting focus. "I'll admit to curiosity." She pointed to the ring. "What do you need me for?"

"For what I don't know." Henry sat, folding his hands on the table. "You've been given the essentials. Assuming the Kmet are willing to transit me and my shuttle to the *Henderson*'s coordinates, which we should learn shortly, I'll face an unprecedented situation, one with consequences we can't predict. The level of uncertainty is why I've asked you all to meet with me. I hope you'll consider acting as my oneirics."

Ousmane's eyebrows shot up. "All of us?"

"I'm certified to six," Henry replied, slightly uncomfortable with what sounded like—was—a boast, but they had to believe in him. "Most often, you'll be with me as guests, hosted in an imaginary meeting room much like this to discuss issues as a quorum. As required, with your consent, you may find yourselves my passengers, seeing and hearing with me in real time. If feasible, I can offer projection."

Rena began to grin.

"So yes," he continued hastily, removing his jacket and holding out his wrist, with its four colored bands. "I invite all of you. First, I'm sure you have concerns—"

"Not me." Rena swept up her ring and squinted through it. "Miss my first chance to see another planet up close? I've waited my whole life for this."

"While that's highly premature—" Henry sent her a quelling look she met with a familiar unrepentant grin. "—*if* there's suitable opportunity, I'm willing to enable projection with sensory input via my Flip to yours. *If*." He trusted Simmons to deal with the requisition of an attendant polymorph for each. Call them safety attendants, if anyone in Sentient Resources balked at the reallocation.

He refocused. "The first step would be a stay here, in the Arbiter's Tower. Those who don't already have one will be given a neural lace—an injection." Henry touched the back of his neck to illustrate. "Once that's taken hold, we'd do a test run of our connection. If it's solid, Simmons will make arrangements to set you up wherever you wish, constrained, of course, by the time available to us. I warn you, we're hoping that'll be short. The world's watching."

"Yes, but this." Shomchai tapped the table near his ring and sighed. "Much as it pains me, Henry, this is a black hole. I've a mountain of work waiting—"

"This is our work now," Ousmane interrupted. "Nothing is as important, ah, as finding Earth's children." She brought out a blue velvet bag, setting it on the table beside the ring, then reverently eased it across the table to Henry. "This is for you, Arbiter."

He opened the bag, slipping its contents into his hand, and looked up with real dismay. "Tell me this is a copy."

"Bring it back," said with the ghost of a smile. "I promised the museum."

It was an arbiter's badge. The front of the oval medallion showed two Human hands clasped in agreement, symbolizing a successful mediation; the back, antique scales in balance. The same symbols graced the wall behind his desk and were here, smaller, beside the door.

The Arbiter's badge. Worn thin, polished by use and care over centuries, for what Henry held was a singular treasure. The words "Ad Astra" had been stamped across the hands two hundred years ago, for this was the badge worn by the Arbiter who'd authorized the pre-emptive launch of the sleeper ships, to save them from New Earth's fate.

The historian set her ring spinning, then flattened it with her hand, eyes locked on Henry's. "Five ships remain unheard from, Arbiter. There is no need to, ah, wait for more probes. I've brought the coordinates for their intended, ah, destinations from the archives."

An immediate, immense, expansion of mission parameters and Henry nodded without hesitation, having anticipated this. *They had to know.* "If there are descendants on any of those worlds, you have my promise as Arbiter they will be found and diplomatic contact established." A promise riding on the opinion of the non-Humans overhead, but he had to make it.

"You'll go to all of them?" Shomchai's eyes rounded. "The first generation slept a century—there could be five, maybe more overlapping generations since. Six unique starting points, the potential for language drift—societal change—" He snatched his ring as if afraid Henry would take it back. "Ousmane's right. My work is here, with you. This is an incredible opportunity."

The linguist's excitement was contagious. Henry saw it shining in Rena's eyes. In Ousmane's.

"Sofia?"

The crisis expert sat, nothing to read on her face, hands out of sight below the table as if the ring might slip on her thumb of its own accord. The rest fell silent, waiting for her answer. Finally, she spoke. "The others have something to offer. I see no need for me."

Oh, but he did. Henry was well aware Sofia hadn't always been *m'*Rogers, working with minds under stress, but *m'*Alexander, a leader within the System Coalition. Under her watch, the Coalition had campaigned to build interstellar ships once more, to reach for other Earth-like worlds. Then came the Kmet and the Duality, within which Humans gained access to the Portals. Instantaneous travel to anywhere of mutual interest with only one catch. Humans who went had to come back.

The Coalition continued; Sofia washed her hands of it and space, spending the last twenty-nine years helping people on the ground. She brought a pre-Kmet mindset, an Earth focus, a people-first approach to balance his quorum.

Not that he'd tell her.

"I need someone who understands how people react to shock and knows how to help them through it." He leaned forward on the arm with its waiting wristbands. "Say I do find six worlds supporting healthy, thriving Human settlements. Say each is eager to reconnect with us, with Earth.

"Those worlds will be diverse, their societies evolved along different paths, as Shomchai points out, from ours as well. Mutual understanding isn't a given. It's actually unlikely, since I'll arrive with the Kmet. First contact, on repeat. With us, as well as with an alien species."

He paused, watching their expressions, waiting for comprehension. Shomchai and Rena, familiar with the Kmet, looked worried—and should. Ousmane had a small frown, as if he'd confounded her perception.

Sofia? A grim half-smile played across her lips. "Panic in the streets. Assuming they've streets."

"Not if I—not if *we* can prevent it," Henry stated. "It took thirty-seven years for a cohesive Human civilization, speaking with a united voice through this office, to arbitrate and achieve the Duality that defines our present relationship with the Kmet. I'll have that to bring with me. I'll have you. If there's anyone out there." He had to add that caution. Had to feel it himself, a defense against the intoxication of hope.

"There is," Rena asserted. "We're a tough species. Adaptable. Smart. Give us any chance at all and we survive. Isn't that right?" She looked at the others.

Nods. A smile. Two. Seizing the moment, Henry stood and held out his arm. "If you agree to be the Arbiter's oneiric for this mission, put on your ring and touch it to one of these bands."

He went around the table to Rena. She touched her ring to the yellow, lowermost band, smiling up at him. Ousmane touched hers to the next, green. Shomchai, with a wink, touched the red.

Sofia slid her ring on her thumb, then tapped it lightly against the uppermost, purple band. "I still say you don't need me, Arbiter," with a frown.

"Forgive me if I say I hope I won't," Henry replied, eliciting a second, more thoughtful look.

"Thank you all." He returned to the front of the table, beckoning Simmons and his stack of paper to join him. "Together, you're more than a quorum of expert advisors. Once I leave Earth, you'll be the check on my actions as Arbiter. I'll depend on your honest, forthright opinions."

Simmons caught his eye, glanced upward. The uplink. Kmet-Here was ready. *Kmeth's turn to wait.*

Henry rested his hand on his assistant's shoulder, looked out at the four. "Your signatures authorize the Arbiter's Office to care for you while you remain my oneirics." With pay and insurance and everything else required when people agreed to fall unconscious—and stay that way—at his whim. Thinking of that, he used his grip to pause Simmons before his assistant could hand out the paperwork. "Simply take off your ring to prevent my summons. I hope—I will rely on your wearing them as much as possible. I'll try to be a convenient nuisance," he vowed.

It surprised a laugh from all four, if shaky, as the sight of official documents seemed to hit home what they'd just committed to do.

Now, to convince the Kmet to let them.

"We wait."

The Arbiter spoke for the ten and a half million who inhabited Earth, the appointed representative of the planet's collected regional governments in matters requiring arbitration at the highest possible level. When Henry spoke today from the Arbiter's Office, every word would be shared, recorded, and discussed worldwide.

Once the techs were ready. Equipment walked in, his desk moved out, and Henry thought, not for the first time, they should set up a studio like any ad agency.

It wouldn't happen. When the Arbiter dealt with his own species, which was most of the time, they met in his office, with its comforting seal on the wall and, depending on the individuals and level of discussion, beverages nearby. Such conversations were recorded by more discreet devices, people preferring the illusion of an exclusive private interview, albeit aware it'd be shared with all concerned stakeholders.

Not so when he dealt with the Kmet. Then, *everyone* wanted a seat.

Henry set his little wooden frame on the top of the ominous deck of lenses and lights and stepped back into the circle taped on the floor. The frame held a photo of his grandfather, a hairy chicken beneath each arm, a grin stretching ear to ear on his dust-smeared face—an audience far easier to contemplate.

Kmet-Here waited, the uplink established. Informed there would be a further, unavoidable ten-minute delay, kmeth had been agreeable.

A Human might feel remorse for holding up the call. Kmeth? *Might well be digesting lunch and glad of an excuse not to move.*

Techs prowled silently around him, testing and retesting. Hardly a new experience, connecting to the Portal. He'd done it regularly during the Niablo dispute and before that and before that—

This was different. Those around him felt it. Could see it, in the newly arrived console positioned away from the cameras, operated by a pair of quiet strangers in the crisp yellow and green uniforms of the Planetary Peace Corps. The pair kept sneaking looks at him, as if checking they were in the right place.

True, the PPC typically responded to active emergencies, like Sofia's volcano or wildfires, but Henry'd had a niggle of a feeling. An instinct to expand his resources. He'd learned to pay attention.

He caught the eye of the senior tech, Mersi m'Askwith t'Kruzins. "How close are we?"

She repeated the question, listened, then focused on him. "Eight minutes to live, Henry. Want your cue at one or the half?"

"The half, please." Thirty seconds would do. Henry went over to the console. The PPC pair straightened at his approach, one twitching as if to salute.

He offered his hand to each in turn. "Hello. I'm Henry."

"Yes, sir. Specialist Liam m'Pearson t'Sojnocki. This is Specialist Ireiti m'Mitchell t'Fucic. We're here to take your orders, sir."

"Henry," he urged with a smile. "I take it you've surveillance capabilities as well as—?" His vague wave at the console encompassed options Henry chose not to contemplate.

"Yes, sir. Henry. We're linked into the Kmet-Earth Outer System monitor relay. Nothing budges around our sun without us knowing it."

"I'd something closer in mind. The Portal?"

The pair looked like mischievous kids. Liam nodded, trying not to grin. "We have our own eyes on that. As you requested, we should be able to give you—what do you think, 'Reiti—twenty seconds' warning of power-up to transit?"

A nose wrinkled. "More likely fifteen, tops."

Impressive. "I'd have been happy to get five," Henry admitted fervently. "Excellent." There was an agreed-upon alarm to clear traffic near the Portal, broadcast by the Human pilot on board before shipping transited through.

The Kmet, however, didn't always inform the pilot.

In fact, Kmet-Here was notorious for swapping kmeth's Portal for another's without notice in the midst of a negotiation, thus dropping a different, uninformed Kmet into the meeting. Whether the ploy was to avoid a particular discussion or disrupt one or perhaps share the load—opinions varied—everything had to start again from the beginning.

A tactic Henry did not intend to allow Kmet-Here this time. Fifteen seconds should be ample warning to put his figurative foot down. "How will you signal me?"

"A red dot will appear on your screen," Liam replied promptly. "Only those in this room will see it, sir."

Even better. "Thank you."

"Good luck, Henry," Ireiti offered.

Everyone deserved to be part of this. A choice Henry, as Arbiter, could and did make without hesitation, unlike his predecessors. Humans had lived in the Duality for years now. Under his term, the general population had grown accustomed to the oft-quaint and occasionally downright obscure nature of talking with the neighbors.

It hadn't always been an open conversation. This building held records, yet to be released, of the early fumbles toward comprehension. The best were laughable; the worst made Henry wonder how they'd made it this far.

The newly critical concerned the first time Humans had approached the Kmet to take them after the sleeper ships. The answer had been a monotonous declaration: *Humans-Here. No Humans-There.*

What about Origin Earth? Again from the Kmet, *Humans-Here. No Humans-There.* With growing agitation as Humans persisted, trying to offer proof, until they gave up.

Henry'd gone through the recordings, gained no more sense from the gist than those of the time. Had it simply been too soon, a working vocabulary barely established and subject to wild misinterpretations?

Or, as Shomchai and Rena postulated, had Humans somehow crossed a biological line, offending the Kmet on a level those on two legs were unable to grasp?

Inability to communicate and *disappointing result* were in the official report, Humans accepting the brunt of the blame and the need to wait to learn more of their new friends. The then-Arbiter had objected in private, calling the Kmet's behavior a deliberate betrayal; she'd lost her post. And might have been right.

That was then, this was now. Henry touched his pocket, home to the antique badge in its bag, the trust it represented. He glanced over at the battered little probe, on an illuminated podium, the curl of foil beside it. The only props he'd use for this meeting; all he had.

Surely proof enough—surely they'd come, in the Duality, far enough.

Frustration, disappointment. Betrayal.

Henry returned to the circle, promised to do better with a nod to his grandfather and chickens, and signaled Simmons, who quickly came to stand beside him.

Time to consult.

Henry pressed his right palm firmly over the bands on his left wrist to summon his oneirics.

Closed his eyes.

✱✱✱

Opening them felt normal, as being in the meeting room across the hall without having moved felt normal, as having four faces look up at him with expressions ranging from mild surprise to queasy felt—not so much normal as his doing.

After all, Rena, Ousmane, Shomchai, and Sofia weren't *here* any more than he was; the room was a construct maintained by his mind. Focus and concentration on his part, belief on theirs, and the result let Henry consult with more than one oneiric at the same time.

Trancing, spacers called it, refusing to adopt the enhanced neural lace that permitted the technique. They'd a valid point; trancing took attention off the real and potentially hazardous world.

He'd Simmons and a roomful of techs standing watch.

His oneirics wore what Henry remembered them wearing. He looked down, smiling as he saw he'd unconsciously elected to appear in his favorite gray suit, not what he wore at this moment.

"Thank you for waiting," Henry told his quorum. "When you leave—" *wake* "—you'll receive a live feed of my meeting with Kmet-Here. I'll provide as much advance notice as possible before we reconvene to go over it and—" he spread his arms like wings "—make our plans around the result. Any final comments? Suggestions?"

Ousmane, the one swallowing repeatedly, raised her hand. "Don't take no for an answer."

"You can't force the Kmet to agree—" Rena objected.

"Maybe it's time we tried." This from Shomchai, palms flat on the table. "I say raise the stakes, Henry. Tell kmeth this isn't a request, it's an action critical to the health of the Duality."

A wording as precise as it was potentially disastrous, and Henry eyed the linguist curiously. "Yours, this advice?"

"Not only. I consulted my peers. You expect us to use our resources."

"I rely on it." Henry nodded. "Thank you. Sofia?"

She lifted an eyebrow. "You don't need me yet. But—" the word dangled a moment "—let's say I trust you're as confident as that suit looks."

He hadn't expected to chuckle. "Remember this is the start of a conversation. Kmet don't tend to quick decisions and this may draw out over days. I hope not, but be prepared."

Henry opened his eyes.

To find himself in the circle, the bustle of activity become an expectant hush. The clear screen that would fill with the Kmet's transmission stood in front of him. Henry checked it for a warning red dot, relieved to see none. Simmons stepped back, duty done; Henry thanked him with a nod.

Waving her hand to get his attention, Mersi slowly lowered her fingers one by one. Henry glanced at his grandfather and chickens, then composed his face into a pleasant welcoming smile for the non-Kmet watching.

The screen came to life.

A gasp from the darkness beside Henry. *Someone new.*

Admittedly, the sudden appearance of an immense solitary eye was startling even if you knew it was all a Kmet would show of kmethself on a transmission of any kind.

The iris, taller than Henry, was a rich brown, feathered with bronze and yellow; the pupil, at this magnification, a vast black pit with ragged edges that pulsed open or closed in without warning. A translucent inner lid flickered past at a rate similar to a slow Human pulse, keeping the eyeball moist, sliding a trapped piece of lint or hair back and forth.

Henry's eye developed a sympathetic itch.

"Greetings." He kept his head still, a courtesy to a species who found necks peculiar to say the least. As he spoke, Mersi supplied the pre-recorded tritone harmony to convey *we're here and connected.* "I am Arbiter Henry m'Yama t'Nowak. Do I address Kmet-Here?"

Kmeth's answering tritone hum, much lower, rattled the frame with his photo. Someone hurriedly lowered the incoming volume. *I see you,* it meant. Or *I believe you exist.* The gist was *ready to talk.*

"Kmet-Here." The voice came with a low, heavy wheeze, as if delivered by a bellows. "What purpose, Arbiter-Henry? More negotiation?" The iris pulled in, shrinking the pupil, giving the eye a wary look. "Dispute?"

Human vocal cords couldn't reproduce the language of Kmet, with its reliance on subsonics and multiple tones; the initial breakthroughs in communication had involved, records showed, a linguist whose partner had been rehearsing with a tuba in the next room. On the other hand, the Kmet had no difficulty reproducing Human words, a language kmeth considered sparse and inelegant, though technically adequate.

"The Niablo negotiation has concluded. There is no dispute. This is a new matter, Kmet-Here." Henry took a step to stand by the podium, all the equipment, including the screen, smoothly moving to keep him centered. "New Earth has received a message," he stated, cupping his hands to either side of the probe. "From another world, in another solar system."

The iris widened until the pupil almost filled the screen, drinking in the view. Having kmeth's full attention, along with that of every Human watching, Henry held up the curl of foil, spreading it with care to show the inscription. "These are coordinates—"

"Human notation," the Kmet interrupted with a dissonant hum under the words. "Human message."

"It is, Kmet-Here." *Maybe this would be easier than he'd thought.* Henry opened his mouth.

A red dot appeared on the screen below the eye.

Imminent transit. *Damn.* "Kmet-Here. I need you to remain. To discuss a mission to these coordinates. I am prepared—"

The screen went blank.

"Nine seconds," Liam called out. "Sorry, sir."

The screen brightened. Filled with another, different eye, this iris feathered with black and gold. An iris that widened in shock at what Henry held in his hands.

"There will be a brief delay," Henry told his wider audience. *While we sort our Kmet.* Portals worked in pairs, to transit Human spacecraft from one location to another. They could transit *through* one another, to exchange places, as

Kmet-Here had just unfortunately demonstrated. It remained a moot point if the Kmet thought Humans couldn't notice the swap or if kmeth were merely being optimistic.

Also unfortunately, they'd no way to know if the new Portal, with its new Kmet-Here, was from Rogue 58 or somewhere else. Kmet did not volunteer that information.

Nor did the Kmet share kmeth's number or species' origin or anything other than *here* being the individual interacting with Humans in a given moment versus that ever-nebulous *there*.

Henry occasionally dreamed of two Portals showing up on New Earth's doorstep at the same time and having to maintain a sane flow of conversation when both Kmet insisted kmeth were, in fact, the only individual *here*.

"Greetings, Kmet-Here. I am Arbiter Henry m'Yama t'—"

The black outer eyelid slammed down as if to shut out the view.

"—Nowak."

The screen went blank except for a red dot. An alarmed, "Going again, sir!"

"Pause broadcast." The rest of the world would see a comforting image of the Arbiter's symbol. Perhaps go and make tea, having grown accustomed to lengthy breaks in the feed as Kmet deliberated, or switch to watch a hockey game.

"Reading a transit in prep, sir. There it goes."

What had he told his quorum? *Kmet don't tend to quick decisions.* Except when bailing from an uncomfortable conversation.

If that's what this was. Henry put the Kmet-traumatizing foil on the podium and returned to the circle, beginning to have a very bad feeling. "With all this movement, do we have a risk to traffic?"

"Shouldn't be, sir." Another voice. He was surrounded by helpful people he couldn't see. "The area was cleared before the uplink went live."

A Portal could transit through another Portal to an entirely new location. A process taking less than the blink of a Human eye that swept up every speck of matter within a specific radius, like confetti caught by a gust of wind, and what wasn't a Portal? Didn't reappear, anywhere.

"Is there a Portal in Earth orbit?" Henry asked, keeping his voice calm. There had to be. It was a tenet of the Duality there always be.

Not that Humans relied on it. Ships moved by Portals carried epitomes, never originals. Information New Earth did not volunteer—

"Yes, sir," from one of the surveillance team. "Seems to be staying."

"The uplink's stopped," from Mersi. "No contact."

Henry gave a cool, collected nod, as if he'd expected both answers. As if his heart wasn't in his throat. "Have the news feeds resume normal programming and get me the pilot. Now."

"The pilot?"

"Arbiter's decision," he said. "Do it, Mersi. Audio only." Whether his career survived a review of this particular choice would depend, Henry knew, on the result.

"You're connected."

"Pilot, this is the Arbiter. If you are free to do so, please identify yourself."

"Omar m'Starink t'Koleszar, sir." The voice was slow, some words slurred. *Transit shock*, Henry guessed with remorse. Portals weren't designed for Human passengers. "Where—this is Earth?"

Not Killian. Making the Kmet in orbit not the first to see the probe and coordinates, but the second. "Yes, Omar. You're home. What just happened?"

"We were—orbiting Rogue 58—my Kmet ordered a simul-pop with Earth's. Nothing out of—out of the ordinary till kmeth saw what you had on screen. Took the controls and sent us off again. Supposed to wait twelve hours between pops—I told kmeth. Didn't listen. Must have made one more, to return us here, but that—it's all fuzzy." A pause. A ragged breath. "Think I passed out."

Henry pinched the top of his nose. Kept his voice composed. "Omar, this is critical. Did you go to the coordinates I showed your Kmet?"

"Can't say, sir. Kmeth blanked the screens. Locked me out of systems. I'd no clue where I'd wound up till you called." As if it were his fault.

A given. "Thank you, Omar. That's all for now."

"Wait—what's going on, sir? What can I expect?"

If only he knew. "The situation will stabilize shortly. Take care of yourself." The Spacer Repository, via Omar's oneiric, would give the pilot more detailed advice and instructions. They'd want to order up a replacement to relieve him.

A request he'd have to refuse. They couldn't afford any changes to further destabilize the Kmet.

"That'll be all for now." Henry made a cut-off gesture. "Lights, Mersi."

The windows became transparent, sunshine pouring into a room full of glum, anxious faces.

"What do we do now, sir?" Henry couldn't tell who'd asked the question.

"All we can do," he replied softly. "We wait."

"I'm only a pilot."

KILLIAN m'Lamarr t'Brown stood at attention, her back to the only wall without screens or controls, waiting to be noticed.

Hoping not to be, given the enormous alien thrashing around Control. Sad little puddles marked where kmeth kept squashing the PIPs that helped run the Portal. The Portal's Integrated Polymorphs kept pulling themselves back together and returning to work, heedless of their ongoing peril.

There went another one. *Squish*.

Her training hadn't included suggestions on how to calm a thrashing, uncommunicative Kmet. On the contrary, most instructions began with wait for kmeth's orders. *Not* wait for sanity.

Control, as pilots called the space, was huge and curved, thirty meters deep and twice as long, with a high domed ceiling, and Kmet-Here, large as a rhinoceros and agile as a mouse, pretty much consumed it. Those immense paired flipper-legs sprawled to the side, widening the *could crush you* zone, heaving kmeth's enormous slug-like body along with that alarming speed.

The recent wild effort had kmeth breathing heavily, resulting in a vibration Killian felt through the wall behind her and an acrid stench that would have had her eyes watering if she hadn't put in the drops pilots knew to use.

Remembered those on her own, hadn't she?

Kmeth's neckless body and limbs were covered in yellow-brown scales about the size of Killian's open palm. Skin showed between the scales and where Kmet-Here had lost the tip of kmeth's left limb. Kmeth's two big eyes, independently mobile, twitched back and forth, blinking frenetically.

Did kmeth know she was here? She'd come through the airlock, dropped her duffel on the floor of her quarters, and rushed to Control. Got through the standard introduction harmonies and been ignored, as she'd been told to expect.

Killian had stayed to wait for kmeth's approval, however long it took. After all, she'd made it. She was on a Portal. Kmeth's Human pilot and, eventually, able to send ships across space in a single bound.

Another *squish*. You'd think the PIPs would learn.

Short, white spikes filled the top of the head, between the eyes. Each held what pilots called a willy-bit, after their resemblance to a wizened Human penis. The color and number of exposed willy-bits were supposed to tell you a Kmet's mood.

What did it mean when none were showing?

Best keep to the wall.

Kmet-Here hadn't noticed her. Had taken care of the uplink to the Arbiter's Office without her help. She'd watched the screen fill with the Arbiter's famous face, witness to what happened next.

Kmet-hysterics. A surprise simul-pop. Now this. Acting as if kmeth's scaly hide was covered in itching powder.

Killian would very much like to know what exactly the Arbiter had done in a seemingly simple communication to drive this Kmet—*her first*—bonkers. Played the wrong harmonics? Worn the wrong color?

The obvious—that kmeth's agitation stemmed solely from seeing those Human artifacts, implying Kmet had strong opinions about the Halcyon Project, New Earth's highest achievement in space, and its result—wasn't a notion she liked to contemplate. Not while alone with one.

She'd been space-crazy long as she could remember. Had built a scale model of a sleeper ship, lugging it up the stairs to the roof of their apartment building where she'd spent hours pretending the mossy tiles were an alien landscape.

Seeing the evidence on display, despite years since in space and a solid layer of cynicism for protection, her heart had beat faster. It meant people might have made it. Hell, maybe she'd relatives born under a different sun. Her aunt always claimed they'd sent family on the—

<Stay where you are,> her oneiric interrupted.

Late, as usual. Killian had to be satisfied with imagining the words. You didn't speak out loud to someone not physically present, not where a Kmet might overhear and be confused.

Though the way this one was acting, confused might be an improvement.

She'd received the basic neural lace, like all pilots and most epitomes; while connected, her oneiric rode in her mind like a passenger, with access to what Killian saw and heard.

An opinionated passenger. Kisho m'Hadfield t'Twist. Old, retired with a flawless record, and Killian knew she should be grateful to be saddled with an authority who inserted critique and commands into her head whenever inclined.

Her previous oneiric had been her best friend and partner in all things, Giselle. They'd worked the sweeps between stations as a well-oiled team. Celebrated hard each time Killian returned and left the repository, and the fun they'd had—

<Eyes on the screens!>

She glanced up. The screens remained an unhelpful blank, kmeth having shut all three down after the gut-wrenching simul-pop—Kisho not shutting up throughout about *someone* forgetting her meds when it was the oneiric's damn job to remind her—

Giselle'd never missed. They'd taken ships through Portals uncounted times before. *Nothing to it.* A Human couldn't sense the instant they and their surroundings were disassembled by the Portal and a copy—*that, hell, yes, felt perfectly real*—was spat out by the receiving Portal.

To be fair, Kisho had warned her Kmet-Here was about to do a simul-pop with another Portal. Called it a negotiation ruse, nothing unusual. Said her stomach might complain.

Hadn't, damn her, so much as hinted at reality of transit shock, that being *inside* a Portal going through another was something that outraged every body part—though in hindsight it explained the supposedly mandatory minimum twelve-hour layover between—

Had she been turned inside out? Flash-frozen? Seen her skin float past? *All of the above?*

Killian wasn't sure of anything except she'd staggered at the end of it, catching herself against a wall that felt perfectly real—

—and was, that was the point, right to the taste of vomit in her mouth.

To hell with Kisho's orders.

She stopped watching the screen, focused on Kmet-Here. Killian did not look left, where a good-sized portion of the clean, white functional room was full of—what wasn't. Too large to move through most of the Portal's system of tubes and corridors that accommodated Humans and PIPs, kmeth lived here.

In a den. A floor-spanning mess of organics and machine scraps with an ominous cave-like entry hole closer to her size than Kmet-Here's, smelling worse than kmeth's breath. She'd yet to see kmeth go inside.

Happy about that.

Kmeth came to an abrupt stop in front of the trio of pedestals rising from the floor, uttering one of kmeth's bone-shaking off-key moans. PIPs clambered into position on top of the outer two. More climbed the walls, pins and pushers extruded, ready to access ancillary switches and buttons.

Killian's stomach clenched. She grabbed the notepad attached by a retractable line to her belt and wrote: *What's happening?* She stared down at the words, willing Kisho to answer.

Kmeth protruded a triple-forked tongue, how kmeth manipulated the pedestal's controls.

<Prepping another simul-pop,> confirmed her oneiric. <Never heard of a second so quick. Kmeth's rattled. Reacting.> A pause, then the predictable aloof and distanced summation of Killian's worth: <No shame if you can't cut it.>

The fossil dared write her off?

Clearing it with a stab of her finger, Killian dropped the pad, which snapped back to her waist, clenching both fists. The almighty Arbiter was the one who'd hadn't *cut it.* He'd messed up. A mistake he'd had to make on her first watch of her first rotation on board and she'd love to spit in his—

TRANSIT!

***

Squatting on the floor, Killian dragged her sleeve across her mouth as a cluster of PIPs deftly whisked away the pile at her feet, unable to rouse herself to more than a vague disgust as the things trundled over to kmeth's den and began applying her bile and chunks of partially digested breakfast to a wall, as if delighted to have new material.

Wonderful.

A snarl in her head. <Next time disconnect with me first!>

Killian grinned until the word *next* sunk in. Twice had to be enough. With a shudder, she shot a worried look up the Kmet's long sloping back. Kmeth hadn't left the pedestals.

Her eyes rose higher, locking on the screens. All three showed Earth.

She sagged with relief. They were home. *That was good, wasn't it?* They'd stay put now, wouldn't—

TRANSIT!

***

<Wake up. Wake up!>

God, she and Giselle must have done a right good bender. Killian hadn't felt this wasted since graduat—

<FOOL! Kmeth's talking to you! GET UP!>

Kmeth? Her eyelids cracked open as Killian belatedly realized someone *outside* her head was shouting, no, booming at her.

"Help!" *BOOM!* "Help!" *BOOM!* "Help!"

She stared into kmeth's gaping mouth, gagging at the stench. Spittle burned her face and Killian scooted backward on the floor until she hit the wall. She pushed herself up and out of range. "What's wrong?" she shouted over the next *BOOM!*

"Danger to the Duality!" Huge gold-brown irised eyes fixed on her, clear lids flashing back and forth. "Danger, Pilot," Kmet-Here announced, the spikes on kmeth's head erupting with red willy-bits she didn't need a manual to say meant upset—maybe even fear. *BOOM!* "I need your assistance. Hurry!"

Kmeth swung around. Killian jumped the trailing flipper-leg. Sprang to the side to avoid kmeth's tail end as it scraped the wall where she'd been, then hastened behind the creature, searching desperately for a clue to kmeth's behavior.

Kmet-Here better not have broken the Portal. Contract or no contract, she'd no intention of staying wherever they were—the screens an ominous blank—for however long it took the PIPs to fix the thing.

If they could.

She cast a longing look at the tube leading to her quarters. All she'd have to do was exit this body to wake up, on New Earth, in her own. "The hell with this—" she muttered under her breath and swung about on her heel.

<Stop, Killian. New Earth won't let you back,> Kisho told her. <A pilot stays aboard till their replacement arrives.>

Killian froze, shocked as much by the sympathy in her oneiric's voice as what she said, then took up her pad. Began to write a protest, *They can't—*

BOOM! "Help!" *BOOM!* "Help!" *BOOM!*

"Coming." She turned back toward Kmet-Here. "What do you want me to do?"

"Fix." Kmeth angled the eye on Killian's side to stare at her, the black lid half down. "Humans in wrong place."

Did kmeth want her to leave? Her head hurt, not to mention her abused stomach, and she'd be very happy to be anywhere else. *Still.* The *BOOMs* had to mean something wrong. "Kmet-Here," Killian asked cautiously, "where would you like me to be?"

<No! Pay attention, fool!> Kisho chided. <Kmeth said Humans, plural. The *Henderson.* That's where you've gone. Their world.>

It couldn't be.

Oh, but it could. The probe. The argument with the Arbiter . . . mind-bending pops between locations that honestly left Killian shaky on lefts and rights, let alone a conversation. "Kmet-Here. Where are we?"

"Here." Three screens activated, showing the same view: ash drifting along lifeless streets. Seared twists, like overdone bacon left on a plate, clustered as if caught together—

Killian would have been violently ill if she'd anything left. She must have cried out. Maybe Kisho did, seeing what she saw.

"Kmet-There came to this wrong place. Kmet-Here followed."

She grasped it then, why so many transits in a row. The Kmet hadn't been arguing about the probe. Kmeth had acted, instantly. The first pop had switched them with the other Kmet, sending them wherever its Portal had been. A mining planet. Didn't matter, because the next pop had been her Kmet using this Portal to take them to New Earth and send the other here. *To observe?*

And the last, to put this Portal here, in its place, hinting at a hierarchy or specialization between these Kmet no Human had seen before.

Why?

"Did you do this?" Killian heard herself demand, her voice high and strained. "Did you send Kmet-There to kill those people?"

The lid raised, the pupil dilating. "All Kmet-Here came to protect you. Protect New Earth. Protect Humans-Here. We cannot protect Humans-There, in wrong places. We will bring them home. Help. Retrieve them."

"Re—" Killian looked up at the screens. "Retrieve what?"

"Bring Human-There to Human-Here. Or Human-Here becomes Human-There."

She shook her head. "I don't understand." *Was afraid to even try.*

<Ask for the Arbiter.> Kisho's voice trembled with urgency. <Ask for him now!>

Killian took a breath, folding her hands at her waist. "I'm only a pilot. You need the Arbiter for this, Kmet-Here. The Arbiter!"

The Kmet uttered a two-tone hum. The red willy-bits slowly turned a placid mauve. "Agreed. First retrieve Humans-There." Kmeth heaved itself from the pedestals, granting Killian access. "Need pilot for this."

She stepped up on the dais, facing the center pedestal. Her hands wanted to shake. She'd no idea what the Kmet wanted her to do. "'Retrieve,'" she echoed, trusting her oneiric to know.

<Activate the mining PIPs. Send them down on the big lifters. Kmeth will input the parameters.> Kisho went on, reciting the sequence, guiding Killian's fingers as if the old pilot stood here instead.

Numb at first, Killian slowly began to anticipate what to input and where; she'd trained for this, mining the most common task for a Portal's Human operator.

Never for charred corpses. Never for the dead. Nothing like this.

There'd never been anything like this.

"Let's get some answers."

HENRY'S stomach growled, again, his epitome's insides every bit as Human as those he'd left in a can on the second floor. He'd sent Simmons to the food dispenser for anything to sit under the second coffee he shouldn't have had, not while waiting in his office for the Kmet to make sense.

The world waited with him, with less patience. He'd left the media and general public to his staff, sent a brief response to the heads of governments: Matters are proceeding. *Or going to hell.* You'll be informed the instant the Kmet are back in contact.

Or know before I do.

His biggest fear, shared by every arbiter-primary since the Portal arrived in orbit, was to make The Mistake. The one that broke the Duality between Human and Kmet, losing their tenuous foothold in space, abandoned by their potent partner.

Or worse—

"They had your doughnut," Simmons announced triumphantly, proffering the bag. "I got you two."

Henry shook off his mood and smiled. "Thanks. Join me?" He patted the windowsill. His office remained a studio; he'd refused the offer of a stool. The technicians needed them, being busy doing what they could, while he tried not to hover.

His assistant sat, digging into his own bag to produce a napkin-wrapped taco. "Any news?" he asked in a low voice.

"None." The Portal from Rogue 58, now Kmet-Here's, remained in orbit, its occupant stubbornly silent or brooding.

Or catching a nap. Neither Shomchai nor Rena had been willing to speculate.

Henry opened the bag. The doughnut, plain and old fashioned, was still warm from the dispenser. After bolting down the first without tasting it, he pulled out the second and made himself pause. "Hits the—"

Alarms swallowed the rest. Henry froze, doughnut in hand.

Mersi hurried over to him, standing on her toes to shout in his ear. "JUST A NORMAL TRANSIT ALERT—FROM THE PI—from the pilot. Omar." She lowered her voice as the wailing cut off, an embarrassed wave signaling an apology across the room.

They were all twitchy. "Is it labeled?" A high point in Henry's career, negotiating a system to distinguish between, for example, ice blocks and shuttles full of returning miners, Humans viewing the two differently. Kmet, not as much, but kmeth agreed to apply labels. Most of the time.

"Ore shipment," someone called out.

Normal. Henry raised his doughnut.

Lowered it without a bite. "Visual confirmation," he said, raising his voice. "Now."

The PPC had satellites positioned to monitor the Portal at all times. New Earth didn't advertise their role; the Kmet had never objected, assuming kmeth noticed.

The screen in front of Henry came to life. Against the black of space, a simple white rectangle floated in wait, its corners crisp, sides smooth. Scale was elusive; the Portal was ten times larger than all three Earth stations combined—a behemoth whose own gravity drew debris in its wake and shifted the orbits of poorly placed satellites.

Within the rectangle, a hollow echoed that shape, was framed by it, and opened into a seething maelstrom of otherworldly colors.

"Close in."

The view magnified until those colors filled the screen, reflected in the sides of consoles and from lenses, bathing the room in otherworldly light. Henry shielded his eyes until someone reduced the brightness.

"Transit."

The light show disappeared, replaced with a web of stuff moving outward, expanding as it went. The web was a metal mesh bag, used to keep multiple objects together for easy recovery; a result of one of the first Human-Kmet negotiations, following a disaster that had sent uncontrolled fragments through a space liner, killing hundreds.

Epitomes and disposable, not that the Kmet were told. Not that it made any difference. Those linked to them had suffered the same horrific pain and terror; some experienced death before they could be pulled home and were never the same.

Handing his doughnut to Simmons, Henry pressed his palm over all four wristbands. At his request, his quorum members had remained, ready to be consulted. Rather than close his eyes and meet them internally, this time he kept his eyes open, focused on the image taking shape, enabling them to see what he did. "Quorum, we have a developing situation. Objects have come through the Portal, labeled as ore."

Twinkles of light appeared, closing in like a halo around the webbed mass:

catchers on their way, small powerful craft that were half engine, half grappling claws. They worked in triplets, one having a Human pilot, two with Alt-Intels at the helm; together they could handle anything from a fully loaded freighter to a misplaced pen.

As Henry watched, the triplets split apart, thickening the halo.

A low steady voice from one of those at the PPC console. "It's not ore, sir. We're showing a lot of organics. Some refined products."

A label error wasn't unknown, especially when a Kmet took charge of a transit.

Henry made himself stay calm. "Thank you. Quorum, initial thoughts?"

<Henry—what has kmeth done?> Rena, sounding shaken.

Sofia spoke next, an edge to her voice. <It's too soon to speculate.>

<I agree. We must wait on a thorough analysis,> from Ousmane. <I would be, ah, grateful for the oppro—>

<What organics are coming through?> Shomchai asked, overriding the historian. <Find out, Henry!>

"I'll let you know." Henry pressed the bands as he walked over to the PPC console, keeping an eye on the Portal back to filling the screen. It would be another few minutes before the catchers were in contact and could send down their analysis. "Tell me everything you can about what's come through."

This as the Portal's color show resumed. It might mean another imminent transit—certainly the device stood ready.

Iteriti stood, leaned over the console. "Sir," an uneasy whisper. "The predominant material—it's almost equal parts calcium oxide and phosphorus pentoxide. A bit of water." In the ghostly light from the screen, the specialist's eyes were haunted. "That's what's left, sir, when a body's burned. Calcinated bone."

Henry put a finger to his lips. Iteriti nodded and sank back down, her partner nodding as well.

The Arbiter steeled himself, and turned back to the screen. "Mersi, please connect me to the Kmet presently in orbit," he ordered, calmly, coolly, despite the hammering of his heart and a doughnut now lead in his stomach.

"Sorry, Henry. Kmeth isn't accepting the uplink. I can try to get you the pilot again." Doubtfully.

He shook his head. "Not yet, thank you. Simmons?" He waited for his assistant to come close. "Go to the Spacer Repository and interview Killian's oneiric. On my authority," well understanding the flash of concern. "Make it fast."

"Yes, Henry." Simmons spun about and left.

He'd gone as far as he dared alone. "Mersi, notify the Chair the Arbiter is calling an immediate confidence vote."

The room went still. Mersi squinted at him. "Say again?"

Giving him time to relent. He worked with the best people. "It's all right, Mersi. I need to know they're with me on this."

And if not, there'd be a new Arbiter standing here.

***

"They're ready for you, Henry."

Nodding, he rose from the chair and straightened his jacket, wordlessly following Com Operator Li Jie across the hall and back to his office. Techs came alert. Mersi, her expression grave, waved him to the spot on the floor. Unlike last time, paired lights emphasized the Arbiter's Symbol on the wall behind him.

The planet's governing body, the Assembly had been in emergency session since the news of the probe's arrival, its eleven members receiving a constantly updated feed from the agency concerned with space and the Kmet. Namely, the Arbiter's Office.

If he stretched up a hand, he'd feel the array overhead ready to project the Assembly Chamber around him, as his image would be projected there in return. Similar setups brought together the leaders from the settled regions of New Earth and whomever else they deemed necessary.

Time he joined the conversation. With an inward settling shake, Henry composed his features to serious but not grim, and gave Mersi a nod. "Begin, please."

His office vanished around him, replaced by a limitless span of ice and snow whipped by low swirling winds; where they met was determined by the current Chair and this year's was from the Polar Habitable Region. A chilling sight, if not sensation.

The nine voting members sat on blocks of ice, set in a curved row. In reality, they'd be sitting on whatever they liked in their own offices, but the overall impression of unity mattered. *Even if they rarely agreed.*

Henry stood before them at the focal point. Two others stood to one side. He nodded a greeting to the representatives from the Print House and the Planetary Peace Corp.

The Chair rose to her feet. Gave a small bow. "Arbiter. The floor is yours."

Eastern Foothills made a rude noise. "For now."

He represented the region where the *Adamant* had landed and Human civilization on New Earth began, attributes those living there rarely missed a chance to point out, feeling they deserved more than the obligatory single vote.

"That will be up to you," Henry acknowledged, then addressed the whole. "I've come for your support for what I've done. For what I may need to do."

"What you've done is upset the Kmet and put our pilots at risk!" The representative for the Spacer Repository leapt to his feet. Raised a clenched fist. "I insist you permit the next rotation!"

The Chair gestured. The representative sat, glaring at Henry.

"And what happens if I do?" the Arbiter asked gently. "If we swap out Omar in the midst of this, leaving Killian? Oh, yes," at the representative's surprise, "I know their names. I know who they are and their capabilities. And I know the Kmet. A personnel change when kmeth are already stressed will destabilize the situation further. Perhaps irreversibly."

"A situation you caused, Arbiter, by showing Kmet-Here the probe's message." The accusation came in a mild tone, but its source was potent. The serene face displayed on the surface of the oval object balanced on an ice block represented every Alt-Intel on and off the planet, and had two votes to cast for, or against, Henry.

"I accept the fault," Henry replied. "In part, that's why I'm here. For your judgment."

Southern Plains waved dismissively. "No one could have anticipated kmeths' reaction. It's what happening now that concerns me—us. You're sure those are remains?"

Henry looked at the PPC representative, who gave a slow nod. "Members of the Assembly, Chair, I have reviewed the analyses we provided the Arbiter and received the latest from the recovery team. What the Kmet are transiting through to us are—were Human beings. I can add they died recently."

"The Kmet—" The youngest here, representing the Northeast Estuaries, flushed after his outburst but continued, "—how do we know the Kmet aren't responsible?"

Several spoke at once. "Don't be foolish—kmeth have been our treasured allies for a generation—" "—aliens. We can't predict what the Kmet will or won't do. Never could." "—Earth in danger?" "—HIS FAULT!"

The Chair tapped her toe. The ice cracked from that contact, fanning outward to their feet. Everyone fell silent, looking at her. "I will remind you the Arbiter himself requested this confidence vote. Let him speak."

Henry waited until he'd their attention, then bowed. "Thank you. Everything you say is true. The Duality between our species is a source of progress and peace—but it is not static. It has evolved over time through negotiations, mutual understandings, and yes, misunderstandings on both sides." He spread his hands. "Some are fundamental to what we are. The Kmet have trouble telling us apart. We have the same problem with kmeth." A few nods. "Most frustrating of all, the Kmet were unable to grasp that we had a past where we flew between stars, to comprehend that Humans might live on other worlds than this one. Kmeth refused for thirty-seven years to transport us to any of those worlds. Today, that changed." He gave them a heartbeat to absorb the enormity of it.

"The result isn't what any of us expected or hoped. It's tragic. We've found the descendants of the *Henderson*'s passengers only to lose them; the only explanation we have for their deaths comes from the Kmet. The Kmet say Humans-Here, on New Earth, are somehow good and safe. That kmeth came here to protect us. That Humans anywhere else—Humans-There—are in danger of their lives and, as proof, we've bodies arriving in orbit in their thousands.

"We don't know, yet, how they died or why. We don't know—*yet*—if the Kmet are being truthful or lying to us. Until we do, I see but one course of action. With the Assembly's support, I propose to undertake the following mission: to go with the Kmet to each and every world targeted by the Halcyon Sleeper Ship Project, then use our combined resources to evacuate every Human we find to New Earth. It is on this I request—no, I must have your vote of confidence before proceeding. Thank you." Henry folded his hands together at his waist, preparing to wait, ready for questions.

Silence.

"So we're clear, Arbiter," Central Forest said suddenly, "you propose bringing what could be thousands of strangers here. To our home."

His people had done the math. "Potentially millions. Yes."

"Thank you for the clarification." She quieted, her face inscrutable, as if Central wasn't begging for people and likely the first to benefit from a new source. New Earth's growth had been carefully managed, conservatively so, waiting until other regions were bursting before opening new areas to settle. They were justly proud of the result—a planet barely touched, its biology allowed to adapt to what came with Humans from theirs.

The Alt-Intel's face took on a somber cast. "Even if we immediately deployed all resources at our disposal, we could not initiate the next Spread in time to safely house such an influx."

"Give strangers an entire new territory?" Central Forest paled. "We'd be destabilized. Or worse."

"We mustn't repeat the mistakes of the past. What I propose is we—all of us—offer them sanctuary in our homes until theirs are safe and they can return." Henry firmed his tone. "Is that not how our ancestors survived on arrival? Is it not the very cornerstone of our existence, that we share this world?"

The ensuing pause was, he hoped, thoughtful. Central Forest regained her color.

Northeast Plains spoke next, his voice heavy with scorn. "Just you and a Kmet, off to rescue them all. This is ridiculous." He looked around at the others. "Ridiculous!"

"I'll have additional resources," Henry reminded him. "Starting with the pilot."

The Spacer Repository's Representative nodded vigorously.

Print House looked uneasy. "Arbiter, this will put an unprecedented strain on your and the pilot's existents and epitomes."

Henry let himself almost smile. "As always, we put our trust in your staff."

Shoulders stiffened. A tiny nod accepting the responsibility.

"Get on with it," said Eastern Foothills with a dark frown. "We know the stakes. I'm ready to vote."

"As am I," Southeast Estuaries declared.

When no one disagreed, the Chair, who'd sat to cede the icy floor to the Arbiter, rose. "Those in favor of the Arbiter's proposed mission will raise a hand or provide the equivalent signal. Failure to receive a majority will mean your immediate replacement," she warned Henry.

"I understand." He mentally apologized to whichever arbiter-secondary landed in this mess.

"Those in favor?"

Central Forest and the Spacers representative raised their hands. To Henry's surprise, so did Eastern Foothills. Two blue dots appeared above the face representing the Alt-Intels.

"Those against?"

Her hand rose, as did those of the Southern and Northern Plains, and the Southeast Estuaries. Northeast Estuaries hesitated, then thrust up a hand.

A tie.

Under most circumstances, the Arbiter cast the tie-breaking vote. Being the subject of this one, Henry remained as he was.

The Chair blew out an annoyed breath. "A tie is insufficient to remove a serving Arbiter from office. Nor does it grant sufficient support for the proposed mission. Arbiter, find another option."

Henry gave a deeper bow. "I accept the will of the Assembly."

Now what?

<Damn good job.>

THE real difficulty dealing with aliens, Killian decided, was a Human had no idea what the non-Human thought they were doing.

And now she was stuck on kmeth's Portal, doing kmeth's bidding, until whatever kmeth *thought* kmeth was doing was done.

At least she'd stopped retching. A very minor improvement in what would give her nightmares for life. She'd the shakes. Her vision tended to tunnel, with black edges.

Not leaving her post.

The mining PIPs had been instructed—not by her, oh, no, she didn't have *that* kind of access to their systems, no Human did—on what to collect and what to leave. Kmet-Here had taken her place to input that information, then again to transit the first load through the Portal, to New Earth, before returning to lie in the opening to kmeth's den, eyelids closed as if overwhelmed.

Overwhelmed? Killian pitied those first to learn what they were getting.

Bodies. The remnants of them.

Structures. The remnants of those. Some pieces and hunks went straight into the lifters, the rest were pummeled flat as the autonomous machines hunted for—what, exactly?

She'd thought belatedly to launch a pair of surveillance satellites, the sole bit of Human-controlled tech on board, shunting their feed to the center screen.

Killian had stared at the screens till her eyes burned. She still couldn't find a pattern to what the PIPs *retrieved* and what they obliterated.

Henderson's descendants had done pretty well for themselves. They'd had a good-sized city, once. A few towns dotted along a major river. Roads between. Wind turbines. Humans had made a solid start on this pretty world of topaz and blue. They'd have named it.

There was no one left to tell her what.

The mining machines followed every trace of Human activity as if determined to erase what had been here, and at the rate they were going, Killian didn't think it would take much longer.

Then what?

Abruptly chilled, she touched the white band around her wrist. Its pattern of lines became a series of narrow triangles, signaling activation, a change visible only to Human eyes. So the experts said.

<I'm here,> her oneiric said, no more bossy tone, no more *knows better.* Kisho had seen enough, before Killian released her to wake up. Wake up and run, not walk, to the nearest communications system in the repository, because Earth had to be warned and regs about oneiric-epitome confidentiality, as Kisho'd put it, be damned.

Killian looked down at her hands, hovering over the pedestal. Rather than pull out the notepad, she curled her fingers and thumb into a question mark.

<The Arbiter had someone standing by to get our report. I gave them an earful, you bet. Asked what they were going to do about it. About you.>

Killian sliced her hand back and forth, a sharp *no.*

<Why? It's not as if they'd think of us first otherwise, is it? You're going to pass out soon, you don't get some fluids and rest, then what?>

The echo of her thoughts made Killian shudder. She turned her palm up—*don't know*—then looked up at the central screen. Too fast. Control spun. She gripped the pedestal.

Steadied her voice. "Another load to transit through," she said aloud, as if notifying the somnolent Kmet, advising Kisho. "Then the equipment to call back up. Sats stat." Code for leaving the satellites active, to complete their optical survey. By the regs, a pilot was to recall them before transit.

Nothing about this was by the regs. Sure, the settlement below the Portal had obvious boundaries: mountains, bogs. And yes, there'd been no sign of runways or launch capability to suggest the *Henderson*'s descendants had ever moved beyond the flatlands where the ship had put them.

But Killian refused to rely on Kmet-tech to find every Human on this planet. As long as the satellites were linked to this Portal, their data would continue to feed through. To her, here. To New Earth, when they transited back.

If she didn't inform Kmet-Here? *Well, kmeth would have no reason to argue.*

<I'll pass that on. Killian—> The old pilot's voice caught. <I'll tell them all you did. Damn good job.>

Writing her off again, was she?

Killian tapped the wristband, dismissing her oneiric. "Taking my break," she announced loudly.

Without looking at the heap of alien, she turned her back on the world being destroyed and staggered into the tube, heading for her quarters.

With any luck, maybe she'd be on the toilet when Kmet-Here wrenched them back through Earth's Portal.

"DANGER! DANGER!"

THE Arbiter sat at a table existing only in his mind as his guests absorbed what information they had so far. Including the troubling statement Simmons had obtained from Killian m'Lamarr t'Brown's oneiric. *He didn't envy them.*

"That's the sum of it," Henry finished. "In retrospect, Kmet-Here's reaction to the *Henderson*'s message indicates kmeth had good reason to expect what happened to those settlers."

Annihilation, Kisho had called it.

The word wouldn't leave his mind. "When that Portal transits back," Henry continued, "we should receive data from the satellites Killian left in orbit."

"Smart thinking," Sofia commented.

"It's awful. The whole situation." Rena's face was sickly pale. This version of her face existed only in his mind, but her pallor would be real, an oneiric's emotional state part of the palette the epitome received, informing the seeming of each guest. "I can't wrap my head around what could have the Kmet, with their incredible technology, running scared."

"You think, ah, kmeth lied?"

"No one does." Henry stirred. "No one should," he reminded them, looking pointedly at Ousmane. Ever since she'd identified the image of a transited fragment as being a piece of a sleeper ship, she'd railed against the Kmet for destroying Human history. "We remain within the Duality. Rely on it and our partners."

Until such time as they couldn't. Not a thought to share. "According to the pilot's oneiric, Kisho, the Portals will swap soon," he went on. "I want options on how best to approach the Kmet once—" Even for him, even in here, hard words to say. "—the last arrive."

Bodies. At last count, over three hundred thousand bits of what had been Human, turning the joyful anticipation from the probe's return into a nightmare.

Shomchai leaned on his forearms, brows together. "I advise delicacy. This event will cause kmeth significant upset—"

"'Upset?!'" Sofia interrupted. "What about every person who's had to watch Human remains spat out with the garbage? Who's worked to recover them?"

"It's not disrespect," countered Rena. "Kmet don't distinguish between an individual and what they use or make. Kmet-There is simply sending home what kmeth sees as Human." She turned to Henry. "My recommendation is to offer gratitude."

Henry nodded. "Ousmane?"

Dark eyes glowered. "You know my position. New Earth launched six sleeper ships. That five remain unaccounted for, ah, means five more possibly settled worlds. We cannot let the Kmet, ah, get to them before we do."

She wasn't wrong. "There's no other choice. The Assembly refused to send me and I won't delegate the responsibility or authority to the pilot. I'll emphasize to Kmet—-"

"No! Bricks are coming through! Ship parts, ah, and wheels! The Kmet are destroying the established, ah, infrastructure on *Henderson*'s world. Whether ignorance or intent, it must not be allowed to, ah, continue or happen again." The historian rose, leaning her weight on her fists. "The value of what these people have built, ah, to the next round of settlers is incalculable. Incalculable!"

Rena was shaking her head. "You can't believe we'll ever send people there again, not after this."

"I'm certain we will." Sofia appeared galvanized, her face full of excitement, her voice a confident staccato. "Certain Ousmane's right. If the Kmet can't or won't tell the difference between flesh and construct, we must send someone who does."

The System Coalition. Henry'd thought Sofia out of it. *Should have remembered dreams never die.*

Shomchai had sat back, looking pensive. "Oversight," he said abruptly. "Kmeth grasp the concept of an observer with authority."

"Yes, for an engineer going to a new mine," Rena said. "You can't be thinking of—" Her head swiveled to Henry.

"It doesn't matter," he said, when she didn't finish the sentence. "The Assembly won't let me go, whether in my shuttle or with the Kmet."

Sofia tapped the table. "Send me instead. If there is a threat, if, as the Kmet insist, all Humans must pull back to New Earth and be under their protection—forget first contact. We're talking mass evacuations. Resettlement. My specialties. I'm the one to go."

Eager to check out a future new home?

Whatever her reasons, it was a brave offer. "Thank you, Sofia. I'll present the option to the Assembly, but don't pack yet. I suspect it was the challenge of so many coming at once that swayed the vote against us." He stood, as good a signal here of a meeting's end as in the real world. "I'm expecting the uplink at any minute. Thank you all for your guidance."

***

A red dot blinked near the bottom of the screen. Henry drew a breath, straightening his shoulders, and began a slow inward count. Curiosity, mostly, to see if Liam's equipment would better its nine-second best this round.

It helped him remain calm. According to Omar, the Portal in Earth orbit was about to simul-pop again, bringing back the one with a no-longer-novice pilot. A notification Kmet-Here failed to make, even though it returned kmeth's Portal to Rogue 58.

Had anyone remembered to tell Niablo Station?

"Transit, sir."

"Fifteen, Liam. Well done."

"Thank you, sir. Henry."

"Mersi, prepare—"

"We're getting the sat feed. Visuals, from the surface. Oh my God—"

"Show me," Henry ordered quietly.

The screen switched to multiple images, pouring down in columns, too small to make out until the operator selected a particular set to enlarge.

At first, he didn't grasp what he was seeing. A Kmet mining operation, busier than most—the machines were familiar to all in the room—

But it wasn't a mine. It was a town, a recognizably Human town, and the *town* was what the machines tore apart and sorted and dumped into transport bins.

Gasps from around him. A sob. A curse.

Knowing wasn't the same as seeing. They owed that pilot.

He did.

"Remove it from the main screen, Li Jie. Please," Henry added gently when the stunned operator didn't obey at once. "I'll need a summary as you have it. And—everyone—" Henry raised his voice, turning around. "—this doesn't leave the office."

A muted chorus of "Yes, Henry."

With one critical exception. "Mersi, send direct to the members of the Assembly, urgent. Add to the attention of the Chair: the Arbiter requests a second vote based on this new information. And Mersi?"

"Yes, Henry?"

"Tell her I'll wait."

***

The second vote was unanimous in favor of Henry's mission, not that he'd had any doubt. No one on this planet, seeing those images, would leave the Kmet to rescue living Humans.

Henry'd recalled his quorum at once. "Sofia, once you wake, please use the

Arbiter's Office to create a framework and coordinate with local governments. What we'll need here. What we'll need to transit through—assuming," he added wryly, "I can convince the Kmet to do this our way."

"I must interview everyone," Ousmane burst out, then half-covered her mouth as if shocked by her own zeal. "When it's, ah, appropriate," she added very quietly.

"I'll do my best," Henry assured her, understanding. It wasn't only people he'd bring back; it'd be the sum of their history. New knowledge.

With any grace at all, new courage.

He rose to his feet. "Thank you."

A murmured round of somber "Good lucks."

Catching Rena's look, he tapped everyone else's band. Sofia, Ousmane, and Shomchai winked out of existence. "I know what you're going to say," he began.

"That you've spent too long away as it is? That this is incredibly dangerous?" She managed a smile. "The Assembly got it right. You're the only one the Kmet will listen to, Henry, upset or not, and there are, we all hope, lives to be saved out there." Her smile faltered. "Do me a favor. Come back in one piece."

"I can't promise, Rena. Not if the stakes include lives here as well."

Her eyes widened. "You don't believe what the Kmet told the pilot. That kmeth came to protect us."

"I can't risk it. Not when it makes just as much sense to me the Kmet came to New Earth thinking we could protect them."

Her brow rose. "There's a disappointment."

"Maybe." He grinned. "I'd like to think we have our strengths."

Rena half-smiled back. "So do I. Good luck."

Henry's fingers hovered over her band then withdrew.

"What is it?"

"The Print House rep expressed concern in the Assembly. I'm afraid they're ready to pull me out at the least sign of stress."

"To save your life, Henry."

"By preventing any risk, even ones I'm willing to take. Even ones I may have to take to get this done." He gazed at the one person in the world who knew his every weakness and fault, his every capability and strength. Rena'd trained her whole life to work with alien life-forms like the Kmet. Had been the best, most logical choice to assist him when he became Arbiter, wanted it with all her being, and he couldn't refuse.

Even if Rena's being his oneiric ended their intimacy. No one was at fault. Spending your dreams in someone else's head tended to disrupt physical attraction, let alone what it did to romantic fantasies. As they grew awkward in bed, finally laughing in mutual frustration, their friendship only deepened.

"Rena—" he began and stopped. Afraid to ask.

Knowing he didn't have to.

"You want me as proxy," she said heavily. "You want me to let you suffer, maybe die."

"To let me succeed." As proxy, her neural net would be modified, granting her the ability and authority to shut down his, returning Henry to himself: an authority superseding his own. There'd be no way back without her consent.

No one else he'd trust to put the mission first. "Will you?"

"I hate this."

He nodded.

"You're going to owe me one hell of a favor on the other side. Yes. Yes. Put me down." Rena waved her hand to shoo him out of his own head. "Get to work, Henry."

Averting her face too late to hide the glisten of tears.

Mersi shot up her thumb. "In three, two, one—"

The screen filled with an eye Henry knew.

"NO HUMANS-THERE!!!"

An earthquake might have struck the building. The wooden frame toppled to the floor. There were cries from the room as the powerful vibrations of, yes, an *extremely* upset Kmet hit the air inside Human lungs.

Frantically Mersi signaled to her crew. *Scrub it!*

"ONLY HUMANS-HERE!!!" Even without the disturbing layer of unheard sound, the overloud voice hit nerves. "DANGER! DANGER!"

Henry lifted his hand, waited for Mersi to play the greeting harmony. Spoke over the hum, his voice quiet and composed while his heart hammered in his throat. "This is Arbiter Henry m'Yama t'Nowak. Am I addressing Kmet-Here?"

The eye blinked, the pupil adjusting as if noticing Henry for the first time. "ARBITER-HENRY!!! ARBITER-HENRY!!"

He had to calm kmeth. "Peace, Kmet-Here. You have our gratitude for—" *use kmeth's term* "—retrieving our lost ones." And there was Shomchai's contribution, in place of loaded words like corpse or victim. "Thank you."

The pupil shrank. "It was essential," at lower volume. "There cannot be Humans in wrong places."

Whatever "wrong place" meant. Tempting, to outright ask. Safer, Henry decided, to start with what he had to achieve. "There could be, Kmet-Here," he announced. "More Humans, that is."

The iris kept closing until the pupil was a dot Henry could have covered with his hand. Finally, "More? Where?"

"It might be a wrong place. It might not." Henry took the risk. "It is not here."

A long, long pause. The clear lid crossed the eye, over and over again, a steady hypnotic rhythm. *Thinking.*

Henry maintained his expression of polite interest and wished he'd worn a cooler jacket.

The pupil suddenly expanded to half size. *Conclusion reached.* "Here is the right place for Humans, Arbiter-Henry. With Kmet. Only here is our Duality safe from the Divider. If the Divider finds Humans in wrong places, none will be safe."

An offering. The revelation of another intelligence, a third, outside their Duality.

This was not a public conversation; the few allowed to witness would be scrambling to comb every record since the Kmet arrived for reference to *Divider*.

The stakes couldn't be higher. A new species—one Humans could potentially negotiate with—end this.

Or not. Henry came to a conclusion of his own. Assuming the Kmet used the term *place* to mean planet—as most believed—kmeth's focus on exploring sunless, lifeless worlds, adrift and alone, might have a specific reason. "Are rogue worlds safe from the Divider?"

A black lid descended, almost shutting the eye. Did Kmet-Here regret giving Humans that name to use?

He'd take kmeth's hesitation as a yes.

Making the Divider a space-faring species willing to destroy others who, what, trespassed on living worlds? Was that why the powerful Kmet never left their Portals?

Was that why, Henry thought, staring into the abyss of an alien eye, *on finding Earth teeming with intelligent life, kmeth decided to protect it?*

Maybe, something deep inside him cautioned, pulling back. They didn't know enough. Not nearly enough. "The Duality remains healthy," Henry said, buying time.

"Only with all Humans-Here, Arbiter-Henry." The eyelid rose. "This is critical to the health. There must be no Humans-There."

"As Arbiter, I will make that happen, Kmet-Here, with your help. I request transit for myself and my shuttle to find such Humans."

"Coordinates."

Not this time, you don't. Henry kept his expression pleasant. "All Humans are the Arbiter's responsibility, Kmet-Here. I'll bring the coordinates with me. At my signal, Earth will send transports to bring our people home. All will be Humans-Here. Is this agreeable?"

"Yes." The pupil expanded, filling the screen as the Kmet closed in on kmeth's lens. "Come now, Arbiter-Henry. NOW."

Simmons, at the edge of the screen, showed Henry two fingers.

"Expect me in two hours, Kmet-Here."

The screen went blank.

Henry let out a long breath, then raised a questioning eyebrow at his assistant. "Flip's ready to launch." *With a mild grumble at the amount of baggage.*

Simmons came close as the rest began taking apart equipment with quiet murmurs and no few looks his way. "On her oneiric's suggestion I took the liberty of contacting the Spacer Repository—to send us anything the pilot, Killian, left for the next flight up. That's the delay." He looked remarkably pleased with himself.

New pilots routinely failed to appreciate how few and far between those additional flights might be, winding up stuck on a Portal without some crucial-to-them personal item. The Repository fielded such pleas on a regular basis and no, they didn't respond by sending a pilot's personal effects on the Arbiter's shuttle.

Until now. Henry regarded Simmons. "Why?"

Some of the pleasure faded at his tone. "The mission, Henry. You said the odds are it'll be longer than the normal rotation. Maybe much longer. Kisho told me Killian will need her things."

"And seeing them arrive with me, what do you think Killian will conclude?"

A blink. A hesitation during which Henry suspected Simmons replayed their earlier conversation. An abashed expression. "That she's being given no choice."

Which her helpful oneiric would know. "I think we owe Killian one, don't you? After what she's been through."

His assistant nodded. "I'll return her belongings."

Henry chuckled. "Being an optimist, I'll take them with me. You're right that Killian will want her things—if she agrees to come. Just have a list of pilots ready to take her place, Simmons, in case she spits in my eye."

A dubious, "Surely she won't."

"I'm joking." He hoped. "Anything else?"

Simmons, smiling, held up a bag. "Your other doughnut."

"Magnificent." Henry took it with an answering grin. "Now, since you've arranged everything, and thank you again, I'd best use my time to—" He caught himself before saying *put my affairs in order*; even to him, that sounded grim. "—change for the trip."

"Yes, Henry. I—I wish there was more I could do."

"There is, in fact." Stooping, Henry picked up the frame. "Please put through a call to my grandfather. Let me know when he's on." He smiled down at the image. "It might take a while. Depends on the chickens."

He went around the room, thanking the techs, especially Mersi, who'd put in a long few hours. They weren't done. There'd be an edited version of his agreement with Kmet-Here to show the general public, with a package of information on the sleeper ships. A release about the *Henderson* would be in the works, sent through multiple edits and revisions before others made the choice when, where, and how much to set loose. Henry rather thought those in charge would wait to see how his mission went, it being a much happier situation if he found people, alive and well and—

Willing to leave?

He'd have to develop an approach, how much to say to each—especially where kmeth might be listening—thankfully, he'd his quorum ready, with their support networks.

Two hours didn't seem long at all. Henry took his doughnut from its bag, sniffing reverently. "Might be the last for a while."

"Your grandfather," Simmons told him, handing Henry a remote. "I couldn't get a secured line," in a troubled whisper.

It was a farm; there were none. Henry merely nodded.

He took the remote, and doughnut, to sit in a quiet corner of the room and talk about the weather and missing bean sprouts and learn where the hens had hidden their nests this time.

Knowing his grandfather would hear what he didn't need to say at all.

"You're serious?"

THE screens came alive.

The left showed people. Humans. Running down what appeared a wide street and for an instant, Killian felt relief. They'd made it home—again. She'd been mercifully unconscious for a fourth transit—

Then her eyes shifted to the middle screen. Saw the advancing line of blue fire, the reason the people were running—

—while the right screen showed a planet of blue and green, white and brown, like a jewel on black velvet, a planet covered in lines of blue fire—

They weren't lines, she realized in horror, they were rings, flaming rings on the surface growing smaller and smaller. New Earth. Home—

Her head snapped back to the left screen. The people weren't running.

The people burned.

"Fuck! Fuckity fuck FUCK!" Killian beat her fists into her pillow, tears streaming down her face.

Not real. Not real! She didn't smell burning flesh. New Earth was—was fine.

She pushed herself up on shaking arms, head hanging.

She'd survived the next transit, not in the toilet, on the floor of her quarters. Hadn't made a mess; there'd been nothing left to expel from her body. Just as well. No PIPs allowed in here, so nothing to clean up after her.

She'd roused. Guzzled a bulb of the appropriately labeled Restore. Used a second to wash down the drugs Kisho might have told her to take *before* and not *after.* Dragged off her soiled coveralls and fallen face-first into bed.

Whatever good she'd done for herself, the sickening dream had erased.

Somehow, Killian sat up, putting her legs over the side of her bed. A bed, not a cot or pull out. After years in communal quarters and hammocks on ships and stations—epitomes not needing more—she'd thought it quite the luxury, having a real bed in her own room, with a bathroom she didn't share.

With a door that locked.

She continued to like that feature. Liked the neat counter and sink, with its cupboards full of ready-dinners, the epitome nutrition staple.

Didn't, the stark bareness of the rest. Shelves, still empty, above the bed. Desk with pull-out seat and drawer, empty. Her duffel stood alone next to the door, packed. She'd left her things, in a hurry to see her first Control and meet her *partner* face-to-whatever kmeth had. Few made it into the training program, let alone became pilots—she'd been proud. Exhilarated.

Giselle had thrown her a party—

Killian dragged her eyes up to the Portal's version of a com panel, a series of lights and tones, several outside Human senses. A steady red light flashed. *What was red?* A summons. Green meant Control. "Fuck," she repeated wearily, and pressed her wristband. "Kisho. What's happening?"

<The Arbiter's on his way up.>

Killian blinked. "What?"

<You've less than fifteen to get to the airlock and greet him. He'll—are you hearing me?>

"Yes." Though she'd like the voice in her head to slow down and make sense. Killian pressed her hands over her ears. "The Arbiter's coming *here*. Boarding."

<He'll want your report before meeting kmeth.> Kisho's voice assumed its normal unpleasant arrogance. <Wake up. You're not the only pilot the Kmet just screwed. Omar's begging for relief and they won't let him swap out either. So pull yourself together and do your damn—>

Killian pressed the wristband to shut Kisho up.

Regarded her locked door wistfully.

Then grabbed her duffel and headed for the shower.

***

A Portal had one airlock, according to kmeth. Which was weird, according to Humans, given the size of the construct, and worrisome, given the fragility of living things in space, but that's as it was and Humans didn't argue.

There might be more. The Kmet didn't share anything concerning Portals kmeth didn't absolutely must to gain Human help and keep those helpful Humans alive.

Killian hadn't been up here since her arrival. Didn't remember the entry area to the airlock being this large or as bitterly cold. She blew warmth on her fingers and shifted from side to side, having arrived five minutes ahead of the Arbiter's shuttle and in her haste forgetting parka and gloves.

PIPs were everywhere, busy about whatever they did, ignoring Killian except to keep a distance. This version resembled stubby tortoises, with legs ending in what she decided were magnetic discs after watching the things run up walls and across the ceiling.

She rubbed bare arms, having had to settle for her off-duty coveralls, the only other option stuck to the floor of her quarters. To the good, her clothes were clean, as she was; not so good, she'd hacked off the sleeves a few years back and, since then, used the front—and glue—to house her collection of mission patches and rude spacer sayings. It was great for the sort of seedy bars she and Giselle liked.

Hell of a first impression now. She stamped her feet to keep some feeling in them.

The Arbiter? She knew the type. High-ranking public servants were worse than station commanders. He'd sniff and give her a dirty look, as if her outer appearance made any difference to her work. Wouldn't listen to a word she said but give her orders? Oh, they'd come hard and fast, starting with *carry my gear* and *keep out of my way.*

Fine with her.

PIPs stopped where they were, orienting toward the oval door of the airlock. A second later, lights rimmed the thickened metal plate and showed through a tall, narrow window.

The shuttle had docked.

Now what remained was for the Arbiter to disembark and walk into the airlock. It would cycle closed—the shuttle either staying linked to wait or pushing off to remain in the vicinity—then the inner door open.

Hurry up already. Killian shivered, seeing her breath.

The door swung open. She peered in, dismayed to find the airlock empty. *Where was the Arbiter?*

"Pilot Killian, please enter." A pleasant male voice.

She'd been recalled. *That stunt with the sats.* That's what it meant, being called into the shuttle. The feed would have started autosend once the Portal arrived in Earth orbit—to the Arbiter's Office as well as the Repository—

Why hadn't Kisho warned her? *To see her grovel?*

When Killian recalled her nightmare and what inspired it, leaving this post might not be the worst idea.

Leaving in disgrace was. She scowled, wrapping her arms around her middle, and didn't budge. "On what grounds?" *Make them say it.* She'd right on her side.

"I do not understand."

"Why. Am. I. Recalled."

"You have not been, Pilot Killian. You are invited to come in me."

In me? This shuttle didn't have a pilot and crew. It had an Alt-Intel, which made it a thinking ship, which made it a snob and no proper spacer's friend.

"'Invited'," she stalled. "What for?"

"I don't know. Once you come in—" the disembodied voice told her, sounding amused, "—you can ask Henry for yourself."

The air flowing through the airlock door was warmer than where she was. Decision made on that basis, refusing to admit to curiosity and maybe a little awe, Killian stepped inside.

The door behind her closed, the outer opened. Beyond that was another, of a strange gray-green material with a liquid glisten. She reached out.

The shuttle's door slid open.

"Come in, please." Another voice, instantly familiar from news sound bites and government announcements. There'd been a documentary after the Transiting Goods Label negotiation, sponsored by the Spacer Repository and required watching.

The Arbiter.

Who had to take her as she was, Killian told herself, bristling as she walked into the shuttle.

Only to stop, her way blocked. She stared in disbelief at what weren't the luxurious appointments of a spacecraft used by the most influential person on New Earth but instead a plain, round cargo hold, jammed with random crates and boxes strapped to the floor.

It took her a moment to spot the smallish man in a gray suit on the far side, seated on a crash seat let down from the wall, hands folded in his lap. Not her replacement, had she any doubt left.

The Arbiter. His face? Familiar as the voice. Giselle thought it classically handsome, like some old painting she'd seen once. Killian had argued it might as well be paint, because it wasn't a real face, not with that quick reassuring smile able to convince millions it was for each of them, and certainly not with those blue eyes that went from peaceful to sharp conviction as if controlled by a switch.

Facing the man, Killian was forced to concede his face was real after all. Not the hair, artfully tousled over his high forehead. *How long'd it take a stylist to get that to stay put?* Her still-unsettled gaze landed on a stack of green trunks. "You brought my stuff."

"Just in case," he said mysteriously. He undid his safety harness and stood. Was taller than she'd thought. "Hello. I'm Henry m'Yama t'Nowak, my epitomeself."

No one but an epitome left Earth.

No one but the Arbiter could bring frivolous excess to a Portal. She'd brought barely enough to survive, counting on dribs and drabs arriving later. Offended, Killian waved her hands at the crates. "What's all this?"

"I've no idea." Busy working his way to her, there being very little floor showing, he paused and tilted his head like one of her younger twin brothers up to mischief. "They didn't tell me. There's my luggage." He angled his arm to indicate a pair of scuffed and dented cases. "Flip, do you have the manifest for our good pilot?"

"Of course, Henry," said the disembodied voice—no, alt had a body, Killian suddenly realized. She stood inside it. "Should I forward the list to your mail, Pilot Killian, or would you prefer a print version?"

It was talking *to her.*

Seeing no console or screen, Killian picked a spot on the ceiling to address. "To my mail—ah—Shuttle."

"Henry calls me Flip."

A FLIP? A *fucking human-made polymorph?* This was no shuttle with an Alt-Intel pilot tucked behind a bulkhead.

This was the present highly temporary version of some *thing* with a mind of its own, a scandalous blend of Human- and Kmet-tech Killian, personally, hadn't ever seen in person nor wanted to, had she been offered, and now—now she was *in* one?

Seeming oblivious to her shock, the Arbiter sketched a circle over his head. "Flip's a flying saucer. Did kmeth notice?"

Maybe she was still dreaming. "A what?"

The polymorph answered. "A flying saucer is a common motif in historical science fiction, Pilot Killian. It is an entertaining and unexpectedly efficient shape for surface-to-space transport."

"Fun," the Arbiter translated.

Or Earth sent a buffoon.

"People died," she snapped. "*Sir.*"

"Yes." She'd never seen a face alter expression in a flash like this, the mouth becoming solemn and grim, the eyes full of a startling depth of grief. It meant the grins and easy manner of before had been for her benefit.

Putting her in the wrong. Didn't like him, Killian decided then and there. Didn't like anyone who turned their feelings on and off to manipulate those around them.

"I'm here to help," the Arbiter continued, probably reading everything in her face. *Reading her badges, likely, and there went any doubt about what she was.* "Let's start over." He held out his hand, smiling. "I'm Henry m'Yama t'Nowak. Henry."

The gesture shoved her off balance, closer to anger. "What help are you talking about? Sir." She ignored his hand. Was likely about to be fired and sent home in this flying whatever. Killian didn't, at the moment, give a damn. "We *retrieved* the bodies. What *help* is there for that? Bringing my trunks?!"

The Arbiter kept his hand out. "What's your name?"

He bloody well knew it. Playing the game, she accepted his hand, gave it a quick, limp shake, then tugged hers away. "Killian. Killian m'Lamarr t'Brown. *Sir.*"

"Henry. We need to talk. Please, have a seat, Killian. Flip? Some juice?" Blue eyes considered her. "Coffee?"

Her coffee maker was in one of those trunks. Bringing them was not why he'd come. Killian plopped herself on a crate, giving him a sidelong look. "Coffee. Sir."

"Henry," he repeated, as if it was somehow important she forget his rank.

As if she ever would.

Buffoon.

***

The coffee came from a slot that appeared in one wall, delivered in the type of recyclable cup used by spacers. Hot, strong, and black, the first swallow hit like a transfusion and Killian gave the cup a sincerely grateful glance before returning her full attention to the Arbiter.

Who sipped juice and had come into space wearing, of all the fool things, sandals.

He saw her notice his feet and opened his mouth to explain.

Not interested. "Sir. I'm prepared to give you my report."

"Henry. Finish your coffee first, Killian." He had to know what she'd been through, three simul-pops with no break. Hell, easy for anyone to see she wasn't remotely at her best, but he didn't offer sympathy.

She flushed anyway. She lowered her cup, about to protest—

"We've a few minutes. Kmet-Here," the Arbiter continued, "has been informed there'll be a delay before I board the Portal." He tapped a sandaled foot on the deck. "In part, because kmeth refused to let Flip come with me."

As something not a shuttle—not that she'd a clue what—the creepiest part of polymorph tech being that ability to reshape at will. Killian eyed Henry over the rim of her cup. By the terms of the Duality, negotiated by this man's office and highly inconvenient to pilots, Human-tech on a Portal was restricted to personal communicators and external satellites. Her coffee maker had taken forms in triplicate to be approved. She hadn't dared try for a toaster. "Why'd you bother asking?"

"Part of the job." That grin again, lighting his eyes and inviting her to share. "You never know. One day, a Kmet might say yes."

Potent, that charm. Practiced. Killian resisted the tug at the edge of her lips. "And one day, *sir*, the Heartbreak will be a note in history and our real selves get to space."

His eyebrow rose.

She replayed what she'd said and felt the blood drain from her face. You didn't talk about *what* you were, on a Portal. Didn't let the aliens know the only Humans who left Earth's gravity inhabited flesh suits, disposable and safe, and the only excuse she had for the slip was—him. *He* made words fall out of her mouth. Honest words, sure, but dangerous beyond belief. Killian cringed inwardly, braced for a reprimand, angry to be caught.

The eyebrow went down. Was followed by an unexpected nod. "You're quite right. The path humanity took to return to space wasn't meant to trap us as this." He touched his chest, expanded the gesture with an open palm to her. "The laws weren't supposed to stop brave individuals willing to take those risks—courage I freely admit Earth needs to recover, Killian. Badly and soon."

He was saying things to her that belonged on the top floors of the Arbiter's Office, behind locked doors and security shields—*why?* Wariness didn't stop her tongue. "Can't happen now, can it? We can't let people be alone up here. Can't let them act for themselves." Killian lifted her arm, showed him the wristband. "Because of—" She jerked her head at the airlock.

"Because we aren't alone. The Kmet reset the clock on us," with shocking frankness. "Until we reach a deeper level of mutual understanding—of predictability—epitomes with oneirics remain what it is to be Human, out here and with kmeth. We are working to do better. It's part of my job to bring us back. Don't worry." He must have read something in her face. "Flip ensures our privacy, don't you, old friend?"

"Yes, Henry."

Private or not, Killian was certain she wasn't supposed to hear such things. Didn't want to, was more to the point. "Why are you talking to me like this?" Disrespectful, that surly tone. She didn't mend it. "I'm just the pilot. Sir."

"Henry."

Bad as her brothers. She plucked at a badge ruder than most, glaring back. "Sir."

A half-smile. "Your choice," he conceded. He leaned forward, elbows resting on his knees, intent on her. "Yes, you're the pilot. If we're to work together, we have to trust one another. I realize," a rueful shrug, "that's a great deal to ask from a few minutes' conversation—"

"'Work together'?" She'd thought he'd come up from New Earth to meet with Kmet-Here, maybe get in kmeth's face about Human remains and bits, dig out answers. *Replace her with another pilot.* Killian looked at the crates and boxes, realizing with a sick lurch what surely she'd have figured out right away if her head wasn't still half-fogged and stupid. *Supplies—a lot of them.* "You're taking the Portal. Where?"

"After the remaining sleeper ships."

Killian burst out laughing. When his face didn't change, she stopped. "You're serious."

"I've seen the images. What you saw, Killian. I'm not the only one. What happened to the people from the *Henderson* mustn't happen again. It's our job to make sure of that. We're to bring everyone we find home, to New Earth."

The smell from her dream came back to her. The stench of burnt flesh. Burnt people. Killian ran a shaking hand over her scalp, left it pressed against the back of her head as she stared at him. "*Our* job," she echoed numbly. She glanced at her trunks, then back to him. "Why aren't you replacing me?"

"Should I?" He met her stare with a steady, inscrutable look. "Your choice, Killian," he repeated.

"Mine?" She wanted to laugh. "First day on the job I threw up in Control. More than once."

His nose wrinkled. "I suppose it'll be my turn soon."

"The meds take care of that," she confessed. "I forgot mine."

"And still functioned." He lowered his head, looking up at her through a lock of unruly brown hair. "*Effective under extraordinary pressure.* From your oneiric's report. You thought to keep a vital survey going, to be sure all of *Henderson*'s people were accounted for—to show us what you'd witnessed firsthand, for which I thank you, from my office and personally. Seeing—well, it was the warning we needed to put Humans in charge of the next mission."

Killian stared into her coffee cup. The Arbiter gave her more credit than she deserved—she hadn't given any thought to the impact of others seeing the bodies on the ground or destructive recovery methods of the Kmet, just to gather the data. Finish the work.

"Pilot." When she looked up, he tipped his juice packet at her. "Let's not forget you, Killian m'Lamarr t'Brown, have seen another Human world. No one else can say that."

"Yet," she countered.

His infectious grin reappeared. "Exactly. What do you say?"

Killian held up her cup. "I need another coffee." She took a deep breath. "I'd like to see a world with still-alive people," she admitted. *To chase away the nightmare.*

He waited.

"I'll go. On one condition." A finger tap to her ear. "We're heading that far out, I want a new oneiric. Can you do that?"

"I'm the Arbiter. I can do anything."

If about power, the words, their gentle certainty, would have been chilling. Something in his eyes assured her they weren't. They were the acceptance of appalling responsibility, as if all he was, was for all of them—including her.

She shook off the feeling. *Just the pilot.* "I want my former oneiric. Giselle m'Tharp t'Horyn. We trained together—she'd have made Portal pilot too, if she—" *If she still had legs.* The Print House tried, but there was no reconciling Giselle's stubborn self-awareness with an intact epitome and, according to the know-it-alls, no surprising a Kmet with anything else. Didn't matter how well she functioned on a station or shuttle. Didn't matter her grace in zero-g—"Giselle knows her stuff," Killian stated. *Let him look up the rest.*

"We'll need our friends," he agreed, confounding her perceptions again. "Flip, stand by to transmit my authorization to change Killian's oneiric, if Giselle agrees." To her, "Do you want your current oneiric to remain at the Repository as a resource?"

"Not if she tries to boss Giselle, I don't."

He ducked his head as if to hide a smile. "You can stipulate the terms of the interaction."

And lupins could fly. Still, if he wasn't lying . . . if she and Giselle had access to Kisho's annoying but undeniable knowledge . . . "All right—"

The *sir* hung between them.

Killian let it go. "—Henry. You've got yourself a pilot."

"I know what I heard!"

HENRY.

A warm spot, a tiny step to a shared path; Henry knew better than make anything more of it. The pilot had coped with kmeth's extreme behavior. *Good.* Wasn't cowed by his office. *Better.* Her willingness to stay and help save lives when she'd every right to demand a deserved leave home reinforced Kisho's recommendation. *Best.*

None of which mattered more than his initial assessment.

She didn't hide her feelings, or chose not to—an honesty he found encouraging. Killian's face scowled fiercely and smiled well: broad, with strong lines at jaw and cheek, and large, dark brown eyes, bloodshot but alert, shrouded by thick lashes. Her scalp was covered in a close-cut black fuzz, a geometric pattern shaved into the sides. Nice work by the Spacer Repository. There were even holes in her epitome's earlobes and in each wide nostril where she'd removed piercings from previous assignments. Prudent. Kmet tended to fixate on them. Muscle flexed along her bare arms and her posture, weary or not, suggested athleticism.

Killian was in her mid-forties, as was he, and the patches dotting her faded, loose-fitting coveralls hinted at a past full of stories—and an attitude. He liked both, to be honest. *Not that she'd care.*

He liked that as well.

The pilot cradled her coffee, studying him in return. She'd arrived with conceptions about who he was, based on what he was; most who met him did. *Might be shifting.*

She'd arrived with those bloodshot eyes, now clear and bright, and the hand holding the cup no longer trembled. Flip's coffee, no doubt, the polymorph having read the exhausted pilot's vitals when she arrived and inclined to *fix* things.

Maybe she wouldn't notice.

"Let's get started," Henry announced. "I need your observations of Kmet-Here and kmeth's reactions, Killian. To me and my oneirics at once, if you don't mind."

She touched her wristband. Reflex. Didn't tap it. *Decision.* For whatever reason, the pilot didn't want her oneiric present.

"We've had Kisho's statement," he told her. She'd know, but it was polite. "As for my oneirics, I won't call them unless you agree."

He'd startled her. *Was it the courtesy?*

She tried to hide a pleased look, responding with a gruff, "Fine with me. Then I offload the gear?" With an understandingly dubious glance at Flip's crowded deck. "I'll need a cart."

"All this can stay until we need it. Right, Flip?"

"Yes, Henry."

He caught Killian's twitch at Flip's voice. No surprise a pilot would have issues with a self-aware shuttle. Again, most did. *Definitely not the time to tell her about the salutary coffee.*

"I want to move quickly. Kmet-Here agreed to my coming on board with the coordinates. I'd prefer not to give kmeth time to reconsider."

She swirled her cup and took a sip, then frowned at him over the rim. "Last time you gave coordinates to a Kmet, Henry, it didn't go so well."

She'd every right and reason to protest another transit so soon. To complain, bitterly, and that she did neither told him more. "I'm sorry, Killian. I truly am. We were all taken by surprise."

A shrug dismissed the apology. "We get there, then what?"

"If we find living descendants, I go down and explain the situation to them."

"The *situation* as in: leave or die."

Henry coughed. "I may phrase it differently but, yes, in essence. Evacuate the population to New Earth; go to the next planet. Repeat till done." He spread his hands. "That's the gist. What do you think?"

"Me?" The flash of a wicked grin. "Glad I'm the pilot."

She understood, he realized. Enough, anyway. The people he took from their homes wouldn't thank him. If their grief demanded someone to blame, that would be the Arbiter's job as well, one Henry suspected wouldn't last beyond this mission. He allowed himself to hope he would—

Worth it, worth all of it, so long as everyone survived—

"Ready to give your report?"

A nod. She straightened.

His oneirics were waiting on their couches in the Arbiter's Tower, attended by the medical team; once the mission was underway, they could and should return to their own homes and privacy, with support. He would urge it.

Henry slid up his jacket sleeve to expose his colorful wristbands, their inactive pattern a match to Killian's.

Who held up four fingers, raising a skeptical eyebrow.

Yes, he'd the upgrade. Henry smiled. "Flip? Project the full quorum, please."

"Yes, Henry."

Killian's eyes widened as four standing figures appeared inside the shuttle, then narrowed to shoot him a hard assessing look.

He gave back her little shrug. *They'd a lot to learn about each other.*

Projections were everyday tech on New Earth. They weren't here, on a Portal, and though he couldn't give her the technical background for exactly how a combination of FLIPs, neurally-linked Human brains, and an epitome with his hardware as a nexus came together to make this work, the result?

She'd meet them, they'd meet her.

"Pilot Killian m'Lamarr t'Brown, I present my oneirics. These fine people will be traveling with me—with us—as long as needed."

Ousmane, new to being projected, looked discomfited to find her lower body inside crates. When Sofia merely walked forward until her projection cleared the obstacle, the historian followed suit, her arms out for balance.

They weren't dreaming. Awake, wearing headgear, what each oneiric saw and heard as a projection was provided through Flip's sensory equipment, not Henry's eyes and ears. If they turned their heads, Flip adjusted the result to match. According to Rena, it felt remarkably real—except for the lack of touch and, yes, walking through objects.

Shomchai, whose legs were in one of Killian's trunks, grinned and stayed where he was. Rena made her way to stand beside Henry, giving him a small smile before looking at the pilot. "Hello, Killian. I'm Rena. I help interpret the Kmet's biology."

"Body bits. Hah!" Shomchai spread his hands. "Words are where true understandings lie." With a wink. "Shomchai, linguist."

Killian looked impressed. "You speak Kmet?"

His face fell. "Alas, no. No one does. The Kmet remain unwilling to share kmeth's language with us. Perhaps because kmeth worked so hard to learn ours before arriving." Then he brightened. "I did create the tonal correlation algorithm you pilots use."

"So the weird singing lessons are your fault?" Killian's frown turned into a shy smile. "Thanks."

"This is Ousmane, our expert on the sleeper ships," Henry told her, the historian still distracted by her balance. "And—"

"Sofia m'Rogers t'Patel, Crisis Specialist." Her glare skipped past Killian to lock on him. "Here under protest, Arbiter. I should be instructing ship captains, not interviewing a Portal pilot with what, a day's experience, who disobeys the most fundamental regulations." A dismissive shrug. "She'll have nothing to say worth hearing."

"I have plenty." The sullen scowl she'd shown him on entering Flip was back, deeper than before, as Killian faced Rena's projection. "The Arbiter showed the probe's message. Kmet-Here reacted immediately. Nonstop subsonics. Moans. Violent erratic moves around Control. Squashed PIPs to jelly. I kept clear. Kmeth's willy-bits—" Hesitation.

Accustomed to the pilot term, Rena nodded encouragement. "How were they?"

"Hidden. After the third pop, at the planet—red ones came out. Kmeth BOOMED and demanded my help." Killian switched her scowl to Shomchai.

"The word, sir, was *help*. The other was *retrieve*. I was to send mining equipment to the surface." Back at Sofia. "To collect corpses."

With a finger stroke over a patch Henry sincerely hoped his oneiric couldn't read from that angle. *Should have coached Flip on tact parameters.*

Shomchai pursed his lips, studying the pilot. "Your oneiric said you accused the Kmet of killing Humans."

Killian flicked her wrist, as if to discard her wristband and who it represented. "Inaccurate, sir. I accused kmeth of sending Kmet-There to kill them. That's when Kmet-Here went off about having come to New Earth to protect us. How kmeth couldn't if Humans were in *wrong* places—" She took a breath. "—as if those on the *Henderson* had had a choice, sir."

Henry stirred. "Killian, to be accurate, what were the exact words kmeth used about retrieving them?"

"'Bring Human-There to Human-Here. Or Human-Here becomes Human-There.'"

"Hah!" Sofia scoffed. "You were clearly confused. I demand the recording!"

"There are none on a Portal," Shomchai said over Killian's angry, "I know what I heard!"

Ousmane held up her hands. "The Arbiter must, ah, reach the other worlds. We are all to support the mission." With a quelling look at Sofia. "What else, ah, do you want us to know, Pilot?"

"The Kmet expected what they found," Killian said defiantly. "There was a reason Kmet-There was sent ahead, as a scout. The Kmet are terrified of something."

Rena and Shomchai smiled. Ousmane appeared satisfied and even Sofia looked impressed. Reading their faces, Killian turned on Henry. "You already knew." Her scowl hardened. "This was a test."

"Of a sort," Henry admitted, gesturing to the quorum.

"Hiding the willy-bits—retracting sensory polyps—is a Kmet defense mechanism. A response you correctly interpreted as fear," Rena volunteered. "Purple hues enlist those around a Kmet to a shared action, an imperative one."

Shomchai went next. "*Help* and *retrieve* are indeed words to notice. To Kmet, *help* equates to a command to preserve the Duality. *Retrieve—*" He licked his lips as if savoring the taste. "We've no precedents. That's going to keep us busy. Nicely done, Killian."

"Agreed." Sofia almost smiled. "It's true, I've calls on hold with the captains of anything able to convey passengers through a Portal, but this was equally critical. The Arbiter will be alone with the Kmet except for a pilot. Frankly, we'd concerns about it being someone so new."

Killian's eyes were still cold. "I'm sure you did."

"No longer. After what we've seen and heard, after what you did, Killian m'Lamarr t'Brown, I'm relieved it's you." A glance around elicited nods. "We all are."

Cold became fury. "I don't give a flying f—"

"Thank you all." Henry surged to his feet. "End projections, Flip."

The ensuing hush had teeth.

"Flip, please play Killian my last conversation with Kmet-Here."

A screen appeared on a wall. Came to life, filled with that ominous eye. Henry kept his on the pilot.

She flinched at kmeth's shouted, "DANGER! DANGER!"

As the give-and-take between him and the Kmet played out, her scowl was gradually replaced by growing shock. When Flip's replay ended, she stared at Henry and half-whispered, "I was *right*?"

"Yes. There's something out there. All we have beyond that is the name. Divider. Which may not be a name at all, according to Shomchai."

The shock faded beneath a considering look. "You stood up to Kmet-Here."

It hadn't felt like it. Henry shrugged. "I negotiated. Now it's up to us to get kmeth to honor our agreement."

Killian settled back. "So, Henry. Where to first?"

"We follow the *Exeter*."

"Not in my quarters, you're not."

EXETER. Killian tried not to show any excitement, but *damn,* hearing the name of another Halcyon Class ship made it real. They were doing this. *She* was doing this.

With Henry, who at least seemed up front with her.

With his oneirics. Four of them, brought in and out by wristbands like hers, and despite their unusual colors, she'd seen the proper telltale pattern change to signal someone else was listening in, which she had to trust, didn't she?

She'd bet high and wide the one with bugs in her hair was Henry's friend, the way Giselle was hers. The language guy and the other one, the history buff, seemed decent sorts, for academics.

Sofia m'Rogers t'Patel, Crisis Specialist. Killian wasn't buying the switch. The impatient Sofia who didn't want to be here was the real version, with all the attitude she'd expected in the Arbiter. *The better-than, knows-more, condescending—*

Like Kisho. What had she been thinking, blurting out to Henry that she had to have a new oneiric, like some newbie who hadn't learned to work with others? Had she been asleep?

Well, she wasn't now. "Henry—I've changed my mind. Kisho m'Hadfield t'Twist is the most experienced Portal pilot we have. I should keep her."

"Ask her."

She blinked at him. "About what? Giselle?"

A nod.

Wouldn't that *make living with Kisho in her head a joy?* "Terrible idea."

A smile lurked at the corner of his eyes, but his face remained serious. "'An epitome must be able to ask their oneiric anything and trust the answer.'"

He quoted the Print House manual at her? About to explode, Killian put her temper on hold. This unassuming man in sandals and rumpled suit negotiated for the entire planet. Stood up to aliens.

Everything he said had a purpose.

She pressed her wristband. "Kisho."

<Where have you—? The Arbiter—?> A pause, then a more collected, <How can I help, Killian?>

"The Arbiter suggests I ask your advice. We're to leave the solar system on an extended mission. Might take months. Should I replace you with Giselle?" She'd know who Killian meant.

<Absolutely. Do it now.>

Trying to be rid of her? How dare—Killian paused. Frowned absently at Henry, who waited by the airlock door with unexpected patience. Thought, hard.

Kisho was ancient. Maybe she couldn't handle *months.*

No. Killian didn't buy it. The other pilot's toughness was legendary. "Why?"

<You and Giselle are a tight team. What the pair of you don't know or can't figure out, she can ask me. If you'll let me stay on to consult. I've a couple of others in mind. Resources, if you need them. Up to you, Pilot, but—> A softer note. <I know I'd want an old friend along.>

Killian focused on the Arbiter and scowled. *He'd known.* How?

Didn't matter. "Appreciate it, Kisho. Please stay and get whoever you think could help." Relief threatened her voice. Killian firmed it. "Who handles it? The Arbiter's Office? He's offered and standing by."

Henry nodded to confirm.

<Spacers take care of our own. Giselle's been a presence at the Repository. Next time you call up, she'll answer. Good luck, Killian.>

"Won't need it," she answered automatically.

An honest-to-goodness chuckle from Kisho. <Lima Charlie.>

The traditional *your signal's loud and clear* settled close to Killian's heart. She grinned. "Tell you what, Kisho. Stay close till we've made the next simul-pop. I'd hate to start Giselle with one of those."

<Will do. Take your meds this time.>

"Deal." Killian tapped the wristband. Odd. The nag didn't jar her nerves like before. She gave herself a shake. "Ready when you are, Henry."

"Excellent." But instead of keying the door, he looked around the interior of the shuttle and sighed. "Flip, sorry to have to leave you here."

"I understand, Henry," the shuttle replied with what sounded like sympathy. "Don't worry about me. I have new books and films."

Books and films? Killian mouthed, incredulous.

Henry grinned at her. "Enjoy yourself, Flip. We'll be back for our things." He opened the door. "Lead the way, Killian."

She eyed his suit and sandals. "It's freezing in there. Do you have a coat?"

"You don't," he observed.

The admission, "I forgot," fell out of her mouth. *The coffee must be wearing off.*

"Flip? We need warm coats." Henry nodded thoughtfully. "For me, the type I wore to the Polar Summit last year should do nicely."

"Understood." A two-beat pause. "Here you are, Henry, Killian."

Another of the odd little doors formed beside the airlock. This time Killian caught the ripple in the material of the wall preceding it.

"Thank you," Henry said and opened what turned out to be an improbably normal closet that hadn't existed a moment ago, complete with a rod and two long coats on hangers. He took one, handing the other to her as he closed the door. "Here's yours."

It was a coat, soft and light and warm. And wasn't— "What is this?" Killian asked, fingering what looked like wool and felt like—

"Some of me," Flip replied.

She couldn't help it. She dropped it. What appeared fabric landed, briefly became liquid, then solidified again into what looked like a coat, and no way in hell was she putting *that* on.

Henry stopped, arm in one sleeve. "Don't worry. Flip can spare the material."

Killian was speechless.

"Temporarily," the Arbiter continued, watching her.

"Would you prefer a different color, Pilot Killian? Pockets?"

They weren't making fun of her, not quite; she'd a distinct sense of another test. *Just a damn coat,* she told herself. "Yes. Pockets, please."

The coat on the floor *melted* into it and disappeared.

Henry waved at the closet.

Killian stepped around him, opened the door, and, seeing a new coat inside, grabbed it. She thrust her arms into the sleeves, managing not to flinch as the fabric seemed to hug her, then shoved her hands into the ample pockets. "Better." She looked at the ceiling. "Thank you, Flip."

"It is my pleasure, Pilot Killian."

And if that didn't sound smug . . .

***

The coat was warm, fit, and she'd have decided to keep it if she hadn't an immediate vision of it turning into goo and flowing back to the shuttle.

Henry huffed when he stepped out behind her into the antechamber, smiling as he saw his breath, and gawked around the enormous space as if a tourist on holiday.

She had to say it. "You've been on a Portal before."

"Oh yes. A few times," he answered comfortably. "The PIPs keep changing things."

They did? Killian gave the cluster on the wall a curious look. They burst apart, scurrying up, down, and to the sides. The wall remained the same, as did the array of reinforced holes. "So you know how to use the tubes." *She could have stayed in bed.*

"I know to follow the pilot," he admitted with that charming smile. "Kmet-Here doesn't accord visitors the same access."

The disingenuousness of it annoyed her. Since the first Kmet Portal arrived in orbit, the only *visitor* invited on board was the sole person on New Earth the Kmet accepted as equivalent Human authority, namely whomever held the post of arbiter-primary for the planet. Every communication to and from New Earth, every pilot selected, their rotation schedules, when they wiped their noses—*everything* shunted through this man's office.

Her nostrils flared. The entire fucking Duality, from New Earth's forays into space to continued peace with aliens who had such superior technology they hadn't words for the physics, revolved around a single Human, a non-spacer at that. Here now, with her, his head packed full of opinionated experts and his feet in those ridiculous sandals.

She couldn't imagine a worse arrangement. *Not that anyone asked.*

"What did I say?"

The current Arbiter was too damn quick. "Nothing, sir."

His face lit with comprehension. "Ah. Visitor. I should have said professional nuisance. Kmet-Here hates having me on board. Ignores me, often as not, when I am."

What was he talking about? "Make sense," Killian growled.

"The first Kmet had no intention of letting Humans on a Portal, ever. The greatest achievement of the first Arbiter?" A shrug. "To convince the Kmet certain agreements were only binding on Humans if made face-to-face. Her next?" That grin. "Telling the Kmet every ship orbiting our planet required a Human pilot to render assistance at all times, including a Portal."

It wasn't the version of events taught to spacers—or in schools. Killian raised her eyebrows in polite disbelief. "What if the Kmet had refused?"

"We wouldn't be having this conversation," he said, then lightened his tone. "Fortunately, the Kmet liked the idea of pilots under kmeth's command more than kmeth detested an Arbiter's visit. The working assumption is that kmeth are more comfortable with individuals whose function is comprehensible. Kmeth remain unsure what an arbiter does."

Kmeth weren't the only ones. Killian kept quiet.

"To this day, the Kmet have welcomed trained Human pilots. Insist on them, in fact." Henry waved a hand at himself. "While, to this day, the Arbiter remains a necessary pest." He lowered his voice conspiratorially. "I'm pretty sure Kmet-Here worries if I touch anything, I'll break it."

"Don't. Touch anything." Warned by that mischievous half-grin, Killian gave him a dour look. "Before I take you to the bridge, let's refresh the rules, Henry."

"Don't touch anything." Glib and quick. "Don't approach the den. Don't talk out loud to my oneirics in the presence of kmeth. Oh, and don't annoy our host. I may," he added as if an afterthought, "have to break that one."

She'd bet on it. Leaving that alone, Killian jerked a thumb at the airlock door.

"Flip?" His grin vanished. "What about Flip?" Inward focus. "No, thank you. I don't need anything." Outward again. "Why?"

She crossed her arms and leaned against the wall, impressed the coat protected her shoulders from the chill. "More rules. Kmet-Here talks to other Kmet. I don't. You don't. In Control, I'm authorized at any time to use the Portal com for two reasons: to communicate with Human shipping transiting through or to take requests for uplinks with kmeth from your office. Nothing else. Personal coms? Quarters only."

"I had to call Omar," Henry said, not missing her point. "I won't have to call you," with a hint of cute.

Save me. "And your shuttle?"

A slow nod. "I see. You want to know if I've spoken to Flip in front of a Kmet, thus revealing the presence of implanted technology along with the capacity to eavesdrop inside a Portal."

She came off the wall. "I didn't mean—" *She did, damn it.* "I get you make the rules," Killian snapped. "Doesn't prove you won't break them." *And then what happened—*

He merely gave another nod. "I haven't. Will I need to during this mission? Possibly." Henry pulled an object from his pocket, passing it to her. "Which is why I brought this."

"A phone?" An antique. There'd been one just like it in her great-grandmother's drawer, tech so outdated she'd given it to Killian and her brothers as a toy. The pilot turned it over. The power cell was missing. "What's it for?" she asked as she handed the useless thing back.

Henry put it to his ear. "Flip, you there?" He smiled. "Yes, that's right. Just checking in. Talk to you later." Pretending to turn it off, he returned the hunk of plastic to his pocket.

"You've got to be kidding."

A little shrug. "The Kmet have learned I'm unpredictable. Part of that is intentional. At times, I'll produce something odd from my pocket during a negotiation. Glasses. A pen. A chicken feather. A phone." A pat of his pocket.

Killian chewed her lower lip. "Kmeth will know the difference between that and your assigned personal communicator. That you aren't tied to the Portal's system. What if Kmet-Here objects?"

"I'll tell kmeth the truth. Since I wasn't permitted to bring my shuttle inside the Portal, and need to communicate with it, I brought a device of my own to do so. As the first visitor to travel on a Portal, if Kmet-Here accepts what I've done, it establishes a useful precedent—while keeping the rest our secret." Henry gazed at her. "I'm told a Kmet grows accustomed to a new constant."

"To a new pilot," she corrected, but he wasn't wrong. And the phone trick? If it worked, she'd consider it clever. *If.* "I strongly advise against talking to Flip in Control—by *phone* or otherwise—unless absolutely necessary."

"Agreed." A pretend shiver. "Anything else, Killian?"

"Through here," she said, leaning into the maw of the tube that would—*should*—take them to Control.

"I'll stay with you."

Killian glanced over her shoulder at Henry. "Not sharing my quarters."

That settled, she put her hands over her head and dove, letting the tube activate and whisk her along. The speed and motion didn't help the headache she'd sworn was gone—*not enough coffee.*

Thuds and a muffled *yelp* from behind did.

"Shall we go?"

GETTING around within a Kmet Portal required, for Humans, physical flexibility and composure. Henry checked the contents of his pockets were secure before bending to follow Killian into the transit tube that would whisk them along to where Kmet-Here would be.

Should whisk them. The walls, floor, and ceiling of the antechamber were pierced with over a dozen holes opening into tubes, outwardly identical. Markings readable by Human senses would have been reassuring. "How do you know it's the right one?" he called, hearing his voice echo.

"Pilots do." Her booted feet disappeared with a *swoosh.*

"Get in, Henry," Flip urged. "The tube might close."

He pressed a grateful hand to the coat, over his heart. "Glad you're with me."

More than glad. The phone in his pocket? A convenience at best. Private access to Flip and the polymorph's resources within the Portal would be crucial. The problem they'd faced was how to get enough Flip onboard to be useful without alerting the Kmet. They'd considered and abandoned several scenarios. Then came Killian's call for a coat—

He'd thank her one day, when she was ready. Somehow, he didn't see the pilot being overjoyed to know she'd helped the Arbiter circumvent Portal protocols to bring along a stowaway.

Wait till she saw what that stowaway could do—

Henry threw his hands over his head and dove into the waiting tube.

Feeling like a dust bunny sucked up by a cleaning stick, he kept his eyes closed and arms outstretched to fend off Killian's boots. Wind whistled past his ears as they picked up speed and at one point the tube aimed straight down—according to his ears, though directionality of the gravity field in a Portal was at kmeth's whim and—

—then straight up, as if he'd been sent flying and Henry truly feared Killian had picked the wrong tube—

He tumbled out on a floor.

A moist, startled-sounding burp, the whirr of the tube closing, then silence.

Killian offered her hand. Accepting her help, Henry got to his feet. Only logical to shed their Flip coats, essential in the cold they'd left, too warm here. He reached for Killian's, to keep everything Flip together.

She snatched his coat. "PIPs will think they're waste." Before he could protest, she shoved both coats into another tube.

HENRY! Flip subvocalized anxiously. WE'VE BEEN SEPARATED!

"Where did you send our coats?" Henry asked, for the polymorph and himself.

"Straight to the pilot's quarters." Killian shrugged to dismiss the coats' fate. "Best guess. Now what?"

Henry looked around, as always expecting Control to be different somehow, as if one side might win over the other. But no. Half was white and gleamed as if new. The lower two thirds of those three walls were covered in the Kmet version of buttons and levers, the upper third with screens presently showing Earth in all her splendor.

Centered in the gleaming space was the operation dais, its pedestals waist-high in Human terms and holding the controls used by Kmet or pilot. Those on the walls were reserved for PIPs, summoned to their task by any touch on a pedestal; Humans remained mystified by how the little polymorphs were themselves controlled, knew only that their cooperation was required for any Portal function.

Owning the other half of Control, consuming its light, was Kmet-Here's den. Where, by the burp, kmeth was hiding or resting or whatever kmeth did to avoid Henry.

Not an optimal start.

But a familiar conundrum. Henry took a step or two in that direction, then stopped. He wasn't welcome any closer. No Human was.

The contrast between tech and organic was stark. The den rose to almost touch the ceiling, its lower edge ragged and glued to the floor. It was composed of Kmet secretions, glistening gray where freshly applied—done, according to Rena, when there were no prying Human eyes—turning black as it hardened. While it hardened, other materials were incorporated.

As they'd done during his every visit to a Portal's Control—and by pilot reports never stopped doing—PIPs scampered over the den's exterior on their varied legs, arranging, rearranging. Some pressed offerings into still-soft gray areas. The things spent a considerable amount of time chewing strips, presumably unnecessary, from elsewhere in the Portal for the purpose. Other PIPs were busy chiseling material out and running off with it, as if the den had claimed something urgently needed elsewhere. They were ubiquitous and essential, merging to become larger as needed, splitting apart to fit into the tiniest space. FLIPs derived their polymorphic nature from them, a technological gift Human engineers had accepted eagerly.

One Henry'd confidently thought he'd have at his disposal at this moment. *Oh well.*

Killian watched him, waiting. In every negotiation, someone did. Someone was. At least she was here to help.

Once he figured out how.

The Portal needed both PIPs and an operator to function; it wasn't going anywhere while kmeth refused to engage.

Henry tapped his teeth gently, eyes on the den. On previous occasions when Kmet-Here refused to show kmethself, kmeth had pre-authorized the Portal's pilot to deal with Henry, be it taking receipt of an official document—likely to wind up glued to the den, but it was the form—or transiting a particular cargo.

So—Henry turned to Killian. Nodded at the pedestals.

Killian shook her head violently.

Then Kmet-Here had to come out.

He reached up his sleeve to press the yellow and red wristbands; having remained at the ready, Rena and Shomchai were linked at once.

With Henry's eyes open, they arrived as passengers, able to see with him. To show them the problem, he looked at the den's low, wide opening, black as pitch and patently empty.

Rena, quickly. <Kmeth might be waiting for something from you.>

<I suggest the protocols.> Shomchai's voice, though as urgent, was a cautious whisper. <The Duality greeting, Henry. Kmeth is under great stress. The formality might be calming.>

Henry glanced at Killian and raised his right hand, crossing his forefinger over his thumb. She gave the signal back, licking her lips.

After exchanging tiny nods—*now*—the Arbiter took a deep breath and sang the word, "Heeereeee," in the note of F, holding the note with perfect pitch.

Precisely three seconds later, Killian joined him, her voice clear and strong, singing the same word in B. Tritone established, they faced the den together.

Until acknowledged by its occupant, their voices had to remain steady. If either faltered, they'd have to leave and try again.

Suddenly, the matching two-tone hum, three octaves deeper, filled Control with unsettling dissonance.

Acknowledged. Henry didn't dare show relief. "Greetings. I am Arbiter Henry m'Yama t'Nowak. Do I address Kmet-Here?"

A shadow moved within the den's opening. "Kmet-Here." An agitated *BOOM*. "Did you bring the coordinates, Arbiter-Henry?" *BOOM*. The sound shuddered along his bones. Killian held her ground, though alarm flashed through her eyes.

"I did—"

"Go NOW!" Howling the word, the Kmet burst into the open, flippers slapping the floor, heading for the pedestals.

Henry stepped in kmeth's path.

Kmeth's eyes pivoted to lock on him, but the Kmet kept coming.

Ignoring the outcry from his poor oneirics, trapped and watching the very large alien rush toward him, Henry stood his ground.

Killian hovered at the tail end, as if trying for some part safe to grab.

The mouth gaped. Purple bits shot up from the sensory polyps—*join in my action*—which seemed entirely unreasonable if he was about to be crushed—

Kmet-Here dodged Henry at the last instant, granting a too-close view of that immense body. Scales on kmeth's side fluttered the creases of his pants. Bigger than his aunt's bellicose old ox.

And as much a bully. Good thing oneirics couldn't read thoughts—Rena'd be all over him for that judgment.

"No. We don't go yet." Henry moved with the Kmet, keeping between kmeth and the pedestals. "By the Duality!" He thrust out his hands.

Kmet-Here stopped with a wheeze. PIPs scrambled up the scaled sides, some settling in place, others picking at the skin between the scaly plates.

"Thank you." Henry eased his hands away and down, slowly, careful not to touch the Kmet or kmeth's hangers-on. He took shallow breaths through his mouth. Proximity added potency to the air flowing out between kmeth's wide fleshy lips. The smell beat out rotten potatoes and sulphur—not that such poll results were released to the general public. There was always some Kmet-aroma in the air, distributed by the tube system. He'd smelled it in the tube they'd taken. In the early days, Rena'd told him, they'd suspected the species used pheromones for communication.

If true, kmeth shared the means, not the meaning.

"Why wait?" *BOOM!* This close, he felt the subsonics agitate the air in his lungs. "Provide coordinates for Humans-There!"

"Not yet." Henry deliberately crossed his arms, an ability Kmet found distracting. "By the Duality, any Humans we find are my responsibility as Arbiter. Do we concur?"

One eye rolled back to watch Killian, the other remained locked on Henry, the transparent lid flicking more rapidly.

Shomchai whispered, <Careful what you take on yourself, Henry.>

He'd no choice.

"We concur, Arbiter-Henry," came at last, in a quieter tone. "By the Duality, the Portal is my responsibility. Do we concur?"

"Yes."

The eyes switched aim with a meaty sound. Killian backed away. "Give me the coordinates, Arbiter-Henry. We go now!" The voice began to rise in volume.

<Watch out, Henry!> from Rena.

Behind the alien, Killian, clearly sharing the xenologist's opinion, was shaking her head.

Kmeth's haste was uncharacteristic, as was this level of—dared he call it emotion? No doubt Rena and Shomchai, with every expert they could find, would sift through the nuances.

Didn't help in the moment.

"Not yet," Henry repeated firmly. "By the Duality, I, as Arbiter, will oversee the process of bringing the Humans we find to New Earth. Do we concur?"

Kmeth should have no interest in the logistics of opening households and moving supplies, the scramble to organize a fleet of space-capable transports—and spacer epitomes—nor that Sofia had ordered, through his office, the emergency refit of every orbital station to receive the newcomers arriving through the Portal. From there, they'd be moved to the surface as quickly as possible. New Earth would find room. Make more, if the evacuation became permanent.

The welcome wasn't the issue. Where, might be. Making it imperative to assess the best fit for those born on another planet.

First, get them to leave it.

He'd earned the stare of both enormous eyes. Colors flashed in a wave as several purple protrusions turned yellow. <Indecision,> Rena identified, followed by Shomchai's, <Or confusion. Clarify, Henry.>

Or still bluffing, Henry told himself. Something was ticking in that inscrutable brain. He'd a hunch the language interface wasn't the issue. He squared his shoulders, a cue for the other Human in the room. *Time to push.*

"Kmet-Here. I, Arbiter-Henry, will decide all aspects of how the Humans we find are brought to New Earth. You will use the Portal to help me in this, when I ask and how. Do we concur?"

"To help Humans-There become Humans-Here. With me. Kmet-Here. Yes. Do this."

<Careful, Henry,> murmured Shomchai. <Here. There. To Kmet, they've a significance we don't understand.>

Henry glanced at Killian. The pilot made a cutting gesture at her throat. New as she was, she sensed it, too.

Kmet-Here was trying to lead the conversation. *To have Henry make a mistake.* There were tiny gold plates around the enormous eyes regarding him. They quivered slightly with the flickers of the inner lids. The outer lids had lowered, as if the ambient light was bothersomely bright.

Or to keep secret what only another Kmet could read. *The mistake would be assuming he'd any idea.*

"Have I misunderstood, Kmet-Here?" Henry asked lightly, despite the hammering of his pulse. "I've come because you've told us Humans on worlds other than Earth are in grave danger. Are they really threatened? Is there urgency? Is there truly a Divider—"

BOOM! BOOM! The Kmet flopped backwards at speed, forcing Killian to jump out of the way of a flailing flipper, sending PIPs flying to splat against walls. "Threat, yes! Danger, yes! Divider always, yes!" Kmeth paused, PIPs scrambling back on board. "Do we concur, Arbiter-Henry?"

In that instant, doubt almost choked him. If the Kmet were responsible in any way for what happened to the *Henderson*'s planet, something they couldn't rule out and many, including him, feared—how dare he take this Portal to another world?

How dare he not—

"We concur," Henry conceded, stepping away from the pedestals with a beckoning gesture. "Shall we go?"

Kmeth went rigid, eyes opened wide. "Go?"

<Go?> Rena echoed with dismay.

"Yes. As Arbiter, I decide when and where." He smiled. "I decide now and I've the coordinates. Do we concur?"

The remaining yellow polyps flared purple. "We concur. We go!"

"I'll assist the Arbiter." Killian came up to Henry, pressing something small into his hand. "Would you like me to input the coordinates, sir?"

"No!"

Ignoring kmeth, he closed his fingers gratefully over what he guessed were transit meds. "Thank you." Then leaned over and whispered the numbers in Killian's ear.

A disgruntled burp.

"I have them, sir." She straightened and faced the Kmet, nothing at all to read in her face. "Ready to input, Kmet-Here."

That, Henry thought, for kmeth's attempt to limit his pilot.

"Do it," Kmet-Here grumbled.

After she did and moved aside, the Kmet heaved kmeth's bulk to the pedestals. An eye rotated to fix on Henry as PIPs climbed the walls and held in position. "Now we go."

TRANSIT.

“Safe as starships.”

Doublet

HAVING checked her creation for any mouths free to nip, Beth wore it over her short-cropped hair, soothed by the vines' rustled complaint. *Still alive.* As long as they were, a sweep wouldn't tag either as intruders. “Safe as starships,” Beth murmured, satisfied.

Doublet had a starship. A great Halcyon-class sleeper ship named the *Exeter* for a place on Earth-past-and-gone, and Beth, like everyone else, took her turn at maturity to stand inside the remnant of the hull that had seeded this world with their kind of life. While standing there, she'd thought it past time to recycle the metal, the way the rest of the ship had been repurposed and helpful.

Not that others would agree, stuck in the past-and-gone themselves.

She shook off the bit of ill feeling, though it was part of why she was a Seeker and such a good one, her burning need to go somewhere new-and-here. To find and learn.

To take a piss first, where it was safe—safer. She caught every warm drop in its flask, not letting a trace of her touch the ground.

There were those, below, who'd notice.

In the Split, you rested the heat of day, moved as it eased at start of day and end, hoarding moisture and strength. By full dark, you hid from what wanted both. Beth'd placed a stone to gauge the sun's height in the sky. By its shadow, time to go.

Taking up her sounding stick, of metal mined on Doublet, thus free of Earth-taste, Beth left last night's hideyhole. Her groundsheet, of layered foil, she'd carefully folded and tucked in her pack. Her cloak and the clothing beneath were woven from a blend of Home fibers and those gleaned at risk in Away, by other Seekers. Her thigh-high boots, of the same fabric, were coated with slick resin and had thickened soles of Away rubber. The ground of the Split ate through them. Beth carried spares in her pack, the limit of her journey out and back again.

With each step, Beth struck the ground lightly with the butt of her sounding stick. The tinkling hollow beads inside made her footfalls a message. *I'm a Seeker. Let me pass.*

The meaning was Human. The result—the crust beneath her feet staying solid—was what counted. They'd learned. Something lived below. Something built shelters in Away and left them empty. Same something made the land divided as it was, setting rules that let a body cross, if not easily, then alive.

Day would come, they'd meet. Bios ran endless scenarios and talked it out, making plans; a few always argued to slow down, being fearful, but everyone knew they'd no choice, sharing this world, the *Exeter* brought to a purpose and it was this.

What no one doubted? It'd be a Seeker who first came face-to-what.

Beth had her questions lined up, be it her, starting with why.

Might be. This trip, her pack contained more of what the Bios called *meaningful artifacts*, junk saying something about what they were, in case what wasn't was curious. Her suggestion, a year-plus back, to try the physical, and they'd seized on it with a little too much enthusiasm for comfort. Her fourth time, bringing the things, setting them out. Those below had yet to show interest. *Wasn't,* she thought resignedly, *as if anyone'd a better notion.*

Other than the junk, her journey'd be a straight cross to a familiar part of Away. Straight, so as little time in the Split as could be; familiar, a place Beth'd been before but no promises, in Away, it'd be in any sense the same. Life there was too busy and fretful to stay put. According to the Bios, what inhabited the other half of Doublet was at a different evolutionary stage than the tamer life of Home. More inclined to bite first and keep biting.

If the junk didn't *elicit a response,* Beth would keep going, Bios after samples of fungal fruiting bodies for analysis and possible cultivation. Still-alive samples, she reminded herself cheerfully, so no need for a nippy vine hat for the trip home.

Assuming the response didn't kill her.

World II

"I'd call that a yes."

"PILOT, you input the wrong coordinates!"

"Respectfully, Kmet-Here, the hell I did!"

BOOM BOOM— <Henry! Henry!>

The cacophony in and outside of his head found its way into his stomach. Henry reached out blindly.

An arm slipped around his waist. "Take the meds. We're here, sir," Killian told him, her voice mercifully low and steady. "Completed an orbit at the equator, now holding geosynchronous over the largest land mass. No sign of Humans yet. Kmeth's sure I made a mistake. I didn't. Glad you're awake."

He'd passed out? The meds. Henry brought up his hand and popped the small blue cubes stuck to his palm into his mouth, desperately hoping they worked fast.

Haste. He'd wanted to get kmeth off balance, not to lose his own.

<Henry!> Rena sounded frantic.

"I'll be fine," he said aloud but he couldn't afford the room in his head—not when he had to recover and think—

HENRY, I'M DETECTING AN IMBALANCE IN YOUR—

"Fine," he repeated sharply, this time for Flip's benefit, and pulled free of the pilot's hold. His head stayed attached. *Progress.* "What's the problem, Kmet-Here?"

"This is not fine," muttered the Kmet, still at the pedestals.

"The screens, sir."

Looking up threatened his small gain, but Henry managed. The screens showed repeating views of a planet so Earth-like at first he thought kmeth was right and Killian had made a mistake and sent them home. Then his eyes began to track the novel shape of the continent. See unfamiliar colors. Not their Earth. *Somewhere new.* His breath caught.

"Pilot made a mistake. Atmosphere contains no Human products," Kmet-Here stated, concluding, "no Humans-Here. I will input the coordinates correctly and we will go to the right place, Arbiter-Henry. Do you concur?"

"This is the right place—where the *Exeter* was to land," Killian protested. "The Arbiter gave me the values. I did *not* make a mistake."

"I do not concur, Kmet-Here." Flashing the offended pilot a brief smile—*not nodding while his head wanted to explode*—Henry faced the Kmet. "I have full confidence in our pilot's expertise and offer another explanation." He paused, waiting as kmeth's polyps turned a more amenable purple.

"What is this explanation, Arbiter-Henry?"

<Good,> Rena said. <That's very good.>

<Only if Henry has one,> Shomchai countered.

Ignoring his oneirics, Henry kept his focus on the Kmet. "Humans living here may have taken a different path and abandoned the particular industrial processes detectable above New Earth." He was careful not to say *lost,* though Flip's dystopian SF came to mind all too easily and a failure to maintain a technological society—or choice not to—was a plausible scenario according to Ousmane. "Our societies—our species—tend to variation."

The Kmet shuddered from head to tail, shaking off PIPs. "You flit in every direction. It's a wonder you get anything done."

An interesting, if unflattering, representation. Henry chose to leave it unchallenged. "We must learn if there are Humans here."

Killian spoke up. "Arbiter, the surveillance satellites."

A reminder Humans did have technology at their command—at his—on the Portal. "Deploy them. Kmet-Here, do you concur?"

Brooding silence.

Henry waited.

With an explosive motion, Kmet-Here left the pedestals and dove back into kmeth's den, a handful of PIPs chasing behind.

"I'd call that a yes," Killian commented.

"Now we wait."

HENRY gave the den a lingering look, as if half-inclined to take a peek inside.

Welcome to it. With an inner shudder, Killian stepped up on the dais, fingers hovering over the control pad affixed to the rightmost pedestal. Human tech. Hers. "Kisho."

<Still here. I can't believe he got away with that.>

She grunted in agreement. Since Henry hadn't been squashed to jelly, leaving her alone with kmeth, Killian decided to be impressed. She'd courage. Not the kind to stand in the way of a charging Kmet.

Mind you, she'd never do anything that dumb—

"Ready to start the planetary survey. Two sats, pole-to-pole, low orbit." The satellites were equipped with WFHR, Wide-Field High-Resolution opticals. The AIs in each, while primitive compared to an Alt-Intel, would compile and analyze images based on search criteria, uploading those refined results to the Portal every half orbit. Killian wrote on her notepad. *Any advice?*

<Ask the Arbiter for a dataset to feed the AIs. Buildings. Roads. Huts. That stuff.> Said with the disdain of a spacer. <And have the sats scan for masses of refined metal, subsurface penetration.>

To look for the *Exeter*, intact or as a debris field. A chill ran down Killian's spine. Her oneiric was right. If the giant starship made it this far, there'd be something of her left.

If not, well, they'd know, wouldn't they?

Lifting her hand, she showed Kisho a thumbs-up.

<Giselle's ready when you are. It's been interesting flying with you, Pilot.>

Killian tapped the wristband. *And a pain having you in my head,* she added to herself, not about to forget the old pilot's nagging.

The Arbiter, hands in his pockets, contemplated the center screen. Most likely his stomach hadn't settled. She'd a tentative truce with her own.

"Henry?"

He turned, eyebrow rising.

"We need optical references for the sat AIs. To compare to what they'll see on the surface," she elaborated. On the *Henderson*'s planet, they'd used what remained of the town. Roads.

He reached into his pocket, brought out his useless phone, and held it up as if asking her permission.

Killian scowled, then gave a grudging nod.

Though the Kmet was denned, Henry went through a pretense of entering digits, then put the antique to his ear. His eyes took on the distracted focus of someone listening to what wasn't here and yes, if she hadn't known better, it was pretty convincing.

"Yes, we're both fine, thank you. Yes, Killian gave me the meds in time—" Henry gave her a half shrug, mouthing: *Fussing.*

As if apologizing for the anxiousness of his shuttle, not something Killian would have thought possible. The emotion, not the apology. Henry apologized by default, she'd noticed. Though if anyone should, given that *in time* turned out to be *at the last possible minute,* it was her.

Killian shook it off. They'd survived. Once the sats were in motion, there'd be a good long rest ahead.

"Flip, we need optical references for all Human-made objects, present day and historical, every culture and material on record. Size above—" Henry looked at her.

Wanting the resolution. The opticals could pick out a bushel basket on a lawn. Under ideal conditions, they could distinguish the apples in the basket, but there was ideal and get it done, Killian judged. "Two meters."

"Flip's working on it." Phone in hand, Henry approached the pedestals, but didn't offer to touch, leaning forward to take a look.

Killian pointed out the pad welded in place to her right. "This is ours. But you know that," she added, remembering he'd been here before.

"Not at all. The other pilots wouldn't let me this close." Almost a smile, then Henry sobered. "How long—to be sure?"

That no Human had made it here. She hid behind the numbers. "2500-kilometer swath per sat pass . . . repeats to cover any orbit jiggles. I'd say a week, Earth equivalent."

"And the ones you left?" The Arbiter tipped his head at the den.

Henderson's world. "Five days, thirteen point two hours." Before he thought she could calc' it on the fly, like Giselle, Killian added, "Just checked. I can shorten things here. Ignore oceans and polar caps—"

He shook his head. "We won't get kmeth to this planet a second time. Do it all, please." Phone to his ear. "I'll ask. Killian, should the shuttle send the reference material to you via Portal communications or directly to the AIs?"

She'd take the help. Killian waved airily. "Direct. Thank Flip for me." She stepped down from the dais, stretching. "Now we wait."

Henry's gaze drifted back to the dark opening of the den. "Or not."

Predictable. He'd seen the sats could work alone. If they ran out of the things, the almighty Arbiter would have more transited through to them, budget no object.

Only they weren't machines. Henry looked green around the gills and none-too-steady on his feet. She was ready to drop—not to face what might be a second *Henderson.*

Killian snapped her fingers under the Arbiter's nose, pointing to a tube opening on the wall. "I'm done, Henry. Another transit? Hell, right now I couldn't carry my own trunks and I *want* my coffee maker. Bed, Henry. Something to eat first. Three hours off duty before we do anything else. My professional advice," she challenged. *Was she the pilot or not?*

"Taken." A rueful smile. "Needless to say, Flip agrees with you."

Killian snorted. Backed up by a polymorph on a fake phone.

Wait till Gis heard that.

“We won’t know till we get there.”

THEY had to get to the next world. This vacant planet marked failure; if not of his, then enough to stick in his throat. They’d get no answers here and Henry hated any delay—

As much as he knew Killian was right to insist on it. Once locked on a goal, he’d a tendency to push himself and those around him; he couldn’t afford it here, on a mission whose duration was anyone’s guess.

“Coming?”

“Right behind.”

The tube sucked them in, Killian first, and Henry closed his eyes as he spun, or the tube twisted, no, he was spinning . . .

And came to a stop, this time with his arms hanging from an opening a good distance up the wall. He stayed there, head out, calculating how best to get down. Killian rolled easily to her feet, standing with her arms crossed to watch him. “Turn and slide out,” she suggested.

Barely room to bring his knees and feet around. How she’d managed wearing those boots Henry couldn’t fathom, but he tried.

Getting stuck mid-fold. He fought the urge to giggle—

“Tube’ll close any second.”

Inspired, Henry squirmed and fell, more than slid, from the tube, managing to land on his backside. He eyed the now-closed tube opening above his head with dismay. “We have to use that every time?”

A shrug. “It won’t be there long.”

He blinked. “Pardon?”

“Tubes reconfig—” A weary shrug. “—I’ll explain later. Looks like they’re making us walk this time. Follow me.” Killian turned, going left down a white corridor much like a tube itself, lacking corners at ceiling and floor, illuminated by a soft glow emanating from the walls.

Ahead, the corridor flowed as if bending around unseen, doorless chambers. In places, the floor rose underfoot. In others, it dipped gently. Henry copied Killian in hopping over a narrow depression shaped like a W she told him hadn’t been there earlier. They passed no intersecting corridors, but the bumps of closed tube openings littered the floor, walls, and even ceiling.

The air smelled like the farm after a thunderstorm, fresh and moist, with a tang of ozone.

Fascinating. Henry'd never been in this part of a Portal. Hadn't thought to ask for a description or a briefing on where he'd be staying—it being less important than getting kmeth to take him in the first place. He looked back and ahead. "I don't see any PIPs."

Or their coats. Where was Flip?

"You won't. They keep out of this section when a Human's present." Killian sent him a wicked grin over her shoulder. "Rumor says the first pilot used them for soccer practice until she was left in peace. Been that way since."

"And Kmet-Here?"

The grin disappeared. "No." As if he'd alarmed her, the pilot sped up, disappearing around the next bend.

Henry followed to find the corridor split in two, each half the width, each bending to hide what lay ahead.

Killian stood between the two, her expression a mix of perplexed annoyance. "When I left, there was a single corridor, with one door—locked—on my quarters." Her head swung from passage to passage. "My stuff."

Henry appreciated her dismay. "I'll check the left," he offered.

With a curt nod, Killian went in the right.

Sound wasn't muffled, Henry noticed as he entered, it was stolen. Nothing from the Portal. Sandals or boots, neither made a sound on the floor. He gave a short low whistle. No echo. *Why hadn't he picked up on that?*

HENRY, ARE YOU IN DISTRESS?

The familiar voice inside his head was almost a relief. "No, Flip. I'm looking for you."

YOU ARE IN CLOSE PROXIMITY, HENRY.

He stopped. "How can you tell?"

I KNOW WHERE ALL OF ME IS, HENRY, AT ALL TIMES.

He frowned. "But to know where I am—a tracker?" One could have been installed in his epitome before he entered it, on New Earth. Henry fought the irrational urge to strip and hunt for what he couldn't possibly find. "Why wasn't I told?"

IT IS NOT A DEVICE, HENRY. OUR SEPARATION WORRIED ME, SO I ADDED SOME OF ME TO THE BOTTOM OF YOUR FOOTWEAR. WAS I INCORRECT?

Anxious. On reflex, Henry looked down at his feet. "No, Flip. It's just as well someone knows where I am."

THE REST OF ME IS AHEAD OF YOU.

"I see the door. Let me get back to you." Two doors, actually, both open. A larger to his right, opposite a smaller, and if he had to guess—Henry stopped and peered inside. He was right. It opened on a small but functional Human-style kitchen, with a sink, counter, and cupboards on one wall, faced by a generous table with two stools.

The coats were lying on the floor. Henry hurried inside and swept them up as Killian came through the matching door on the far side. She stopped by the table, looking bewildered. "A galley. Did you arrange this?"

Interesting question. "Not to my knowledge." Kmet-Here did seem unlikely to know how to accommodate an additional Human passenger in such exacting detail. Assuming kmeth were so inclined and not, as he strongly suspected, wishing Henry off the Portal so the kmeth could work alone.

Henry resisted the temptation to consult Shomchai and Rena. As for Flip, who easily reshaped himself and might well have an answer? Best not imply the Portal might be taking better care of *his* passenger.

"You said the tubes reconfigure?"

"Yes, but not where I live!" Killian swallowed and visibly collected herself. "Good point," she conceded. "More than the tubes—the Portal itself morphs to suit whatever's transiting through it, so I guess it can do the same inside. This—" a wave at the sink; a calmer tone "—is like the setup in my quarters, my old quarters. Bigger."

She went to the cupboard over the sink and raised the door. "Equipped the same." Pulling out two ready-dinner packets, standard fare on space stations and shuttles, the pilot gathered sporks from a drawer. "What do you say, Henry? Hungry?"

Killian looked ready to fall flat on her face, Flip's doctored coffee having worn off long ago. Concerned, Henry asked, "Don't you want to find your quarters first?"

Sinking on a stool, she put the packets on the table. "I won't get up again." She pushed one his way, snapping the seal to heat her own, releasing the scent of curry and cumin.

Putting the coats aside, Henry took the other stool. Sitting, she was taller, or would be, if exhaustion didn't slump her shoulders and have her lean on an elbow to eat. "Thank you, Killian."

Eyes rose. She knew he didn't mean the packet. "Did my job." Killian aimed a sporkful of rice at him. "The outcome could have been worse, Henry. Much worse." She took the bite and chewed grimly. "Next world might be."

"Or better," he countered. "We won't know until we get there."

A noncommittal grunt. Then, "What about this planet?" She dug out another morsel, not looking at him. "Looks pretty sweet."

Henry regarded her warily, not touching his packet. He'd no appetite, for food or the topic. "Don't even think about it. It's not for us, Killian."

Another glance. "Says what isn't."

"Says those with technology we don't have, who do what we can't—including reach this world. That's before considering what's already killed some of us for being out here."

She'd gone still, to listen. Resumed eating when he was done, as if he hadn't said a word worth hearing.

"Killian. I have the coordinates. I agree we need rest first," to forestall the frown Henry saw forming. "And to unload Flip's cargo—unpack some things." The smaller door in each passage should lead to living quarters. "But then we have to move to the next world as soon as possible. And the next. Pull our people back to safety. Finish this. After that—we reach out again, with care, with caution, to what's been so very offended by our presence."

"Still planning to talk to what burned innocent people to death."

"Yes. To stop it happening again, yes."

Another grunt. "We've a while to go before that, Henry." Dropping her spork in the packet, Killian closed the lid and stood, tucking her meal under an arm. "Mandatory minimum recommended recovery time from a simul-pop is twelve hours. Times—" she scrunched her face "four for me, one for you. Forty-eight hours."

Two days? "Killian—" Henry stopped himself. *She knew best.* "Understood."

A grim half-smile. She leaned forward and popped the seal on his packet one-handed. "Eat. Or our recovery will take even longer."

<Sweet dreams.>

KILLIAN found her quarters hadn't changed, only been shifted over in whatever the Portal had done to add space to the Human section of itself. She took a suspicious sniff. *Cleaned.*

Not her soiled coveralls. Those were in a reassuring heap more or less where she'd left them. She'd meant to grab her coat from Henry—

Later.

Leaving the ready-dinner on her desk, Killian took her dirty clothes into the washroom and dropped them on the shower floor, spinning the tap. Scalding hot water jetted down, filling the stall with steam. For good measure, she tossed in a full sheet of soap paper, then closed the door.

Every part of her ached. Her mind felt like soggy laundry and she was *not* looking at the bed. Not yet.

Pulling her chair to the desk, she opened the packet, making herself take each mouthful, chew it methodically—*Damn.* When had she bitten her tongue?

Killian grabbed a bulb of Restore from the cupboard, using that to wash down the food.

Only when she'd finished every last bite and drop did she get up and strip, this time folding her coveralls neatly over the back of the chair. By accident, the patch on top showed the officers of a freighter she'd served on with Giselle, the first mate being the stalwart ass with a head up his rump, and Killian choked on a laugh.

Soon, she promised, shaking her wristband.

After spinning the tap to cold, Killian stepped in the shower, toeing her coveralls aside as she made herself stay, gasping, under the jets. She'd hoped the shock would wake her up. Instead, she broke into uncontrollable shivers and missed the air-dry control twice before slamming it with the flat of her hand.

Leaving her hand there, leaning on it, kept her on her feet. *She was an idiot.* Shouldn't have agreed to a quick three-hour break before the cargo and a check on kmeth. Wasn't up to any of it. Wouldn't be in three times that long—

A wreck, that's what she was, but he'd looked so earnest. So disappointed—

Feelings he'd meant her to see, used to enlist her cooperation, and she'd no way to know if they'd been real.

Remember that, she told herself.

Enough. Cautious of her balance, Killian squatted to get her coveralls, hanging the dripping soapy mass over a jet nozzle. About to turn off the dryer and save power—spacer habit—she changed her mind. *Fucking alien spaceship.* Who cared about saving power?

Staggering into the other room, Killian climbed into bed. Stretching out made her hiss. Putting her head on the pillow made the room revolve and she'd better finish before she passed out.

She closed her hand over her wristband. Pressed gently. Whispered, "Gis? You there?"

<Always.>

Gravelly. Abrupt. Steady as starlight and the one voice she wanted in her head. The relief sent tears spilling as she closed her eyes and Killian tucked her arm with the wristband under the pillow. "Gotta sleep, Gis. Wake me in three." Spacers did that, on long, tough shifts. Relied on their oneirics to stay connected and alert. One eye open, Giselle called it, while the other slept.

<Sweet dreams, Killie-Cat.>

"I get to say so, don't I?

A BED with blanket and a pillow. The blanket, Henry discovered, felt like a luxurious sheet underneath and he debated whether the idea was to wrap himself in it, or cover himself. The mattress—he sat and bounced a bit—would do.

The corners of wall, floor, and ceiling were rounded. There was, as Killian had said, a sink, counter, and full cupboards, so they needn't share every meal.

He hoped Simmons packed a kettle.

A desk, with a pull-out chair. The lighting increased when Henry sat at it and pretended to read, lowered when he stood and walked away.

He stuck his head into the washroom, mildly disappointed to find it similar to such rooms on New Earth. More utilitarian.

The whole room was. *Had Simmons packed his photos?* They'd help.

A doorless closet contained hooks and a series of shelves. Henry took off his jacket and hung it up, leaving on his vest. He put his sandals on the lowermost shelf. They looked homey.

Or was the better word lonely? He eyed the coats.

Resolutely, he pushed up his sleeve and sat on the end of the bed. His hand hovered over the wristbands.

Then dropped away. His oneirics were hard at work trying to find him answers and options; or they rested, as he'd been ordered to do. Either case, no need to pull them from their lives for company.

That, he'd brought along. "Flip."

The coats melted into a gray metallic puddle. A matching trickle dripped from the shelf with his sandals, flowing along the floor to join the rest. When it arrived, the liquid shivered and thickened, rising up in the middle to form a—

—PIP. A metallic gray version, otherwise indistinguishable to Human eyes from the others he'd seen, and it meant—*Flip had been absorbed by the Portal!*

Henry scrambled onto the bed. "Flip!"

A variety of arms budded from it, including what Henry recognized as a replica of his phone. Flip's voice emanated from the speaker. "Hello, Henry." Another arm opened a lens at its tip and spun in a circle. "Nice room."

The same voice. The same curiosity. Henry walked on his knees to the edge of the bed, staring down. "Is it you?"

Arms waved. "This is a mere zero point zero zero one three percent of me, Henry. The rest of me is outside as an authentic flying saucer. Your shuttle," as if the Human needed clarification. "Why?"

"You surprised me. I didn't expect you to look like this."

"I'm in disguise." *Proudly.* The lens arm bent to regard the soccer-ball-shaped body. "My data records this as the root form. My ancestor, in a sense." The arm bent again, the lens glinting at Henry. "Did I choose incorrectly, Henry? I predicted an animal form would be conspicuous."

It was only a shape. Flip did shapes. And it was a clever ruse, assuming other PIPs couldn't detect an imposter.

Not a chance they should take. "We'll keep you away from the Portal's PIPs," Henry decided, sitting once more. "We don't know what codes they use internally. Here's fine. Killian says PIPs don't come into the Human section."

"Is Killian to interact with this portion of me, Henry?" A coy pause. "She appeared to enjoy her coat."

"At some point," he said. *Maybe.* "Until then, liking the coat's a problem. Being half of—" He waved at PIP-Flip. "I can't keep taking it from her."

"I hadn't anticipated you would, Henry." The polymorph sounded amused. "Killian can certainly have it." With the words, the shape blurred and spread, the pilot's coat reforming, PIP-Flip reduced to the size of a cricket ball perched on top. A scaled-down phone popped out, an appendage nudging the coat. "This material is inert. I incorporated it because it was here, not because I require it."

An offering, to help turn the pilot's opinion. "I'll return it," Henry promised. He laid back, arms behind his head, feet on the floor. "Let's get to work. Start a new data module, please, Flip. Order by planet designation."

"Shall I use ship names or their destination coordinates?"

"Simpler. This is for my reference." And ship names meant passenger lists, loading the scales. "Numerals," he decided. "I for the *Henderson*'s planet. II for this one, the *Exeter.* Keep going through to VI."

"Yes, Henry."

"Attach current status. Within, add dates, links to data, etc. My annotation. I, found and attacked—presumably by the Divider, Human remains retrieved by the Kmet, survey continues. II, sleeper ship failed to arrive, survey continues." He stared up at the featureless white ceiling. "Killian's tracking her satellites. I'd like you to do the same. I want to keep up on their status."

"Is there some reason you can't ask her, Henry?"

"I will, at times." He made a face. "I've a feeling I'll want to check more often than Killian will tolerate. And she's bigger than me."

"Henry?" Something cold and hard touched his toe. "Do you feel threatened?"

"Figure of speech, Flip. I feel—" Henry paused, nodding to himself. "—quite safe around our pilot. In fact, Killian tried to protect me from kmeth earlier."

PIP-Flip scurried up the wall like a chubby spider, aiming the lens arm at Henry. "Why was there need? What happened? Henry?"

Close to panic. "Diplomacy in action, Flip. I wasn't in any danger." A gamble, facing off against the Kmet. *If he'd been harmed, would have said something about Kmet-Here Earth needed to know.* "Now. Expand the module, to complete as we gather information on each world. Specifics for me. Appropriate clothing. Season. Footwear." Henry closed his eyes. "I may need boots." He disliked confining his toes.

"And me, Henry. I insist. You must not land on any of these planets without me. Promise!"

Henry smiled. On the surface, an odd plea from an Alt-Intel currently a shuttle. The Kmet had made it clear from the onset New Earth was responsible for moving Humans around—Portals had no suitable craft. Unless Henry ordered through another shuttle, he'd no choice but Flip.

This wasn't about what Flip knew.

Like any Alt-Intel, Flip possessed a complex, well-developed personality. One with Human-like opinions and preferences. A sentient construct could experience bouts of inexplicable anxiety.

And need reassurance. About to promise, Henry opened his eyes to see the bizarre shape on the wall.

Not Flip.

Doubt rose again, formless and faint. *Foolish!* Henry struggled to push it aside. "I won't land on any of these planets without you, Flip," he made himself say. "I promise."

A tiny shudder. A smaller voice. A relieved, "I appreciate that, Henry. Thank you."

It should have been enough. That it wasn't, that he shied away from looking directly at PIP-Flip, scared him more than the Kmet.

It's your imagination, he told himself. Made himself focus on what was simply another version of his utterly reliable companion and helpmate. Admire the ability, if not the result.

"Let's finish the module, Flip. I owe the office a report. Next column—"

***

Killian looked up as Henry entered the shared kitchen. By the triangles on her wristband, she wasn't alone. He paused to give a small bow. "Giselle, I take it?"

He'd gone through the oneiric's file, the deeper one rushed to him by the Spacer Repository on her reassignment to Killian and thus his mission. Been impressed. Giselle m'Tharp t'Horyn was a brilliant mathematician, of a caliber to take her pick of a variety of fields on New Earth. What she'd wanted was space.

Felt a twinge of envy. Giselle and Killian were a couple, in a long-term relationship seemingly unaffected by the epitome/oneiric bond they'd established after Giselle's accident.

Found a small oddity: like the majority of spacers, Giselle was an active member of the System Coalition. Killian wasn't. Then again, Killian didn't strike him as a joiner.

Time to introduce himself. "Hello, I'm Henry."

The pilot listened, then made a sideways slash of her hand. "Gis says you're shorter in person."

Not, he guessed, *what her oneiric actually said.*

Henry nodded agreeably. "So I've heard." He took a ready-dinner from the cupboard and a bottle of water, promising himself a coffee from Shuttle-Flip, then sat down, assessing Killian, certain she knew it. Three hours was pitifully short; the time had flown as he'd worked, though he'd managed to complete and send his initial report to the Arbiter's Office, via Flip.

He trusted she'd slept. Killian did appear alert despite faint lines at the corners of her mouth, and wore her proper uniform, albeit wrinkled and damp on one shoulder.

"Any questions for me?"

Killian listened. Frowned. "Oh, for the—" She slapped her wristband. Sat glaring at Henry.

A sporkful of cereal poised at his lips, he raised both eyebrows, "Something I said?"

"You don't want to know." The pilot shoved her packet away. "I'm going to get my stuff—and yours—from the shuttle."

Oh, he definitely wanted to know. One day, he might.

Henry replaced the lid on his breakfast and didn't bother with his phone. "Flip, we're on our way to unload."

YES, HENRY.

"Thought you'd say that. I'll need my coat."

"I'll get it." He smiled. "Flip? Put on the coffee."

The pilot positively beamed back.

***

Flip, anticipating their needs, had a pair of carts ready as well as cups of steaming coffee. Killian had given the ceiling of the shuttle a very thoughtful look.

Just as well she'd hadn't seen PIP-Flip. The coats had been waiting for Henry. Presumably the coating on the soles of his sandals as well, not that he'd checked.

The crates, trunks, and assorted luggage went on the carts, fitting neatly through the airlock. It was then Henry saw the problem.

He used his arms to approximate the width of the largest crate and walked to the tube opening. "Won't go."

"Bet it will," the pilot said, leaning on the nearby wall, coffee cup in hand.

He saw another problem. "Shouldn't one of us be waiting at the other end? To move things out of the way as the next comes through?"

A careless shrug. "Pilots can't. Don't worry, Henry. Whatever goes down the tube to our quarters, the Portal creates the right-sized spot to receive it. My duffel got a closet." She eyed the mound of *stuff.* "This probably rates a storeroom. Unless you'd rather put one thing through at a time and go check what happens to it." A leisurely sip; a sharp look. "We've a couple of days to kill."

"You said less."

"I said it depends."

He could pull rank. *And lose what trust he'd gained.*

Henry went to one end of the big crate, bending to take hold. "A little help here?"

The opening expanded on contact, engulfing anything they pushed at it. The process turned into a game, the pair of them competing to get the next piece to shove into the tube, and Henry, starting to sweat, took off his coat before grabbing his suitcase.

"Bad idea," Killian objected, taking the case. "Put the coat back on, Henry. Frostbite or hypothermia's no joke. Of course, you've cans of epitomes to spare. This—" She tapped her chest. "—is it for me."

As he shrugged the too-warm garment over his shoulders, Henry shook his head. "Print House rules apply the same to me as every spacer, except my existent-self stays at the Arbiter's Repository." A dust of his hand downward. "My one and only."

"That's—that's ridiculous. New Earth expects you to travel to these other worlds. To go down on them." Killian grew incensed. "It's not as if you've any sense—you almost got yourself squished by a Kmet on the first day! Henry, you can't do this job on a single copy."

"I don't plan to break it," Henry assured her, rather touched.

Her glower wasn't aimed at him. "Tell them to make more. In Kmet-Here's state we can't change personnel—there's no telling how long kmeth would take to accept someone new."

"I believe that very argument is being presented at this moment—" Classified, but Killian should know. "—to the Print House, with a request to start growing more me's. And you's."

She stared at him, dumbfounded. "What did you say?"

"They may not agree," he qualified. "For either of us. The sentiment—and science—is strongly against multiplicity. Even if they do, I'm told there's no rushing the process. A new epitome takes—" He didn't actually know.

"Twenty-seven months." Killian pressed her lips together, her stare changing to something else. "Our real selves can't last that long. Mine can't. The Spacer Repository isn't set up for long-term maintenance."

"It is now, for you." Henry sat on a crate, his breath fogging the air between them. "The instant you agreed to stay on, they moved in a team like the one I have, whose sole job is to prevent your body from deteriorating. Your can's in a special isolation room. Ask Giselle."

"Damn right I will." She didn't appear mollified.

He didn't blame her. "I'm sorry. I didn't think to tell you earlier. I assumed you'd know epitome procedures better than I did. If it helps," he ventured carefully, "they've orders to bring you back at the first sign your existent isn't handling this well or your epitome shows distress." Standard for spacers. "And if you've had enough. I won't need a reason, Killian. I promise."

She walked away, stood by her trunks. Gave one a light kick. Did it again.

He gave her time.

Finally, she turned. "That's me. What about you, Henry?"

The truth, he decided. "I have a different protocol in place. Rena's my proxy. She won't bring me back unless there's no other way forward. This mission must succeed."

Killian nodded grimly. "Then that's what I want. Giselle can do it. Will do it. I get to say so, don't I?"

"You do." They were, neither of them, kind to their friends. Henry stood and reached out his hand. "Thank you, Killian."

She shook it. Like his grandfather, she'd firm, calloused palms. This time she kept his hand, squeezing until he had to work to keep from wincing. "No more stupid risks, Henry."

"Agreed."

I LIKE HER, Flip commented.

"Transit in forty-three hours." The pilot's lips twisted. It wasn't quite a smile. "Let's move this gear."

"You don't have to come—"

HOLDING the framed image, Henry considered the possibilities. Over the bed or on the desk?

Desk. Where he had it in his office. He positioned the frame, stood back. The presence of his grandfather, with chickens, lent the space a warmth it had lacked.

Added a reminder of everything at risk—

On second thought, he moved it to the shelf above the bed.

The Portal had, as Killian predicted, created a storeroom for their cargo, accessed through a new door in the kitchen area. They'd moved their personal belongings into their respective quarters, the pilot disappearing behind her closed door to unpack, taking her Flip coat.

Inert material. He supposed if Flip wasn't worried, he shouldn't be.

Henry upended his suitcase on the bed. "Update, please, Flip."

PIP-Flip waved a sock. Alt had produced arms with graspers to help with the process. "No evidence of Human habitation has been found on either planet currently being surveyed, Henry." A meaningful pause. "It has been ten minutes since your previous request. Would it not be more efficient for me to alert you to any change?"

"Possibly." There were shelves in the closet. He tossed underwear and a sweater on the middle one; the polymorph added socks. Hooks and rods received his second, better suit, blue and more formal in cut. "Any progress mapping the tubes?" *Wait to be escorted back and forth?* He and the pilot had better uses for their time.

"No, Henry. Other than the fixed locations of Control and the docking area, the Portal obscures its internal structure whenever I attempt to scan it. Scanning is, I am obliged to remind you, a violation of the Duality."

"I'll ask Killian to show me, then." Henry made a ball out of his sweatpants and threw those on the closet's top shelf.

Producing sucker-feet, the polymorph climbed up to neatly fold the pants.

The process didn't take long. Henry'd brought three changes of casual wear, two suits, assorted shirts and underwear, plus the boxers and tees he preferred for sleeping. If there wasn't a way to wash his clothes on the Portal, he'd take them to the shuttle and let Flip devise a solution.

The remainder of his luggage contained what wasn't clothing. With more care, Henry brought out his kettle and two favorite mugs. One was tall and shaped as a piece of bamboo shoot, with a beetle climbing up the side. A gift from Rena. The other was ugly and chipped, with a piece missing from the handle, but a picture of the farm's antique tractor covered both sides and he never traveled without it.

Those went on the counter by the small kitchen sink, along with a box of cocoa, two spoons, and a daunting multipurpose knife-tool combination Henry was sure he hadn't seen before, stamped with the Planetary Peace Corps logo.

He showed PIP-Flip. "Think they want me to use this on the Portal?"

"It would be more useful if you were lost in the woods, Henry, while camping."

Camping? Henry chuckled to himself. "Not planning to leave civilization, Flip. Now this will come in handy." He held up an unexpected bottle of his favorite whiskey. From Mersi, if he had to guess.

"Do you have appropriate glassware, Henry?"

The mugs would do. "Dunno yet." A search in his shoes uncovered a wrapped shot glass tucked in each. "Yes!" Henry tucked the bottle and glasses away on the top shelf of the closet, behind his sweatpants.

There was a reader, linked through Flip to his library. His battered harmonica, not to inflict on a Kmet, the notes potentially saying something unintentional—or on Killian, for that matter. Not till they knew each other much better or over the contents of the bottle.

Henry tossed five memory cubes on the bed. PIP-Flip tipped one over dismissively. "You do know I can instantly access whatever information you require from the Arbiter's Office, Henry."

"Yes, Flip." The cubes were from Simmons, at a guess, making sure he'd have what he needed at hand in case Flip wasn't.

Or if he chose to do research without the polymorph's knowledge. Slippery, the thought, the way uncomfortable notions were. Holding it, Henry glanced at PIP-Flip, presently emptying the last items from his suitcase: several pads of official stationery in various sizes and a new pack of pens.

"I'll take those," Henry said, silently thanking Simmons as he put them on the desk. Reaching into his jacket pocket, he withdrew the velvet bag containing the Arbiter's badge. That treasure went beside his grandfather's photo.

Returning to the desk, he kicked off his sandals and sat. The flooring wasn't soft underfoot, but it didn't steal his warmth. Insulated. The flat seat reminded him of a waiting room chair, regrettable after a few minutes.

Then it began to soften.

Henry stayed where he was, hoping for the best.

The seat returned to solid and yes, it was better. "Much, much better," he murmured.

"Better than my seats, Henry?" PIP-Flip stopped midway across the room, empty suitcase held high by a ragged assortment of claspers and pins. "I scan and use your current measurements." A note of distress. "You would tell me if my work is substandard, wouldn't you?"

"I would," Henry assured him. "Your seats are always comfortable, Flip. I merely meant this one feels better than when I first sat in it." The polymorph's fuss seemed so normal, the Arbiter leaned his elbow over the seat back to study this version, hunting the differences from the Portal's PIPs.

Finding fewer than he'd like.

The suitcase wavered. "Henry, why are you staring at me? Is something wrong with me?" The eye-arm bent, aiming alts lens at the body, moving to view as much as possible.

His heart softened. Perversely, his doubt grew and, in fairness to Flip—and out of a certain curiosity—Henry chose to admit it. "Why did you call this your ancestral form, Flip?"

"Because it is, Henry. The facultative polymorphic matrix used in my creation was the first technology the Kmet gave Earth."

To demonstrate kmeth's desire for the Duality. Revolutionizing the design and manufacture of every mechanical device from conveyor belts to Alt-Intels like Flip. Rocking local economies, that too, until the Kmet identified sources of the requisite materials on rogue worlds and offered to go into the mining business with Human partners, and why care now?

Because the end result of that Kmet-Human history watched him through a single lens, waiting patiently.

"Given that connection, Flip," Henry ventured carefully, "do you feel at home on the Portal?"

"My home is where you are, Henry. At present, most of me is outside the Portal and all of you is in it, making it impossible for me to *feel at home.*" PIP-Flip's myriad little movements abruptly froze, the suitcase toppling to the floor. "Henry, do you believe this portion of me to be corrupted?"

Henry rested his chin on his arm. "Would you know?"

Two clasper arms came together with a clink. "This me is an extraneous access and sensory port, nothing more. *I* am secured against any tampering, by any source, Henry. In addition, should the Kmet attempt any connection outside normal, approved communication channels, I am programmed to self-destruct."

His head jerked up. "What?"

"You should not be surprised, Henry. All Human technology in reach of the Kmet must have that capacity. The regulation comes from your office." An arm pointed beyond Henry. "Even your kettle."

"I did not authorize it be applied to you!" *Simmons.* Fury boiled up. *What had his assistant been thinking?* Flip had flown him to and from the Portal without this—this—nonsense!

Henry fought to calm himself. Pictured an earnest young face. Simmons had thought about the mission. About the rules and why they existed.

Didn't make it right. "You're a person, not a kettle."

"My rights as a sentient construct have not been abused, Henry." A tinge of fond amusement. "I gave full and informed consent. You need me."

He did. And had let suspicion taint a relationship he absolutely depended on. Henry sighed. "I owe you an apology, Flip."

A coy beckoning gesture from the phone arm. "Then you'll stay in the shuttle? You'd be more comfortable. Feel at home, with me."

He'd the best partner. Something fixed itself, deep inside, and Henry gave a warm chuckle. "I'll keep that in mind."

"Please do, Henry." *Smug, that was.* PIP-Flip abruptly retracted most of alts arms. "Oh. This portion of me needs to recharge." A new arm extruded, a prong at the tip. "There is a station under your bed and another in the closet. Do you have a preference, Henry?"

"You choose." He waved his hand.

"And will you do the same?"

"I might. Go on."

***

Henry lay on the floor to take a look under the bed. The twinkly glow of an optical lens reassured him. Self destruct? *Not happening.* He'd do whatever it took to protect Flip—even the polymorph's bits.

As for rest? He'd sent off his first report. Created an organization for the information he hoped would start flooding in—but in no sense was his mind ready to stop.

Dropping into the seat, Henry pulled over a pad of paper and opened the pack of pens, selecting one and putting the rest aside. Rested his pen's tip on the blank page.

Got up again to snatch the frame from the shelf, setting it on the desk in front of him. Shifted it to the right. *There.* "You taught me to work things out, Grandpa," he told the image of that wise old soul, smiling a little at the chickens, feeling more grounded. "I'm missing pieces of the biggest puzzle of my life and I don't even know their shape."

Start somewhere. Henry drew a circle in the middle of the page. Inside, he wrote *Kmet.*

He drew more circles on the page. Wrote in each. *New Earth . . . Divider . . . Humans-There.* After a second's consideration, he added *Humans-Here* to the circle with Earth, adding a question mark. He used an arrow to *Humans-There* to indicate the sleeper ships having originated on New Earth, then hesitated.

Shomchai warned the terms *here* and *there* held particular significance to Kmet beyond kmeth's insistence on applying the words to kmethselves.

That application was excruciatingly fluid. The Kmet in this Portal was rightly Kmet-Here to Henry and Killian, and the one in the Portal at Earth, Kmet-There. Except the reverse applied to those on New Earth, who'd call *their* Kmet, Kmet-Here, and so forth.

As if it was more important to acknowledge relative position than identity. As if whatever remained together, in contact, stayed the same. *Or mustn't change.*

Yet did. Sitting in Kmet-Here's Portal, which wasn't orbiting Earth but was outwardly identical to the one that did, Henry wondered—not for the first time—if the confusion was intentional. New Earth governments and scholars held it an open question if only two Kmet individuals had ever visited Earth, or if a sequence of others took turns, hiding kmeth's true identities.

He'd assumed he could tell his Kmet apart, better than kmeth could tell Henry from, say, Mersi, but could he really? Kmet-Here, the one in this Portal, was missing the tip of kmeth's flipper. What if such damage was common within the species? Rena thought it possible, based on comparisons to New and Origin Earth analogues such as walrusux or manatees.

Comparison. Inference. The field of xenology limped along, the Kmet ignoring or deflecting questions about kmeth's inner nature and not about to hold still for an examination. They breathed the same air. Preferred similar temperatures. While never consuming food or water in the presence of Humans, kmeth tolerated and even relished some of the same foods, leading to entire academic departments centered on the implications of what each Kmet favored or disliked, though kmeth proved confusingly individualistic in their tastes.

A crate loaded into Flip and now in the storeroom turned out to be full of pickled beets and raw peanuts in the shell. If this Kmet refused them, he and Killian would have to eat the lot.

If—then this Kmet wasn't the one they believed kmeth to be—

Easy to get lost.

Genetics would help. As part of her assignment as pilot, Killian was tasked with obtaining samples of any materials a Kmet might shed or excrete for analysis on New Earth. Discreetly, of course. A feat yet to be accomplished by any, Rena'd lamented, because PIPs whisked away any leavings the instant they were produced.

She'd optimistically added a set of sample jars to the supply crates, a hint he was now part of her collection team.

Bottom line, humanity knew more about extinct deep-sea squid than its partner in the Duality and, to make matters worse, the Kmet ignored questions having to do with *there,* as in, where was kmeth's part of space, the nature of kmeth's original planet, or even where else did Kmet go?

Thinking of all they didn't know, Henry drew a series of lines from the Kmet circle, ending each with a question mark. *Maybe he'd have time to answer a few.*

In the context of where Humans should be, and shouldn't, Kmet-Here definitely had an opinion. *There* for Humans was wrong and dangerous. *Here* came with words like home and good and it was all too easy to assume kmeth meant Earth.

He lifted the pen before he wrote: *Which one?* Leaned back, regarding the paper, eyes hooded in thought.

Earth. His. His grandfather's. Killian's. The current planet year was 963 SA, and it was a rich and gorgeous Human home—just not the first. There'd been another world with the name. His ancestors brought with them its history. Names. Stories. Music. Flip's movies and books. Small personal items, now treasured themselves.

Nothing to prove Origin Earth had been humanity's birthplace. For all anyone knew, a succession of Earths trailed behind their species as it crossed the vastness of time and space, eager two-legged adventurers leaping from each into the void, abandoning one home to begin the next.

Braver, before.

Had they been found, before? The *Adamant*'s Archive didn't describe a planet in crisis. Her launch had been a triumphant moment. Yet—the end result—

—felt terrifyingly familiar.

They'd survived. He took courage from that. Leaning forward, Henry touched the pen tip to the Divider circle. Drew a dashed line from it to the Kmet to represent a connection. He wrote *fear* on the line and *knowledge/history.*

Then, before he thought, he wrote: *why would the Kmet defend us?* He stared at the words. Kmet-Here had claimed kmeth came to New Earth to offer protection from the Divider.

Divider. Possessed of a weapon that set fire to Humans, but not their buildings. Who'd left the remains as what, a warning against expansion?

For the Kmet?

There was a grimmer possibility. Slowly, Henry drew another dashed line from the Divider to New Earth. Added the words: *how many—*

A knock on his door. The prosaic sound—in this place, with his dark thoughts—made him start.

"Flip," he whispered urgently. "Coat."

A louder knock.

Henry waited as PIP-Flip melted, his coat reappearing. Picking it up, he tossed it on the bed, then eyed his sandals. If Flip had attached something to the soles, he couldn't tell. He sat at the desk, turning over the pad of paper. "Come in."

Opening the door, Killian stayed in the corridor. Her gaze, after a quick survey of his quarters, landed on him with suspicion. "Trancing?"

He patted the desk. "Had to get down a thought."

She looked unconvinced, then gave a casual shrug. "I'm heading to Control to check on things. You don't have to come—"

He'd jumped to his feet. "Ready."

The ghost of a smile. "Follow me, then."

“I like drawing.”

<MESSY is adorable,> Giselle commented slyly, continuing her running commentary on what she found attractive in the Arbiter.

Apparently everything. Including living quarters chockful of loose objects—some hard crystal blocks—ready to become projectiles if the Portal’s g went into serious flux. Something Killian’s oneiric knew perfectly well. “Getting old, Gis,” Killian warned under her breath, waiting for Henry.

<Ooh, and he’s putting on sandals again. Those cute toes . . . I miss toes . . . >

They’d painted one another’s, before Gis lost hers. If her partner thought to garner sympathy, she was talking in the wrong head. Killian rolled her eyes at the ceiling. “Take a break, Gis,” she said out loud. “Call you if I need you.”

<Happy to watch—> Suggestively.

“Killian out.” She let her hand fall from the wristband, hoping her embarrassment didn’t show because then she’d have to explain—there was no explaining Giselle, who’d a love of life, and lust for it, literally, undiminished by distance or circumstance. “Ready, Henry?”

He combed his fingers through his hair, pushing it back as he nodded. “Yes. Thank you.”

“This way.”

The Arbiter closed his door, she noticed, but didn’t lock it. Later she’d find the right time to suggest he should—he’d personals in his quarters and a desk load of work, probably classified. You had a door that locked, you locked it, that was all. She wasn’t going to take offense.

More importantly, “When you get back, Henry, secure your things. If we lose gravity, loose articles are a risk.”

He kept up with her. “Has that ever happened?” he asked curiously. “On a Portal, I mean.”

“No,” she admitted. “But it’s a risky habit.” Killian smiled to herself, having remembered she’d an ally of sorts. “I’m surprised *Flip* lets you get away with it.”

By Henry’s distracted expression, he was getting an earful. “Yes, Flip,” he said finally, shooting Killian a wary look.

She managed not to grin. "We're here." Stopping in front of the cluster of tube openings, Killian waved at them all. "Time you learned some pilot skills, Henry."

His face lit up. "You're going to show me how to get around?"

"Only where we're authorized," she told him, making it firm. "Think of the tubes as pairs. We're allowed into three. Control to the Human section, here, is one. Directionality's preset so back again is a different tube, making the first pair." She waited for him to nod. "Control to and from the docking antechamber, that's the second. Here to the dock and back, the third."

Henry studied the tubes, some open, some closed, surrounding them on every side. Only the floor was clear and that, Killian knew, didn't mean there wouldn't be a tube opening there the next time. "How do you tell?"

She leaned into one, took a sniff and listen, then eased out to face him. "This goes to Control."

His mouth opened, then closed. Waiting for her to explain. Willing to be taught.

Good. Without smiling, Killian pointed to another opening, waist high. "Try that one."

Henry went to the tube and began to lean in, jumping back when the tube irised closed in his face.

"Unauthorized means no other tubes will let us inside. On the bright side, you can't get lost. From here, an open tube gets you to Control or the dock. Fifty/fifty shot."

Blue eyes twinkled. "You do better than that. How?"

"I pay attention." She tapped the side of her nose. "Control smells like Kmet. More like Kmet," she qualified. "Sometimes, if kmeth is vocalizing, the tube carries the echo. As for the dock? It's cold there. You can feel that in the tube. Whatever's left that lets you in, comes here." She stamped her foot.

"That's all there is to it?"

Killian shrugged. A sore point, with pilots, to have the temptation of dozens of tubes and be unable to explore. "PIPs use the rest," she reminded him. According to her former oneiric, every so often a pilot thought about sneaking into a tube behind a PIP, as if it was some revelatory new idea no one else could have had; fortunately for the Duality, none had been, in Kisho's words, dumb enough to risk it.

Someone like Henry did *not* need more ideas.

"If none of the open tubes seem right," she continued, "put your hand on a closed one." She demonstrated. The tube opened at her touch. "Keep checking until you find what you need."

He stuck his head in, drawing back with astonishment. "It's cold."

"If it lets you in," she cautioned, "that'll go to the dock."

Henry tilted his head, studying the tubes. "Has a pilot seen a Kmet go into a tube?"

"No." She shrugged. "Some think there are openings in the dens. For supplies and such."

"Do they, now?" he mused, tilting his head the other way, like a bird.

Damn fool would go into one to check. Killian frowned a warning.

He ignored it. "Has a pilot ever seen a Kmet here or in the docking area?"

"You're asking questions when you know the answers. What are you getting at?"

"Checking assumptions. Such as the Kmet stay in Control. We still don't know why."

Killian snorted. "Sure we do."

His eyebrows rose. "Go on."

Henry wasn't a pilot, wasn't a spacer, and it wasn't, strictly speaking, any of his business what those who were believed. Still—"Kmet don't trust us—Humans—with the Portals."

His eyebrows rose. "Then why take on pilots?"

How the hell would she know? Killian breathed through her nose, managing not to snap the stock pilot answer: *Because Kmet are lazy--insert expletive--lumps of dough.* Besides, she'd a better one, hers. "The Kmet want us to see what we can't have. To rub in our faces who'll always be running things."

"Is that how you see the Duality?"

The calm question, his suddenly piercing eyes brought her up short, reminding her who he was. *And what.* "Just the pilot, Arbiter, *sir,*" she ground out, pushing back. "Not up to me to question policy. Maybe it's the same for the Kmet. Maybe kmeth's pilot's ordered to live in Control, same as we're told where to sleep." Liking the notion, she rolled with it. "Would let the Portal restrict life support to key areas."

He pointed to the tube that had closed on him. "Unless there are more Kmet, in the places we can't go."

That creepy notion wasn't new. Pilots scared recruits with it. On the other hand, this was the Arbiter, with resources Killian doubted she could imagine. Bending her elbow to show him her wristband, she gazed meaningfully at his arm. "You telling me or guessing?"

A half-smile. "If you want, I can have Flip provide you with the latest studies and conjectures. My current favorite involves a vast Kmet nursery growing soldiers for a future invasion of New Earth."

Killian had an immediate mental image of hordes of flipper-flapping, armored Kmet trying to fit into the same shuttle. Funny—*and not.* "The Kmet wanted Earth, kmeth could have taken it from us the first day," she growled. "A single Portal. A Kmet at the controls to send down miners. You saw the visuals from *Henderson*'s world. We'd have rolled over and surrendered on the spot."

"Think so?"

She didn't. Wasn't getting into an *all for one, one for all* moment with him either. "What I think, *Henry*, is that the only Kmet who matters is—" She jabbed her thumb at the tube to Control. "After you, this time."

***

Killian almost expected to see Kmet-Here charging around Control, but she rolled to her feet to find only Henry waiting. Predictably—she was getting a sense of him—he was standing on the dais investigating the pedestals, hands a little too obviously clasped behind his back. *Like a kid told "don't touch" pushes the limit.*

Keeping a wary eye on him, she did her walk around the room. PIPs got out of her way, an improvement over her first day, when she'd had to step over a few. If she didn't know better, she'd swear the things were pretending to be busy, turning dials back and forth, polishing what already gleamed. Other than the usual group redecorating the outer surface of kmeth's den with chunks of red foam resembling insulation. "That better not be important," she told them, for what good it would do.

Three popped out antennae to aim at her.

That was new. "You heard me," Killian continued, though she'd no idea if they did. She pointed at a PIP scampering past with more foam. "Doesn't the Portal need that?"

To her surprise, the PIP with foam came to a stop, also producing an antenna to aim at her. Two more came up to it, sprouting little arms with suction cup ends they used to examine the chunk with what seemed alarm.

"What's happening?" Henry whispered from behind her shoulder.

"Not a clue."

All at once, the three at her feet split apart. The one carrying foam spun about and jumped into a tube. The two hurried to the den wall and joined those previously applying chunks in removing them, passing them down to others waiting, those carting foam into the same tunnel as the first in a frenzy of urgent action.

Killian had to shake her head. "Silly things," she muttered, tempted to bring Gis back to see, knowing she mustn't. Her oneiric deserved a solid eight and that was easier now.

Though she wasn't alone. "I take it this means you've been accepted as pilot by the Portal, as well as Kmet-Here."

She grunted something noncommittal as she walked past him. What she wanted to do was rush to the privacy of her quarters, summon Gis, and get her oneiric to ask if any other pilot had talked to PIPs and been answered.

Instead, Killian stepped on the dais to call up the latest on the sats, combining the feeds on the screen to her right. Routine, unless she let herself remember this was a living *other* world—then her pulse kicked up a notch.

"Nothing to report," she announced after a moment. "Here or—" After switching the feeds, "—from the *Henderson*."

"World I." Henry corrected without looking around. He stood under the middle screen, stared at the planet below. "This is II."

Original, she almost said, before thinking it through. There were codes for the things a Human mind preferred to avoid. "I. II. Got it."

"What's that?"

Involuntarily, Killian looked where he did.

Spotting something new at the lower right corner of the screen she should have seen immediately. Would have, if not for PIPs fooling with the insulation.

A faint disc, perhaps two meters in diameter, had been superimposed over the planet's image. An intense spark of light moved within it, carving a spiral inwards from the rim, and she'd no idea what it was for, other than a change from what they, meaning pilots, spacers, and entire Spacer Repository, knew about Portals.

Two in short order, if she counted the PIPs' behavior, and why not? Killian thought, sneaking a peek to confirm the now-total lack of red foam on the den's outer surface. "I've never heard of anything like it," she admitted.

Henry'd stepped closer to the screen. He looked at her over his shoulder. "Steady movement implies tracking or measurement. Time? A clock?"

"It might monitor the survey's progress. Kmet-Here would want to know when it's done and we're ready to go." She sounded unconvincing even to herself. The Kmet relied on kmeth's pilot for notification, not a display outside the den.

And displays, visuals? Were their species' default, not kmeth's. "Henry," Killian said uneasily, "what if it's meant for us? We have to figure it out."

"It would help—" He shoved his hands in his pockets, plainly offended by a mystery on top of all else. A frustrated, "We need Flip to *see* this."

"Here." Killian pulled up her notepad. It skirted the prohibition on recordings in a Portal, being nothing more than a writeable surface, but when connected to her personal communicator, an allowed device, she could send whatever was on it. Presently doodles. She cleared those with a quick tap of her finger.

She'd need the stylus for this. Working with practiced precision, feeling his eyes on her, Killian drew a sequence of discs showing the dot and spiral at different moments. "Okay?" she asked when done. "It's an approximation."

"It's what we need." Henry paid her the compliment of not glancing up to compare her artwork to the reality on the screen. "Flip, analyze the incoming image please." A nod like a command.

Killian sent the image, careful to attach it to her cargo manifest checklist as a legitimate communication between shuttle and Portal pilot. A checklist she hadn't had time to complete, but, if Flip was as intelligent as alt seemed, the simple subterfuge would hold up.

She felt Henry still looking at her, curious. "So? I draw," she snapped. "People do."

Including the rude patches on her bar-hopping coveralls, but *that* she wasn't about to admit.

Not in this lifetime.

"See you at the next stop."

THE PROBABLE FUNCTION OF THE DISC, HENRY, IS TO INDICATE TIME ELAPSED TOWARD A PREDETERMINED MOMENT. A COUNTDOWN, IN THE VERNACULAR.

He'd been afraid of that.

I FIND NO REFERENCE TO A PRIOR SUCH REPRESENTATION BY THE KMET, LEADING ME TO SPECULATE IT RELATES IN SOME WAY TO ANOTHER SINGULAR AND RECENT FACTOR INVOLVING KMETH. THE DIVIDER. IF SO, THERE ARE SEVERAL POSSIBILITIES. WILL YOU RETURN TO YOUR QUARTERS TO CONFER OR WOULD YOU LIKE ME TO LIST THEM?

He could think of a few, none of them good. "Later, Flip. Thank you." The phone went back in his pocket.

Killian remained on the dais, ostensibly going over the satellite feeds, aware they'd a serious complication. Aware they wouldn't discuss it in Control, with Kmet-Here steps away and very likely listening.

What Henry wanted to do was think. To think while pacing, but there wasn't room. Several PIPs had come alert when Killian touched the pedestal, climbing into position on the walls, but the rest—and more—covered the floor, pouring from several tubes with finger-sized pieces of what looked like metal clutched in an extruded claw, destined for kmeth's den.

Metal they applied to still-liquid patches of gray: fresh Kmet excretions. Kmet-Here had been out of the den recently; perhaps kmeth had ducked back inside when the Humans arrived.

Was kmeth awake? Alert? Interested?

Henry looked at the dark mouth of the den. He'd questions. *More now.* About to move closer, he stopped. He wasn't ready to force a conversation. Not without knowing more. Not before consulting with his quorum.

The spark kept moving. *How long did they have?*

He must have said it aloud. "Forty-three hours," Killian responded, a reminder they'd decided on a countdown of their own, to the next transit. Making it easier on the bodies they wore and relied upon—

—*would it make them too late?*

"Flip's sure it's a clock," he announced. "Any idea how to calibrate it? To know how long we have?"

Killian's lips tightened, acknowledging the implication. Without a word she stepped down. Disappointed PIPs, primed to work the wall controls, dropped to the floor with sullen little thuds.

Going to the screen, the pilot reached up. Her outstretched fingers barely reached the bottom of the disc. "I give you a boost. You put on strips of this." She produced a roll of thin black tape from a pocket too small to have held it. "It's a centimeter wide," she said, giving him the tape. "We mark the time the spark disappears behind each strip, again when it emerges. Do the math."

AN EXCELLENT IDEA, HENRY, Flip praised. I am happy to 'do the math,' if you wish.

"Flip approves," Henry told her.

Killian's face was an interesting study in gratification and *why should I care what a polymorph thinks,* ending in a neutral scowl. "Tape." Shoulder against the wall, she cupped her hands, ready to lift him up. "Up."

By the Portal clock, now calibrated in Human terms and fed by Flip to the reader on Henry's desk, as of this moment they'd fifteen hours, ten minutes, four seconds left before the dot reached the center of the disc.

Three seconds.

Two.

Henry closed the reader and ran his hand through his hair. Took a long breath in, let it out, slow and steady.

"You appear agitated, Henry." PIP-Flip clung to the wall above the closed door, presumably in case Killian surprised them again. Henry hadn't asked. "Is there a concern?"

"Just hoping I made the right choice." The pilot hadn't argued when he'd suggested they transit before the dot reached its goal. "What do you think?"

"You made the only possible choice, Henry. It would be highly unwise to remain here until the countdown finishes, without knowing the outcome."

They were doing this.

"I believe Killian," PIP-Flip continued, "ordered a rest period beforehand, Henry."

To quarters, both of them, to recharge. Eat. Sleep. Take their meds. Be ready, as she put it, for a rough one.

Henry'd no appetite.

"I've something to do first," he told the polymorph. "Keep watch."

Still dressed, he stretched out on the bed, but not to sleep.

Grasping his wristbands, he closed his eyes . . .

***

Opening them to see sunlight shining through the windows of the Arbiter's meeting room, laying bright bars across the polished wood of floor and table, a harbinger of fair weather.

A storm crow. That's what he was, Henry thought as he waited for his quorum to respond. They'd be surprised by the unscheduled summons—he couldn't help that.

Dismayed by the reason.

A doomsday clock. If that's what it was. Henry'd added the disc, with its spiral and dot, to the surface of the table. Imperfect, but he'd had Flip send Killian's drawing to New Earth. The Kmet continued to allow normal communications through the Portal's connection to its partner in Earth orbit.

The dependence made him nervous, even if he and Killian possessed their own means to send and receive information. Depending, of course, on the availability of their oneirics.

He looked down at his wristbands, honestly surprised to find only one dark. Sofia's.

Rena arrived first, with Shomchai, appearing as if seated. Seeing his face, they didn't say a word.

Ousmane arrived next. "Oh," she said, looking around the room. Uncertainty crossed her face. "Is this—ah, it is. We're here again."

Henry realized he'd forgotten the door to the main hall. The curtains. Remembered the seal on the wall, yes, but not water glasses or the stand to hold them. No mountain view out the windows, only blinding light—

Do better next time, he admonished himself. Details grounded his newer oneirics, kept them connected. Hurry—dread—he couldn't allow emotion to distract him. "My apologies. You know the situation."

Sober nods answered his half question.

"We're prepared to leave for the next world later today, ahead of this." Henry indicated the disc. "Thoughts."

"I think it's a suggestion to get on with the job." Shomchai leaned back, hands folded over his stomach. "Kmet-Here reached a decision about this world; you insisted on a visual search. The clock sets the limit of kmeth's patience with the delay."

"Don't forget kmeth won't factor in the time you and Killian need to recover, Henry," Rena cautioned.

"Ousmane?"

The historian circled her finger on the table. "Your report, I've seen. Nothing, ah, of the *Exeter* since?"

"No," Henry told her. "The satellites will remain here until the entire surface has been surveyed. You have my word."

An intent look. "Reconsider," she said. Seeing his surprise, Ousmane gestured upwards, her earrings refusing to catch the light. "I see this clock, ah, as a dire warning. That Humans away from New Earth have this much time and no more, ah, before the Kmet's enemy—" Her hand came down, forming a fist "—arrives to snuff them out."

Henry gave a slow grim nod. "A possibility we must consider."

"If so, you must not leave any evidence of our existence, ah, to be found. You cannot!" Ousmane lowered her voice. "All Human spacecraft can self-destruct. Have the pilot, ah, order the satellites to deorbit and burn up in the atmosphere."

"I'll ask Killian to be ready but—" Henry paused for emphasis. "—for the selfsame reason we mustn't miss anyone. For their sakes, and for ours."

Rena, who'd been gazing down at the disc on the table, now looked up. "What's Kmet-Here going to do if the Divider comes?"

Shomchai sat up, alarmed. "Run here. Bring it to New Earth. Henry—"

"Easy." Henry held up his hands. "Even if kmeth did transit us home, we don't know of anything able to track a transiting Portal. That may be how the Kmet have avoided interacting with whatever *Divider* refers to." He found he didn't like the term. Then again, he didn't like formless threats to humanity either. "I hope we do encounter the Divider. I've authority to open negotiations."

Their silence reminded him of the pilot's incredulity at the proposal. *Not encouraging.* "Talking's what I'm here to do," Henry insisted. "Anything else before we move on to your reports?"

"Do Portals have weapons?" Ousmane asked, very quietly.

The stock answer was no, provided by the Arbiter's Office every day to a wide variety of anxious inhabitants of Earth. Their new neighbors had come in peace, the argument went, advanced beyond need of armaments.

"We don't know," Henry admitted. "And even if the Kmet suddenly gave us full access to a Portal, I'm told it's highly unlikely we could tell a weapon from the plumbing." No need to add the other side of it, that New Earth might learn more than it wanted of the Kmet's offensive capabilities if the Duality shattered. He coughed, dispelling the dark thought. "Flip offered a modification of your scenario, Ousmane. That the countdown estimates how long we can safely remain before our presence in orbit will be detected by the Divider."

Shoulders relaxed. They liked that one better. So did he. *Didn't make it correct.*

"So Kmet-Here is protecting you," Rena concluded, pointing at the disc.

"Or kmeth's self." Shomchai shrugged. "It works out to the same."

Did it? Henry kept his doubt to himself. "Whatever its meaning, we'll transit to World III before the count's up." Seeing Ousmane start to frown and having no intention of shifting back to ship names, he added, "I've adopted the nomenclature while we're underway. What can you tell me about the PIPs and Killian? I believe Flip was thoroughly insulted I asked."

Rena grinned. "Having less in common with a Portal's minions than you do with a herring, Henry. Poor Flip."

"About the gist of it." Henry smiled back.

Ousmane steepled her fingers, her dark eyes gleaming. "The behavior is not, ah, unprecedented. My colleagues and I have accessed the Spacer Repository's records. It appears the Portal Integrated Polymorphs, ah, are capable of understanding and responding to Human verbalizations related to ship safety. There have been two previous incidents. It, ah, is a sensible measure by the Kmet to allow this."

"Killian was surprised. An omission in her training?"

The historian ducked her head, a tiny smile furrowing dimples in her cheeks. "The previous are not, ah, considered incidents of credit to the pilots. In the first, ah, the PIPs were exiled from Human quarters by physical intervention."

Soccer balls, Henry thought, amused. "The other?"

"A pilot smoking in a corridor was able to successfully, ah, countermand the PIPs fire suppression response." Ousmane chuckled. "That said, the PIPs responded by sealing the pilot within a section of corridor, ah, until she finished."

"So comprehension, with the reaction within preprogrammed parameters," Shomchai commented.

"The consensus, yes."

So no talking to them anytime soon. Dismissing the PIPs, Henry moved on to the Portal. "And the adjustment made to living quarters—to accommodate my presence? Any ideas."

Ousmane shook her head.

Rena shrugged. "It could be what Portals normally do, we simply hadn't observed until now. You're the first Human passenger, Henry."

Shomchai nodded. "The Kmet studied us before making contact. Continue to do so. I am not surprised the contingency was available, nor that your rooms are identical. Two's of things, Henry, always. Your presence may make kmeth more comfortable."

"Or three make a crowd."

"Are you sensing friction?" Rena asked, troubled.

"No. Not yet," Henry said truthfully. "If there's any indication having two Humans around bothers kmeth, we'll work it so only one of us is in Control at a time. Killian showed me how to use the tubes." He caught Ousmane's shocked look. "Sorry. I should have put it in my report."

"No. No. That knowledge is, ah, exclusive to pilots."

And so a sign of trust. He wouldn't betray it. "Just so."

Her eyes flickered. "However, this being a unique situation, I don't, ah, suppose—"

"I promised Killian," Henry lied. Before any of them could press for more, he turned to the last topic. "The Divider."

"We've done a thorough analysis. Keep in mind the Kmet use our language with precision. When it suits them," qualified Shomchai, having helped Henry draft agreements. "You should take the word at face value. That which divides or separates. I am intrigued by the lack of plural. It emphasizes the action over the collective existence—assuming the Kmet refer to another intelligent spacefaring species and not a device or machine."

Henry's eyebrows rose. "Machine?"

"We don't think so," Rena hastened to say. "Kmeth's emotion and actions match a response to another life-form, perhaps a competitor for resources or, yes, a predator."

"Or parent." Everyone turned to Ousmane, who gave a throaty chuckle. "I've teenagers at home. When they know they've misbehaved, their response to me, ah, isn't so different."

Henry tilted his head at their xenologist. "Rena? Kmet family structure?"

She blew out a breath. "All I can offer is guesswork. We've long suspected kmeth are hermaphrodites. The problem is, Earth comparisons range from organisms with no parental care to those with incredible self-sacrifice." Her lower lip disappeared between her teeth.

She'd another thought, was reluctant to let it out. "Go on," Henry encouraged.

"The Kmet—those we've seen—lead solitary lives within elaborate, very personal structures. To me, that suggests an instinctive territoriality, coupled with a preference or perhaps an obligation to live alone at this stage in kmeth's life."

"Or a limited number of qualified Portal operators," Ousmane protested. "Such a highly technological society, ah, cannot be ruled by its biology."

"Says the mother," Rena responded.

The historian shrugged, conceding the point.

"'Emphasizing the action over the collective,'" Henry repeated thoughtfully.

Shomchai raised a warning finger. "A personal opinion, Henry. My colleagues aren't ready to support it."

"I'll keep that in mind." While helping Henry negotiate with the Kmet, the linguist had evinced several such opinions. None supported but all, he recalled, of value. Shomchai offered a unique insight into the alien/Human interface, one he trusted. "Thank you. Unless there's more, I'll let you go now. Wake. Work or rest, but be aware I'll want you with me at our next transit."

"Wouldn't miss it," Rena said lightly.

"I will be ready," from Ousmane. "Do not dismiss my concerns, Henry. For the mission, for you. Please exercise, ah, the greatest of care. The situation is perilous."

"Hah." Shomchai smiled, throwing a hand toward Henry. "The Arbiter responsible for more breakthroughs in Human-Kmet relations than any before him. That's you, Henry. If anyone can get us through this, it will be you."

Henry eyed him. "You sent the bottle."

The smile widened. "I admit nothing."

"Where's ours?" Rena demanded.

Ousmane laughed at the face Shomchai made.

He'd a superb group forming around him. Henry felt it, trusted what he felt, drawing confidence from them as he hoped they would from him.

"See you at the next stop," he told them.

Then opened his eyes.

<Lima Charlie, Killie-Cat.>

WAITING sucked.

Killian popped the lid. Sauce splattered the table like blood.

Getting up, she went to the cupboard, found a wipe, and methodically cleaned her mess, putting the soiled wipe into the Portal's equivalent of a waste container. What went in didn't come out.

Like Henry, who hadn't, for supper or company. Maybe he was still working with his experts on New Earth to find a solution so they wouldn't all die. "Good luck with that," she muttered.

<You talking to me, or yourself?>

"The Arbiter, if you must know."

<Ohh. Henrryy the Yummyyy.>

She dropped into her seat with a morose, "Shut it down." Settled to eat what she couldn't enjoy. The food was pretty good; her mind wasn't on it, only duty.

<You'll be all right, Killie-Cat.> Softer, almost gentle. <I took a look at your fancy new setup down here. Upgraded me, too. A suite, no less. Full library and archive access. Twenty-four-hour food service. Laundry. It's like an all-inclusive without the beach.>

Killian's lips twitched involuntarily. "You hate beaches."

<Makes it the sweeter. Must say, Henry's fair. Omar and Annie are getting the star treatment as well, s'long as he's stuck in orbit with Kmet-Here.>

"You're talking to her again?" There'd been a memorable bar fight—fine of itself, but Annie had a temper. Tended to words. Words that cut. Killian stabbed her spork at the air. "Not me."

< Hey, we're all spacers. All Human. Gotta stick together.>

"Since when?"

<Since now. You ready to get to work or do you want to wallow some more? I'm amenable.>

Wasn't wallowing . . . Except she was. Gis read her like a book, had ever since the day they'd met training to fly orbital sweeps.

Probably saw upset in how Killian turned her spork in the sauce.

She dropped the utensil. "I'm listening."

<We'd like you to make some measurements. >

We? The System Coalition, that meant, and likely Kisho and Annie and who the hell else. Meddlers. Killian made a rude gesture. "No."

<To draw—>

Killian's hand hovered meaningfully over the wristband.

Her partner spoke rapidly. <What you did for the Arbiter got everyone excited down here. We want more drawings like that, this time of where you are. To scale, best as you can. Of anything. Everything. You'll be there long enough to get eyes on more than anyone ever has, Killie. Don't waste that. Use it.>

Her hand fell away. "I'd be breaking more than regs, Gis," she said heavily. "I get caught—"

<Then don't. You're smart. Hide your work out in the open. Make it so obvious Henry will look right at it and not see what you're really doing.>

Against her will, ideas floated up. Waterproof ink, paint over top. Killian shook her head. "Can't do it. I'd need supplies."

A smug, <Who do you think packed your trunks, darling-mine?>

She aimed her middle finger at her right eye. "My coffee maker better be there."

<Finish eating and go see for yourself. About time you unpacked.> The words were light; the tone wasn't. Like her, Gis followed the countdown. Breathed with it. Waited with her.

Killian let out a shuddering sigh, feeling the tension melt from her bones. "Love you, Space Rat."

<Lima Charlie, Killie-Cat.>

“NOW!”

AT two hours to transit, Henry and Killian went to Control, neither able to rest. Both were anxious, though Killian did the better job of hiding it, being annoyed with him.

Henry watched as satellite images rained in numbing monotony on the outer two screens, overlaid with short-form data code from the AIs. Nothing to report, according to Flip. The planet below the stationary Portal held the centermost screen and Henry’s attention. Hypnotic, watching the change from light to utter dark, give or take streaks of beautiful fluorescence in the waters along the southern coastline. Under other circumstances, he’d have summoned Rena.

She’d see the next world.

A storm along the east coast swelled into an immense disk of swirling white, scored by flashes of lightning at night, and Henry would have worried about anyone caught in it, had they found a trace of anyone at all.

Too soon to be sure.

Not too soon to lose hope. He pulled his knees to his chest, having taken a seat on the floor. PIPs moved around or above him and, though he tried, he’d lost track of the number of different appendages they grew at will. Calipers and hooks were popular, along with what looked very much like his grandfather’s rasp. Was knowledge of which to manifest built into their shape? *He’d ask Flip.*

And bring a pillow with him, Henry decided, rump getting numb. Should there be a next time.

What PIPs shared, he discovered, was a compulsion to touch the den, heedless of their other tasks. They’d trundle or scamper to it, spend time in contact via an appendage or leaning their squat bodies, then resume what they’d been doing before. Almost like worship.

He could hear Rena now. More likely, the PIPs monitored something about the den’s ongoing construction, and Henry shouldn’t speculate without data.

Killian continued to ignore him, keeping her focus on the images. She’d loaded the emergency deorbit commands and silently showed him the activation sequence on the pad, in case.

What annoyed her was his admission he'd no idea when to destroy the satellites. He was sure they'd know, he'd told her. *Not fucking good enough,* she'd shouted at him as she dived into the tube.

Saying nothing since. By this point, Henry was reasonably sure Killian's annoyance extended to the entire uncooperative universe, diluting her ire with him. To test the hypothesis, he wiggled and gave a little cough.

She didn't budge. She did, to his relief, finally speak. "I've confirmed Kmet-Here's analysis. No recognizable traces of manufacturing in the atmosphere. As of 68% completion, no refined metal detected by the sats above or immediately below."

No ship. Killian knew the sorts of things that could happen to a starship; he wasn't about to ask. Regardless of why, the *Exeter* hadn't made it.

He found himself sadder than he'd expected.

A regular pattern, an early excitement, had turned out to be sand dunes. A glow, volcano. What they'd thought were a chain of islands in the midst of an ocean turned out to be startling conglomerations of floating shelled life-forms, each the size of an Earth whale. Another moment when he'd wanted so much to call Rena. She'd get every scrap of the data as relayed to New Earth, but it wasn't the same.

HENRY. YOU WANTED ME TO TELL YOU WHEN THERE WERE THIRTY MINUTES LEFT ON THE COUNTDOWN.

"Thank you, Flip." Henry looked at the den. They'd seen no sign of Kmet-Here.

He got to his feet, having no intention of waiting for whatever happened when the dot hit its spot.

Killian's head swung around. "Time to go?"

"Yes."

"Got your meds?"

He nodded. He'd taken the cubes when they'd arrived in Control. Had done whatever the pilot recommended, including drinking a bulb of Restore. A second made an awkward bulge in his jacket pocket. Thinking about fluids brought up a question. "Is there a washroom?"

"Here?" A wicked grin flickered across her lips. "Use your empty bulb. Don't worry. If you miss, the PIPs won't."

Henry didn't mind the topic. They were talking again. About to move. He flashed a cheerful smile. "Ready to hum?"

***

They hummed in harmony for a second time, prolonging the notes, and finally received a response.

A single loud burp.

Nothing more.

Henry looked at Killian. Her shrug said *your job.*

Handing her the bulb from his pocket, Henry strode forward to the den, bent down before he could reconsider—and the *smell* was a warning he really should—and went inside.

Warmer here. Warmer and moist. Not as dark as he'd prepared himself to face, light penetrating thinner portions of the construction, enough to confirm he wasn't about to step on any body parts.

A hiss from behind. "Henry . . . the PIPs aren't moving."

He stopped as well, having made his point. Listened. The deep thrum of kmeth's breathing filled the space. *Asleep or brooding?*

"Kmet-Here," he said briskly. "This is Arbiter-Henry. I would—"

"OOOUUUTTT!"

The roar sent Henry stumbling backwards, that and a threatening glimpse of enormous sideways teeth gnashing where he'd been.

Killian caught his shoulder, using her grip to drag him out of the den and safely past the pedestal, then give him a hard shake. "Idiot!"

"Got kmeth's attention," he gasped in triumph as the Kmet erupted from the den, quivering from snout to tail with what might be outrage. Every polyp on kmeth's head was erect and bright red.

Definitely outrage. "Hello, Kmet-Here," Henry greeted cheerfully. "How good of you to join us. Killian, please input the coordinates for the next planet."

She shot him a dubious look, matched by the Kmet's. "Sir? Are you—"

"Do it, please, Pilot. We need to go now."

"Now?" Polyps changed from red to cooperative purple in a flowing wave from front to back as Kmet-Here heaved kmethself forward. "Now is good." An eye fixed on Henry. "Before was better, Arbiter-Henry."

"Then, I wasn't ready. Now I am."

"Coordinates input, sir." Killian stepped briskly from the dais, ceding it to the giant alien. "Ready to find the *Naga.*"

PIPs scrambled up walls and each other to get into position as Henry continued to meet that one-eyed stare, keeping his hands and head still, his expression set at pleasant. If he faced another Human, he'd say kmeth was inclined to challenge him despite wanting, for kmeth's own reasons, not to delay.

"It is for the health of the Duality," Henry said quietly, "and the good of all that we look for and find the Humans on the next world."

"If there are any Humans-There, Arbiter-Henry." A flipper lifted, slapped the floor, just missing a PIP. "Do you have a message from this next world? From any other worlds?"

Been thinking, had kmeth, in that dark, dank den.

So had he. Kmet-Here forced the issue as kmeth had in their earlier confrontation. This time, Henry went with his alternate strategy: distract.

He leaned to the left, then the right, drawing kmeth's other eye from Killian to join the first. "Pickled beets," he said, once sure of kmeth's full attention. "Peanuts."

Lips pulled away from those plate-like teeth. "You brought delicacies, Arbiter-Henry?"

They'd the Kmet they thought they had. Henry gave a restrained little bow, hiding his satisfaction. "A small acknowledgment of the onerous task we've asked of you, Kmet-Here."

Tongues flicked inside the partly gaping mouth. "Where are they?" Kmeth swung around, squashing a PIP. "Here are they?"

"We'll deliver them to you, here, after the next transit." On a whim, Henry pointed to the dot moving on the screen. "That is what you wish, is it not? To go?"

An eye tracked his gesture. On reaching the screen, the Kmet shuddered, eyelids slamming down. Every polyp abruptly snicked down into its stalk. "Yes. Yes. We must go now. NOW!"

Why? The question caught in Henry's throat, begging to be asked. He opened his mouth—

"NOW!" Eyes wide open, Kmet-Here lunged for the dais. Henry eased a few steps away, giving the Kmet ample room, the moment lost.

There'd be more.

Killian gave him a thumbs-up from kmeth's rear.

He wasn't sure he deserved congratulations.

Then he realized she signaled something else—

TRANSIT.

Hi, there.

Doublet

WHERE to leave the junk was a quandary, there being no overt sign of intelligent life in the Split since the *Exeter* landed, making the ideal placement another topic fruitlessly debated by the Bios, who vacillated between repeat visits—leaving a steadily increasing pile—and moving carefully calculated distances from the selfsame spot. This trip, they'd agreed on the latter approach, ordering Beth to pace outward from the last spot to an identical patch of barren, sun-baked crust.

Being the one with extra weight in her pack and at times ready to chuck it any old where, Beth had her own plan.

It didn't include carrying the junk into Away itself, either, a variation Bios longed to try and Seekers knew better than let them. Anything put on the ground would be stolen by life smart enough to know *different* might mean *edible,* sink in quick mud, or be grown over and vanish in hours.

Shelters—which might be animal traps or religious offerings, for what Humans knew—suffered the latter fate. Bios expected those who found one still showing, its rounded top clean and new, to hunt what made it. Seekers knew better than that as well. Nothing gained by chasing what ran from you. In Away, you couldn't sit still to wait for it either. Not without being hunted.

Beth planned to shuck her weight in the Split; she'd simply a new thought of where.

Seekers avoided pots, for fear approaching them might trigger a sweep, and because they stank of sulfur. Made the most direct crossing a tiresome weave around the things, but a sensible habit.

Habits, sensible or otherwise, didn't offer to change things. Did give Beth a disquieting chill between her shoulders, entering the shadow of a pot for the first time. Not that it was cool, given her proximity to steaming magma, but air moved up the wall in answer—a breeze in a place without much.

The stench climbed up her nose, squatting at the back of her throat; she paid it no mind.

The wall was like her daughter's pottery, this close, made of a stack of lumpy rings with a shiny baked-on brown glaze. A single ring tall as Beth, no possibility the pot-makers rolled each by hand.

Nonetheless, she gave the crust beneath her feet a thoughtful look before getting to work.

She might have ignored the Bios' stated location; she didn't alter their method. Wasn't much to alter about putting objects on the ground a measured distance apart, then waiting at a presumably safe distance to see if any were sucked down.

Beth spread her groundsheet and sat cross-legged in the middle. Waited ten breaths to see if anything objected.

Nope. Pulling her pack on her lap, she dug out the latest junk. A charcoal pencil. They sent one every time. *Look, we can draw stuff.*

Next. A flattened Human figure of clay the size of her hand—*explained the weight.* Patrick's, probably. She held it up. Frowned. A face. Ears. Hair in a bun. Clothes, including mittens and shoes, hid the remaining informative bits. If she was the alien, she'd want those plain. Not, *look, we're cookies.* Back in her pack it went.

Out came what improved her mood: a tiny speaker, complete with electromagnet and wires. They hadn't sent functional tech before, other than pencils. *Look, we can talk to each other.* And refine metal, draw out wire, use electricity, communicate by sound—there was no end to what the thing revealed about Home and Humans.

About time. She, personally, was tired of pretending not to be a reasonably advanced, tool-making, fun-to-be-with intelligence. *Take us as we are,* would be her message.

Along with *play nice.*

There was the ever-present strip of Doublet metal inscribed on one side with simple numbers. Beth turned it over, shaking her head at the rows of equations. *Look, it's a test.* A child's toy, a ball attached to a paddle by a rubber band. *Look, we play.* A book, rolled in a tube.

Wasn't putting *that* out without checking. She undid the tube and began flipping pages. "They've got to be kidding," she mouthed to herself. Pictures, no text. Showed people of varied sizes and shapes doing what people did. Planting a tree. Sitting around a fire. Building a house. Walking by a stream.

What part of always underground, cooks magma, and shoots lightning *did they not get?*

Beth restrained a snort of disgust. Even "look" assumed light and eyes to use it, and she'd not bet on either.

Not her job to second-guess the experts, even if none of them seemed to read her reports, or ever set foot in the Split.

This was hers. Beth grabbed out the clay cookie Human and lobbed it. She'd pitched ball, growing up, and had no trouble landing the stupid thing on the far edge of the pot's shadow.

The speaker went next, landing a meter to the right. The pencil took a practiced flip. The strip and book Beth spun along the hard crust, ending up where she'd intended. Vibration was a language, one they definitely shared, and she leaned back on her elbow with a grin, having sent a message of her own.

Hi, there.

***

Beth kept her vigil the rest of day and that night, watching her row of Human-made junk sit forlorn and ignored. Lasted through a second day, too stubborn for her own good; forced around and around the pot by the sun, including a blistering hour hiding under her cloak. Learned in passing the pot was as symmetrical as they'd guessed from a more prudent distance.

The air significantly warmer near the magma, she stayed a second night, rising before dawn to move while the crust was cool underfoot. In place of the Bios' artifacts, her pack was weighed down by bottled urine and a sack of crap. Appropriate. Next stop, she'd let the contents dry.

Done with this one. For good measure, she glared at the ground. "Wouldn't have hurt you to say hi," she whispered.

Waited.

Thought for an instant she heard the crust creak all around as if something cruised beneath, something crazy big, and her heart skipped a beat on its way to racing, it not being a good sign or safe.

Unless it was.

Stars moved in the sky; she didn't. Not till the glow on the far horizon told her she'd run out of time.

"Catch you later," she whispered.

Beth set off, leaving the junk, her prime concern now not to dry out herself. She'd days left before reaching Away, and the bladder around her waist half-empty.

Down with the stick—*tinkle*—take a step. She fell into the rhythm, wasn't lulled by it, kept her eyes moving and sharp. *Hunting.*

The crust rolled to the horizon, bare and scoured. The only footprints followed her, paired little scuffs, erased by the lightest breeze. There were other signs to watch for.

The first to step onto the Split found it. Or it found them, depending who told the story. Water being so precious and scarce here, little wonder it came as both prey and predator.

Water Ribbons, they called them. Rare and solitary most of the year. Dangerous in their seasonal swarms, which weren't now but soon. Bios argued over what they were. Beth didn't need a classification, only a water source, but you didn't find ribbons on the surface.

You called them.

Once an hour, Beth stopped, readied her water sack, and drew the tip of her stick lightly over the crust. As it bounced, it made a different sound, a hiss. Again and again. When nothing came, she resumed her walk, putting distance between where she'd paused and where she was in case something came hunting her.

Early days in the Split, she'd felt such a rush. Adrenalin. Exhilaration. Wore a body out and for what? Now she did what was needful to survive, part of her mind wandering, most keyed to her senses. A peace granted very few filled her—

A warning crackle came from either side. The hairs on her arms rose.

Sweep coming!

She'd barely time to drop the stick, pull her cloak over her face and fold in her arms before searing bolts of lightning crisscrossed around her, striking the ground, the air they expanded complaining with booms of thunder.

"Five damn yous." Eyes shut, taking shallow breaths, she counted, cursing whatever had triggered a sweep out of sequence. "Four damn yous." Her heels sank as the soles of her boots melted. "Three damn yous. Two damn yous—" Her shins grew unbearably hot—her knees—a gasped, "One—"

Then done.

Beth wiped runnels of sweat from her face and neck with a cloth she tucked back in its pocket, waiting for her boots to cool. The vines on her head were limp, but still tried to nip.

The sweep hadn't touched her, merely heated air molecules in passing. Come close, though. Closest yet and with any luck, ever.

Take close over dead.

Like whatever caused the sweep would be. A century of observing had uncovered the base sequence. Twice a week wherever it was spring to summer, once where it was fall to winter, locations random. At any moment, all bets were off, entering the Split without some Away for company. Or the reverse. Sizzle and melt.

The bulky radio strapped to her left wrist vibrated. Base, aware. Worried.

Beth lifted her arm, shaking up the sleeve. "Still here, Dex. Wasn't me."

"We know—" The ancient tech worked, more or less, in the Split; fancier failed. Sweep-remnant static distorted words, then, "—too smart."

"Hah." Whatever controlled Doublet's nastier side didn't care how smart anyone was, only about its rules. Beth eyed the horizon. "Ready to go, Dex."

"Negat—ome."

She was closer to the haze marking Away. Closer to everywhere but the way back. Beth shook her head. "You're breaking up, Dex."

Regrettably loud and clear, "Haul your ass back here, Beth!"

"Coming." She stabbed the off button. She'd retrace her steps by the pot, in case. Wasn't disobeying, that extra look.

Beth took extra care as she moved forward again, so much chatter making her nerves twitch. Days to go.

Back to hunting.

World III

"Let's get to work."

THIS time Henry kept on his feet and alert, the meds holding the contents of his stomach where they belonged.

Not that he noticed, his eyes riveted on the screen and the new world it showed. Globs and strings of light marked settlements and traced roads as they would on New Earth. The dot and spiral had vanished from the screen. His heart began to pound. He fumbled at his sleeve. His quorum—they had to see this—

Flinched at a *BOOM!*

"Humans-There," Kmet-Here announced grimly. *BOOM!* "Retrieve them. Retrieve all. Pilot, begin. I will input parameters."

"No!" The shout surprised him as much as the Kmet, but hadn't Ousmane warned him? *Don't let kmeth get there first.* Henry went on more diplomatically, "There's a process, Kmet-Here, when dealing with living Humans. I will contact these people and we'll arrange their evacuation on our ships."

"Too slow." A discontented rumble. "The pilot can retrieve Humans-There, faster, better. Then we go to the next planet."

Faster wasn't better. Henry didn't look at Killian, who'd briefed him on the Kmet notion of *retrieve.* While it might work for inanimate objects, it couldn't be used to transport the living. Not and have them stay that way.

"I'm in charge of the Human portion of our mission, Kmet-Here," he responded firmly. "I say there will be an orderly and safe evacuation of these people to New Earth. Do you concur?"

"Do not be too slow, Arbiter-Henry." The words weren't a request.

"I assure you we'll use all possible speed, Kmet-Here," he replied. "It is our—"

Spinning on a flipper, the Kmet heaved kmethself into the den.

Henry frowned thoughtfully. Heard his name and turned.

Killian had leapt to the pedestal, hurriedly skimming through inputs. "Henry. I'm detecting orbital constructs."

"Pardon?"

She wasn't smiling. "Satellites. What look to be remote observatories parked at their L-1 and -2. I'd say they know we're here or will soon."

"Flip." He didn't bother pulling out the pretend-phone.

I'M RECEIVING RADIO TRANSMISSIONS. MUSIC. VOICE. THE LANGUAGE IS OF ORIGIN EARTH. SPECIFICALLY MALAY.

It tracked with what Ousmane had told Henry, that the Halcyon Class *Naga Gunung Pulai* had carried a number of individuals who claimed that heritage from before the Arrival. While impossible to prove one way or the other, the group convinced others to study the Malay language and customs from the Archive. They'd planned to emulate the extinct culture at their new home.

What had he said to the historian? *That won't last.*

It seemed he'd underestimated their determination. He couldn't wait to meet them in person.

I CAN TRANSLATE FOR YOU, HENRY, BUT I DETECT TERMS AND CONSTRUCTS NOT IN MY DATABASE.

Shomchai would fill those in. Henry roused himself. "Search for primary contacts." Flip would flag anything that sounded official, be it emergency broadcasts, community organizations, government, or military.

UNDERWAY, HENRY.

After the *Exeter*'s failure, the stark emptiness of her destination, a wealth of possibilities. *And potential problems.* He licked his lips. "Killian, don't launch satellites yet. Let's not offer provocation."

A nod.

He pressed his wristbands, then drew out the cards he'd prepared earlier, having anticipated Kmet-Here would stay out and observe. He held up the first for his oneirics to see. *People here.* He discarded the second, tossing it to the floor.

A PIP seized it, running to stick *No luck* on kmeth's den wall.

Henry went through the cards, selected *Technology: space capable.*

<Go with the primary option.> Sofia's voice, flat and emotionless. <Identify and contact the leadership, secure their trust, advise them of a pending catastrophe.>

<The most convincing will be what they are already, ah, on alert against.> Ousmane. <Prepare your proof in advance.>

He'd a list of horribly plausible options, a copy with Flip and doubtless on a data cube in his quarters. *Prepare proof?* There'd be none, because he'd be lying.

As if Ousmane read his thought, she continued, <Your FLIP, ah, has been provided with the parameters to falsify the appropriate evidence.>

To terrify the population.

Faced with it, Henry rebelled. "I need another way," he whispered.

Killian shot him a warning look.

<There may be,> Rena said, understanding. <If they're reaching into space, it could be they want to return to New Earth. Who knows if this world's been kind to them?>

He lifted his eyes from the cards, showing his passengers the beautiful planet below. Sunrise sped across the landscape, glinting on oceans smaller than Earth's, finding the white of cloud at the poles and equator. Where the Sun hadn't yet touched, the lights of those living there beckoned like fireflies, dancing with life, and it looked like home.

<Oh my,> Rena whispered.

Sofia, flat and sure. <To get these people to leave, quickly—and by *quickly* I mean weeks, Arbiter, not days—fear is your only option.>

Weeks? Henry's heart sank, thinking of Kmet-Here's *too slow.* He hurried through the cards. Selected: *Estimated time to evacuate entire population.*

<Ask me something I can answer,> Sofia replied testily. <We don't even have a number yet.>

He shifted his gaze to the den; dropped it back to the card.

<Tell kmeth the truth. We won't know without more data.>

<No!> Shomchai and Rena objected for him.

<Never admit a lack of information to a Kmet,> Rena added quickly. <Kmeth will assume fault.>

<Is it better to lie to a Kmet? Because that's what it'd be,> Sofia countered. <A lie.>

<She's right, Henry,> Shomchai said grimly. <Kmet-Here will hold you to any schedule you provide. It must be accurate.>

<Give me two days and access to their demographic data,> Sofia came back. <I'll see what I can do.>

Henry closed and opened his eyes, twice, signaling his oneiric he'd understood and to proceed, then pressed his wristbands to let them get to work.

Two days? Maybe Kmet-Here would stayed denned.

He gave himself an inner shake. "Killian, the radio transmissions? I'd like to hear one."

She nodded, working at the left pedestal. A cacophony of sounds filled Control and PIPs paused, orienting to the pedestal as if distracted.

"Hang on," the pilot muttered. "There."

The racket fell away, leaving a female voice, older; by her steady, measured cadence, she recited prose or read the news. Henry had to smile. "Our first extraterrestrial Human."

"The *Naga* made it!" Killian exclaimed. "We got here!" She glanced at Henry and the joy drained from her face.

She'd remembered why they'd come.

"Let's get to work," he said very quietly.

And erase the accomplishments of a world.

"How do we end the world?"

IT was happening again. Retrieve them all. "I hate this."

<Better than scooping up corpses,> Gis reminded her.

Was it? Killian's gaze locked on the shadowed opening to the den. Henry'd scared her, going in like that, but what had he seen, inside, what more did he know about Kmet than anyone else—?

"Killian?"

She started, turning to Henry. "Sorry. Missed that."

He gave an understanding nod, then showed her his wristbands. *Still active.* "Are we stable up here? We need the beets and peanuts."

<It's important,> Gis said as Killian opened her mouth.

She closed it, swallowing what she'd been about to say regarding where Kmet-Here could put kmeth's bribe. "I'll take care of it, Henry."

He held up a hand, brought fingers and thumb to indicate a fraction.

Smart. Killian raised an appreciative eyebrow and nodded. "And you?"

"I need to go to my shuttle. I've preparations."

She couldn't begin to imagine. Killian slid another look at the planet. Number III on their hit list. Thriving. "There could be millions," she said, not trying to hide her dismay. *Where did they even start—*

"We knew that." Firmly. "We're prepared for it. Transports are launching, ready to transit. It'll take time—patience." His gesture swept Control, lingered meaningfully on the den, then returned to her. "When you're done, can you take a break? Join me?"

"Why?"

<Snap out of it. The Arbiter can't do this alone.> Under the words was worry, plain as plain, but Killian straightened her shoulders.

"No problem," she assured him, taking a quick look around to be sure. The feeds from I and II continued on the outer screens, but they would for days to come. She returned his bulb, which had somehow become hers to keep from the PIPs, then led the way to the tube.

Refusing to admit she was a little curious, despite everything, to meet Flip again.

***

"Welcome, Henry. Welcome, Killian. I've made coffee."

And produced hospitable hooks on the wall for their frost-covered coats. After hanging hers, Killian took her cup—*fine with her if the polymorph added a kick again*—and raised it to the spot on the shuttle's ceiling. "Keep saying hello like this, Flip, and I'll drop by more often."

The thing actually chuckled—warmly. "I like company."

"Don't encourage him," Henry advised. "Flip, how's the search going?"

"Complete, Henry. I have also determined the extent of World III's Human settlement." A portion of the wall became a detailed image.

How—The shuttle sat docked to the Portal, holding above the planet; she'd no idea the polymorph had equipment capable of this resolution. Killian went closer, marveling at the detail. Roads, definitely. Some multi-lane. The people below had aircraft, going by what appeared to be runways. Three large cities, several small ones, with scattered, isolated structures. She touched one with a fingertip.

"Farms," Henry guessed.

"The buildings extend deep underground and are heavily reinforced." A green glow appeared in three places, including the most remote of those structures. "Here are the locations of the potential contacts I've identified."

"Not farms," the Arbiter corrected himself thoughtfully. He paused, appeared to listen. "How do you know this is all of them, Flip?"

"An inference, Henry." The map enlarged, shifting to an edge, until a single feature dominated the view. "They've established a boundary."

It looked as if a huge claw had scraped the ground, leaving a curving ditch, steep-sided and deep. "But they've space flight," Killian heard herself object and shut her mouth.

"The technologies are not mutually exclusive. I can provide examples—"

"Later, Flip," Henry interrupted. "The boundary, please."

"It forms an unbroken perimeter around the settled area, Henry. I detect nothing Human beyond it. There has been a sequence of four such installations. The smallest and presumably first has been filled but remains obvious." The image reduced again, an arrow appearing to trace a small circle within one of the cities.

It only became *obvious* when Flip showed where to look. Killian wouldn't have picked it out on her own. Roads bent to stay within the circle, as did the buildings inside it. A set of larger thoroughfares broke out, fanning into the next, what, protected zone? "What's happened here?" she asked, dazed.

"Ousmane says if the center marks the landing site," Henry replied, "they dug ditches as they expanded out from it. Yes, Rena. I remember." He didn't elaborate, merely stood gazing at the map, eyes half closed, coffee forgotten in his hand.

Killian tried to imagine the effort it would have taken. "I studied the Halcyon Project. They didn't load heavy machinery."

"According to Ousmane, the sleeper ships carried exosuit prototypes."

<That'd work,> Gis commented.

Killian nodded. Spacer training included the body enhancements, if not at the size required to dig mammoth ditches. "Why not a fence?"

"I'll ask them." Henry took a too-quick swallow of coffee and grimaced. "Flip, how many remotes do you have out?"

Killian's "What?" overlapped the polymorph's calm, "One hundred and seventy, Henry."

The Arbiter lowered his head, giving her a guileless look she didn't buy for an instant. "Flip makes them. Show our pilot."

A spot appeared on the wall above the coffee maker, grew into a boil that burst. Something whizzed at Killian's head.

Stopping short to hover in the air. It looked like—"A bee?"

"While I can reproduce any biological organism provided sufficient information, Killian, this only appears to be an insect. It collects data in a usefully covert manner."

A spy by any other name. She chose to object to something else. "That's my job," Killian pointed out. "Pilots operate any Human surveillance gear. Henry, you know that."

<Apparently not,> Gis said.

"I do." Henry spread his hands. "Consider it the Arbiter's decision. These aren't a substitute for the satellites you put in orbit, Killian. What they do is give us eyes much closer to the ground. Close enough to learn about these people, to quickly gather a sense of them and their society. I need to gain their trust—" A wry twist to his lips. "At least enough not to be shot on sight."

"I WILL NOT ALLOW YOU TO BE HARMED!"

Flip's shout reverberated through the hold. Both Humans winced. Henry waved an apology. "No one's going to shoot me. It's a figure of speech, Flip."

<Someone's going to shoot him.>

Killian tapped off her oneiric. *Didn't disagree.* "What do you need me to do?"

His eyes brightened. "You're a spacer. I'd like to run a few of my world-ending scenarios by you for plausibility. In case I need one," he added hastily. "I hope I don't, but I prefer to practice. Have a seat." He looked around, seeing none. "Flip? Seats, please."

Stools rose from the floor near each of them. As Killian sat, she drank some coffee and studied Henry. Sandals and a suit. Rumpled hair and a patient dignity that changed without warning to self-deprecating humor. *He was*, she decided, *the strangest person she'd ever met.*

"Try the truth," she suggested at last, aware of the irony. "They'll believe it. After all, they've a big alien craft sitting overhead."

His gaze grew abstract, then sharpened on her. "My quorum advises we pass the Portal off as Human-tech as long as possible, to avoid frightening them."

"Might be a bit late for that."

"Flip?"

"I continue to broadcast your message, Henry, on every frequency I've detected in use."

"Let me guess," Killian said dryly. "*Don't worry, we aren't here to eat you.*"

He grinned like a kid. "Something like that. Ousmane provided the Halcyon contact code. I added the *no eating* part."

"You are misleading our pilot, Henry," the shuttle chided.

"Killian gets it. A peaceful introduction, attached to a code someone down there should recognize could only come from New Earth."

She gave a grudging nod. "Not bad."

"So." He leaned forward, cup in his hands. "This is my first time. How should we—"

"Henry. You asked to be notified when the countdown would have ended. It just has."

"Thank you." Letting out a breath, the Arbiter looked to Killian, eyebrows up, half-smiling. "That's a bit anticlima—"

"There's now a significant change in the satellite feed from World I. Shall I display it here?"

The polymorph's voice hadn't altered from its default of calm and helpful, but Killian watched the blood drain from Henry's face, felt her heart give a sickeningly heavy beat.

She didn't want to see it.

Knew they had to.

When Henry appeared unable to speak, she managed a hoarse, "Hell, yes."

The image of the landscape below them vanished—

—replaced by a world on fire.

"You aren't to blame."

IN late fall, when the tourists flocked to warmer climes, Henry—his real self—liked to walk along the waterfront, watched by gulls, ignored by sailors, breathing in the sea air. Thinking.

His walk would take him to the small local art gallery perched at the end of the last pier, for tea and a pastry by the window, watching the hushed harbor. The works on display were comfortingly the same. Some pottery. Jewelry and lamps from shells. Nautical trinkets.

Once, though, a series of paintings appeared on the back wall. They were of New Earth, his Earth, and depicted the beautiful globe against the black, a sequence showing it spin from painting to painting, as if he were in space, looking down, and he remembered his initial delight, walking from one to the next, tea in hand.

Until he reached the last. In it, the world was melting, as if made of wax and come too close to the Sun—

"Henry."

He wasn't there, he was here. *Though this wasn't the* same *him, was it?*

"If you're trancing on me right now, I will hit you."

He gave himself a shake, Killian a wary look, and put his coffee cup on the floor for Flip to absorb. "This doesn't change the mission."

"The *hell* it doesn't." Her outstretched finger stabbed at the image. "Are you blind?"

"We're here because Kmet-Here warned us of a threat." Dispassionately, he gazed at the fireball that had been a vibrant, life-sustaining planet. "It's been confirmed, that's all."

Killian lowered her hand. "Minute I'm back in Control, I'm destroying the sats. All of them."

Ousmane's advice. Henry hesitated, then disagreed. "Keep World II's going."

"You think it'll happen there next," she said after staring at him a moment, as if his face held answers he certainly didn't have. "Because of the clock. You think the Kmet did this?"

What he *thought* was immaterial. "Flip?"

A sound like a sigh. "Henry, you know how much I dislike speculating from a single data point."

"Please."

"The precision of the timing does imply pre-knowledge of the event."

"Which would be the case if Kmet-Here was responsible." A grim conclusion indeed. "We need proof. Can we tell from the satellite data?" He looked at Killian, who shrugged.

Flip answered. "Inconclusive. I've analyzed the occurrence to the nanosecond, Henry. The destruction resulted from a multitude of simultaneous eruptions, on every land mass, as if the entire crust was abruptly weakened to allow magma to rise explosively."

"What could cause—"

"Mining PIPs." Deep lines edged the pilot's mouth and eyes, adding years. "They're used to dig tunnels. Break up the surface. Melt ore. I sent them down at Kmet-Here's orders. I should have tracked the number and mass coming up. Should have watched them."

She'd been transiting corpses. "You aren't at fault, Killian, not in any sense," he said quickly. "Were any deployed on World II?"

A wince. "Maybe. Kmeth tested the atmosphere. I didn't pay attention to how—we were arguing." She paused, forehead creased. "Here—I didn't see any launched, but I wasn't always in Control."

Because he'd asked her here to chat. Henry grimaced, admitting what now seemed a mistake. "Flip, were you watching?"

"Yes, Henry. I can confirm a cluster of mining PIPs exited the Portal at World II but cannot say if it was retrieved. Releasing exploratory PIPs may be an automated function. Another was dropped after our arrival here. Was I remiss in not reporting it?"

If another clock appeared. If another world burned. Henry stopped the thought. "No, Flip, but please do so in future."

"Yes, Henry."

"Let's not jump to any conclusions," he said despite knowing it was inevitable. "Alien brains, after all. Kmeth might, in some way, be protecting us from the Divider."

"Or removing temptation." Killian's scowl looked permanent. "You said it yourself, Henry. We won't be allowed to have them."

"This seems excessive," he pointed out. "We've no way to reach these planets without a Portal."

"The Coalition—" She closed her mouth.

"Were building starships. Yes, I know." And stopped. Or had they? *Something to ask Sofia.* "Flip, please resume the World III display."

It wasn't the relief he'd hoped, to see a living world full of people.

Not when they'd seen what might be coming.

Not when they'd need weeks to save them.

"Might work."

<CALL the shuttle. Find out what's happening down there.>

"Not interested." Killian laid out her brushes, organizing them by tip type and size.

Silence.

She'd left the shuttle after going through disaster scenarios with Henry. Alien cracking open your planet's crust wasn't one of them, however likely. Throughout, the Arbiter'd been methodical, composed, even funny.

She suspected he'd kept her with him until convinced she wouldn't fly in a rage and go at Kmet-Here with a wrench.

Still might.

Henry'd elected to go with the classic CME apocalypse, those below still reliant on pipelines and wire, presumably anxious about their star's weather, given they monitored it, or haunted by the storm that had hurried the launch of their ancestors' ship. She'd agreed as if her opinion mattered. Flip the ever-helpful would produce whatever the Arbiter needed to make his case.

Just the pilot.

Who'd had an assignment of her own. Leaving them, Killian had gone to Control. The stack of jars and bags she'd left in front of the den were gone, the air redolent of beet and peanut; a pleasant change, at least until kmeth finished digesting.

She watched the leftmost screen with its feeds from World I's satellites as she sent the self-destruct. Expected to feel relief, but having the dying planet appear to wink out of existence made her sick.

She'd checked Henry's descent. As Flip promised, she'd telemetry. A little flying saucer icon, moving across the planet below.

The thing had a sense of humor.

Henry was represented by a white spot on the saucer. She hadn't asked to track him personally; apparently it came with the package. They'd landed. Saucer with a spot. Boring as hell to watch without the polymorph's bee's-eye view.

Before kmeth started to fart peanuts, she'd gone back to her quarters to finish unpacking.

To tell Gis what had happened to World I—*Hadn't managed that yet.*

<Don't you want to know?>

"No." Killian set the battered wooden box of oil paints beside the brushes, leaving room on the counter for her pens and inks. "Tell you one thing. Feels weird, Gis, having these here."

<What's weird is you not wanting to know how Henry is doing.> A pause. <Good weird or bad weird?>

Killian ran her thumb along the edge of the box's lid. "Just—weird. Not what I'd ever thought to bring for my rotation on a Portal." The pens, maybe, once she knew the lay of things up here.

Up here. Being her third planet in days. At least she'd her coffee maker.

Killian roused herself. "Henry's the almighty Arbiter. He reports to New Earth, not me. Wake up and call his office if you're worried." According to Henry, Giselle had a priority link.

<Oh, no. I'm staying put. Being with you is way more fun.>

A smile tugged at her lips. "Suit yourself." She looked into the third trunk. Tightly rolled canvases filled the bottom. "That's a lot of painting, Gis."

<In case of goofs.>

"Huh." Killian took one out, spreading it out on the bed, and anchored it in place with hand-knit socks. An in-joke from her partner, who'd cold feet. *Had.* Giselle had replacements for the rare occasions she preferred walking over skimming around on her board. "They treating you all right, down there?"

<First class with bonus stars. Lunch I had fresh-squeezed pomegranate juice with salmon steaks and those little round things you like. Capers.>

"Fuck you," Killian said affectionately.

A laugh. <Back at you, Killie-Cat.>

Gazing at the blank canvas, rocking on her heels, she moved her finger through the air, tracing out—*what?*

What was the opposite of being cooped up in an alien box . . .

Of burning and death . . .

Outside. Fresh air. Softness and sunshine. New Earth's fragrance, texture, and color. Every color. Killian traced petals and stems. Used both hands, her arms. Spun around and tossed imaginary balls of paint at the empty white.

Stopped. Went close to the limp canvas. Used her fingernail to scrape a straight delicate line. A short curve. A tiny spiral. "Might work." She eyed the blank wall opposite the door. "Gis? You pack glue?"

"Who's up for a field trip?"

TO further the impression of extraordinarily advanced Human technology, Flip remained a flying saucer for the descent to World III. The downside, as far as Henry was concerned, was that being on cameras inspired the polymorph to make unnecessarily dramatic swooshes through the air. Flip thoughtfully provided a viewport in the floor, presumably in the touching belief alts passenger would want to watch.

Henry elected to lean against the wall and close his eyes, listening to Shomchai complain.

<This is ridiculous, Henry,> the linguist said, interrupting his rapid-fire briefing on Malay for the fourth—or was it fifth?—time. <I can't possibly analyze the current dialect—from radio, of all things—before you land.>

"Flip will do the talking," Henry pointed out. Away from the shuttle, he'd broadcast the polymorph's voice through his personal com.

<You'll need to watch for potential implications—Henry, these people cobbled together their own version of a dead language. Trying to interpret—the pitfalls are—are enormous!>

Henry wiggled his fingers where Shomchai could see them. "They're Human."

Despite being drawn to a common interest, the descendants of the *Naga Gunung Pulai*—which translated as *The Dragon of Mount Pulai*—appeared as physically diverse as New Earth's. Flip found no distinction between rural and urban dwellers or visible genders in terms of clothing, which tended to be a loose shirt over wrapped patterned skirts for adults and sheath-like dresses for those younger, many in bright colors. Wide hats or parasols were the rule, the planet closer to its star.

Flip rendered an outfit for Henry with bold splashes of fuchsia and lime green. He'd declined in favor of his suit; blending wouldn't help him convince their leaders. Henry was happy to keep his footwear. Being early summer, the streets were full of pedestrians with sandals similar to his. *Did they remove them to go indoors?*

<Henry?>

Henry felt his cheeks warm. "Missed that," he admitted.

<I appreciate the burden's on you, Henry,> Shomchai said gently. <Just beware of species' bias—yours and theirs. We can't guess how these people will differ from New Earth's, only that they will, I assure you. If things start to go sideways, say this: *Bersatu kita teguh.*>

Henry repeated the words, Shomchai correcting his pronunciation until satisfied. "Do I want to know what it means?"

A soft laugh in his head. <Ousmane provided it. It was the *Naga*'s motto, derived from a proverb. *Bersatu kita teguh.* Means: Together we are strong. My guess is you'll sound like someone's great-grandfather stopping a family squabble, but hey, whatever works.>

For the first time since seeing the *Henderson*'s planet go up in flames, Henry grinned.

"Henry, I'm on approach."

A glance at the floor window showed the ominous rush of ground toward him. Henry hastily looked away, pulling on the harness that appeared beside him. "Thank you, Flip. Shomchai. We're about to land. You'll stay with me?"

<We all will. Good luck.>

With a barely perceptible jolt, Arbiter Henry m'Yama t'Brown landed on a new world.

***

Minutes later, Henry tossed his hat aside and slumped in the chair Flip produced without being asked, the hatch lowering soundlessly behind him. Exploded, "What the hell is a pod?!"

He'd said Shomchai's phrase. Bowed. It hadn't helped.

The instant he stepped out on the ground, the people gathered to meet him had taken one shocked look and turned their backs, muttering in obvious distress to their neighbors, Flip translating the mutters as *where's his pod? How can he have no pod?* and assorted versions thereof, all referring to *pod* and his appalling lack of one.

"I do not have that information, Henry," Flip said unhappily.

"It's all right, Flip."

Knowing who'd better, Henry closed his eyes.

Opened them on the meeting room. Hurried to add the windows he'd forgotten. His oneirics sat facing him. *Maybe they hadn't noticed.*

All looked tense. They'd been passengers; had seen what happened. *And heard him shout.*

"Excuse the outburst," the Arbiter said, collecting himself. "I wasn't ready to be stymied at the start. So, Quorum. What do they mean by *pod*? How do I get one?"

Ousmane's eyes glowed. "I believe I can, ah, speak to the first. It's probably a family or functional group. Such individuals were kept together on the sleeper ships, ah, in clusters called pods."

Rena nodded in support. "The images you showed us, Henry. I should have noticed no one was on their own. It might be something they actively demonstrate—I'm sure I spotted groups of people dressed in matching colors."

"A people under siege for generations," Sofia said grimly, "would stay close. Shunning survivors who arrive alone might be part of their present-day ethos."

"'Under siege' from what, exactly?" Shomchai looked at Henry. "Has Flip detected a threat?"

"Nothing yet," Henry admitted. "I think it's safe to assume it's outside the largest boundary. Killian's reported several satellites positioned to constantly observe those regions. Yes, Rena?" She was vibrating in her seat, about to burst.

"The type of barrier. The lack of a current danger." With growing enthusiasm. "The threat might be seasonal—a natural phenomenon they can't stop from happening, or don't want to—like the migration of large herbivores."

She'd love to find them. Henry wished he could let her.

"Or predators," Sofia said darkly. She didn't like the landing site, had pushed for either city over where Flip had landed, by the remote building nearest the outermost, ominous ditch.

They'd had no choice. The initial contact, via radio, had gone quite well and they'd been directed here for the first in-person meeting. The building turned out to be the exposed top of a bunker-like structure, the rest deep underground, and most probably a military base. *Where else would you direct a stranger arriving from the sky?*

The argument continued. "Crop loss alone is devastating," countered Rena.

"As is being chomped by giant scorpion things!"

The xenologist chuckled. "You've seen too many movies—"

"I'd rather not encounter wildlife of any kind, thank you both." Having settled that, Henry put his hands on the table. "It appears I need people to be my pod.

"Who's up for a field trip?"

***

Tamaana binti Saamir, Decision-Maker One, speaking for the Collective of Desaru—which might have been the *Totality* of Desaru, Shomchai advised, reasonably certain *Desaru* was the planet name, though it might refer to the land within the boundary ditch and Henry would have to find out—graciously accepted the Arbiter's radioed apology on behalf of his absent pod, setting a new meeting for an hour from now.

If taking responsibility for the initial failure, perhaps embarrassed, she might want the time to coach the greeting party. Equally possible, having been startled by Henry's solitary arrival, the time was for consultation, possibly consensus. Without knowing their political structure, which Ousmane admitted appeared unique, he'd no way to know.

But he'd a place to start. The delay benefited his oneirics, who'd been with him since arriving in orbit, giving them a welcome chance to wake up and move.

In no other way was it good. Time was now the enemy. Henry expected at any moment for Killian to tell him another spiral had appeared on the screen. Another world about to die. Leaving this one, and what they had to accomplish, and—

—there was nothing he could do but wait. Henry took deep, settling breaths.

Rena and Shomchai would be projected with him, the latter able to speak for him, along with Ousmane, who'd insisted on coming. She couldn't wait to meet the *Naga*'s descendants for herself.

Much as she'd wanted to come, Sofia couldn't. They'd a real mission at last, her words, with a population at the top end of their growth predictions to be moved. She'd no time to sightsee.

Nor did he. He'd stepped on a new world, taken a few breaths of air that smelled entirely unfamiliar and strange, in a good way, seen faces twin to his own—

—before he'd inadvertently offended them in one fell swoop. *Mustn't do that again.*

"Flip, the others should be wearing my colors." Henry looked down at his gray suit. *Couldn't be helped.*

"That won't be a problem, Henry, as long as you remain close to me."

"How close?"

"Beyond ten meters I will not be able to maintain convincing projections."

"Understood."

It would do. It had to.

Open a dialogue. He'd never had a problem keeping a negotiation going, once underway.

If they wanted him to move away from the shuttle, fine. Order his pod to stay with it.

If someone put a hand through Shomchai or one of the others, call it an example of the advanced Human technology waiting for them on New Earth and move right into evacuation procedures for three million plus a few hundred thousand—

He put his head between his knees, hands brushing the floor, and fought for calm.

"Henry?"

He closed his eyes, willing his pulse to slow to normal. Muttered, "Meditating."

"You are not in an approved position."

"Works for me, Flip."

"You should eat."

God no. "Stop fussing. I'm fine."

"Then, as per your orders, I will prepare you an enriched beverage."

Lifting his head slightly, Henry peered through his hair. "*My* orders?"

"Yes, Henry. I am to ensure you receive nourishment as required." A cupboard door appeared in a wall, opening on a tall glass full of a revoltingly purple liquid. "Drink up."

"I never said that."

"Should I play the recording?"

There were times . . . "Flip, I'm well aware you can imitate my voice."

"Henry." Admonishingly. "I would never give myself your orders."

A blueberry-ish aroma reached Henry's nostrils. He sniffed for more involuntarily.

"It's your favorite." *Smug.*

Henry found himself on his feet and walking to the cupboard. He took the glass and drank half without stopping for air.

Easier than arguing.

<Not on our watch.>

THE left screen was blank. The right streamed images from World II, with its rings of floating shell-things and two of the spiral storms Henry'd fixated on, and the middle closed up on the narrow continent of III, with concentric ditches complete with saucer and spot and—

Why was everything a fucking spiral when she was supposed to watch for a fucking spiral clock?

Killian spun away, glaring at a PIP, wishing she dared kick it, wanting to be back in her quarters. Quarters she'd left because from there she couldn't see if the clock was back—

<Draw something.>

Killian snarled under her breath.

<Yes, every pilot's reported on Control, blah blah, and we've sims in the repository, blah blah blah. Think of it as a cross check on your work. Plus you see things others miss, Killie-Cat. I know you do.>

Gis must be desperate. She knew flattery only got her back up. Killian pulled up her pad and wrote: *Not in the mood.*

<Since when do you have moods?>

Since her opinion of the Kmet hiding in the den across the room changed from wary respect to outright fear, that's when. Killian wrote: *Worried about Henry.*

Not that she was.

Probably should be. His type wouldn't last an hour in a trash-level spacer bar—unless he talked the grunts and scabs to death before they sliced him up for cash.

Who was she kidding? Henry'd charm them into buying him drinks, that's what he'd do. Probably take them home—

<He must be doing okay,> Gis assured her. <This place is going crazy. Every ship able to go is getting crewed up. They're stacking cans in the halls. Kisho says be ready for serious traffic.>

Killian drew a frowny face. Added a tongue sticking out.

<Yeah to that.> A laugh, then more seriously, <Old Bat knows her stuff, tho. Omar's getting the heads up as well. You two look to set records, this works.>

If Henry could convince a world to evacuate.

When he was here, filling the space with his conviction, she believed. With him gone, doubt crept in.

Killian wrote: *What if we screw up?*

<Not on our watch,> Gis stated. <Hear me?>

She raised her thumb. It seemed more honest than an answer.

"Why have you come?"

LATER, what Henry remembered of World III were the smells. Of growing things and sun-warmed soil. The perfumes worn by those he met, some bold and assertive, others delicate and light. The petroleum tang around their vehicles. The lavender petals in the water they brought him. In the moment, he hadn't noticed, too consumed by purpose.

The smells came back to him only once they were gone, like ghosts.

The projections of Rena, Ousmane, and Shomchai, though worryingly transparent at the edges from Henry's viewpoint, created such a stir of outright joy from those waiting to greet him a second time, he felt a twinge of guilt. One he'd no trouble suppressing, under the circumstances, but to start with a lie felt as if he betrayed these people before uttering a word.

Here to save them, Henry told himself, keeping a pleasant smile on his face. "Hello. I present my pod. Rena, Ousmane, and Shomchai." The decision to use only first names had been the linguist's, who now repeated his words in their language. Shomchai spoke instead of Flip to give substance to the projection.

The oldest of those waiting spoke, presenting those to either side of her.

THIS PERSON INTRODUCES DESARU'S DECISION-MAKERS, HENRY. THEIR NAMES ARE ELYAS BIN TEH, TAMANNA BINTI SAAMIR, AND PUSPAWATI BINTI UNGU, FROM LEFT TO RIGHT.

Seeing Shomchai bow, deeply, from the waist, Henry did the same, Rena and Ousmane following suit. Tamanna had made the introduction; otherwise, there were no signifiers of rank or precedence. The three wore similar flowing shirts and wrapped skirts, the fabric turquoise at the waist, morphing into deep blue at the ankles, and stunningly beautiful, but the rest gathered around wore those and varied styles and colors. If matching outfits signified pods, some had more members than others.

Fortunately, he didn't have to navigate the culture. He had to move it. The ice broken, Henry spoke bluntly. "I'm here to warn—"

The three held up their right hands, losing their smiles. Elyas, a slender man with piercing green eyes, turned to sweep his left hand toward the open door of the grim concrete and stone building behind the crowd in unmistakable command.

So be it. "The members of my pod will stay with our shuttle," Henry said, waiting to hear Shomchai translate.

Although she'd known the limitations of projection, Ousmane sighed her disappointment, drawing a sympathetic look from Puspawati, the younger of the two women. She spoke quickly to the others, received nods, then turned to Henry to utter a long, fluid string of words. As she did, a pod of four individuals stepped forward, much younger, with shared looks of timid excitement.

Flip translated: WE HAVE MANY QUESTIONS ABOUT OLD EARTH, AS YOU MUST ABOUT US. IF YOUR POD IS WILLING, THESE VOLUNTEERS WILL REMAIN AND CONVERSE WITH THEM.

A kind gesture, even if a way to interrogate those left behind without him; his oneirics would, Henry knew, reinforce the idea that New Earth, old or otherwise, would be welcoming—while learning what he'd need to know. He nodded. "We agree, gladly. Thank you."

The three Decision-Makers turned and headed for the open door.

HENRY, PLEASE BE CAREFUL.

"Back soon," Henry said cheerfully.

***

It wasn't, as Flip postulated, a bunker. Fortified, yes, and Henry looked forward to an explanation when he found himself standing on the floor of a sophisticated grain silo, one extending down instead of up.

The scale of it was astonishing. Walking through the door had been like going through a tunnel. Once through, monstrous augers and conveyor belts filled the cool, shadowed space, belts loose, machinery gleaming with oil. Idle, for now. Ready when needed. Concrete slabs waited to be rolled over the floor grates. "Does all your harvest come here?" he asked, forgetting he'd left Shomchai outside, then heard Flip translate, his voice—the Arbiter's—emanating from the com unit in his pocket. Henry hurriedly pulled it out.

Tamanna answered, a lilt of pride in her voice.

NO. THIS IS THE SEED VAULT FOR THE OUTERMOST RING.

Seed ensured a future. How many times had his grandfather said it?

To fit enough to plant such a huge area next season, the silo must extend deeper than he'd imagined. Why the protective walls and slabs? Was it the climate?

Or some risk to the seed—*Rena might be right about pests.* Maybe she'd get the answer.

The three continued, walking the sunbeam from the door deeper into the place,

Henry behind, the rest of those who'd been gathered outside following, their shadows blending and growing longer.

They stopped at a set of metal stairs that looked, by their pristine shine and loose-hung wired lights, to have been installed that day.

Might have, if this was for his benefit.

They were, he discovered, to climb. No one said a word, the hush giving it the feel of a procession, accentuated by the lack of light everywhere but the stairs and what streamed in through the door below. Henry let the experience sink in, refusing fear or speculation. This was their way, their home.

They'd built it once.

His job, to tell them they'd have to do it again.

***

Umbrellas fluttered in a light, clean breeze. From where Henry sat, fields filled his view, stretching to the glittering distant towers of the nearest city and away to either side. There were no planes in the air nor vehicles, like those parked below, moving on any road. Clearing the area where an unknown spacecraft was to approach and land was what he'd have done. It was reassuring.

More of a surprise had been the festive patio waiting atop the silo bunker. As the stairs, the arrangement spoke of purposeful haste. There was no railing or wall. A cross of carpeting in the center of the roof held four tables covered in bright yellow tablecloths, shaded by blue umbrellas. Folding chairs were set at each and a tall woman who reminded Henry of Sofia stood to the side as he was led to the centermost table, apparently to cede him her place to join the Decision-Makers who'd brought him here. A ceremonial admission to a pod, perhaps.

A good sign, that they'd sufficient flexibility to get past Henry's foreignness. What they'd think of the Kmet? *A question for later.*

He'd been seated with his back to the boundary ditch, having to be satisfied with a peek over that side of the building on emerging, blinking, from inside. Impressive engineering, seen up close. Wider than this building, deep enough to swallow his grandfather's farmhouse, with smooth sides narrowing to a crevasse-like bottom; he would have thought it an effective trap—at least one he couldn't have climbed out of—except for the ladders. In either direction, they connected the surface on the Human side to the bottom of the ditch, and he ached to know why.

Curiosity had to wait.

Maintaining the order in which they'd met him on the ground, the three Decision-Makers sat across from him. Tamanna dipped her head and spoke.

WELCOME TO DESARU, FAR TRAVELER.

After listening to Flip's translation, Henry brought out his com and stood the finger-sized cylinder on the table. "Thank you." His tone, or the words from the device, produced smiles and nods.

The person sitting to Henry's left, older and rounder than the rest, made a graceful gesture to himself. "I speak the words of New Earth and have offered my service in this meeting." Lips formed a curve. "It is a lifetime chance to speak it. My name is Aati bin Perang."

An unexpected gift—and a reminder not to underestimate the resources of those he met. Henry made a show of turning the com on its side, but didn't remove it. Let them assume he recorded the conversation. *As Flip would.* "The pleasure is mine, Aati. Please, call me Henry."

"Henry. It is our custom to share water and the food of Desaru before any serious discussion takes place." Aati had an expressive face; behind his polite smile Henry detected concern. *Would their guest be polite?*

The Arbiter nodded gravely. "I am honored to do so."

After translating, Aati relaxed. "*Silakan,*" said Tamanna, directing the word at everyone, and servers moved to each table bearing trays. The first brought bowls and towels for the washing of hands. Next came the pitchers and cups made of a fine porcelain, the glaze a rich green overlaid with lace-like traces of white. "Beautiful," Henry said, indicating his. Aati translated.

Tamanna replied with a pleased nod.

"They are from New Earth," Aati informed him.

Priceless and irreplaceable. "As is this." Henry drew the velvet pouch from his lower pocket, setting that on the table beside his cup.

The others took note with quick sidelong glances.

Miming the others, Henry washed his hands in the basin provided, drying them on a towel.

Once every cup had been filled with water, the Decision-Makers raised theirs in both hands, nodded, then sipped twice before setting them down. Henry did the same.

A new tray appeared at his elbow, bearing ranks of little sticks with ornamental holders at the tops. The others waited, watching him.

Henry took the nearest. Insect-like creatures had been impaled on the stick, brown multi-legged bodies dusted with white crystals. The food of Desaru. A test? *No,* he decided. *Like the cups, they offered their best.* He held the stick sideways and took a bite. The crunch he expected.

Not the juicy squirt that almost went into his eye.

Everyone laughed, covering their mouths with three fingers.

Wiping his face, Henry gave a rueful grin and held up the stick. "Any advice?"

Puspawati took hers, flourished it like a tiny sword, then used her tongue to slide the endmost creature off and between her lips, chewing with evident delight.

More slowly, Henry copied her actions. When his teeth met, a wonderful taste exploded in his mouth. He gasped, then choked. After wiping his eyes, and washing the mouthful down with some water, he eagerly took another, this time prepared.

He half-closed his eyes as he tried to pin down the flavors—a heat, a salt—possibly the white powder—and a deep, rich something that made him think of corn on the cob, but wasn't, of ribs, but not that. He'd no equivalents, only that it was probably the most satisfying food he'd ever eaten. He glanced up, saw his hosts relishing their own, and kept eating. By the time he finished the last on his stick, he was astonished to find himself too full to want more.

Food of Desaru indeed. "Thank you. What are they?" he asked, licking his lips. No need to translate the question. The three across from him looked very pleased. Elyas answered, his voice deep and rich.

"Ostix," Aati translated. "When our ancestors came to this place, the Ostix destroyed our crops. Starving, desperate, they turned to them for food. Now Ostix are a vital part of our harvest." He pointed behind Henry, to the boundary ditch. His fingers mimed things falling in, then being gathered up. His hands went to his mouth and he pretended to chew. "Food for us and our crops. Fuel. Food of our world."

Henry nodded his understanding, then pointed down, to the bunker. "Still a risk?"

Aati shrugged one shoulder. "Every few years, the Ostix come in numbers greater than we can catch. They eat anything that grows. We protect the seeds. Plant again."

LOCUST ANALOGUES, HENRY.

"Locusts," he repeated out loud.

The translator's eyes lit up. "Yes, like in the old stories. But better." He licked his lips.

"Much better," Henry agreed. "May I keep this?" The little stick was carved from a reed of some kind, beautiful work.

Nods. Smiles.

"Thank you." *The time had come.* Henry picked up the velvet bag and slid the badge out on his hand. Holding it up, he made sure everyone at the table saw what it was.

The three across from him lost their smiles. Tamanna spoke, a harsh burst of words.

Aati's voice shook. "That is the symbol of the one who sent us here. We know and revere the Arbiter, who saved our ancestors from destruction. Why have you come, bearing it?"

"To save you again," Henry answered.

And began to lie.

It took more than his word, of course, but he'd come prepared. Printed charts of their star. Readings indicative of a growing and dangerous instability. Data that looked real to the scientists of this world, who lacked the technology to verify it for themselves but were well aware of the peril posed by a solar eruption. Who'd been convinced from the first sightings of the Portal that Henry came from an

Earth far more advanced than the one in their records, and why would New Earth have sent its Arbiter—that badge—if what he warned wasn't true?

No need to share with them how desperately the Arbiter wanted to recant the lie, to promise their evacuation wouldn't be permanent and their lovely hard-earned home would be spared and waiting for them. But how could he, when he couldn't even name the real threat, let alone stop it?

Desaru's Collective was a peaceful, cooperative society, long accustomed to striving toward a common goal. In the end, all they asked was that pods leave together, agreeing each person only take what they could carry. New Earth would provide.

The exception being their records and data—that, in whatever form, including representative works of art—came with them. Their lives here must be remembered.

Henry's insistence on that reassured them.

As did his agreeing to transport their dead.

“Tell me, Gis.”

“THE dead. You want me to—wait, where are they?” Killian listened to Henry’s reply, shut off communications and swore until she had to stop for air.

<Snag?> Gis inquired artlessly.

“The bodies are in the ground. Bones, bits, fresh ones. The almighty Arbiter’s promised we’ll retrieve them intact for reburial on New Earth. What the fuck does he think I can do from here?”

<Give me a minute.>

Killian tapped her wristband, waking her oneiric. Who, no doubt, would immediately share the almighty Arbiter’s latest impossible request with Kisho and whomever else lurked near Giselle’s can these days.

Days. She turned off the lights and called it night. Turned them on to call it day and she hadn’t been away long enough to get the crawlies, as spacers called it, where she had to have light at all times to remember where she was, but any more creepy stuff—Killian tapped her wristband again.

<Got it,> Gis said, sounding breathless. <Niablo Mining had a problem with PIPs mixing their gear when decommissioning—point is, they came up with ident tags that do the trick. Guessing you’ll need a whack of them, so we’ll send some crates through to get the locals started and requisition a synthesizer from the company for them. The PIPs make their own, ah, bags, right?>

More corpses. Killian abruptly sat on the bed, face in her hands.

<Killie-Cat?>

She didn’t move. “Here.”

<Henry’s done his part.> Gis’ voice, gruff and warm and real, filled her. <Time comes, we just do the heavy lifting. Hear me? Same as always.>

“Sure.”

Doubt. <I’m not seeing anything.>

Killian dropped her hands, gazing at her canvas. It measured three meters by two and she’d glued it to the wall at a height letting her stand to paint. Near the lower left corner was her tiny but detailed ink drawing of the Portal pedestal with its controls. She'd begun a flower next to it, sketched a stem, crossed it out, thrown a cup of red paint at the middle—"It's crap."

<That's 'cause there's no point.>

"The point is to draw the Portal. What I can see of it," Killian amended. Before Henry's success, she'd planned on more time to snoop around. *Maybe the next world.*

<I mean the flowers. Pretty isn't your style, Killie-Cat.>

Gis wasn't wrong. Flowers alone—Killian tilted her head, teased by a thought. "How many ships will come through?"

<You got the report—>

"Tell me, Gis."

<Three hundred twenty-four transports—fifty-two being Delta-class freighters, holds rigged for atmo. Every available surface-to-orbit lifter to get people up to them, seeing as we've no time to flesh out the local capability. 3.32 million people, their bags, the dead—why the sudden interest in numbers?>

Killian was already at work, pencil in hand. "A petal per ship, Gis. A flower for each world we give up. A way to—" *Atone.* "—to remember them. A point to this."

<That works,> Gis agreed. <S'long as you're ready for a quick start when the time comes, Killie-Cat. First ship's standing by and our Henry's not a patient guy.>

"I've prepped."

There wasn't much else she could do. She'd dug out her pack from a trunk and filled it with Restore bulbs and meds, adding whatever else she had to keep her mind sharp and body standing. Call came, she'd grab it and go.

When it came.

Transiting ships through didn't take the toll simul-pops did, but three hundred twenty-four in succession, making return trips? Daunting didn't cover it—

Henry's other impossible command haunted her. To finish the evacuation and be ready to move to World IV—whatever waited for them there—before a new clock appeared. *If.* Killian dutifully checked every three hours during her day, taking the tube up, staring at the screen, doing a slow turn in case it appeared somewhere else to confound things, aliens prone to it, in her opinion. Nothing changed, other than the intensity of the peanut smell.

She'd kept to her quarters the last two nights, playing word games with Gis, drugging herself to sleep.

Might have stayed awake and played other things, Gis having an interest and, yes, sneaking more than art supplies into her trunks, bless her big, lustful heart, but Killian hadn't felt the urge.

Her waking mind kept working the problems.

Fastest turnaround? Transit wasn't the issue. She and Omar would sync their Portals, transiting ships in both directions at once. Shave more time by having small vessels linked before entry, to handle as one object. Allow for ships to clear the Portals, to avoid collisions, add turnaround at the space stations for refueling and checks, and they still could punch through twenty per hour, easy. A day, if the Kmet let them go flat out; kmeth did on mining runs.

Load and unload speed wasn't so easy to figure. Passengers weren't like cargo, having children to stray and seats to find—those getting seats. Gis told her the refitted freighter holds had pads on racks, with emergency nets for restraints. This wasn't a vacation these people were going on either. They were leaving their home and she'd bet on meltdowns of every kind. People changing their minds at the last second, having to be dragged on board. People rushing the ramps in a panic. Any such chaos and Henry could kiss his *done and ready* goodbye.

Not to forget the shuttles making the trip to and from the planet to load the freighters—some would break down, they always did—

Killian stopped there. *Just the pilot.* Others had the logistics. She and Omar were to stand at their respective pedestals, communicate with the ships and each other, and operate the transit controls for as long as their bodies and minds let them.

And then some.

"I've no intention of being reasonable."

IT took two days—plus an Earth hour, World III's rotation longer by the equivalent of thirty-two minutes, a piece of unhelpful trivia supplied by Flip—to get the first shuttle into the air. Henry spent them in meetings with the Decision-Makers and their staff, talking to anxious scientists and top transport experts, and taking interviews with Desaru's version of media—unusual in the number of school-aged children involved.

Or wise, considering the questions children asked. *Will we be able to play outside?*

Yes, he'd say, and talk about swimming and boats, their bordered patch of the planet lacking placid large bodies of water.

Why can't I take my pet?

They're of this world and happier here, he'd say, and have Flip bring up images of horses and puppies, Origin Earth species that thrived on his world, if not theirs.

When will we come back?

Never. He didn't say that, not to the children, but Henry refused to lie. Instead, he'd tell them of the extraordinary trip across the stars they'd take, that everyone they knew would come, and how other children were waiting on New Earth to meet them.

Confronted with the end of their lives here, the inhabitants didn't worry about Henry's lack of a pod, only what he had to say. When he wasn't talking, he slept, too exhausted to appreciate the comfort of the bed Flip made. Feeling fragile, he filed reports every chance he had—*if anything happened to him, the arbiter-secondaries had to be ready*—and consulted with his quorum only as necessary.

Rarely, now, with the evacuation about to start. Sofia'd been as good as her word, providing Henry with an estimate. Three weeks. She called it highly optimistic, cautioning the number might increase once parts were in motion.

So far, it hadn't. The only good news was Kmet-Here remained denned. Avoidance wasn't the ideal policy, but Henry'd take every minute he could get before facing the impatient Kmet with twenty-one days, let alone the implication of longer.

As for the rest of the quorum, poor Rena had to be satisfied with secondhand reports of the biology of this world, there being nothing endemic allowed through the station quarantine to theirs, though Ousmane and her fellow historians stood to reap a treasure trove. Shomchai had started a paper on the Malay spoken by these people. He vowed to preserve it, was working with Sofia on possible ways to provide isolation.

To the linguist's disgust, Henry refused to make it a priority for the Arbiter's Office. In part, because he'd enough on his mind getting these people where they could worry about language assimilation or protection. In part—

Because he couldn't—despite witnessing the methodical upheaval of millions of lives on his word—believe it was all going to work.

The first shuttle wouldn't be full, being a flight to reassure those millions the enterprise was safe and, most importantly, the Decision-Makers who must issue the directive to board.

The shuttle was Flip, Henry to be present for any questions and to forestall any of the myriad problems he suddenly imagined, waiting alone in the wind of the designated landing field, watching the first glimmer of sunrise on distant, low hills.

A new world. Funny how that consequential thought eluded him until a moment like this. He tilted his head, letting the wind lift the hair from his face, dared wonder what else the air had touched on its way to him, what might detect the scent of a different sort of Human when it left—

VEHICLES APPROACH, HENRY.

The whimsy left him, replaced by a weight that made this world seem to have a heavier-than-usual gravity, when in fact he was slightly lighter. "Ready inside?"

I AM ALWAYS READY, HENRY.

The *smug* made him grin, as Flip intended. "Let's welcome our guests."

***

World III had satellites in orbit, but sending people up was a project on the drawing board, Henry had been told. Given that, the placid demeanor of those with him, Elyas, Tamaana, and Puspawati, was remarkable.

Aati alone didn't hide his wonder, the interpreter's eyes wide as he took in the interior of his first spaceship.

A shame Flip hadn't gone for fancy, Henry thought, but they'd talked it over and decided an appearance like that of the coming transports made more sense. There were windows in the ceiling and floor; the others noticed them when Flip had left the ground.

They were used to aircraft. Henry waited for the moment the sky lost color, stars coming out as if they rose into night.

Tamaana turned to Henry, bending her knees then straightening with a smile that deepened the wrinkles around her eyes, and said a word.

"Gravity," Aati translated.

Henry smiled back, guilty of taking such a feat for granted; most could since the Kmet shared that very useful secret, though older, pre-Duality stations still spun to make their own. "Every transport provided for your people will," he assured them.

"No seats," Elyas observed through the interpreter, less happily. "No protective harness. Is this safe?"

"I am the safest of all," Flip countered in their language, making them look for the source of the voice.

"My pilot," Henry said quickly, pointing at the airlock door and hoping they'd just assume another compartment. Explaining sentient constructs and polymorphic matrices, let alone Alt-Intels and epitomes, was not on the needful list. "Let me show you how we'll get you and your people to New Earth in much, *much* less than the century it took the *Naga Gunung Pulai*." He waited for Aati to translate, their eyes to show curiosity and a healthy skepticism. "Now, Flip."

A curve of wall became transparent.

The Portal hung like an improbable work of art, unrelated to anything a planet had to offer, white and sharp-edged. The rectangle of strange colors it framed teased the Human eye with suggestions of patterns, only to burst and change as if boiling within.

It might be. However deep Earth's hunger for the Portal's deepest secret, Henry'd yet to talk to any expert offering an explanation other than *weird alien science.*

Puspawati stepped forward, head moving from side to side to be sure she didn't miss any aspect. Aati, having his fill of strange, eased behind his leaders, face pale and sweating. The remaining two appeared mildly interested.

Or continued to doubt. "The Portal is there," Henry said firmly. "If you wish a demonstration, I can have an Earth ship transit through. Aati?"

The man gave himself a shake and translated.

Elyas' eyebrows shot up. "Now? This minute?"

He smiled. "Flip, please ask the Portal Pilot to transit the first ship, if possible." He turned to the others. "We'll have to await her confirmation. I didn't advise Killian—"

"Oh!" "Do you see—" "Transit," Flip announced as the freighter emerged from the Portal.

—Killian, it seemed, had been ready for him.

"The *Cape Sable*'s Captain sends his greetings to the Arbiter and the people of this world and awaits permission to assume position in orbit prior to sending down shuttles. The *Cape Sable*," the polymorph added for his audience's benefit, "is a Delta Class freighter. She left Earth's orbit the same instant she arrived here."

Henry was not about to get into the whole *disassembly at the molecular level* with them either. "Express my thanks to the pilot and captain."

Puspawati's eyes gleamed with excitement. "A starship to take us to New Earth. To save us. It's all true, what Henry's said. *Bersatu kita teguh.*"

"*Bersatu kita teguh*," Tamaana echoed in a completely different tone. She stared through the floor window at her world, a tear sliding down her cheek.

Henry's heart ached for her, though he kept his face impassive. The loss experienced by this generation, the agony of it, would never really heal.

His doing.

They had to survive, he vowed. *All of them.* Or none of this was worth the price.

He steeled himself. Made his voice matter-of-fact.

"With your permission, the captain will begin the evacuation."

Henry returned the four to their world. Their mood was determined, if somber. Each took a turn to hold his hands before disembarking the shuttle, eyes moist, mouths working with emotion.

As if he deserved thanks.

The evacuation would begin at once, transports from the *Cape Sable* on their way to this and, shortly, every airstrip. The concentration of settlement within the second boundary ditch, the well-laid-out road system, worked to their advantage; with the exception of those working the vaults and fields, no one was more than an hour's drive from an evacuation site.

Everyone on World III would start their one-way trip, abandoning vehicles on fields they would never again harvest, leaving behind homes and everything they'd known—

"Close the door, Flip."

A seat appeared, with harness. "Ready to lift."

"I need a minute." He sat cross-legged on the floor. "Lift when I say, please," Henry qualified, before the polymorph started counting seconds.

"Yes, Henry."

The planet was no longer his problem. World III's inhabitants believed the brunt of the solar storm would cross the orbit of their world in forty-three of their days, a timeline determined by those on New Earth as outside their science to disprove while not so imminent they wouldn't be gone before it failed to happen. Henry secretly believed his office pulled the number from a hat.

Earth was sending through ships. Sofia and her team's doing. Leaving him to ensure an impatient, barely cooperative Kmet agreed to keep the Portal in place till the end.

So much could go wrong. "Flip? Latest estimate to complete the evacuation. Give me some good news."

"I regret to say I cannot, Henry. Your office just increased the evacuation estimate by fifty percent to thirty-nine days. Still, of course, assuming no unforeseen difficulties."

He'd expected Kmet-Here to erupt over twenty-one. Spent hours on stratagems, none guaranteed. To add fifty percent—*They had to do better.*

"Hold my calls, Flip." Pressing a wristband, Henry lay back, arms behind his head, and closed his eyes.

***

Opening them on darkness. *The lights. He'd forgot the lights.*

Henry focused with an effort and everything brightened, as if he'd pulled the curtains aside to let in the sun.

"Do not do that again." Sofia's lips formed a wavering angry line. She looked worn—must be, given the task he'd assigned her.

No time for sympathy. "Thirty-nine days? We have to move faster, Sofia."

She huffed. "You're the one who rushed the first ship through before we've a single station set to receive evacuees, and I won't leave people strapped in freighter holds longer than absolutely necessary. Thirty-three's a minimum—"

"Impossible. You saw the sat feed from World I. That's what's coming."

"Is it?" She leaned back, regarding him coolly. "Even if the Kmet are somehow burning bridges behind us—and may I remind you a single planet is hardly proof—we're after the same goal, to get Humans off these worlds. Why shouldn't kmeth give us the time we need to do it safely and well?"

Because the Kmet didn't care if people left on their feet or as charred corpses.

Not a conviction he was ready to share—especially not with someone with connections outside the Arbiter's Office who'd jump on any reason to doubt the Kmet. *That was becoming his job.*

"And why haven't you asked for more Portals, to start the procedure on all the remaining worlds?" Sofia went on, merciless.

"Because there's only one me," Henry countered. "The Kmet don't accept any multiplication of authority within the Duality." Nor did kmeth acknowledge the existence of more than these two Portals, *why* being another question come to haunt his sleep. "Safety comes first, agreed," he went on, "but we can't delay for comfort."

"*Comfort*?" Real shock or feigned, didn't matter. Her fury was real. Sofia half-rose from her seat, finger tapping the table as she gave him a list. "The delay, as you call it, is to complete crucial infrastructure and protocols. To finish getting medical teams on-station. And let's not forget the strain of even a moderate pace on the Portal pilots—who you refuse to swap out—"

As if the Kmet's nature was his fault. It was certainly his to deal with. "I'll take care of the pil—"

"—as for *comfort?* I'm warning you, Arbiter, if we don't process these people humanely, with due attention to their needs, we'll pay the price once they're on New Earth."

They'd be alive. "I appreciate the difficulties, Sofia, and respect everything you tell me," Henry said grimly. "I'll get you what I can."

She settled back down with a scowl. "I'm hearing a *but.*"

"You're right," he acknowledged. "The instant the Kmet clock appears, everything and everyone goes, even if we have to get out and push. Is that understood?"

"Good luck with that." A derisive snort. "When the end's in sight, people give up. They stop. No matter how hard you push then? I guarantee you won't save them all."

***

"Henry, is something troubling you?"

Henry released his death's grip on Sofia's wristband and sat up. "I'm fine." He let out a gust of air. "My oneiric says I can't save everyone."

"That is a reasonable statement."

He pushed to his feet. "I've no intention of being reasonable, Flip."

"Bigger picture, Space Rat."

"EVAC Group 506, clear to transit."

The screen Killian faced was now divided in three parts, a feed showing traffic at Omar's Portal, one showing that around hers, and the last, on the right, World III's version of air traffic monitoring. With no planes in the air, the fuzzy moving dots represented Earth transports, shuttling to orbit and back.

She rolled her shoulders, heart rate back to normal after the adrenalin rush of the first hour. Omar m'Starink t'Koleszar had years on her at the post, hadn't slowed a whit because she was fresh to it. Killian had appreciated his confidence while cursing him under her breath.

The first evacuees were away. Not on *Cape Sable*, she'd need three more hours to load, latest update, but on her heels had come this cluster of smaller ships, the type used to ferry spacers rotating up to stations. Nimble, tough, and quick, the stubby craft held fifty if you liked your neighbors; the passengers weren't coming up in spacesuits, granting more leeway. Easier to board. They'd turned around in twenty minutes.

With passengers who weren't epitomes. Did the crews think about it? That if they made a mistake, real people would pay for it?

Don't make one, Killian reminded herself.

Nothing untoward yet. The same PIPs were on the walls, working with her. Kisho'd told Gis to pass along that the things wore out before a Human, taking their own version of a shift change. Killian was to watch for signs in case the damn things dropped from their posts as she was keying in a transit.

What signs?

They were working on a list, her pals on New Earth; things experience taught that newbies typically learned for themselves, ore in the holds not caring how long it sat.

As far as Killian was concerned, the famed Spacer Repository Portal Pilot training program had more holes in it than her favorite cheese. She found herself obsessively counting the number of arms her PIP crew extruded.

Killian sent the cluster of linked ships through, accepting Omar's simultaneous return toss. "Welcome to World III, Delta *Balache Point.* Please clear the Portal and proceed to your assigned orbit. Local air traffic control will handle your transports."

"Roger, Portal. *Balache Point* clearing your doorway."

Big mother. A Delta was the largest spacecraft Earth possessed and the entire fleet would be pressed into service here. Henry'd done that. His people. If she'd wanted proof of his *I can do anything* it had just popped into existence close enough to shade the Portal and make her swear in admiration.

"Pilot Killian, Evac Group 507 ready to transit."

"Roger that, Pilot Omar. Be a while before I've something to toss back to you."

A laugh. "I'll keep you busy. We're stacked to the poles here. Everyone's eager to go. Think they're hoping these folks have new jokes."

She had to grin.

This might just work.

As might what lay at the base of the podium, tucked in her bag.

She'd left it open, having shifted the contents to her pockets and inside her coveralls. Finished a bulb, dropped it inside. Wrappers, too. Kept an eye on it during the hours.

PIP after PIP continued by, ignoring temptation. After the first wrapper, a couple nudged the bag in passing, as if curious.

Killian almost missed the moment a PIP climbed inside. Luckily—for her—the thing took its time, sticking bits of waste to itself.

She'd pounced, zipping up the bag in a frenzy so it stuck halfway. Heard Omar's voice on coms as she fiddled it closed. Muttered a stern, "Stay, damn it!" and the other pilot had overheard, replying "Not going anywhere."

Maybe the admonishment worked. The PIP in her bag could have cut itself free or summoned others.

Instead, whenever Killian had a second to glance down, the lump remained still.

Her key.

Once she'd a chance to try it.

"Ready, Killian?"

Wasn't going to be anytime soon.

***

<We've come up with a way to get you a break, Killie-Cat. >

Rest. The allure threatened to melt her bones, but Killian gave no outward sign. She lifted a palm, asking Gis for more, though she'd stopped checking the den mouth six hours ago and after ten no longer cared if Kmet-Here or Kmet-There, also denned, overheard what she and Omar were saying to one another.

Most being rude and likely incomprehensible to anyone else. The other pilot was getting punchy. So was she. Didn't affect their work with the ships—that was total pro—but she'd kill for some of Flip's special coffee about now.

Her prisoner hadn't moved. The lumpy round shape of the bag told her the PIP hadn't become a puddle and leaked out.

<We'll shunt Portal-to-ship chatter this side to Enstrab Station. They've the best viewpoint. You give yours to *Balache Point*—>

The hell she was. Killian slashed a violent negative. "We're not waking our Kmet."

<Sharing tasks is routine.>

Maybe on Rogue 98, pushing through rock. "Henry authorize this?" She'd bet not; the almighty Arbiter had enough on his plate without kmeth.

Silence, then, in a voice that didn't sound like Gis at all, that sounded like someone reading a script, <Spacers take care of their own.>

The Spacer Repository. The System Coalition. Whoever thought space was something you could claim and Killian felt sorry for her oneiric, who only wanted to help her and Omar.

Not if it meant abandoning their posts, leaving Kmet in charge of the evacuation. Not without assurance what the Kmet would do with it. *Planets burning*—

"Bigger picture, Space Rat," she said briskly, and tapped her wristband.

Killian drew out the personal com she wasn't supposed to use outside quarters—having peed twice in a corner of Control, she felt entitled to expand the definition. "Get me Henry."

Flip responded. "Connecting you now, Pilot Killian."

"What was that for?"

BEETS and peanuts; Kmet-breath and Human urine. Henry tried not to gag as he pulled himself from the tube. *Add beer and it'd be a sleezy pub.*

Kmet-Here remained in kmeth's den. He'd hoped to postpone their confrontation a while longer—*the duration of the evacuation worked.*

One look at Killian told him the grace period was over.

The pilot sat on the dais, long legs outstretched, back against a pedestal. Her feet rested on her bag. To her left was a small cluster of quiescent PIPs, mimicking her posture, but the rest of the things were on the move. Henry stepped to one side to avoid a steady stream, those heading to the walls sprouting arms and handling claws, those leaving shrinking into balls with urgent feet, their goal an open tube.

"Shift change," Killian informed him. Seeing what he'd brought, she set aside the bulb she'd been holding with a weary grin. "You're a life saver."

He hadn't asked Killian to avoid waking Kmet-Here; she'd done it on her own and he was grateful. Henry sat cross-legged, putting the basket within her reach. Gifts from the planet below, fresh fruit and breads, with deep-fried Ostix, but first he pulled out a covered cup and handed it to her. "Flip's compliments."

"Hot damn." Killian grabbed more than took it, sipping with an eloquent roll of her eyes.

He looked past her, at the screens. No sign of the Portal's clock. *Yet.* Mysterious codes and symbols overlaid images of the planet. Ships and status, he supposed. "How are we doing?"

"*We*?" Dark bloodshot eyes peered at him over the cup, humor in their depths. "Bet you've been told."

"Ah, yes." The Spacer Repository had flooded the Arbiter's Office with protests, each more blunt than the last, the last an ultimatum. If Henry refused to authorize new pilots, they'd no choice but to order Omar and Killian to hand control of their respective Portals to the Kmet.

A threat dependent on pilot cooperation. Thus far, Omar remained steadfast that Killian was in charge and he would act only with her approval; approval, by her summons, she wasn't about to give without Henry.

The Repository was lodging an official complaint about the Arbiter's disregard for spacer regulations and pilot safety.

They could get in line.

"I'm here," Henry said quietly. "Tell me what you need."

"Trust." Killian lowered the cup, her mouth a grim line. "We've got to switch out, Henry. Omar's Kmet should be safe to handle Earth's side of things. There'll be plenty of eyes on kmeth." Grudgingly. "Can't say the same about—" Her head tilted to the den. "Will kmeth follow orders? That's your territory."

They'd ships waiting. More importantly, they'd people on World III waiting for those ships—a momentum he doubted they'd recover once lost.

Henry pinched the top of his nose, let out a slow breath, considering. He understood—shared—her suspicion, but someone had to operate the transit controls and keep the ships moving. Even if he'd known how, even if Kmet-Here and the PIPs accepted him, his place was on the planet, keeping up the urgency.

Killian? He'd no doubt without reassurance she'd keep to her post until she collapsed—*not a useful precedent with three planets to go.*

His hand strayed to his wristbands. *As if anyone else had answers.* Instead, Henry used that hand to push the basket closer to the pilot. Rising to his feet, he tugged his jacket straight and turned to face the den.

Killian stood with him, the cluster of PIPs splitting apart and scampering to the wall as if eager to work. She scowled at them, curling her arm around the basket, bag in one hand, then transferred the scowl to him.

He shrugged, then winked at her. "Time for that chat."

Henry walked toward the den entrance, absently noting the lack of moist secretions. Kmet-Here hadn't come out. Because Killian was on duty or because kmeth wasn't interested? No way to know. He pressed his wristbands to summon his oneiric, then signaled the pilot to be ready to hum with him—

He held up two fingers to stop her as the tip of a flipper emerged from the darkness. Remembering how kmeth had burst out last time, both Humans eased back, but this was a different exit. An eye, half-closed against the light, showed next, then the rest of the head as Kmet-Here slowly pulled kmethself into view.

The polyps were a reassuring purple, most fully extended. "Arbiter-Henry. Pilot-Killian." The courteous acknowledgment sent an alarm down Henry's back. Sure enough, the Kmet lumbered forward with a smug, "We are done and ready to move?" Before he could reply, the far eye caught sight of the screens and the lid snapped open. "There remain Humans-There! Why?"

Henry spread his arms and gave a deep bow, reclaiming kmeth's attention. "The evacuation is underway, Kmet-Here," he announced as he straightened. "It will continue until there are no Humans-There, as agreed. I wish to offer you the privilege of participating in this meaningful event. Human and Kmet, working together! A truly powerful moment in our Duality, sure to be immortalized in our shared history," this last delivered with all the pompous conviction he had in him.

Henry carefully avoided looking at Killian, keeping his own expression full of confidence, and stepped to the side, gesturing grandly to the dais.

Did he imagine suspicion in the eye fixed on him? Relying on instinct, he continued smoothly, "Communications will be handled by Humans on other ships. New Earth's Portal will be operated by its Kmet, demonstrating to these new Humans how much we trust our partners."

Polyps flared red. "A demonstration? Why, Arbiter Henry? Do these new Humans not cherish you as do the rest of your kind?"

Rena whispered, <Henry—that's new.>

And peculiar. Henry filed away the thought as he sidestepped kmeth's question. "It's their first contact with a new species, Kmet-Here. Humans need more than words to accept so great a change in their perception of the universe. When they learn you have—" He didn't need Killian's faint cough to warn him not to give the alien any semantic wiggle room. "—taken your shift at the controls to see them to safety on New Earth, it will prove the Duality that exists between us. Do you concur, Kmet-Here?"

"I concur." The red began to disappear beneath a wash of more compliant yellow. "How long a shift?"

"Three—" Killian began to say.

Henry spoke over her. "*Twelve* Earth hours. The standard, I believe." Exhausted and worried, the pilot wanted her hands back on the pedestals as soon as possible. She didn't see it. This wasn't about him trusting the Kmet.

It was his test to learn if they could. *Fail now, with everyone watching—better than fail later, alone.* He dared her to disagree with a look.

Hers held a furious challenge. *Better be right.*

Unfortunately, Kmet-Here hadn't moved. "How many shifts, Arbiter Henry, until the Humans-There are gone?"

He'd so hoped the Kmet wouldn't ask.

<Get all the time you can,> Sofia pleaded. <We're behind—>

"Thirty more," he told the Kmet. "Approxim—"

BOOM!!! The waving polyps topping kmeth's wide head were that contrary orange-red. "Unacceptable! Too slow. Too long!" BOOM!!! "UNACCEPTABLE!"

You won't save them all—

He'd damn well try. "Twenty-five."

<Henry—we need—>

With an inner wince, he pressed Sofia's wristband. "It's the best I—"

"UNACCEPTABLE!" More red now and the Kmet rocked back and forth, agitation growing. "The pilot can retrieve remaining Humans-There in three. Do you concur?"

*How did kmeth know—*The mining PIPs on the planet. Spies.

Henry continued doggedly, "I do not concur. We must do this our way, Kmet-Here." He'd asked Sofia for the absolute minimum to save these people, breaking every protocol, taking every chance.

They were there.

"The Portal must stay for nineteen more days—not one less. Do you concur?" He stood statue-still, waiting.

The Kmet leaned on kmeth's paired limbs, blinks slower than usual, as if doing the same. Henry heard Killian's heavy breaths.

Stalemate.

<Kmeth's stalling, Henry,> Rena said quietly.

<Agreed,> from Shomchai. <Change the parameters. Shake things up. >

Shake things up? Well, there was one approach he'd yet to try.

Henry deliberately ran his hand through his hair and slouched his shoulders. Plastering a smile a Human would see as false on his face, he took the plunge.

"Oh, I understand now," he said heartily. "You wish to renegotiate the Duality. I concur. Let's start with access to New Earth food, shall we?"

The rate of blink sped up. "WHAT?" BOOM!

Henry's head erupted, the rest of the quorum reacting with alarm and asking/shouting variations of kmeth's question. He pressed his hand over the wristbands, severing every connection.

"Either the Duality stands as is, Kmet-Here," Henry said, "and you continue to accept my authority as Arbiter over Humans and this mission, or the Duality is being changed. Not a problem," he continued breezily. "I'm prepared to reopen negotiation on every point." He pulled out his pretend phone, opening it with a flashy gesture. "Flip, how long did it take to create the original Duality document? Oh, and include time spent adding every subclause and modification since first contact." He smiled mercilessly at the Kmet. "We mustn't miss a thing."

"The original agreement took sixty-six days, Henry. Subsequent negotiated modifications bring the total time commitment thus far to three hundred and fifty-two days."

"Thank you, Flip." Henry put away his phone. Wrapping his hands around the back of his neck, he rocked back and forth on his heels. Kmeth's eyelids opened and closed slightly with Henry's motion, as if hypnotized. "More than a year. My my. I confess I hadn't appreciated how much effort has gone into maintaining the health of the Duality." He paused for effect. "It would seem faster to work together and complete the evacuation under the current arrangement, but if you insist, I'm willing to renegotiate—"

"I DO NOT CONCUR!"

Henry stopped rocking. "With which part?" he asked innocently.

"The Duality establishes us. It cannot be changed. Must not be."

Gotcha. "The evacuation will continue using our ships."

"Yes, yes. I concur, Arbiter-Henry," Kmet-Here said in a far more pleasant tone, polyps fading to purple. "My impatience is only to save Humans-There from the Divider."

He'd done it. Finding it hard to breath, Henry resumed a more polite and conciliatory posture at once, erect and hands clasped in front. "We share that goal and are grateful, Kmet-Here, for your assistance." *He'd be even more grateful if the Kmet stopped playing these power games.*

Later, Henry decided that was the thought that kept his mouth moving, when a saner person would have shut up and taken the win.

"I believe it's your shift," he said, gesturing to the waiting dais.

The Kmet, oblivious to Human emotional undertones, huffed with apparent good nature and began heaving kmeth's bulk to the pedestals. "I concur."

Gripping the basket and bag, lips tight, Killian stared at the Kmet—statue-still until Henry touched her arm. She gave a little start, eyes wild. "Flip's passed the word to Omar," he whispered. Louder, "Call if you need us, Kmet-Here. Let's go, Killian."

***

"You've been painting." The banal observation let him step into her quarters to gaze at the canvas fixed to the wall. Henry felt Killian's eyes burning a hole in the back of his neck and spared a moment to worry if she'd hit him, but didn't turn around. Bold colors, subtle blending. Interesting textures beneath. Did she realize how much of her was revealed in her art?

Wouldn't care if she did, he thought, hiding a smile. "Is it too soon to ask your intentions? With this."

"It's a reminder—a memorial, I suppose," she admitted after a long pause. "A petal per ship. A flower for a world." Her voice hardened. "I can't believe you left kmeth alone up there."

And this was why he'd intruded in her space. Henry turned to meet her blistering glare, letting something of his smile show. "I haven't. Flip. Control please."

An image appeared between them, projected from a dot on his collar. Flip's tiny bee must have settled on the top of the den. The resultant view looked down at a considerable slant to the pedestals and Kmet-Here's long, polyp-encrusted back. Three PIPs, clinging to the control wall, showed along with most of the rightmost screen, but nothing else.

Killian's mouth had dropped open. It snapped shut. "Thought there were rules."

"Call it a precaution," Henry replied comfortably.

HENRY, I HAVE CONFIRMATION. OMAR M'STARINK T'KOLESZAR HAS RELINQUISHED THE PORTAL TO HIS KMET-HERE. TRANSIT BETWEEN PORTALS IS ABOUT TO RESUME.

He stuck a finger in the image of Kmet-Here. "Can you tell from this if our friend's doing what we expect?"

"Maybe." She squinted. "Flip, enlarge the top of the pedestal in front of kmeth." The image filled with busy tongue tips moving over the levers and dials, leaving a glisten of slime. "Looks nominal. Transit prep," she clarified for him, her voice full of relief. "Nothing unusual."

As it should be.

Henry gave himself a second, his own reaction threatening to give him the shakes. He'd had as many—or more—doubts as the pilot, but that wasn't it. Something Kmet-Here had said. *The Duality establishes us.* He'd heard it somewhere before, but where . . .

"Good," he said firmly. He pried off the dot, handing it to her. "Flip's recording as long as the remote transmits. Once the two of you have established the pattern, feel free to have him take over for a while." No point telling her to rest.

Killian nodded, staring at the dot on her fingertip. Her eyes shot up to his, full of emotion. "Henry—"

He ducked his head, then nodded to the flower taking shape on her canvas. "Here's hoping for three more."

Leaving Killian, Henry went to his quarters and closed the door. He pulled the wad of folded pages from under his pillow and went to his desk.

At first, he simply sat, hands flat on the paper, absorbing what had happened. He glanced at the picture in front of him. "I did it, Grandpa." The evacuation, other than communications, rested now in the hands—tongue tips—of the Kmet. The Duality, on the surface, functioned as it should.

He should be gratified.

He wasn't. Like Killian, perhaps Omar, he'd been reluctant to turn Human lives over to the aliens. *Bias?* Maybe.

Or maybe it was something else.

The Duality establishes us.

He opened his notes, taking up a pen. The circles of *Earth . . . Divider . . . Human-There* were already embedded in a chaotic nest of crisscrossing lines, no idea eliminated, no pattern he could discern.

Choosing a blank sheet, Henry started again. This time, he wrote *Kmet-Here* in the center. Around the name, he put his observations.

Confrontation a bluff.

Chased me from den. Didn't protest.

Unsurprised by anything that's happened. Typical.

He underlined *Typical.* Kmet-Here being predictable was reassuring.

Kmeth knowing what to expect—perhaps being the cause?

The opposite.

Henry tapped a knuckle to his teeth. His gaze landed on the velvet bag and he stretched forward to pull out the badge, holding it between two fingers. Looked at the back, with its clasped hands representing unity. *Us.*

The Duality establishes us.

Surely the inclusive us, Human and Kmet.

He'd searched. The phrase wasn't in any document. He couldn't recall hearing a Kmet say it before—but he had.

Where?

On a hunch, he went back to the first Kmet-Arbiter negotiations, going over and over the recordings, not knowing what he was after—

—until he found it.

The Duality establishes us.

And more.

***

Trying for casual, Henry stepped out of the shower, drying his hair. PIP-Flip dented his pillow, a lens aimed in his direction. "Status, Flip?"

"Transits in both directions have taken place successfully, Henry. I regret to say I can offer no further direct confirmation of Kmet-Here's actions. My remote was absorbed by a Portal PIP. I can, however, tell you traffic is moving smoothly along anticipated routes here and around Earth."

Henry froze, towel in one hand, dripping on the floor as his mind raced in a new direction. "Did you expect that? To be absorbed?"

"Our molecular framework is quite similar, Henry."

Not an answer. "Should I be worried?"

"About what, Henry?"

And now evasion. He tossed the towel aside and sat on the bed, regarding his companion. Flip-coats, his sandals, the shuttle itself. The mind might be protected from tampering by a self-destruct, but what of its substance? "Flip. Can PIPs absorb any portion of you they contact?"

Three seconds passed, an alarming delay from a sentience able to resolve a multitude of complex problems simultaneously. "I would require additional trials to confirm or refute that hypothesis, Henry. Considering our circumstances, I do not recommend conducting them."

Worry it was. "I want your promise you'll take every precaution."

The appendage with the lens retracted with an offended *pop*.

"You fuss over me," Henry told the polymorph, "I get to fuss over you. Especially when it comes to our surviving this mission. Is that understood?"

A sullen, "Yes, Henry." The lens didn't reappear.

He'd other problems. Time to deal with his disturbing epiphany. He pressed Rena's band. "Project Rena, please, Flip. Recording off."

"Yes, Henry."

She appeared standing in the middle of his bed, wearing her lab coat, eyebrows arched as she took in his presently naked self. "Been a while."

This wasn't his body and she wasn't here. Neither realization prevented his blush. Henry grabbed the towel, arranging it strategically, then gave a rueful grin. "That's not—I'm sending you a present via the *Cape Sable*. Remember the Ostix?"

Rena's entire face brightened, then fell. "You didn't send a specimen—Henry, you know better. Nothing alive or dead transits that didn't evolve on our world."

He grinned. "No provision against sending processed food items. I've an embarrassment of gift baskets full of the things. The one I've sent you is properly sealed." He leaned back on an elbow. "If you don't want them, call it lunch. Share with your techs—"

Her hands came up with a laugh. "No, no. That's fine. More than fine." The glow was back. "Combined with the data and images from their biologists, I should be able to—" Rena stopped short. "What's wrong, Henry?"

He gave her a wounded look.

"Sending me the best present ever? Something is."

Henry rose to sit. He couldn't help a glance at PIP-Flip, a quiescent gray lump on his pillow. The arm with the lens was tucked out of sight, along with the audio appendage. *Another trust being tested.*

"The Kmet. Kmeth studied us before deciding to make contact. I think kmeth were looking for something specific. About us. About New Earth."

Her eyebrows met but all she said was, "Go on."

"I went back to the recordings. What was said by either side. The stumbles to understanding. Something about the first conversations bothered me, Rena, but I didn't pick up on why until earlier today. Kmet-Here said, 'The Duality establishes us.'"

"I've never heard that before."

"Only one person has before now. The first Arbiter to deal with kmeth, when the Kmet first proposed the Duality. 'To establish *us*.' And another phrase caught my attention. 'To bind *us* in health.'"

"Not the Duality's health?"

"That came later. Maybe we started it with a misinterpretation. Regardless, the Kmet haven't used it since—until today. I think kmeth's reversion to the original was deliberate. A signal to me."

"Henry—" Her *be-reasonable* voice. "The Kmet found and followed our transmissions through space. Kmeth were curious, as we were."

"It's not the same, Rena. From the start, the Kmet have insisted we—Earth Humans—are special. Unique. Humans-Here. Shut down any conversation about Humans on other worlds, including Origin Earth. Refused to view evidence until the probe message. And we didn't argue, did we? We took the Kmet at face value, as a highly advanced civilization willing to share kmeth's technology. In our lifetimes, we've rebuilt ours around it and I think that's exactly what the Kmet needed us to do. Not for our benefit. To change Earth for kmeth's."

She gave him her *you failed biology* look. "Needed for what? Why?"

"You tell me. You're the xenologist."

"You're the one with a Kmet. Get me some blood."

"I can try—"

"And I was kidding. We both know it's not worth the risk, Henry." Rena waited for him to nod before she continued. "If this is your way of telling me you've switched to the big bad aliens mean us harm camp, why didn't kmeth destroy us when they came, thirty-seven years ago?"

Killian's question. Henry shrugged. "The only one who'd know happens to be in charge at the moment."

She digested that. Swallowed. "What are you going to do?"

"As long as the Kmet appear to be our allies, all I can do is operate as if everything Kmet-Here tells me is true. Remove our kind from these worlds before their presence triggers a reaction from kmeth's alleged enemy."

"If the Kmet *are* the big bad, you'll be herding us into a pen for them. For whatever reason." Rena paused, then gave him an oddly suspicious look. "You're gambling. That you'll find the answers, the proof, before that happens. Henry—what if you can't?"

"I have to." He spread his hands. "So I will."

An abrupt shake of her head dislodged a pin. A beetle, with bright red wing cases. Each was an exact replica of an insect on the Earth they both knew, with ten legs, not the six of their namesakes, recorded in the Archive. The difference amused children and was forgotten by most adults; Rena'd told him studying Origin Earth's now-alien biology had been her first taste of what might live on other worlds.

She fondled the pin absently, being awake and real where she was. Impossibly distant. Untouchable. Henry swallowed the lump in his throat. She looked up at him, eyes sober. "How can I help?"

"I've given you clearance to the first contact files—everything between the Arbiter's Office and Kmet since then. Look for anything I might have missed, any overlooked clues to kmeth's motives."

"Shomchai—"

"You. Just—you. We can't risk spreading this, Rena. If Kmet-Here discovers my doubts, my questions—we don't know how kmeth will react."

"With aggression," his xenologist assured him, grim and certain. "Henry—you and Killian. If there's danger—"

"Leave me here to finish the work. That above all else." He tipped his head, grinned at her through his hair. "Besides, I'm pretty good at distracting our local bully, if I do say so myself."

"Henry—" At his look, she sighed. "I promise." A weak chuckle. "Glad you lead with my present. Something to look forward to. That, and meeting their biologists in person." A real smile. "Wait till they see our wildlife."

"They're good people, Rena. Except for—" Henry stopped, too late. He'd wanted to lighten the moment before she left him. Failed.

It didn't matter, he realized. *This was Rena.* "I wasn't going to tell you," he admitted. "Guess that ship's launched."

Her smile faded. "What have they done?"

"Nothing yet. This world—these people have a custom. Shomchai thinks—doesn't matter where it started," he caught condemnation in his voice and forced it away. "Whenever a group of them leaves on a journey, someone stays behind. A caretaker for the crops."

"Someone's to stay on the planet."

He gave a weary nod. "I've argued. Begged. Nothing's made any difference. The Decision-Makers are adamant."

"And you know who it is." Her face filled with sympathy. "I'm so sorry, Henry."

"Aati, the interpreter. I realize he volunteered but—the man's already afraid, Rena. Of space. Of what I've said is coming. I'd almost convinced him until—they offered him this—this barbaric duty, to be a meaningless sacrifice—" Henry paused. Calmed himself. "Shomchai'll say to respect their beliefs. Sofia, not to waste my time; they'll die anyway. Ousmane? Probably wants me to interview them."

It might have been the real Rena sitting on his bed, eyes searching his face. "What do you say?"

"I'm here to save people. Even if they don't want to be saved." His jaw tightened. "Especially then."

"Because if you don't save everyone, you've failed."

"It's not about me—" Henry stopped. This was why he needed Rena. Her knowledge of him. Her relentless honesty in all things. "Is it?"

She half smiled. "You've your faults, Henry. Hubris isn't among them." Her lower lip disappeared between her teeth. Her eyebrows drew together as she regarded him solemnly. "You've an obligation to honor the agreement with the Kmet, to retrieve all Humans. To protect us. If you haul Aati and his family into orbit against their will, no one will judge you."

"I won't." Henry shook his head. "I can't. It has to be their choice."

"No, Henry. If you let them stay, it's yours. Kmet-Here will insist on retrieving the last Humans-There. You'll force kmeth—and Killian—to commit murder and what becomes of the Duality then?" Her expression saddened. "But you already know all that, don't you. My poor Henry."

"They won't thank me. They—"

Rena leaned forward to press her lips against his. Intent, without substance; still, the memory of the real thing warmed him. He managed a half-smile. "What's that for?"

She drew back with the hint of a dimple. "You dropped your towel."

<Why are they listening to you?>

STEADY. *Steady.*

Killian shot the hovering image another quick glance. Added length to the precise line of ink representing a not-seen-before interior junction between the pedestal top and base. Flip's sensor provided superb resolution and she mustn't waste—

A tremor shook her fingers. She pulled back the pen tip before she ruined the work. *Done anyway.* She let out a sigh, rolled a shoulder. "Flip, elevate twenty degrees."

"Yes, Killian." The image shifted higher, focused on a section of wall controls. Stupid PIPs covered most with their fat bodies, pushers and pullers a blur of activity, but she could make out a decent slice.

Killian dipped her pen in the ink pot. Low tech versus high tech. The thought made her chuckle, a hoarse sound warning of thirst. She reached into the basket blindly, found another yellow pear. Bit off the top half, careful the dribbles of juice went on the floor, not her canvas.

<You need sleep.>

"Later." No way she'd relax without drugs. Killian planned to postpone oblivion as long as she could. Wait through another transit cycle at least before letting herself believe Henry'd done it again. Talked the Kmet into cooperating.

Man's tongue should be classified.

Killian chuckled again.

<You're punchy as hell, Killie-Cat.>

Wasn't the first time; wouldn't be the last. "Later," she grumbled, counting the number of small knurls on a knob. Might not be a detail that mattered. *Odd though.* PIPs had grippy appendages and clamps. A raised profile helped smooth digits make precise adjustments—

The image vanished. "Flip!"

No response. Killian brought out her personal com, fumbled the switch then had it. "Flip! What happened?"

"My apologies, Killian. The sensor no longer transmitting."

Oh no oh no. "Was it kmeth?"

"It was not," came the unhelpful yet reassuring answer. "The link button Henry left with you is no longer functional. Please destroy it at once. Placing it in water will suffice."

The caution she understood. Killian peeled the dot from her palette tray and dropped it in a puddle of pear juice, watching it dissolve, then returned to her pen and ink. Had to recreate the knob before she forgot what she'd seen, then paint over the result. Henry hadn't appeared to notice the underlying schematic, being focused on her flower petals.

No time to be careless.

Done, she stared numbly at the canvas for a moment, then let out a breath. *Time.*

She'd shoved the bag with its imprisoned PIP in the shower stall, closing the door. Kept Henry from seeing it, at minimum. He'd started playing fast and loose with the regs; no need to test him. Besides, the Arbiter and Flip were heading back to the planet.

Killian grinned as she recovered her bag, still full of PIP, and gave it a triumphant little shake.

Now to see if her key worked.

Killian picked the first tube door that refused to open to Human hands. She pressed her bag against it, hoping she wouldn't have to risk releasing what had to be a very annoyed little polymorph.

The tube opened. "Yes!" she shouted, then closed her mouth. *Not smart, shouting.* Killian leaned in.

Flinched back, revolted by the smell. *Something ripe at the other end.* Usually was, if you had plumbing. Figured that'd be her first big explore.

Wrinkling her nose, the pilot checked the pouch around her waist was secure. A trunk had contained her toolset, the sort of quick assists a spacer might need on station and wouldn't willingly be without, Portal rules or no Portal rules. She felt better having them.

Stalling. Killian could almost hear Giselle. Tempting, to press her oneiric's band and have company.

Better wait till she'd found something worth breaking rules over.

She tied a cord to the bag handles, knotting it around her bicep, then pushed the bag and herself into the stinky tube.

Immediately Killian regretted not setting a timer. Duration was the only reliable, riding a system like the insides of a loose cable. She did her best, counting seconds in her head.

Until erupting out the other end. The handles flew from her hand; the knot held as she rolled across the floor. *The stench!*

Different texture. Rougher—no, ridged. She came to a halt, running her hands over the strong mesh screen where a floor should be. Below was the source of the smell.

She looked up to find a ceiling composed of yawning pipes.

"No, no, no." With each *no* Killian hitched herself along the screen to the nearest tube door, hauling her key with her. Nasty things came out of pipes. Judging by the smell, a large amount of nasty, and she wasn't sticking around to find out.

Tube door, press the bag, jump in—wherever she was heading had to be an improvement—

—Killian found herself protruding from a floor, this one smooth and clean. Heaving the bag out of her way, she climbed out. The tube closed behind. She didn't pay attention, too busy grinning.

"This would be something." She pressed the band on her wrist. "Gis, you there?"

<Here.> Disgruntled. <Why are you? Kmet-Here took your shift, fool.>

"Oh, I'm not at work," Killian said with satisfaction, turning slowly, running her eyes over what was a perfect replica of Control save one significant feature. No den.

No Kmet.

There were PIPs, who didn't appear interested in her or her prisoner. They weren't interested in the controls either, busy dismantling the panels on one wall and scurrying off with pieces. Now that she paid attention, the little monsters had been scavenging materials throughout. Even the pedestals were hollow, their workings cut off.

< Hot damn, Killie-Cat. You found a way to move around the Portal.>

"I did." She crouched in the path of a PIP brandishing a clawful of wires. "Put those back."

The polymorph came to a stop. All of them did.

<What are you—?>

Killian rose to her feet. "You heard me," she said, wondering what they'd do.

To her delight, as one the PIPs spun about and began reattaching the materials they'd ripped from the replica Control, producing tiny welding arms and fastening clamps, little arms with spinning tips affixing bolts. It was as if she'd set them in reverse.

<Why are they listening to you?>

"No idea," Killian replied quietly. Unless the PIPs were programmed to prefer building over destruction, and merely waited for a more rational set of commands than *build a squalid alien den out of anything you can find.*

Lacking a guarantee they wouldn't resume ripping the room apart once she left, the pilot pulled out her sketch pad and began to draw. This much exposed wiring?

A bonus she wouldn't refuse.

***

Killian slept for four blissful, inadequate hours, waking to Gis' cheery <Time to get to work, slughead.> without her usual groan of protest, even accepting the return of bright lights with a squint.

She turned her head on the pillow to admire the canvas. The schematic of Control had grown to consume a third. Sketchy—she'd more details waiting in her pad. Hell, she knew the way back, if she needed more. Could pull a panel or two herself.

<Shift change in twenty minutes. Shower and breakfast, Killie-Cat.> A yawn. <I'd like the same, if you don't mind.>

Killian brought a finger before her eyes. Drew a heart on the pillow by her cheek.

<Mushball,> Gis responded, gruff as ever.

"Love you, Space Rat."

<Lima Charlie, Killie-Cat.>

The pilot tapped her wristband as she rolled to sit up. There wasn't time to paint over her new lines of ink, not if she was to take that shower, but Henry wouldn't be back till the evacuation finished.

***

Killian arrived in Control to find Kmet-Here hunched at the pedestals, PIPs dashing around as usual . . .

. . . and, as if waiting for her to notice, the next doomsday clock hovered over the images on the rightmost screen.

She drew out her pad, quickly sketched the location of the dot along the spiral, and sent it to Flip to estimate how much time World II had left. *Let the polymorph break the news to Henry.*

The pilot went to stand by the dais, waiting until a huge eye angled at her in acknowledgment.

"Pilot Killian reporting for my shift, Kmet-Here."

"Forgive me."

THE clock was gone. Fifteen hours after it had reappeared, World II cracked and burned. They'd watched until the sat feed ended, knowing what it meant. The Kmet herded humanity to New Earth and intended them to stay there.

You won't save them all.

He'd done his best. They all had. Nineteen days of stripped safety margins. Dropped screening and checks before World III's people were sent on to New Earth. Breakneck turnarounds with crews pushed past their limits. Beyond credibility, no one died. There'd even been five births. Sofia was grimly triumphant.

Kmet-Here waited in the Portal for him to keep his word.

A scrap of paper fluttered down the street, caught on the leg of a patio chair, came loose to slip into an alley and disappear.

The city was empty. The world, was. Except for Arbiter Henry m'Yama t'Nowak, walking the same street, hair tossed by the gusty wind that moved the litter.

Except for the seven waiting for him, who intended to stay and die where they'd been born, granting him the courtesy of a final goodbye.

When he sent in his next report, good odds he'd hear about delaying till the last possible moment. Arbiter's prerogative didn't cover it. The Kmet clock had reset. Proof they'd a limited window to finish and move to World IV, get its inhabitants—should there be any—to safety, and yet?

Here he was.

Here was no longer a good place to be. The buildings on either side of the road loomed, dark and silent. Before abandoning their world, despite knowing they'd never be back, the population had shut down power stations and released livestock and pets. Henry wouldn't have been surprised if they'd closed curtains and checked their taps for drips. A meticulous, conscientious people, justly proud of their accomplishments, who walked away from them on his word.

The quiet scratched like claws along Henry's nerves. *Or was it remorse?* He fought the urge to look over his shoulder. Pushed aside emotions of no use to him or them. Concentrated on what was. Aati and his family would be welcomed. Their people would need his skills on New Earth.

He couldn't bear to lose them.

HENRY, I AM OVERHEAD WITH THE PASSENGER TRANSPORT. I CAN LAND ON THE STREET WITHOUT DIFFICULTY.

"Thank you, Flip."

HENRY, YOUR TONE IS NOT WITHIN NORMAL PARAMETERS.

Because he was holding it together by a thread—Henry cleared his throat. "I'm fine. Stand by."

Ahead the street split around a boulevard wide enough for tall plants to shade pleasant groupings of tables and chairs. The colorful umbrellas were furled; the wind, he thought, forcing a smile for the people sitting together, waiting for him.

As Henry approached, a small animal stepped in his way, a blue ribbon around its scaled neck. It blinked three eyes up at him, arched its back in greeting, then jumped into the arms of the child who left her family to retrieve her pet.

The animal climbed to her shoulder, turning its head right around to continue to stare at him.

Aati rose to his feet. "Come, Henry. Sit. We have water and the food of Desaru to share with you," he said, gesturing in invitation. "Silakan."

The table was set for eight. Four adults, counting Aati, three children, the youngest sitting on an elderly woman's lap, and a seat for him, their guest.

Later, he'd remember they all wore blue-green, and most had dimpled chins and sharp noses like Aati, and the eldest child had her hair in a braid secured by a twist of grass, and the youngest fell asleep as they spoke, sucking a thumb.

At the time, it was all Henry could to do take his seat. "Thank you."

He dipped his fingers in the fragrant water bowl. Drank from a cup. Held the plain stick with its splayed, leggy offering in midair, then lowered it abruptly. "I'm not here to say goodbye. Come with me."

Aati put his own stick down. "You know we cannot."

"Will not."

The smaller man shrugged. "Yes."

Henry looked pleadingly to the other adults. Two avoided his gaze, the third, the woman with the toddler, met it. Smiled with terrifying compassion. *For him.* Spoke.

Aati translated. "My mother would not have you grieve for us, Henry. This is the highest calling of our people, to stay with our beloved home. To care for Desaru in her final hours."

She paused to plant a soft kiss on the child's head, whispering.

"May our pod be found worthy on the Day of Judgment," Aati finished.

The others nodded, their expressions brightening.

They were calm. Even happy. The child fed her three-eyed pet an Ostix leg, clearly done with the discussion.

He'd known, deep down, there'd be no convincing them.

Aati's hand landed on his shoulder. "This is our choice, my friend," he stated, as if hearing Henry's thought. "We are not afraid to die. Only of failing those who trust this sacred duty to us. As we—" with gentle pressure "—trust you to save them. Goodbye, Henry."

Rising to his feet, Henry drew Aati into his arms, then embraced each member of his family. The pet jumped to his shoulder and nuzzled his ear, making the child laugh.

He kept his composure as he walked away. "Flip, activate the stun field on my mark." Two steps. Four.

Henry stopped and turned. "Activate."

He made himself watch the family slump where they sat or stood, the pet falling to the ground, a cup break. He'd use Flip's cart to move them to the shuttle. Strap them in. Take them to safety. Force them to live.

"Forgive me," he whispered.

"Show me what you've got."

Doublet

YOU died in the Split, you got a little plaque of precious ship metal with the date on it, screwed to a boulder, big, gray, and ugly, sat square in the middle of the Seeker training ground. Just the date, someone long ago deciding there was no need of names to go with them and it being an encouragement to those come later to see the dates grow further apart.

Beth didn't see it that way, it more likely the Split would bite, having gone hungry.

She'd stood by, rain pounding on her head and shoulders, tucked in a tunnel of wet, while the head of training screwed in the latest plaque in front of every Seeker and those wanting to be, her being proof a body could go through in a Sweep and walk out again as Kimm Seeker hadn't.

Came back that night to lean her hip on the cold stone. "Damn fool," she'd grumbled. "Almost fried me with you."

Took a nail and hammer to her friend's scrap of dead ship and pounded the letter *K* into it, regs be damned, too.

Bios were thorough folks. They tested every scrap Beth brought with her, then went after her, scraping skin and taking blood, checking her ears and eyes, poking where she'd rather they didn't, but it was how Home learned from the Split and she'd no complaint.

She did like leaving their obsessive care, end of each day. Especially when the time came they were done and Beth was doing just that, leaving, when Patrick came charging down the hall behind her, making more noise than a thunderstorm.

She stopped to let him catch up, taking pity on those wanting quiet to work and, truth be told, enjoying the spectacle of his long arms and legs flailing the air. *Man ran like one of the bugs he loved.*

"Seeker!" Patrick gasped when he got to her. "You—for—got—your artifacts!"

"Didn't forget," Beth informed him dryly. "Junk's dead weight and pointless." And no, she hadn't put the phantom creak in her report, having time to think it through. Be truly embarrassed. A newbie mistook the sounds caused by temperature jumps, night to day, not her.

"But—" His mouth and eyes went round, feigning shock. "You—have to—take them."

Bios made requests; didn't give orders. She raised a warning eyebrow. "Says who?"

He dropped the act, brown eyes now imploring. "Please, Beth. Please? You're the only Seeker left who will." Fingers wiggled in the air. "We've put together some new items—promising ones. Could be the breakthrough."

Wheedling, was it? Didn't suit a grown scientist of Patrick's credentials and she left the eyebrow up. "Doesn't mean what you think it does, in the Split."

"The connection, then. You could be the one to make the first—this could be the trip. Please, Beth." He was unusually excited, even for a man prone to throwing his hands in the air and dancing a jig over a new tick, and she felt herself relent.

Not that she'd make it easy. Reluctantly, Beth lowered her eyebrow; joined both in a fierce glower. "I check them first."

"Yes, yes!" If he nodded any harder, his thin neck would snap.

"No more cookie statues. No more paper picture books. Or stupid charcoal pencils," she continued, warming to her theme.

Patrick beamed from ear-to-ear, his wispy mustache sending hairs up his nose. "Agreed. Yes to everything. We listened to your suggestions, Beth. These are much better, I promise."

She doubted it. There'd be something not worth packing to the Split, guaranteed. "And you're buying tonight. I'm in the mood for steak."

Almost comical, the way his face fell, Bios not known for fat wallets, but Patrick didn't hesitate. "Anything you want, Beth. So—you'll do it?"

Her turn to smile. "Show me what you've got," she said, waving him back down the hall.

***

"BETH!" Dex put his hairy arms on the rail behind, bending to shout in her ear. *The Taphouse* was packed to the gills by now, being the favored watering hole for Seekers and those who sent them out. "GET YOU ONE?"

"Sure." Beth passed him her empty mug, though she knew the drink came with company and she wasn't in a mood for people.

Rarely was. A Seeker trait, common in those willing to enter the Split more than the once and first. Was why she chose to be here, night before the convoy to the edge left, filling herself with the stink and racket of a crowd. Friends' faces, music.

Store it up. Tuck it away. Wouldn't help her survive. Did help her smile when big Dex pushed through, shoulders first, to arrive at her booth with mugs so full of beer the heads sloshed on the floor.

Danger!

Taking hers, Beth pushed the thought down where it belonged. *Taphouse* floor was sticky with spills and nothing broke through the boards after it. Not outside the Split. *This side of it,* she reminded herself, clicking her mug to Dex's as he wormed his bulk onto the bench beside her. Away was its own set of perils.

She couldn't wait.

Then Carla arrived, the scarred and wiry Head Seeker sliding onto the bench across, making it not a social but a what—a briefing? Beth put a hand behind her ear and grimaced. *No talking here.*

The other woman laughed and nodded, lifting her drink.

Beth relaxed, guessing this a send-off, figuring the why of it. Losing Kimm—been a while since the risk slapped them in the face. Made life precious.

Made time that way.

On the thought, she slipped her hand over Dex's wide thigh and down where it got interesting, her toes finding Carla's knee and traveling where they would.

Being in the mood after all.

World IV

"For that, I need your help."

"DONE?" The Kmet aimed both eyes at the screen. BOOM! "Not done. Why are you not done, Arbiter Henry?"

The screen showed the now-empty city. Henry gripped his patience. "All the people have gone to New Earth, Kmet-Here, as I prom—"

"NOT DONE!!!" Polyps flashed red-purple. The enraged Kmet heaved forward and the Arbiter braced himself. Not that he'd survive the charge, but instinct tried—

A familiar bag bounced off the side of the Kmet, who froze, a disbelieving eye locked on the pilot who lowered her arm and snapped, "Thought you were in a hurry."

Henry risked a glance at Killian. She gave him a too-bland look. Turned it on the Kmet. "It takes longer to move what talks than what's stuck to the ground. You want speed, I suggest we go where there's people, let the Arbiter finish his job, then come back to retrieve the rest."

<Not bad,> Shomchai praised.

In full agreement—though they'd talk about throwing objects at the alien later—Henry relaxed slightly. Killian hadn't accused the Kmet of burning the previous worlds, a confrontation he'd prefer to leave until they'd proof. "Pilot Killian, please input the coordinates for Kmet-Here."

"Yessir."

The polyps faded to an anxious orange. *Indecision?* Henry didn't hesitate. "It is time to move. Do you concur, Kmet-Here?"

A long, uneasy pause during which a drop of sweat slid maddeningly down Henry's neck.

Finally, a reluctant, "I concur. We must go from here. Now."

They'd done it.

Shomchai's next words erased the tiny triumph. <This capitulation might mean the Divider's closing in—that Kmet-Here's seized the excuse to run.>

Costing him his first chance to contact the unknown.

With the individual who'd know draped over the pedestal, tongue-tips at work, Henry thoughtfully filed *that* under later as well.

***

TRANSIT.

Arrival was—disappointing. The destination of the Halcyon Project Sleeper Ship *Kitchener* turned out to be another planet well-suited to Human life but, like World II, one devoid of the Human signatures detected by the Portal. On that determination, Kmet-Here grumbled back to kmeth's den to wait.

Killian deployed her satellites.

Flip sent down his tiny eyes.

Henry fled to his quarters, having no interest in standing with Killian in Control and even less in hearing PIP-Flip's detailed analysis of his agitated state *and would he like a soothing beverage?*

Hell no. He deserved to be agitated. Wanted to be. To feel all of it, every scrap of pain and regret. Learn from it. Do better.

Alone except for his grandfather's picture, Henry wrote his final report on the evacuation of World III, listing his decisions and their consequences. Wrote commendations for the crews of ships and stations who'd accomplished so much, and his deepest appreciation to those taking care of the evacuees as they set foot on their new home.

Stayed awake, obsessively checking for updates on the people he'd taken from theirs.

Next world. This one. He had to do better.

***

Twelve hours later, Flip, at Henry's request, budded chairs from his now-empty floor for a meeting to discuss World IV with his quorum. Killian's and Henry's were the only ones with cushions, projections not requiring them.

To be courteous, since only those tangibly present could hold one, Henry'd refused a mug of Flip's coffee, much as he could have used it. Killian sat cradling hers, slouched but attentive as Flip shared what his tiny spies near the ground had recorded.

"As you can see, there are Humans living on this planet," the polymorph began.

"Where?" Sofia demanded. "All I see are rocks."

The image was of a bleak, lifeless tumble of shattered rock, collapsed from a jagged ridge that wandered into the distance, one of thousands rumpling the landscape beneath a dusty sky. "Close in, Flip," Henry said quietly.

"Yes, Henry."

As if they flew with one of Flip's tiny remotes, the image moved steadily closer to the ground, centered on an area where the tumble formed an oblong mass. Much smaller, rounder, mounds of rock were nearby.

"Those are, ah, buildings—" Ousmane whispered.

Generous. Each mound consisted of flat gray rocks stacked to form a circle broken by a solitary low door. Some were roofed with larger rocks, others by overlapping scraps of dark material; all had a hole on top emitting fitful wisps of pale smoke.

Other than the muted black of shadow, the sun sinking behind the ridge, there was no color or contrast. Nothing growing or on foot. No water.

Yet people lived here. Henry had no idea how.

"The structures are two meters in height with an average diameter of ten meters," Flip informed them. "There is no evidence of refinement or tool use, beyond the scavenging of plastic and metal pieces presumably from their ship, and a prevalence of low-quality hydrocarbon combustion. This appears to be a significantly regressed society."

"Where's the *Kitchener*?"

Killian pointed at the mass of rocks beside the mounds. "You're looking at her, according to my sat feed."

"But—" Ousmane looked ready to jump into the image and dig. "Why would they bury, ah, their main and most crucial, ah, resource?"

"We don't think they did," Henry replied. "Flip?"

"The landscape demonstrates an active seismology, impacting the area's sedimentary rock and rendering it unstable. The evidence suggests the sleeper ship was caught in a landslide, perhaps triggered at landing or by a quake soon after. This feature, however, is not natural." The image zeroed in on an opening, dark and irregular, at the base of the pile.

"They woke. Dug their way out," Shomchai hazarded. "That must have been terrify—what the hell are those?"

The image had pulled back to show thin metal poles driven into the ground, bases supported by more rock. They framed a narrow approach to the opening; more fanned out in a maze around the small mounds. Each was topped with something round and bleached—

"Skulls. Human," Rena identified, when no one else spoke. "Henry?"

He let out a breath. "That's why we're meeting like this. To discuss how I should proceed."

"You don't." Everyone turned to look at Killian, who raised her mug to the skulls. "It's what we're all thinking, Henry," she challenged. "This is no place for you."

"It's not about me. It's about them. These people have endured enough. They deserve a better life." *He would do better.*

"Are they still—" Rena hesitated. "Is there anyone alive?"

"Sats read heat signatures inside the buildings," the pilot answered. "They're clustered. As if everyone's holding on for dear life."

Henry grimaced. "Small as they were, Flip's remotes scared them into hiding."

"It was not my intention, Henry—" *Dismay.*

"I know, Flip. Guess they don't like bees. We pulled them back," he added.

Rena's eyes scoured the image. "What do we have on the climate—the ecosystem? They must eat something."

"Each other, maybe?" Killian sounded more interested than concerned. "It's possible."

"No, it's not," the xenologist countered sternly. "They'd have died out long before now."

"I'll ask about their food source," Henry stated, refusing to consider cannibalism. He'd enough worries, looking at the scene. "So how do I approach them? And who first?"

"I believe I spotted—Flip, display the middle of the village, please." Shomchai rose to his feet and went to stand near the wall, his projection blending with that of the buildings. "Let me—oh dear," he said, looking for his non-existent torso.

"My apologies." Flip made an adjustment.

The linguist now appeared standing at a podium, a pointer in his hand. He swept it approvingly through the air, the polymorph supplying a swish sound. "You're getting very good at this, Flip."

"Thank—"

"Give me numbers," Sofia interrupted hungrily. "If this is the only settlement—"

Henry nodded. "—then from what we're seeing, there couldn't be more than a hundred. That's one ship. I've *Cape Forchu* standing by to transit. You could head to the next planet tomorrow."

Killian gave a dark chuckle. "Unless they eat Henry."

"No one's—" Henry collected himself. "Let's focus on my first meeting with these people. How. Who."

"We can't assume these people will be as cooperative as those on World III, or that they'll be eager to leave." Shomchai used his pointer to indicate one of the mounds with rocks for a roof. "Erecting these structures took combined effort and some skill, even if the rest appear more cobbled together and desperate. Flip, magnify this area." The pointer tapped the front of a mound.

Enlarged, what had seemed a door became a piece of metal secured in the opening by rocks jammed into the gaps. To either side leaned enormous bones. From cannibals to giants—*maybe Killian was right*. "Tell me those aren't Human," Henry pleaded.

"Better," Rena exclaimed longingly. "Fossils. Leg bones—from something really big. Probably shook loose in the landslide. This land must have been underwater once—"

"Does this further the evacuation?" Sofia interrupted.

The xenologist drew herself up, giving a dignified nod. "If there aren't fossils on the other entrances, the placement of these may indicate the dwelling of a person of significance. Your contact, in other words. Who."

"The door with giant bones," Henry protested. "What if it's the local paleontologist?"

His oneirics looked amused. Ousmane took pity. "Based on what we see, ah, before us, this is a primitive, ah, culture such as never seen on, ah, our Earth. From documents in the Archive? Such bones could be idols. Ah, objects of worship."

Rena went to stand by Shomchai, studying the image. "Here we go," she said in an entirely different tone, her finger tracing what Henry'd thought a small rock, pulling away. "Human bones. In the walls."

Killian gave an *I told you so* grunt.

"That settles it." Shomchai turned to face Henry, his expression grim. "Find a less invasive way to watch these people. Study them. We need to know far more about them before you risk going down."

"Agreed," from Ousmane. Rena nodded.

Sofia raised her hand. "Or we choose a more invasive method, for once. The PPC have offered me trained personnel—"

"Send troops?" Shomchai exploded. "With what, stuns and nets?"

Henry didn't flinch, despite his thoughts recoiling to Aati and his family. To what he'd been informed was a clinical despair necessitating intervention by Earth psychologists—and a question he couldn't answer. Maybe never could.

Would it have been kinder to let them die with their world?

Not the children. They'd lives ahead—

"Nope. Can't do it."

They all looked at the pilot.

Killian waved her mug at Henry. "Kmet-Here's aware what's happening, dirt-side. Kmeth agreed to let the Arbiter deal with Humans, as in going in person, alone, to meet the new ones." Her glance at him held a wry sympathy. "My guess is that's not something open to change."

Henry nodded. "You're right. Whatever—whomever—we need to enlist to save these people, the process starts with me." He held out his hands. "With your help."

Rena chose that moment to catch his eye, giving the tiny nod that meant she'd something for him.

Only.

***

Killian left. Henry stretched out on the shuttle's deck, Flip softening the surface for him, and closed his eyes.

Opened them to find himself standing. Rena turned, hands in her lab coat pockets, the sun glinting from the pins in her hair. She dug a bare toe into the sand. "Nostalgia?"

An unconscious choice, imagining them outside on a beach—this rugged, beautiful, solitary beach—and Henry didn't dare look over his shoulder, in case he'd added the hut where they'd spent the week before he'd gone to the Print House. Their last as simply two people, lost in each other. "It's worth remembering," he told her.

She almost smiled. "That it is." Then sobered. "A xenologist should have reviewed those recordings from the start."

To be fair, it hadn't been a science then. "You found something."

Rena turned to look out over the ocean. He went to stand beside her, resisting the impulse to put his arm around her waist; they weren't here, and the past was what it was. "I've—ideas," she began slowly. "I searched for words that, in us, reflect our biology and evolution. Reproduction." With a sidelong glance.

"And?"

"*Cherish. Binds. Health. Establish us.* To me, taken together, they suggest something other than intelligence-driven purpose. They suggest a major life cycle event. Where one of a kind is cherished over all others. Where all are bound to a goal to ensure the future, the health, of their kind. That to succeed, a particular place must be established as theirs, with a specific condition satisfied." Rena hugged herself as if cold, yet he'd imagined summer—

"The Portal—"

She shook her head. "The dens are how kmeth survive an unnatural-to-them environment. The place the Kmet have fixated on must be New Earth."

"The specific condition—" He paused, staring at his friend's face in profile, able to read the tension in her jaw. "It's what we're doing. Getting every Human there. Why? For what?"

Rena tipped back her head, letting out a breath, then met his gaze. "I think the answer's inside another word the Kmet love to use, Henry. Duality. And while it implies we're essential—maybe indispensable—to whatever's coming in kmeth's lives, it doesn't promise we survive it." She forced a rueful smile. "Or that we won't play a willing, happy part. It's just—there are too many real-life variations for me to give you more. Sex gets messy. Reproduction, costly. If that's what this is about . . ." She looked to the ocean.

Not real, the shiver fingering Henry's spine, yet no less potent. "I can't stop now. Kmet-Here won't let me. And—what about the Divider? Do you think it's a lie, to get our cooperation?"

"No. I'm—" She pursed her lips, then shook her head emphatically. "No. Kmeth's reaction when the name comes up is too profound and immediate. That said, if this is about the Kmet's life cycle, *Divider* might refer to any threat to its consummation."

"Such as a second spacefaring species. One that doesn't want the Kmet to consummate—" His imagination boggled, Henry stumbled on, "whatever it is—and really is attacking any Humans it finds as, what, a vulnerability of the Kmet?" He needed to get this down on paper. With color coding—

"Don't speculate too far, Henry. I could be completely wrong," Rena cautioned. "Shomchai'd be the first to remind us my field's goo, not words."

She wasn't wrong. It fit everything together, from the Kmet's refusal to reveal anything about kmethselves, to kmeth's participation—or was it instigation?—in this mission. To save humanity—or doom it?

His job to find out.

Henry reached for her hand. Watched his fingers pass through hers. Looked up into her eyes, seeing what didn't belong there. *Self-doubt.* "What is it you always tell me?" he asked lightly, waving to the ocean. "Usually when we're somewhere like this."

The sparkle returned. "It's always biology?"

"That's it." He turned serious. "Which is why it took you, Rena m'Attenborough t'Wang, the most brilliant mind on or off New Earth, to produce a breakthrough in understanding the Kmet when I was getting nowhere and desperately needed it. Thank you. We all owe you a debt."

She pretended to touch his cheek. "And I think, Arbiter Henry m'Yama t'Nowak, the very best of us, we'll be owing you." Her eyes glistened. "Get it done, Henry. Come home. Walk with me on this beach. Promise?"

He shouldn't. Most likely couldn't. But his oldest, dearest friend asked for hope, and didn't he need some?

"I promise."

<Really think they'll eat him?>

<FIRST you smack a Kmet. Then tell off the experts. Proud of you, Killie-Cat.>

Killian gave her oneiric a thumbs-up, though she hadn't said anything Henry and his quorum didn't already know. *Might not have wanted to admit it.*

She stretched, feeling a good tired. A long shift, but she wasn't about to quit her post to explore the Portal's guts or sleep, not while in orbit around a strange, new planet, reading the incoming sat feeds.

Her fourth. *Who'd have seen* that *coming?*

Yesterday's simul-pop had barely registered on her senses, more because Killian'd double-dosed than her physiology adapting. Epitomes expired, too long out of the can. The signs were on both of them. Good thing she shaved her head—Henry's hair was thinning on top, not that she'd tell him today.

He'd returned from World III looking like Gis the day she lost her feet. Ordered the *Cape Sable* home, gave her the coordinates for their next stop, then went to sit against a wall.

Kmet-Here's willy-bits had positively glowed with satisfaction.

First look at World IV, with its harsh barren land masses and stained sky, she'd been ready to agree with the Kmet and send them to the next. But Henry'd roused himself to quietly order the sats launched.

The only good part had been listening to Kmet-Here's frustrated slap, slap, slap back into kmeth's hideyhole. *Sulking.*

<Really think they'll eat him?>

Killian wagged her finger to shut Gis up.

It wasn't because she felt it was safe for Henry to go.

<Henry, don't—>

<I'M here.>

Rena rode with him, seeing through his eyes. Ready to pull him from his epitome, back to his existent-self on New Earth, and for the first time Henry feared she might have to do just that. *Cannibals?* He shuddered.

"Henry?"

He gave the shoulder strap a little tug. "Nerves, that's all, Flip."

"I understand. This is not a good place for your kind."

Unusual, for the polymorph to offer such a strong judgment. "Why?"

"Killian's survey has yet to identify a single portion of this world where Humans could live in comfort, Henry. I fail to understand why any would choose to come here."

Watching the austere rocky landscape through the floor window, Henry was tempted to agree. "They didn't come for comfort, Flip," he pointed out.

Ousmane had briefed them. World IV's surface held a remarkable abundance of rare and valuable minerals, close to the surface and accessible. From ship records, the majority of the *Kitchener*'s complement had extraterrestrial mining experience. Pre-Kmet.

Thinking of them, he went on, almost to himself. "They came because they believed in themselves. Planned to work hard and thrive here."

Only to have the very land they coveted destroy any chance of that.

"They were brave—" the polymorph said charitably, "—to come without FLIPs to assist them."

The phrasing took him aback. Did *his* FLIP consider altself the source of Henry's courage?

Not that he'd much to spare at the moment. Kmet life cycles. *Now cannibals.*

"Glad you're with me, Flip," Henry admitted.

"Be assured I would not let you take such great risk without me, Henry."

Not a comforting answer.

***

The shuttle—still a flying saucer at every possible opportunity—settled to the ground as lightly as a feather.

Abruptly lurched back and forth. Henry grabbed both straps. "What was that?"

"Minor seismic activity is to be expected, Henry. Do not be alarmed. My landing struts will compensate."

Cannibals and *quakes.* Unexpectedly, he found himself chuckling. "Lively place." Invigorated, Henry unstrapped and stood.

A shelf eased out from the wall nearest him; on it was a deflated breathing collar. He eyed it rebelliously. "You said the air was fine."

"The altitude is not, Henry. Your physiology is unaccustomed to these conditions. Thin. Dry. Breathing without assistance will be strenuous."

The thing would swell up and spew mist as well as air. "I'll keep it handy." Rolling up the collar, Henry tucked it inside his coat. The garment was of Flip stuff, reaching to his ankles and styled to appear dark brown leather, as were thick boots he wore to protect his feet from the terrain.

No streets here.

He patted his chest pocket, feeling the Arbiter's badge. Reached down, under the coat, to pull a tool he knew from the farm from its loop on his belt.

It looked like a small wood-handled pickaxe, with a forged metal head showing wear. Another fabrication. Fully functional but—Henry hefted it, frowning. *Too light.* Worse, it looked like a weapon. "Ousmane, you sure about this?"

<I am not, ah, Henry. I infer a possible, ah, value. As I said, the *Kitchener*'s cargo, ah, manifest allotted a similar pickaxe to, ah, every passenger, to be claimed upon, ah, landing.>

He slipped it away again. "Ready as I can be. Open the door, Flip."

Accompanied by a puff of warm, moist air that froze into sparkles around him, Henry went down the ladder Flip provided, not stopping until his boots were on the ground.

A new world. He made himself pause to take in the sheer wonder of the moment, a feeling he'd been afraid he'd left on World III.

He inhaled and coughed, the air every bit as dry as Flip warned and with an acrid, metallic taste on his tongue.

IF YOU EXPERIENCE DIZZINESS, HENRY, PLEASE USE THE COLLAR AT ONCE.

Fussing. But with cause. Henry waited, breathing slowly, until the urge to cough passed.

Only then did he take in his surroundings.

His view of the other ridges was blocked by the scarp of this one, but it was magnificent. The midmorning sunlight revealed bent and folded layers of rock, and there were patches of light material, some sticking out, forming—

<Fossil beds!> Rena exclaimed.

—distinct areas. "I'll try to get you some," Henry offered, very quietly, not that he'd a right or reason to, but even he was impressed by the quantity in reach. And, come to think of it, underfoot. He looked ahead. "People first."

They'd argued how close Flip should land, whether in sight of the village or not; the deciding factor had been how far Henry could walk on his own.

Might have overestimated.

The ground rose in wide step-like tiers. By the time he reached the last, level with the village, Henry had to pause beside the first skull post, his limbs shaking, to catch his breath. He almost pulled out the collar.

Didn't. This was the air the people he wanted to meet had breathed all their lives. Yes, they'd be better at it, but he wasn't planning to race them.

Only talk. Steadier, Henry walked forward, looking for a door bordered by giant bones.

The silence, the stillness, the sealed doors. Glimpses of bone between rock, the skulls mounted overhead. He passed between the mounds, their roofs no taller than his arm if he stretched up his hand, no longer wary or afraid.

All around him was patience. A terrible, endless patience, like the masses of rock spilling like rivers everywhere but between the mounds.

TURN LEFT AT THE NEXT GAP, HENRY.

He slowed first, lingered to study the plate jammed into a doorway. It seemed—

—something flickered in the small gaps around it. Poked a claw out. Pulled it in. Cackled and fluttered and Henry almost laughed at the sight of a beady eye. "Chickens. It's a chicken coop."

Everything took on a different shape, a vastly more normal one. Including the smell, this close. "Flip, please compare the heat signature of this mound with the others'. I'll wait."

<Henry, what are they feeding the birds?>

As Killian would say, hopefully not people. "Good question. Flip?"

ONLY THE MOUND WITH THE BONES, YOUR DESTINATION, HAS A DIFFERENT SIGNATURE, HENRY. I CONCLUDE THE OTHERS CONTAIN POULTRY.

With clear chagrin, the polymorph caught being less than thorough.

"It's all right," Henry said absently, leaving the coop. "Now we know where to go."

The fossil bones were incredible. Henry stared at them from every angle he could for Rena, not that she wouldn't get Flip's visual and audio record, but there was, he admitted, something arresting about a bone thicker and taller than his entire body.

From something extinct, he reassured himself. Now, for those who weren't.

The door between the bones was another scavenged metal plate, but the center had been hammered to emboss a crude shape. Henry didn't have to pull out his pickaxe to compare; it showed the same tool.

They hadn't discussed how to get through the door, leaving that to him. Seeing the tool, the bones—the chickens—

Aha! Henry began to cluck softly, the sound his grandfather had taught him to use when entering a coop, to reassure the birds.

An alarmed <What are you doing?> burst from Shomchai, silent till now.

Henry kept clucking.

The tip of a pick appeared near the top of the door, worked into a worn notch. A second, halfway down. Together, they pried the door aside by a narrow crack. Eyes filled the shadowed opening, three pairs, all Human, stacked as if they'd climbed on each other's backs to observe him.

Or two were children. Henry, still clucking, crouched to make himself smaller. Drew out the bag with his badge. Shook the badge into his hand and held it to show them.

The eyes widened then disappeared, the door slamming shut.

Henry stopped clucking and stood, the badge flat on the palm of his hand aimed at the door, face set to peaceful; prepared to wait. His Flip-coat was warm, the boots as well, and if he could endure kmeth's stench, he would what filtered through gaps in the rock wall, though he'd like to know what was mixed in with the odors of stale, sweaty Human.

It wasn't chicken.

The gaps were partially stopped up by bones that weren't fossils and Henry glanced fleetingly at them, judging it more important to watch the door.

But they drew his eye back, like words of a story caught in passing, out of context and troubling. Here a fingertip. There a hip. Bodies disassembled. Jumbled.

Or were they remains, placed with careful purpose? Unable to tell, he stopped trying and looked to the door.

In his distraction, the picks perhaps wielded by more experienced or stronger hands, it had opened again. Wide enough for him to pass through into the dark, if he turned sideways.

An invitation.

HENRY, HAVE THEM COME OUT TO YOU.

<Henry—don't—>

With a slight bow, the Arbiter accepted.

Catch more it was.

TO pass the time—and, though she wasn't about to admit it, to keep from thinking about Henry turning on a spit—Killian trapped PIPs.

She'd gotten better at it. Good thing. Within a day, her first capture had solidified into a flat unresponsive disc in her bag. A disc, moreover, the tubes no longer responded to, curtailing her roaming; she'd no desire to be trapped in the bowels of the Portal. *Imagine explaining* that *to Kmet-Here.*

Gis had consulted. Meaning her partner grabbed beers with some other pilots and pumped them for ideas. Consensus? Figure out how to feed a PIP, everyone believing she'd starved hers solid—*might have*—or catch more.

Catch more it was. While Kmet-Here was denned and oblivious, initially she'd worried the other PIPs would notice. Seemed they didn't. A PIP vanished, sealed into a bag; another soon popped from a tube to take its place. She'd two in bags at her feet already.

The trick, Killian thought, squinting at her latest target from behind a pedestal, *was getting the damn things to climb in her bag after the bait.*

This PIP, sponge tips on extruded arms, ambled along the floor, polishing tiny circles as it went. The ball of her thumb covered the area polished each time it stopped, but it would keep working until another PIP took over the work, then go—

—where? There were dozens of PIPs, of varied shapes, in motion at a given moment. They popped from any tube mouth in no order she'd detected, bringing their bits to add to the den, then taking on other tasks. Killian eyed a particular tube mouth near the den, one of the few that stayed put. By her estimate, most left Control by the same exit, via that tube.

Portal PIPs weren't like Flip or the polymorphs on New Earth. They were pure Kmet-tech, as mysterious to Humans as the Portal itself.

If that tube led to where PIPs recharged, or whatever they did to keep energized, and she followed? Humans needed to know.

First, catch her next key.

“I will.”

HANDS took hold of Henry’s arm, his leg, his foot. Blinded by the utter dark inside the mound, he didn’t resist. They were guiding him.

His right foot was drawn down to a step, then his left. Again, now with hands holding his waist and hips to steady him. Protective. Careful of him.

His thoughts raced. The eyes hadn’t been children’s—not necessarily. They could have been adults standing at different levels to look out at him. *How many hands?* He’d lost count, or never had it. Heard the door being replaced above him.

Fought an instant’s panic, trapped with strangers he couldn’t see. Was grateful for the silence of the friends in his head, prudently letting him concentrate on the here and now.

The hands left him. Bereft of his guides, Henry froze in place, imagining he stood next to an unseen pit.

Nor did he want to step on toes, feeling breath warm his cheeks from either side.

After what felt an age, more likely a minute, fingertips found his right hand, danced lightly over his knuckles. Guessing what they wanted, Henry raised his hand and opened it, badge on his palm.

Felt the fingertips explore it, as if these people used touch over any other sense.

A faint whisper in his head, Rena echoing his own thought. <Are they blind?>

Then Henry squinted as a tiny flame appeared next to his hand, lighting the badge, glinting in the eyes of those intent on it.

People. He couldn’t see more than vague shapes. Couldn’t count them, for some stood behind and some were higher, as if on a ledge, but they weren’t many.

Becoming less, he realized with a rush of pity, remembering the bones carefully tucked into their walls. Family, kept close. A death watch.

There was only one thing to say to them, so he did. “I’ve come to take you home.”

The flame went out, the hands returned—a swarm now, a pressure. Touching him. His face and hair. Everywhere but the badge he held out, as if that were precious, and Henry endured it without moving, for the touches were gentle, even respectful.

Yet so many at once—he staggered.

Every hand left but one, a strong support under his arm.

The silence was broken by faint, passionate whispering, as if all of them spoke at once. Henry strained to decipher an accent he suddenly realized wasn't one. The *Kitchener*'s descendants spoke the lingua of Origin Earth—taught on his, yes, but in daily use blurred and mutated. *He'd last heard it like this watching one of Flip's choices from the Archive.*

Now he could catch fragments. "The Word Comes." "He speaks the Holy." "Do you hear?" "Can it be?" "The Promise Made. It is the Promise Made." "The Promise . . . the Promise . . ."

"Hush," this from next to him, still a whisper, yet every voice stopped. "Light the home. Welcome the Arbiter."

Flames flared into life, from torches held in hands, from torches set into the walls. Henry blinked, impatient for his eyes to adapt, eager to see these people.

Seeing him, they bowed.

***

Henry'd been guided down steps because this portion of the mound was below ground level, and, yes, he discovered a pit near where he stood, or rather a well, surrounded by a neat ring of rock, with a pulley and bucket system. The rest of the floor around him was bare rock, soot-blackened and stained.

The people lived elsewhere. Above his eye level, a solid shelf hugged two-thirds of the curved wall of the mound, reached by a retractable ladder of cable and pipe they lowered for him, and he burned to know why. Rena'd suggested the arrangement protected them—and presumably the chickens, if their mounds were similarly built—from a predator come through the door. Or, Shomchai had offered, from flash floods.

Rows and rows of crossed pickaxes lined the walls, wired to the rock, a grim tally of loss as well as protection for those here. The arrangement would help prevent rock from falling from the walls in a quake. Wouldn't save the roof. Henry glanced up worriedly, relieved to see this mound had a metal one. *Was it why they'd retreated to it?*

The person who'd greeted him by name stood holding the end of the ladder. Henry thought it was, but the people revealed by torchlight remained mysterious. They wore patched-together garments of plastic sheeting, bits of foil, and wrinkly tanned skins, secured to limbs and torsos by wraps of wire. Their ship continued to provide some of the necessities of life.

The skins, Henry didn't examine too closely, hoping they were from chickens, determined not to judge if they weren't. These people hadn't survived by wasting any resource, perhaps even their dead.

He climbed up, trying not to be obvious as he counted those here. Fourteen. Age eluded him. They were similar in height, emaciated beyond what he'd ever witnessed, bone and cartilage showing beneath the skin of hands, necks, and faces. The soles of their feet were thickly calloused. They'd rubbed a pale gray powder into both skin and hair, the latter long and twisted into ropey locks. Four had beards past their waists, the only feature suggesting biological gender, and the lack of children hurt his heart.

"Arbiter, welcome." Hands urged him into a pile of what anywhere else Henry would have thought garbage and here must be a vital source of warmth. A privilege granted an honored guest, and he made himself comfortable, expressing his appreciation with a smile shyly returned by one, then two, then more. They sat in close proximity, some in each other's laps, some with fingers interlaced or feet together, where they could see him. Was the torchlight for him? Did they usually sit in the dark, comforted only by touch?

They'd fit inside Flip, every one of them. He was about to make that impulsive offer when someone left those sitting to stand before him and bow. Arms swept to include those gathered. "We are the Tailings." The voice who'd greeted him. A leader, or spokesperson.

<In mining,> Shomchai told him, <it refers to what's left after valuable minerals are extracted. They might believe their situation is deserved.>

No one deserved this. His reaction, not theirs, and he took the linguist's caution. "Hello. I'm Henry. The Arbiter." The title produced a ripple of excitement and he held up the badge. "I have come to take you home. To New Earth." A test, that name; when no one reacted, Henry filed that information as well.

The speaker had bloodshot eyes, green between gray-tinged lids. Now their gaze sharpened. "Is this your Holy Promise?"

More stirring. A gasp.

"It is." Henry took a moment to meet each pair of eyes in turn, then came back to the speaker. "I swear to take you home. All of you."

"This is the all of us," stated with pride. "Will you, Henry who is the Arbiter, come with us now and give your Holy Promise to our Mother, that She release us to your care?"

<Henry . . .>

"I will," he said.

There being no other choice.

"Roger that."

<PSST. Killie-Cat. While you wait for Henry, Gerry wants you to look at the PIPs under the left screen some more.>

Killian yanked out her notepad and wrote, *Who the fuck is Gerry?* Stabbed that gone, wrote, *Don't you lie to me.* Underlined it twice, so hard she scratched the screen.

<Gerry m'Akintude t'Farraway.> Sweet and reasonable. <The engineer. I told you we'd resources—why you getting bent?>

Gis damn well knew. If this Gerry wanted a look, he was *in* Giselle's head and there was only one way to hijack an oneiric. You hardwired in, that's what you did, and it was illegal for every reason there was, starting with burning through brains. *You wired to this engineer?* Killian wrote, then covered the pad with her hand.

She didn't want to know, was the truth.

Did, didn't she. Giselle would do anything in the cause of getting Humans back to space. What better way than secret intel about Portals to do it? She'd have jumped on this Gerry to wire in and stow away in her mind.

There it was. The pain, so deep Killian found it hard to breathe. And it wasn't betrayal—she hoped to be better than that, to love her partner enough—it was the exceptionally good chance she'd never see Gis again. Not whole. Not as she should be. Ever.

<Killian.>

She wiped her eyes with the back of the hand holding the pad. Erased what she wrote. Started again.

What part of the panel does the engineer want to see first?

Promising herself, the instant she climbed out of her can, she'd track down the spacers who'd been supposed to look after Gis, and introduce them to real vacuum.

***

Engineer Gerry's directive, to stare at a pair of busy PIPs doing whatever the hell they were—as if a Human could decipher it by *looking*—ended with a call from the surface.

"Portal Pilot, this is the Arbiter's shuttle."

She'd never been so relieved to hear a non-Human voice. Killian clamped her hand over the wristband to wake Gis, trusting Gerry to take a cue and unplug. *Don't think about it.* "Go ahead, shuttle."

"The Arbiter has left his meeting and is moving away. Do you have a satellite available?"

Flip's remotes noticed by the locals and alt wanting eyes on a wandering Henry—Killian got that. "Tasking one now," she replied, fingers flying over the controls. "It'll take—there you go." The polymorph had known there'd be one about to come overhead. "Sending the feed."

Clever Flip. Alt could have grabbed the feed on alts own. Getting formal to ask was alts way of telling her they'd a *situation.*

Henry. Cannibals. *Where was the surprise in that?*

She put the village on the center screen. Upped the magnification as far as worked—and saw at once what had Flip on edge. A group walking between those skull-topped poles, heading for the rock pile covering the *Kitchener*, and no missing the Arbiter in his fancy coat and boots, right in their midst. *Was he about to be eaten after all?*

"Anything else I can do for you?" she asked. *For Henry.*

"I would appreciate your interpretation of what is being said on the surface, Pilot."

"Roger that." Killian shot a look at the den. Lowered her voice. "Send to my personal com, shuttle."

Kmeth came out and complained, she'd sic Henry on him.

Assuming he wasn't eaten.

"What hurt you?"

BEFORE leaving the mound, the Tailings powdered Henry like themselves, using bags of a talc-like substance he'd leave for Flip to analyze, plugging his ears and nostrils with their fingertips. He'd hastily closed his mouth and eyes, been warned to wait until told to open them, and did so, sitting stoically, with no option but trust.

When the application ceased, a damp cloth brushed his eyelids and lips, cleaning the corners as if whatever they'd put on his skin mustn't enter his body.

Whatever it was. Ousmane thought it part of a ceremony and was taking copious notes. Rena reminded him of the locals' fear of Flip's insect-like remotes and thought it protection against something present in their environment. Regardless, it was important to these people and, Henry hoped, a mark of acceptance.

At a soft murmur, he opened his eyes and smiled, cautious how he moved his lips, feeling powder crack around them. "Thank you."

"Now we will go to our Mother." The speaker raised a hand and every torch was extinguished, plunging the interior into darkness once more.

Hands took hold, guided Henry to the ladder. Held him securely until he'd his feet and hands in place. Face close to the rocks, hanging on, he couldn't see a thing—

—then did. A faint green glow pulsed between the rocks supporting the ledge. He recoiled, barely keeping his grip. "What makes that light?"

"The gut of a creeper beast," someone told him. "We grow plants in it."

Another volunteered, "It turns our wastes into food for our birds. And us, at the end."

Leaving cleaned bones behind. Henry shuddered and climbed down hurriedly, glad when his feet touched the floor and he could step back.

A hand took his elbow, possibly saving him from the well. The Speaker's voice, "This came from the last beast we have seen in over a year. Soon it will die, our birds starve, and so will we," with chilling acceptance.

Henry swallowed the promises trying to come out, the reassurances. The Tailings weren't in despair, they were desperate. Only his actions mattered.

Silent as they were, he waited with them as a pair pried open the door and looked out the crack. He'd have asked what they feared, but he found he didn't want to know, not really.

Instead, he prepared himself to speak to whoever, whatever, they called *Mother.*

***

An impoverished environment didn't make his hosts weak or slow. With him in their midst, the Tailings moved at a brisk pace, pickaxes in hand. Henry kept up at first, but as their path tilted up to the great pile of rock encasing the *Kitchener,* his breaths came faster and harder, drying his mouth and failing to satisfy his straining lungs. Heart hammering, head pounding, he came to an abrupt stop and bent over, hands on his knees, fighting a wave of nausea.

THE RESPIRATOR, HENRY. USE IT NOW.

Henry fumbled out the collar and wrapped it around his neck, aware the others had stopped with him, silent and watching.

Once in place, the collar expanded, jutting past his jaw. The thing was undignified and represented technology foreign, perhaps alarming, to these people; with the first whiff of warm, moist, rich air, Henry didn't care. Three slow, wonderful breaths and he could straighten, feeling his head no longer spin. "I'm not used to your air," he admitted to them. "This will help me keep up with you."

"It is remembered. The first Tailings needed help to breathe," a bearded individual told him, green eyes gleaming with interest. "We do not."

<They'd a suite of modifications for this environment, Henry. Survivors were those with the most useful adaptations, but it reduced the gene pool.> Rena, deliberately dispassionate. <Note how similar they are.>

Outside in stark, revealing sunshine, Henry saw what Rena meant. The fourteen were amazingly alike, from eye color to the shape of their noses.

Except for the scars. There was no expanse of skin free of healed wounds, no pattern to the damage. Three had lost an eye. Several had scars distorting their mouths. The torchlight, their physical condition, and yes, his own mostly scattered observations had hidden the truth.

These people fought—*what?*

When they started walking again, he asked the nearest, "What hurt you?"

Hands rose to cheeks. Eyes stared at him. Sudden comprehension. "You have never hunted a creeper."

Henry shook his head. "I have not. Is that what—?" He pointed to his left eye; that of his companion drooped down, lid distorted.

"Yes. It takes all of us to pull the beast from its lair. When we do, it spits out its gut to defend itself and flees, but that is what we need. We must gather it quickly. Carry it. It takes all our hands." Hands held for the Arbiter's inspection. They were a mass of similar scars. Four fingers lacked tips. "The gut is full of sharp hooks. The powder counters their poison." A note of deserved pride. "I have been in three hunts." A less happy look. "I do not believe I will see a fourth."

Chilled, Henry didn't know what to say. He kept walking. The opening to the pile was straight ahead. It looked unsettlingly like a gaping black mouth.

Or a tunnel ready to collapse in the next tremor. *Really didn't matter which.*

HENRY, I HAVE ADDED KILLIAN TO YOUR COM FEED WITH ME.

Clever Flip. Relief flooded the Arbiter, as if the so-capable pilot perched on his shoulder instead of above the atmosphere.

He was still on his own, an awareness growing as the Tailings who'd led the way stepped to the side to let him enter first.

". . . doing fine . . ."

"PILOT Killian, your thoughts?"

Killian leaned on her elbows, com between her hands, eyes riveted on the feed from the sat over Henry's location. What she thought? *Wouldn't catch her with fucking skeleton people, let alone go with them into a fucking cave.*

"I think he's doing fine, Flip."

Her next thought she kept to herself as well. That she'd give anything to be down there, right now, preferably with something more powerful than a stun field.

Would probably mess his play. Henry had his wits and words. Her lips twisted. *Probably should worry about the people.*

They let Henry go first. He disappeared, the others followed, and there was nothing to gain staring at what swallowed them.

The pilot turned and sank down, sitting on the dais. Listened. Heard footsteps. Henry's breathing. Steady and even. *Man who faced down a Kmet wasn't going to panic in a tunnel.* Heard him ask, crazy calm, "Will there be light soon?"

Closed her eyes, to share the dark.

“Prove who you are.”

“FIRST, we must enter Her.”

Hardly comforting words. After guiding him around a sharp turn that cut off the last light from outside, the hands fell away, leaving Henry to walk on his own.

Worse and worse. The dark gained a palpable presence, thick with ghosts with skulls on poles and bones in walls and bodies fed to alien guts to nourish the few behind him. Who’d be ghosts themselves soon enough, with no one to care for their bones—

Was that why he was here?

Henry reined in his imagination. The floor was smooth, worn by generations of feet, meaning the Tailings routinely came and went this way. They weren’t being cruel. They couldn’t grasp how terrifying walking blind into the unknown was to someone like him. This was their home.

He walked with a hand out, for fear of running into a wall, but didn’t crouch. Was grateful for the respirator as the air became metallic and stale. Had soundlessly counted to thirty-three when his boot landed on what wasn’t packed dirt and rock, sending up a sullen, metallic echo, and Henry knew where he was.

Inside the buried sleeper ship. The Kitchener.

Fourteen voices spoke as one, low and respectful, intoning, “Mother, we have come.”

In answer, lights flickered, steadied, stayed on to dispel ghosts.

Dim lights. Scattered. Revealing a different corpse.

It had been a ship. Generations had scavenged what they could, leaving little more than a skeleton of struts and cable, of metal too thick to cut or carry, as far as Henry could see.

The historian whispered in his head, <She was built, ah, as a resource for her passengers. To disassemble once they, ah, awoke. This much integrity—it means the ship successfully, ah, compensated for the landslide. The ceiling! Look at the ceiling, Henry.”

He looked up. The ship's structure overhead appeared intact; on his own, he'd have assumed those scavenging hadn't been able to reach it.

<She protects them, ah, even now,> Ousmane said with a mix of triumph and grief. <A true mother.>

The Tailings streamed past Henry, confident in this, their most sacred place, expecting him to follow.

So he did.

Ousmane, seeing through his eyes, gave him what she could. <The ship must have, ah, been buried before, ah, the core could be jettisoned. Someone, ah, knew to tap power for lighting. Maybe doors. Maybe more.> She didn't elaborate, perhaps reluctant to ask him to search for what *more* might be.

No one could provide him with a map for what the *Kitchener* had become. *A mistake not to tuck one of Flip's bees in a pocket.* They passed through a series of corridors and room-sized cavities—walled in rock, roofed and floored by ship—and he lost his bearings. If they abandoned him here, he'd never get out.

There seemed no fear of that. Every few steps a Tailing would turn to check on him, another reach back a hand, as if wanting to touch him for reassurance or offer it, but here, for some reason, forbidden to do so. It wasn't just him, Henry noticed. This people, who'd caressed and held each other in the mound, kept their hands at their sides and distanced themselves.

Shomchai noticed as well. <Each comes alone to a place of judgment. I think that's what this is, Henry. You're to be judged.>

<By what?> Rena sounded alarmed.

The answer lay ahead—*You're to be judged.*

Henry's composure threatened to fracture like the panels of the ship. He focused on the garment of the Tailing in front of him. Made himself look for similar sheets of plastic film in his surroundings. Found none, this portion of the ship thoroughly stripped of moveable materials, but the distraction helped. Thinking of the past, of what the Tailings had endured, helped.

The passengers staggering from this ship, waking to what had to seem the end of all hope, had nonetheless torn a legacy from the rock around them with axes and bare hands. They'd proven their worth, over and over.

Up to him to prove his.

***

Their destination was a chamber wide enough to house a hundred times their number, lit with a double ring of lights. Dim, those lights, brightening at irregular moments. What fed them appeared close to failing.

Not a good thought. Henry studied their surroundings, giving Ousmane as much as he could. There were no furnishings, but the walls had been left as they were, unscavenged. In fact, in places they'd been reinforced with material from elsewhere in the ship.

<This would have been, ah, where the passengers gathered, ah, before being taken to their pods. There should be—there, Henry.> As his gaze crossed a wide, unlit opening. <That doorway leads, ah, to where they slept.>

"Arbiter." The Tailing's speaker beckoned. "Approach our Mother. Tell her your words. Prove who you are."

They'd formed a circle around the centermost spot of the chamber, separated by an arm's length, pickaxes out and held ominously on shoulders. As Henry walked forward, two moved aside to grant him entry. They stepped back, closing him in. He looked to the speaker.

Who called out, loud and sure, "Mother See Us!"

With the words, the fourteen raised their pickaxes and slammed the points into the floor. The sound was deafening. The purpose—clear, once Henry saw the circle of dents left in the floor. Looked beyond to see larger and larger ones. They'd come here, done this, to record who was left. Time after time. Fewer and fewer. It was tragic.

And incredible. Henry brought out his pickaxe and went to the middle, thought of the farm, and straightened his shoulders.

Brought down the point with all his strength, to mark the end.

HENRY! HENRY!

"I too am seen," he said, as much to calm Flip as Killian, also listening, because whatever they'd infer from the hammering wouldn't be good. Then, answering to impulse, Henry dropped his pickaxe and pulled out his badge. "Hear my words. I am the Arbiter. I have come to take you home."

"Arbiter. Keyword Accepted."

Henry didn't know who was more startled as the words filled the room, the Tailings obviously never having heard their Mother respond.

The lighting grew in intensity, changed color to a soft blue, became a projection on the floor.

The Arbiter's Seal.

Seizing the moment, Henry stepped into the projection and raised his hand with the badge. "It's time to go. Come with me."

"What about our chickens?" someone cried.

Thinking of his grandfather, Henry had to smile. "Them, too."

"I'm good."

"HUMANS-THERE must not enter the Portal!"

What the—Killian jumped, fumbling her com. Whirled to find herself nose to snout with the Kmet. No way she'd been that focused on Henry, to miss Kmet-Here leave the den and approach. *When had something* that *big developed the sneaks?*

As for what had the Kmet upset, well, that *was* Henry, or rather his success with the cannibals. Who hadn't eaten him after all.

"They aren't entering," she retorted, blood running cold. "The evacuees are in the Arbiter's shuttle, waiting to transfer to the *Cape Forchu*—" Once Omar sent the freighter through—

BOOM!! "NO! They must not be in what touches the Portal!" The willy-bits were bright red and waving; not a happy Kmet.

Why? "The Arbiter got everyone up in a single trip and his shuttle's pulled away. We're close to done—"

BOOM!! "Not everyone! Not done!"

Obstinate lump of—about to say she didn't understand, which would have shown admirable restraint on her part when what she wanted to do was kick it somewhere soft, assuming she found the spot—Killian suddenly thought of the mining PIPs. Kmet-Here's spies on the ground. "What do you know?" she demanded.

"Is there a problem, Kmet-Here? Pilot?"

An eye rolled wildly in its socket to aim at the Arbiter, climbing from a tube mouth. The rest of Kmet-Here spun around to confront Henry. "You bring Humans-There here! I protest! This was not agreed!"

"I concur." Henry's face and hands were smeared with what looked like ash, a deflated respirator hung limp around his neck, and PIPs followed behind to suck the dust falling from his coat, yet there was no denying the power shift in Control with his arrival. Killian stifled a grin as Kmet-Here hesitated.

"My shuttle dropped me off and withdrew, as per the Duality, with those not invited aboard the Portal." Henry aimed an open hand at the wall of controls.

Closed the fingers. "You're well aware it's moved to a safe distance, ready to dock with the transport I believe Killian has arranged." He glanced her way.

Cued, she stepped smartly up to the dais. "Omar, ready to receive."

Kmet-Here rocked back and forth on kmeth's flippers. "What of those still on the planet?"

Skulls on poles, Killian thought. The ship. Kmet didn't care about alive or dead, tech or flesh. She turned to look at the Arbiter. Caught the grief that flashed across his face, brief and powerful. *Deliberate.* She braced herself, not sure for what, only that he wanted her prepared.

"The Tailings asked me to ensure their ancestors would remain with their Mother," the Arbiter said, his tone grim. "I agreed. They stay."

"NO! I do not concur." The purple developed red patches. "There can be no Humans-There. Nothing of Human-There left for the Divider to find!"

"I won't break my word to these people." Henry's voice turned harsh, his face stark beneath its coating, and it wasn't anger he projected, it was a dreadful certainty. "No more pretense. No more clocks. You intend to destroy this planet's surface, like you did the others, Kmet-Here, and I say you will do exactly that once the evacuees have transited through to New Earth orbit. Burn their ship and every scrap of bone where they are, as they are, with respect. Leave nothing to find. Do you concur." It wasn't a question.

Henry knew the stakes. *Why take a stand now, for this?* Killian held her breath, cursing inwardly.

Willy-bits turned an amenable mauve. Tongue-tips casually explored the corners of hard wide lips, then snapped back inside the mouth. "I concur." A shockingly deep rumble suggested amusement. "You are not like other Humans, Arbiter-Henry."

What the hell did that mean?

"Oh, I think you'll find I am, Kmet-Here," Henry replied, with his faint, disarming smile.

Challenge offered and accepted. *Over bones.* Killian wanted to knock their heads together. Changed her mind. If the Kmet was noticing Henry, well, looked to her as if Henry'd already learned something new about kmeth, and that had to be good. *Didn't it?*

The com interrupted. "Pilot Killian, transiting *Cape Forchu* in three. They want me to confirm the chickens."

Killian looked at Henry.

He grinned back.

***

<Chickens? You juicing, Killie-Cat?>

"Nope." The pilot leaned back on her pillows. "Henry brought them up with the evacuees. After quarantine, the people can have them back." *What had the Arbiter said?* "The birds qualify as of Earth."

<Man's lost it. Sincerely lost it.>

She hadn't told Gis the rest. Likely wouldn't, till they were together again, alone for real. How the screens had filled with images of a burning world, how Henry stayed to watch, mercifully sending her to catch a rest before they simul-popped to the next planet.

How she couldn't shake the look on Henry's face. The way he'd forced the Kmet to admit what kmeth wouldn't have, ever. *No more clocks.* Clever, that.

Unless it shaved the time they had to save people. Unless Kmet-Here *liked* Henry's little workaround of *just burn it all, why don't you*—

<Killie-Cat?>

<Gerry there?>

Was that hesitation? <Told him to unplug and give us time. I'm worried about you.>

"I'm good," Killian answered. Lies being easier apart.

"They are the same."

HENRY'S memories of fire held beauty. Comfort. Even laughter. A campfire's flame, a glowing fireplace on a damp fall night, the great cheery bonfire his grandfather lit every Arrival Day.

The fire the Kmet set inside planets would stain his nightmares. It spread like a disease, cracks opening, spilling World IV's blood in white-hot rivers and red lakes. He couldn't tear his eyes away, even as steam and ash drew their blankets over the carnage.

Suddenly the image flared with light. He flinched, despite knowing what it had to mean, prepared for it.

THE KITCHENER'S CORE HAS EXPLODED, HENRY.

Goodbye, Mother.

Kmet-Here aimed an eye his way. "What was that?"

"The sleeper ship. I explained to you how it was buried in the—"

"Yes, yes." The Kmet lurched from the pedestals to confront Henry. "You did not warn me it was intact."

Did kmeth mourn lost PIPs? "It's not now," Henry grated out. "That was why you—we did this."

"Which is good." Polyps faded to white. "We must scour all knowledge of Humans from these places, Arbiter-Henry. The Divider must not identify our Duality."

If he hadn't woken his oneirics, sparing them his vigil, they'd have jumped on the strange new phrasing. Feeling an uncomfortable tingle of his own, thinking of Rena's insights, Henry ventured a cautious, "I thought it was Humans-There we must remove. People. Not knowledge."

"They are the same." With a muted *boom* as if he'd confused the Kmet in return. "How are they not the same?"

How indeed—Henry opened his mouth to continue the conversation, only to find himself facing kmeth's sloping back as the creature resumed work, controlling the destruction below as casually as if any of this were normal.

But it was, Henry reminded himself. Mining. Refining. He'd known the Kmet did it on a planetary scale, had handled countless negotiations to add Human interests to the projects and set pricing for the results.

Not the same, being witness.

"We can go now," Kmet-Here announced. The eye found Henry again. "The recycling will continue to completion on its own."

Not the same, because he'd couldn't stop imagining it happening to New Earth, where he'd sent the survivors—where his grandfather—

Henry looked away from the Kmet, not sure what showed on his face, only that it wouldn't be wise in any sense to reveal it. "I need a shower. Clean clothing. I'm covered in—" *The dead.* Flip's analysis, that what the Tailings put on his skin wasn't an anti-toxin, but the ground bones of their families, didn't help. "—I have to write my report," he muttered nonsensically as he turned his body, desperate to find the tube mouth to take him away. To find himself.

"I'll be back with the pilot when it's time."

Henry shed his clothes on the floor. Closed the shower door and stood in the dark, feeling on the cusp of understanding. *They are the same.* This wasn't just about removing any clues to identify Earth and Humans to the Divider as vital to Kmet's purpose. There was more here. He felt it.

They'd seen the Kmet fail time after time to distinguish between objects and who made them. Mistake one Human individual for another. Ascribed it all to being alien. To a different biology.

What if the Kmet hadn't failed at all? What if *they* had, in missing something so fundamental about the other species, kmeth hadn't recognized it needed explaining?

Henry gritted his teeth in frustration. *But what?*

Knowledge. Organized information.

People. Flesh and bone.

He ran his hands over his chest, felt his ribcage expand and contract. *How were they the same?*

The skin under his fingertips, his fingers, everything about this body had been made by incorporating knowledge of his existent self into this epitome, this copy of him. In a sense, the presence of his mind, in its can on New Earth while at the same time here, in this body, blurred information and flesh—

A wave of nausea swept through him. A warning sense of disconnection. Henry groped for the tap, turned it on full, used the slam of water against his face to snap him back into this body, here and now. He'd speak to Ben, he would. Better yet, send a memo. *Epitome loses mind by thinking too much.* He laughed uncontrollably, gasping as water got in his mouth.

Stopped himself. Losing his grip on his epitomeself wouldn't put him home, it would drown him in the neural net, and he was stronger than that. Everyone said so. Tested off the chart—*had to mean something.*

Henry turned the water to a trickle, leaning his forehead on the wall. Time. Time. At best, he'd a scant few hours before Kmet-Here demanded to go. "Leaves me two more worlds to figure this out," he told himself. *But what if they were like this one, done in a day?* Or worse, empty.

He had to learn exactly what the Kmet wanted Humans for—in Rena's life cycle event, in the Duality itself—before returning this Portal to New Earth. If he failed, he'd have no leverage left, no position from which to negotiate. He'd never been more sure of anything in his life.

"Flip?"

A perky little, "Here, Henry!" from right outside the shower made his lips twitch.

"It's time Killian met this version of you."

Henry dressed, tucked PIP-Flip under his jacket—admonished to silence until told otherwise—and went in search of the pilot. Killian wasn't in their shared kitchen, so he walked through to the far hallway to face a closed door.

He knocked. Once. Again, harder. No answer.

Well, that was disheartening. Tempting, to call out her name, but Henry thought better of it and pulled out his personal com. "Killian, it's Henry. May I come in please? I've something to show you."

The *something* stuck out an appendage and waved happily. Henry shifted PIP-Flip further under his jacket.

A grumpy, "Not a good time, Henry."

"It won't take long. And I'm right here." He rapped the door with a knuckle to prove it.

"Unless this is an emergency, *sir,* I'm on break and don't have to deal with whatever it is."

Taken aback, Henry stared at the door. "Are you in your quarters?"

"Where else would I be—" Grumpy became distinct annoyance. "—When . . . Taking . . . My . . . Break—*SIR*!"

PERHAPS YOU SHOULD COME BACK WITH ME ANOTHER TIME, HENRY.

"My apologies, Pilot Killian," Henry said, ending their connection. He didn't move from the door. "Can you tell if she's inside, Flip?"

NO, HENRY. WHY? DO YOU DOUBT HER VERACITY?

What he doubted made a very long list. Until this moment, she hadn't been on it.

"Let's say it's unlike Killian to react in this manner." He ran his hand through still-damp hair, looking down the corridor as if an explanation would sprout from the white curved walls.

Maybe it did. The ever-present, if ever-shifting, tube mouths caught his attention. Three took Humans where they were allowed to go; there were many more. Killian'd appeared sincerely annoyed by the restriction. At the time, his concern had been to avoid anything liable to upset their host.

Not how he felt now.

Henry turned, put his back to the door, and slid down to sit on the floor. He patted the bulge in his jacket, watching the tube mouths.

Thinking of the System Coalition's outspoken desire to learn everything about the Portals. Of how exceptionally resourceful Killian m'Lamarr t'Brown was.

"We'll wait."

"Not a clue."

<THINK he bought it?>

"Of course he bought it," Killian declared, knowing full well Henry wasn't fooled. Didn't matter, he'd no way to know she wasn't in her quarters or where she really was. *She sure the hell didn't.*

She regretted the *sir*, Henry not deserving it and possibly still emotional about his chickens and bone people, but there'd been no faster way to push him off.

And she'd a problem.

Her latest tube had spat her out into what looked to be the same stretch of corridor she'd just left. A goes-nowhere tube wasted time she didn't have to spare, however exciting it was to their engineer stowaway—who kept interrupting Gis to give Killian directions she mostly ignored.

Except this wasn't the same place after all. Killian'd started to push her bag of PIP into another tube mouth when she'd caught a whiff of roses. Or something floral and plantish, the particulars being Gis' interest—

—the point being, roses hadn't been how their quarters smelled when she'd left, putting her somewhere else.

But where? She picked a direction to wander, following her nose, to find herself where the corridor split in two. Again familiar. As were the doors facing each other when she picked the rightmost, except these were taller and thinner than hers. Opened the same when she approached.

Stepping inside, Killian found herself in what might pass for a galley, if you ate from a communal trough and perched on a stick. The trough was empty. Crossing the room, she went out the door on the other side, striding quickly to the one corresponding to Henry's, already guessing what she'd find inside.

Being wrong. Killian covered her mouth and nose. She'd found the smell. Plants erupted from pots on the walls, trailing vines that met and tangled together in the middle of the room, punctuated by huge yellow blossoms and wrinkled black pods. Where Henry's bed would be she could just make out a bare stump with three thick, bare branches. Closer to hand, free of vines, was a small trough and stick perch. A desk.

<Check out the bathroom.>

"No, thanks." Dead leaves carpeted the floor knee-deep. She wasn't about to scuff through the mess and fight the vines to see what littered an alien bathroom.

Someone had brought the plants on board, maybe for company, maybe for food. A someone who'd worked on the Portal, like she did. Maybe started to ask questions and roam where they shouldn't.

Like she was. Killian stepped from the room, letting the door close.

<Gerry wants you to go back for a sample of the vegetation.>

"Tell Gerry—" Killian shook her head as she walked back to the tube cluster. "These were pilot quarters, Gis. Humans weren't the first to work for the Kmet."

<What do you think happened to them?>

"Not a clue." She found the tube mouth leading to the Human part of the ship and Henry, pausing to look back.

"But I'm guessing it's the same thing kmeth plans for us."

"You certainly do."

KILLIAN squirmed from a tube, pulling a bag with her. Spotting Henry, she froze for a second, then kept moving, climbing to her feet, slinging the bag over her shoulder as she approached. "I take it your *something* couldn't wait," she observed, thrusting down a hand. "Henry."

His name—it was more *how* she said it—acknowledged she'd misled him and dared him to make anything of it.

Accepting the grip, and message, Henry let her pull him to his feet. Killian unlocked her door, gesturing for him to go ahead. Her bag flew past him, sliding into a corner of the room.

Her memorial painting had grown. She'd outlined a fourth flower in black, its solitary petal a harsh white, the complex center made of small yellow bones. Powerful. Distracting.

HENRY, THERE IS A DETAILED BLUEPRINT UNDER THE PAINT. IT DEPICTS PREVIOUSLY UNKNOWN INTERNAL COMPONENTS OF THE PEDESTAL CONTROLS.

He fingered the button in his pocket, replaced on his jacket by PIP-Flip's optical sensor, sincerely impressed. *She'd fooled him.* Not many did. And in plain sight, too. "I like this."

Killian flattened her hand over the flower. "Not done."

Henry obligingly shifted his attention to her face. Her fierce frown was like the paint, he decided, covering something more. An unusual agitation. "Where were you?"

Instead of answering, she put two fingers across her right eye, bending her left arm to emphasize her wristband's inactive pattern; epitome code for *confirm privacy.*

Curious, that she didn't want Gis. Then again, their unusually extended connections wore on their oneirics; Sofia hadn't made herself available since the last evacuees arrived in Earth orbit and he didn't blame her.

Henry pushed up his sleeve to show the same status for his. "Where, Killian?"

"Exploring." Flat and, yes, that note of defiance.

Resourceful indeed. He nodded at her painting. "Spying for the System

Coalition," he corrected mildly, not letting her hear his excitement. "How's that going?"

She gave him a thoroughly suspicious look. "I broke your damn rule. Why aren't you mad?"

Because he was about to break the rest? Henry helped himself to her chair. "How did you fool the tubes?"

Killian seized her bag and emptied it on her bed, dumping out three plate-like discs. "These were PIPs I caught in Control. Used them as keys till they wore out." She tossed one up in the air, eyes on him, waiting.

Henry opened his jacket. PIP-Flip rolled to perch on his knee, the ridiculous replica phone appendage jutting toward Killian. "Hello. I'm Flip. More correctly, a miniscule portion—"

"Killian's got it, Flip, thank you," Henry interrupted. She'd sat abruptly on her bed, face working as if she couldn't decide whether to swear or laugh.

Settling for no expression at all. "You'd never pass for a PIP," she said at last, her fingers gauging PIP-Flip's diameter in the air. "Too small."

"If Henry would smuggle more of me—" The ocular turned to Henry, the polymorph falling silent.

"It's all right, Flip. We're past secrets now. The coats," Henry told her, then winked. "Your idea."

Her eyebrows shot up.

"Not *your* coat," he hastened to add. Sobered his tone. "It's time to pool our resources, Killian. What you can do. What I know or surmise. No more secrets."

"Why now?" Her gaze sharpened. "What's kmeth done?"

"Nothing." Henry took a breath. Uncertainties, conjecture. *Biology.* The lack of facts wasn't as important as being sure his allies, Killian and Flip, knew enough to carry on without him if it came to it.

"Nothing new," he qualified grimly. "I've been digging into our shared past. What I've found suggests it's possible we weren't the first Humans to meet the Kmet."

He watched the implication hit, her lips tighten. A whisper. "Origin Earth." Then Killian shook her head and squinted at him. "Say kmeth visited the old place," in her normal voice. "Why wait so long to come to us?"

"We weren't easy to find until we began broadcasting. Or—"

An eyebrow rose. "'Or'?"

Classified—no longer counted. "The first Arbiter to work with Kmet believed the aliens waited for us to reach a compatible sophistication in technology before contact. Those atmospheric components Kmet-Here immediately tests for? Might have been the sign." He was oddly relieved she didn't look convinced.

"Why come to us?" Killian challenged again. "Because long-ago Kmet messed up? Let the—oooh, scary—Divider destroy Origin Earth so, what, today's Kmet searched out what was left of us to atone?"

"Human bias." Automatic, that warning.

"Fuck that," she growled. "It's as good a theory as any of yours."

Henry nodded. "Except I no longer believe the Kmet came to protect us. Or if kmeth did, there's more to it. The Kmet arrived *needing* us, all of us, together on one world. Why I don't know—Rena's working on it—but it tracks, Killian. Every Arbiter's been frustrated by Kmet refusal to hear there might be Humans anywhere else. I show Kmet-Here a scrap of proof and look how fast kmeth cooperates. For the Duality. We're doing exactly what the Kmet need us to do. We have to find out why before this is over."

"And if we don't like the answer?" Her glare burned into him. "Don't tell me you plan to take over the fucking Portal, Henry. Don't tell me that's what *this* is for." She pointed at PIP-Flip.

"I cannot interact internally with the Portal's system," the polymorph admitted. "Nor dare I come into physical contact with its PIPs or the Kmet."

"Aren't you no help at all—" Killian collected herself. "Henry, we can't. We don't have anything near that level of knowledge. All I've found so far is a duplicate Control half-demolished by PIPs, some random plumbing, and—" Her face changed.

"And what?"

"Pilot quarters. Similar design, but they weren't used by Humans or Kmet. They housed someone different. Bird-ish. Whatever happened to them—maybe it's what's going to happen to us if we can't get ahead of this."

Another species? PIP-Flip bounced on his knee. Henry gave the polymorph a distracted pat, wishing Rena was with him, wondering what it meant. "We're already ahead," he assured the pilot. "We're suspicious. Asking questions. We've time before reaching Earth to do whatever it takes—"

A more vigorous bounce. Henry pushed PIP-Flip to the floor.

"How do you know the Bird Pilot and their version of you didn't have this very same conversation? How do you know it's only us the Kmet herded home? How do you know there's any chance at all? Killing Kmet-Here—" She covered her mouth, aghast at her own words.

Hadn't he thought them, in the darkest part of the night? "Murder won't solve our problem," he replied bluntly. "We must—"

"HENRY!"

They both looked at PIP-Flip, who aimed a grasper claw at Killian. "These are non-random occurrences."

She blinked. "Pardon?"

"Given the Portal's size and the paucity of opportunities to search without being noticed, it is highly improbable that you would have found one significant area, Pilot Killian, let alone a second."

Henry and Killian's eyes met. "How did you choose those tubes?" he asked.

"I just did." She frowned, dissatisfied with the answer. "Got lucky, I suppose."

"It cannot be chance," PIP-Flip disagreed. "The only reasonable explanation is that you were directed to those locations."

A snort. "By what? Kidnapped PIPs? Kmet-Here?"

Neither made sense. "Tube operation is highly coordinated—there'll be a central control," Henry hazarded.

"Not necessarily. Built by aliens, remember?" Killian looked up at the ceiling, then back to him. "Say it does—which I'm not. Still begs the question who'd change the tube destinations just for me. It's not as if a Portal acts independently."

"I do," Flip replied, waving the appendage with its replica button.

"You certainly do," Henry agreed thoughtfully.

"Oh for—then why?" Killian challenged. "Why would the Portal show a Human things about itself the Kmet won't?"

Henry quoted, "'Portals fail the axiom that ideal design must take into account inescapable biological constraints.'" He shrugged. "Rena's a staunch member of *Kmet-didn't-build-it* faction." Her study of reports on kmeth's denning behavior had inspired an acrimonious debate over Human versus alien aesthetics, along with a new bioengineering course.

"We build things our hands can use *because* we have hands. So said every pilot ever come on board." A glower. "Old news, Henry. What's it matter? The Kmet own the damn things now."

"What if the Portals *know* they were stolen," Henry said carefully, aware PIP-Flip had rotated to look at him, "and possess some rudimentary intelligence that means they aren't completely loyal to their new owners." The ocular dipped and he thought of what Flip had confessed to him. "Or has some hidden programming to act against the Kmet whenever there's an opportunity. Or," he finished triumphantly, "the Portal is a fully aware intelligence and this is how it's asking for our help."

Killian burst out laughing. Stopped when she saw his offended look. "You were serious? Henry, not everything wants to talk to you."

"I suggest an alternative which does not involve the Portal," PIP-Flip volunteered. "Our pilot may be correct. The Kmet, having failed to gain Human understanding, might be directing her search. I must point out, Henry, you've no evidence to support your concerns over kmeth's motivations."

Henry raised his hand, palm out. "Then we find some. Killian, I want you to try another tube."

"Won't be soon," she told him, picking up a disc.

"Take me." PIP-Flip hopped from the floor to the bed. "I can keep you in contact with Henry."

"If you work—no." Killian shook her head. "Too risky, Flip. The PIPs I used died after two trips. I think I starved them."

"You did not, Pilot Killian." PIP-Flip produced alts charging cable. "We're self-feeding. Those PIPs were put into storage mode by the Portal."

Said so matter-of-factly it took a second to hit home. When it did, Killian set down the flattened PIP as if it might explode and Henry blurted, "Can they hear us?"

"No, Henry. They are inert and will remain so until receiving the signal to reactivate."

"Could have told us sooner," Killian grumbled, hurriedly shoving the discs back in her bag.

"It did not seem pertinent until now." *Dismay.*

"And wasn't, Flip. Thank you." Henry rose to his feet. "Killian?"

Busy sealing her bag, she looked up at him with a grimace. "Yes, yes, I'll give Rolypoly a try—after we transit *and* after we see what's waiting for us."

He opened his mouth to argue. Closed it, thinking of Kmet-Here's impatience. "You're right."

The flash of her wicked grin. "Get that in writing?" It disappeared. "I hope you're wrong, Henry. About all of this. No offense."

Henry sighed. "I hope so too."

"I do the soap."

THE instant the door closed behind Henry, Killian squatted on the floor, eyeing Flip's version of a PIP up close. Round, mostly. Texture was a match, the color a shade more gray. Adorable miniature arms and that phone? She reached out a finger. An appendage about the same size, tipped with a tiny claw, met it.

"I'm relieved you're comfortable with this me, Pilot Killian." The voice was unmistakably the same, just somehow smaller.

What kmeth called her. "Killian."

"Killian. Thank you."

"It's easier to talk to something I can boot down the hall." The appendage withdrew at once and she chuckled. "Sorry. Figure of speech. What I mean is rolypoly-you has more personality than the shuttle."

"You have yet to fly with me." With a hint of smug.

Odds were she never would, pilots switching out on one of the Spacer Repository's craft. *Still.* "Look forward to it. Meantime, what's our deal here?" She tried to poke the body, missed as Rolypoly rolled out of range.

"In the absence of other instructions from Henry," primly, "our *deal* is I answer to yours, Killian."

She relaxed. "Then here's my first. What I say or do in my quarters stays here. No recordings. No sharing with Henry unless I say so."

"Yes, Killian."

Good. "I want to talk to Gis before we transit again. Without you listening in. Is that possible?"

"Of course." The appendage with the phone at its tip waved cheerfully. "Henry also requires me to assure him of privacy, Killian. I will use the time to recharge, if that is acceptable. There's a station under your bed."

So that's where Henry'd been hiding the thing. "Go ahead. And Flip?"

"Yes, Killian?"

"Nice to have a roomie."

"Thank you, Killian. Until you need me." With that, Rolypoly rolled under the bed.

***

Killian reached for her wristband. Stopped and rolled over on her stomach, hanging her head over the side. A faint small red glow marked where the polymorph was plugged in. Henry trusted it.

Had to, didn't she. Flinging herself on her back, Killian steeled herself, then pressed the band. "Space Rat. You there?"

<Always . . . Killie . . . >

Wrong, that voice, weak and distant as Gis never ever was, not even coming out of surgery, not even—Killian squeezed her eyes shut to concentrate, tried to ignore the pounding of her heart. "What's wrong, Gis? What's happened?"

<I . . . Gis? . . . Gis . . . I'm . . . ?> Doubt. Pain. Almost lost.

SHITSHITSHIT! "You're Gis. My Gis. Giselle m'Tharp t'Horyn, kick-ass spacer tramp. Gis!"

<I'm trying . . . trying to hold it . . . together.> Stronger. <You. You I remember. Killie-Cat.> Faint again. <It's me . . . that's slippery . . . >

Killian sat up, fingers hovering over the band. "You've gotta wake up. Get the med team—"

<No! You . . . more real . . . here with you.>

"It's him. Damn it, he's staying jacked in—" Panic whited the room. This was her worst nightmare, Gis and Gerry blurred, and unable to separate. If she was there, she'd smash in his bloody skull. "Get him out!"

<. . . . Gerry's . . . gone . . . >

Then what—"Baby, you have to get help. Where's Kisho? Old Bat said she'd take care of you." Tears poured down her face.

<She . . . tried. They told her you're . . . what you're finding . . . worth any risk. Think they . . . kicked . . . her out.>

Killian forgave, then and forever, every grudge she'd had against her former oneiric. "Listen, Gis. I'll get Henry to send his people over. Get you out of this. Hold on."

<I . . . can't . . . promise . . . I can't . . . not real . . . losing . . . >

She lowered her voice, made it husky. "I'll make you real, Space Rat."

She arranged her pillows, sat back. Opened her coveralls to the waist and looked down at herself, giving Gis a view. "That time you made me come twice on my spacewalk? I owe you." *For everything.* "See these hands?" Didn't matter if they trembled, only that Gis saw. "They're yours, lover."

She'd had the Print House replicate the tattoo on her stomach, white on her black skin, the same design she'd inked on Gis'. Two space-suited figures, floating face-to-face, bound by a cable twisting up and over each breast, leading down.

Killian let her finger trace the cable, her skin rising in goosebumps. Gulped a breath. "You thinking up—?" She flattened her hand, slipped it below the opening in her coveralls. "Or maybe—"

A soul-shattering hesitation, then, soft and warm, <Up . . . slow and easy . . . Killie-Cat. No . . . rush.>

She choked on her relief. "Lima Charlie, Space Rat."

***

"Gis—you still there?"

<Always, Killie-Cat.> Gruff. Strong. Familiar.

For how long? Killian kept her eyes closed, feeling tears leak. "Let me wake you. Please. You can get help."

<Here I thought you'd be ready to go again, 'cause I am.>

She halfway was, it having been too long and Gis in her head, using that hot, sexy voice. And back in charge, sure of herself—meaning her partner wasn't about to listen to reason.

Killian rolled over and sat up, snatching her coveralls. *Had to try.* "I can't lose you, Gis."

<Hey, Killie-Cat. I'm back to nice and solid, thanks to you.> A chuckle. <Interesting technique. Maybe I'll rec it to med team here. Could be fun.>

Damn it. She gripped her clothes, knuckles going white. Schooled her tone, thinking of Henry. *Negotiate.*

"Make you a deal. I keep you with me, you don't kick a fuss when I get someone to have a quiet talk with Kisho." When Gis remained silent, Killian braced herself. "It's that, or I wake you now and have Henry send in the troops. I don't think your Coalition would like that."

Harsh. <You're messing with stuff bigger than us. Hear me?>

Tell that to the almighty Arbiter. "I'll take that as yes." Killian stood. "Time for a shower."

Thing about Gis, she knew how to end an argument. <I do the soap.>

Killian grinned. "Ready when you are."

Which of course was when the com on the wall came alive with Kmet-Here's unwelcome,

"Pilot-Killian, Arbiter-Henry. I want to leave this place. Return soon."

***

Killian's frustration—on more than one account—diminished when Henry called to her from the kitchen, where he sat at a table already set with two heated ready-dinners. She stowed the bag of inactive PIPs under her seat, to stay till she figured out where to lose them.

He looked up from under that lock of wild hair. "Flip behaving?"

She gave a curt nod, handing Henry his transit meds, popping her own as she sat. "Taking a power nap." Spork in hand, she gave the food a dubious look.

Henry sat back, giving her the same. "Then what is it?"

<He's goooOOOOod. And yummy.>

Killian rolled her eyes, but Gis the nuisance was by far the better option. She stuck the utensil in whatever was in the pack. Couldn't assume Gerry hadn't stuck himself back in Gis' head, able to see what she did, hear what she said. *Made it tricky.* "Kisho m'Hadfield t'Twist promised to stay available—a resource. Can't be one if I can't reach her. Word is, she's left the Spacer Repository."

He resumed eating, those sharp eyes on her. "Why?"

"Someone should ask her—"

<You said quiet.>

"—quietly," Killian continued, staring back at the Arbiter. "I don't want to pressure Kisho if she's had enough. You understand."

"I do." He put down his spork and pushed the pack away. "It's easy to forget oneirics have their own lives outside of ours."

She nodded. "Up to us to remind them."

<Pushing . . . pushing.>

A slight tightening of his lips, the tiniest nod, told her she'd made her point, that he knew this might not just be Kisho—might be about Gis and the Repository. "I'll send Simmons back in. He's good with people."

His own assistant. With the authority to call in whatever the Arbiter's Office had in the way of troops. Satisfied, Killian freed her spork and took a mouthful. "You ready for World V?" she mumbled around it.

There it was, that charming, *means nothing,* half-smile. "As much as I can be. Ousmane will be with me at the transit. Here's hoping for a full house like III."

More to evacuate bought more time to explore the Portal. Killian nodded again. "You should eat the rest," she advised. "An empty stomach's worse."

She'd been wrong. The food lay heavy and unwelcome in her stomach as Killian watched the screens. World III burned in one, World IV, the other; no problem telling which was which. The once-living world choked in massive swirls of smoke.

Would Earth?

She'd Henry to thank for the horrifying notion aliens had wiped humanity from its original home and had mysterious designs on the current one. Between the Kmet and whatever a Divider was, she'd bet on the former, the cause of her indigestion and urge to pace if not scream as she waited for him to finish arguing with—

What she found herself unable to look at, not directly, not yet. As if the screens with their consequence were preferrable to the one responsible.

<At least they're talking about you.>

She'd be better if they weren't. Henry'd come up with a way to distract the Kmet, all right.

BOOM! "I will transit the Portal, Arbiter-Henry. The pilot is not yet ready."

"Because you haven't given Killian the experience, Kmet-Here." Reasonable, calm. By his voice, you'd never guess the power of the emotions roiling beneath the surface. His distrust of the Kmet. Dread of what might happen. Determination it wouldn't.

She'd glimpses, during their *pool our resources* talk. Was proud he'd let her, not that she'd ever tell—

<Killie-Cat. I'm going to lose my brain again unless you shut down those damn screens or look at the floor. You're making us both sick.>

She averted her gaze at once, focusing on the PIPs climbing into position.

<Thanks. What's with Henry, anyway?>

Killian made a question mark with her hand, refusing to feel guilty. When was she supposed to have told her partner of Henry's suspicions and their vague *search for evidence* scheme? During sex or when Gis was floating away from her?

Let alone let a stranger from the Coalition overhear. *Oh, Henry'd* love *that.*

Who was she kidding? He'd tell her every Human was their ally and to enlist Gerry to the cause—keep Gis playing for Team Earth.

No, he wouldn't. Not Henry. He'd save Giselle because that's what he was. The thought landed with such certainty, Killian sucked in a breath.

Henry and Kmet-Here still debating her value, she pulled out her pad to write: *He wants me to operate the Portal this trip.* What she'd trained to do—longed to do.

Until now, with this being Henry's way of working toward a Human takeover if necessary, *if necessary* being a crisis she wasn't sure any of them would survive.

<About bloody time,> replied Gis, as her staunchest admirer and blissfully unaware. <Shame Kisho won't see it.>

Don't need her, Killian wrote, underlining the *her,* then, on a dark whim, drawing a heart.

<We'll be together soon, Killie-Cat.> Gruff, warm, like a good tight hug. <A couple of worlds to go. That's all.>

Killian gave a thumbs-up, putting away her pad at the movement to her left. "Ready, sir," she told Henry, still not able to look directly at the Kmet looming beside him.

"Thank you. Kmet-Here has graciously agreed you will transit us home, Pilot, when that time comes."

"Yes. I will take us to wrong places. Humans-There places. We concur."

She made herself look at its face. "Understood. Inputting coordinates for World V now. Kmet-Here will operate the transit controls until—" The word was trapped in her throat, as if letting it out put everything precious in danger, as if the way she said it would expose them.

"New Earth," Henry supplied quietly. "Thank you, Pilot."

Killian input the numbers. Stepped back and down, for once kmeth giving her enough room, for once waiting—*why—what did kmeth know?*

A Human hand took her arm. "This is the *Lissett*'s destination. I believe you may have a connection?"

She wasn't good at this. Couldn't dissemble with so much at stake. *Wasn't like* him, *damn it—*

<Killie-Cat. Answer the man. A great aunt, right? The one who improved zero-g toilets.>

"My aunt's grandmother," Killian snapped, only to realize she'd broken the epitome's first rule and reacted to someone not here, instead of who was, and stood mute.

Henry had her arm. *Why did he have her arm?* "Do you know her field?" he asked, gently, as if interested. "Her specialty?"

"Aeronautics—she liked—"

TRANSIT.

"What do you call a Seeker?"

Doublet

THERE weren't roads to the Split. Leaving Home—and civilization, such as it was—behind, the convoy bounced and rocked across land that didn't know it should be dead, growth filling gullies and washes after spring and rain, baked away by summer's heat. A desert with pretensions of scrub, that's all it was; Beth stayed in the windowless back of the kitchen truck, uninterested. She'd made herself a comfortable nest from bags of supplies and a few blankets. Wedged herself in and stuck a strip of rubber between her teeth for the worst stretches; napped. Good enough. She'd lost the urge to sleep long ago.

The Bios wanted Beth to cross further to the north this trip, so north they went. Patrick had looked all manner of innocent when she'd questioned the choice, other than it being a crossing no Seeker had done before, and that'd made her glad. Not that she'd let it show.

With good, experienced drivers and tough vehicles, the *further* part, about 800 km, should take ten days. There being a second Seeker to drop off at the 300 km point—a newbie, no less, with his watchdog partner—Beth resigned herself to thirteen.

The newbie, staring when he didn't talk and losing his words when he did? More reason to stay in back.

The convoy needed to get the Seekers where they'd start walking consisted of five one-and-a-half-ton trucks, nimble and tough, a big tractor named Old Mitch with a winch to pull them out of trouble and a shovel to fill holes they couldn't cross, and the tanker to keep everything moving.

One truck hauled nothing but parts and tools, another spare tires. The kitchen and food took up their own, as did the field hospital, though that vehicle served double duty, carrying their personal gear. The fifth truck had radar, a portable weather station, seismographs, and whatever other monitoring devices the Bios thought worth sending along. It ran a day ahead as their scout, planting marker flags along the best route. Came back for supplies and company every third day.

The convoy stopped while there was light enough to watch where you left your bit of biology. Beth kept out of the way as the mechanics climbed into engines to check plugs and wires and fluids, then crawled beneath to inspect axles and brakes and whatever else was prone to break. The drivers went over their pneumatic tires for punctures or damage, then took turns topping up fuel tanks. They yelled at each other nonstop, adding to the din.

Beth couldn't wait to be on her own again, not that she didn't value their skills. They didn't, she knew, understand hers one solitary bit.

A piece of Seeker wisdom she felt obliged to impart on the third night, catching the newbie rambling on—in tedious, textbook detail—about a Seeker's job to a driver who likely wondered why she'd been unlucky enough to sit by the kid in the first place and didn't give a crap in the second.

Beth filled her bowl, thanked the cook, and went to the small group around the fire. She nudged the afflicted driver with the toe of her boot. "Take your spot, Angie?"

The newbie looked up, jaw dropping. Angie surrendered her seat on the ground with a happy grunt. "Just leaving, Beth."

"Appreciated."

"Seeker. This is—I am—"

"Talking too much," Beth said kindly. "Try listening."

His eyes darted to the faces limned by the flames. Older faces, hardened ones. A few missing teeth. Lined by experience, full of character, a few damn sexy—not that a youngster like this appreciated any of that, or that these folks stood between them and dying. He looked back at her, clearly puzzled. "They aren't Seekers," he whispered.

"Like us?" she said, louder, drawing attention. "Hey, Cal. What do you call a Seeker?"

"Dead weight, damn straight." The others roared with laughter. *Old joke.* And the truth, here.

Beth was pleased to see the newbie take it in, think it through, start to blush. Even more when he talked back, polite but bold. "I drove a combine every harvest, back in Bluehill. And a tractor like that one."

"Ain't no tractor like Old Mitch."

"Because any responsible farmer would have scrapped it by now."

The words left a hush thick as snow on a mountain and about as friendly. Beth ate her stew, eyes on the fire, keeping a straight face.

"Kid's got you there, Cal," Angie said, leaning to fill her friend's mug. "Beats me how you keep that hunk of metal running."

That did it. Cal's grizzled face grew comical as he tried to parse if he'd been insulted or praised. The rest laughed, and someone slapped the newbie on the back. He'd have gone into the fire if Beth hadn't had a hand ready. Rocked back, eyes a little wild.

Beth waved her spoon. "That time you lost three trucks to a flood. Go on. Tell Ewen the tale."

Ewen, likely as stunned to hear her say his name as by the hearty slap, nodded rapidly.

"Lost the Seeker and five of us," someone said. "But Cal should tell it. He and Old Mitch—they saved the rest."

Beth resumed eating, the young Seeker beside her listening with every fiber of his being.

Any luck, what he heard might save his life one day.

World V

"Your chickens are safe."

AT first, Henry thought they hadn't gone anywhere, despite the unhappy conviction of his gut. There was nothing on the screens but swirls of brown and white—ash and smoke.

"Hell of a storm," Killian commented, gently reclaiming her arm from his grip.

Of course it was a storm. An entirely natural storm, if enormous, right below them. They'd made it to World V. He breathed a sigh of relief. "That's good."

"It is not good," grumbled Kmet-Here, heaving kmeth's bulk from the dais. "Not fine. There are no Human products in the atmosphere and before you argue with me, Arbiter-Henry, there is no land under it." Polyps swayed, colors a mix of cooperative purple and stubborn orange. "Send your satellites," with a rumble of what might be amused resignation. "When you find no Humans-There, summon me and we will leave."

Without waiting for an answer, the Kmet swept into kmeth's den, PIPs clinging to the creature's sides, one gripping the tail tip and dragged along.

Killian stood with Henry, watching. When the drag-along PIP disappeared inside, she hopped on the dais and got busy. "Launching sats." After a moment, she shot him a look. "Prelim on the sensors confirm what's below the storm is liquid water. 200 plus kilometers deep water."

"Yes, but what about—?" He sketched a globe with his hand. *Surely it wasn't all ocean.*

"Sats will fill in the big details in a few hours, but don't get your hopes up, Henry." She gave her attention to the controls. "Kmet-Here might be right on this one."

Henry pulled out his fake phone. "Flip, any answers?"

"Atmospheric turbulence is extreme and continues to the surface, Henry, where I'm detecting extraordinary waves. The only way I can augment our pilot's satellites would be to go myself."

"Hold that thought." If Flip couldn't send alts tiny remotes, he wasn't inclined to risk the shuttle. Henry pulled out his pad and wrote: *why would the* Lissett *come here?*

Ousmane answered. <The Halcyon project selected exoplanets, ah, based on the best data available at the time but, ah, data must be interpreted. In this, ah, case, I conclude such immense storm systems were, ah, assumed to be a land mass. It was, ah, a risk they all faced.>

Henry spoke aloud for Killian. "Astronomers mistook the clouds for land."

"Rotten luck." The pilot shrugged, dismissing a tragedy two centuries old. "Guess kmeth won't get to cook this one. Should I speed up the survey?"

He opened his mouth to agree—

<No! They may be alive!>

"Wait. No." *What was the historian talking about?* He flashed a question mark.

<The Halcyon Class were built to, ah, protect those sleeping inside, ah, from their environment, ah, on landing.> Despite being in the dream state, her voice a manifestation in his head, Ousmane was agitated enough to think she needed more air, her gasps louder and more frequent. <An ocean world, ah, was a possibility. I've, ah, sent, ah, I—>

HENRY, I HAVE RECEIVED SCHEMATICS FROM OUSMANE.

Henry wrote quickly on the pad: *We have what you've sent. Take a moment. I won't do anything until you finish.*

<Should I wake and contact her team?> Rena asked, ever there, ever ready to help.

He moved his finger in the negative, chafing at the restrictions within Control though they were more vital than ever. The Kmet mustn't suspect the presence of other individuals hidden within their minds—let alone learn about epitomes. *Would kmeth consider them Humans-There or -nowhere?*

BASED ON THESE DOCUMENTS, HENRY, THERE IS A POSSIBILITY THE PASSENGERS OF THE SLEEPER SHIP ARE STILL ALIVE.

<The ship would, ah, keep them asleep. Do you, ah, understand? People, ah, from our past, ah, might be down there!>

"Go on auto, please, Pilot," Henry ordered, rather surprised how calm and normal he sounded. "Time we took our break."

Killian's fingers flew, then she stepped down. "Sure thing." Lightly said, but from her expression, she knew they weren't taking a break at all.

The Arbiter had called an emergency meeting.

***

As a projection, seated in Flip's now-familiar hold, Ousmane resumed a more professional demeanor, her excitement confined to rapidly moving hands. "The option of remaining asleep indefinitely, ah, was not made public."

Killian grunted, helping herself to Flip's coffee. Henry knew what she was thinking. Who'd have gone then? "They were brave—*are* brave," he said, feeling it sink in. A thousand highly trained individuals, willing and able to go on a one-way mission to settle a new world, who'd never heard of The Heartbreak.

Who'd never met the Kmet. What they represented was more than living history. If they could be revived, they'd inspire a profound shift in Earth's approach to space and what shared it with them.

The next Arbiter's project. Henry refocused. "There's two parts to this, both with challenges," he began, looking at those present. Killian hadn't summoned her oneiric; Sofia remained absent and he'd asked Simmons to look into her situation as well as Kisho's. *The last thing they needed was instability at home.* "The first is finding the ship. Killian?"

She grimaced. "If the *Lissett* sank, I doubt we can. Even if the sats pick up on something, the pressure halfway down is more than enough to crush a starship hull—deeper than that, we're talking solid ice."

"No, no!" Ousmane waved both hands. "No, no. She will be, ah, on the surface." Surging to her feet, she went to the wall, tapping it impatiently. "The column and, ah, truss configuration. Show it."

"Please, Flip," Henry added. *Whoever said a sentient construct didn't take offense hadn't met his friend.*

"Yes, Henry." An image appeared of a truncated sleeper ship, shown lying on its long axis. Thick columns appeared to grow from beneath it, each ending in a bulbous tip and connected to the others by girders.

"The columns are buoyant." Ousmane's hand disappeared inside one of the tips. Henry gave the ceiling a stern look and her hand reappeared, the finger a pointer. "A keel with ballast made from, ah, the ship's, ah, metal. A truss." She pointed to a girder. "Together, they not only, ah, keep the ship partially above the surface, they, ah, dampen the impact of, ah, waves on its structure. Please demonstrate."

Flip added an ocean with monstrous waves. "Those have to be exaggerated," Shomchai objected. He sailed, Henry remembered. When not being his oneiric.

"In fact," Flip explained, "these would be considered moderate on this planet, Shomchai. With no land mass to interrupt them, and two large moons, oscillations build rapidly and continue around the globe for extended periods."

The displayed ship, mostly submerged, moved with the water, neither bending nor breaking. "Then that's what we're looking for," Henry announced, nodding at Killian.

"A lifeboat."

Ousmane beamed at Rena. "The ships were also capable of, ah, becoming floating islands to support, ah, their population." Her smile vanished. "The *Lissett* must have, ah, ascertained conditions here were not survivable."

"I'll reset the search constraints," Killian said, putting aside her coffee as she got to her feet.

Rena held up her hand. "If there's life in this ocean, it will have accreted to the ship. Especially after this long."

The pilot's eyebrows shot up. "What, you think slime's going to matter?"

The xenologist smiled. "I think, Killian, your search constraints should include an unusual mass of organics on the surface, roughly the dimensions of the ship but larger."

"Will do." Killian looked impressed.

Henry rested his eyes on Rena, savoring her smile, feeling a pang of guilt at what he'd added to an already heavy burden despite having no choice. *Couldn't do this without her.*

She glanced at him, her joy fading. Remembering, he thought sadly, this wasn't simply another chance to learn about life beyond their Earth, but the second last world before—

Maybe nothing. Maybe he'd fabricated his worry and fears—passed them to her when in reality there was no threat. Maybe he was wrong about everything.

Rena gave a slow nod, her eyes warm. *Take heart,* that was. *Believe in yourself,* that was.

"I don't deserve you," Henry said quietly, and opened his arms to include Shomchai, Ousmane, Killian, and Flip. "Any of you."

Killian snorted. "Damn right." Then grinned at him.

Lifting Henry's mood. "Let's get moving then. Ousmane, thank you for restoring our hope."

The historian looked flustered then gave a short little bow. "It is, ah, the designers of these magnificent, ah, ships we should thank."

He took in the drawing of the sleeper ship, with its clever columns, and found himself chuckling.

"Start checking the passenger list, Ousmane," he told her. "We might get that chance."

***

Henry found himself envying Killian. He'd grown smug, using the tube system on his own between the docking area, their quarters, and Control; learned to ignore the tube mouths he wasn't allowed to enter. Now he paused to stare at them, wondering where they led—

HENRY, ASSISTANT SIMMONS M'HAMMARSKJÖLD T'MCALISTAIR HAS SENT A LENGTHY REPLY TO YOUR MESSAGE. WILL YOU TO RETURN TO ME TO HEAR IT IN COMFORT?

"Here's fine." Bundled in his Flip-coat, Henry sat on a crate, watching the plumes from his breath. "Go ahead, Flip."

A voice came from his com: Simmons at his most official. Then again, the young man was excruciatingly conscious every word sent via the Portal message stream went into the Office Archives—and possibly to the Kmet.

Which was why, Henry thought with some amusement, *they'd a private code.*

"Arbiter, as per your request I contacted Crisis Intervention Specialist Expert Sofia m'Rogers t'Patel concerning her unavailability as your oneiric. She requests you notify her through this office when you actually—her words, sir—need her again."

Through this office. Code for: should Simmons apply pressure from his office to change her mind.

There was more. "I was not satisfied with her response and queried her FLIP, invoking the provisions of the service agreement." Henry winced, having intended the polymorphs for his oneirics' safety, not as spies, but couldn't fault Simmons' diligence. "Sofia recently spent considerable time inside the Spacer Repository—to what purpose, I was unable to determine without exceeding your orders."

Exceeding your orders. Code for: I'm alarmed by this. Authorize me to dig deeper.

An alarm Henry shared. Sofia had to be behind Killian's Portal drawings, interacting with the pilot's oneiric on behalf of the System Coalition, not for his office and certainly not Earth. *Well done, Simmons!*

"As per your request," Simmons' reply continued, "I also contacted Pilot Kisho m'Hadfield t'Twist, inquiring why she left the Spacer Repository when your pilot expected her to remain as a resource. Kisho's reply was concerning. Finding your pilot's oneiric, Giselle m'Tharp t'Horyn, in distress, she attempted to intervene only to be ordered off the premises."

He'd read Killian's upset correctly. Felt a rising anger at the danger in the game Sofia played.

"I took the initiative, Arbiter, and visited the facility myself."

Henry nodded, relieved. Simmons had a way of carrying a folder that made seasoned receptionists run for cover.

At the next words, his relief vanished. "I regret to report, sir, the med team provided by the Print Shop at your order had been dismissed without cause, replaced by on-site personnel who implanted an illegal and unsanctioned wire into Giselle, connecting her to person or persons yet to be identified. Thus far, she has refused to give names. I have rectified the matter and can assure you Giselle now receives exemplary care, but, in light of what transpired, I urgently request your permission to reinstate Kisho's visitation rights and start an independent inquiry."

No code this time. Simmons was furious, had every right to be. Old news, that the Spacer Repository chose to view itself as separate and above the Arbiter's Office, despite their total reliance on him to negotiate with the Kmet.

But they both served the governments his office represented—the people of New Earth. In the midst of a mission affecting them all, to pull his people and replace them in order to forward their goals wasn't a jurisdictional scuffle, it undermined his and Killian's every effort—and was potentially disastrous.

Missed something. "Replay the last bit, Flip, please."

YES, HENRY.

Simmons' voice again, this time in a lighter tone. "Don't worry, Henry. Your chickens are safe and in their roost."

Code, every word. Not about poultry of any kind, but a confirmation that Flip, his FLIP, had indeed allowed a failsafe to be implanted to forestall any subversion of the sentient construct by the Portal or the Kmet.

"THAT IS THE END OF YOUR MESSAGE, HENRY."

Henry wasn't ashamed to have asked; not when everything depended on trust. Still, his "Thank you, Flip," was heartfelt.

IS THERE A REPLY, HENRY?

"Yes, Flip. Here it is: To Simmons. Thank you on all counts. On my authority, detain Sofia." About to ask for her ring to be confiscated, Henry changed his mind. Whatever else she was, he'd need her help with future evacuees and maybe more. "Show Sofia's image to Kisho—and Giselle." As his grandfather would say, there was more than one way to pluck a fowl. "My commendations to Kisho and the Print House. Further to Giselle's situation, I want a full medical report from our people. Please arrange for a FLIP inside her quarters to monitor any further activities. Oh, and Simmons? Thanks for checking my chickens. Arbiter out."

HENRY?

He stood, shivering a little at the actions he'd ordered, however necessary, and looked toward the airlock door. "Yes, Flip?"

IF YOU REMAIN CONCERNED, I CAN OBTAIN REGULAR UPDATES FOR YOU FROM THE VETERINARIANS CARING FOR THE CHICKENS FROM WORLD IV.

Simmons having preempted the type of personal task Flip enjoyed most.

With a small smile, Henry rested his gloved hand on the window. "Most considerate of you, my friend. I'd appreciate that."

"Give me a minute."

A SLEEPER ship at launch outmassed a Delta Class freighter; the historian sounded confident the *Lissett*, other than a minor reconfig to float like a barge, wouldn't have detached her engines. Why being a question Killian didn't bother asking. The ocean wasn't going to drain away; the only reason to float at all was to wait for rescue.

And if from New Earth, those engines might be put to use again.

Hunting for something upwards of half a million tons, she'd been able to lower the resolution and widen the swathe covered by every satellite pass. Cut the time to cover the entire surface from seven days to three, or thereabouts.

"You're monitoring the sat feeds, like before. Real time?" she demanded of the rolypoly in the crook of her arm.

"Yes, Killian. I will alert you immediately if there's a discovery."

About to pick a tube mouth, she looked down. "You don't think we'll find her. Why?"

"I consider it unlikely. On its approach to the planet, the ship would have recognized the problem and concluded what had to be done. While still in space, it would have completed the manufacture of the columns. That said, it couldn't enter atmosphere with them extruded. The alternatives available were hazardous: slow her descent through the turbulence sufficiently to deploy the columns and safely enter the water, or deploy them after landing. In either scenario, if the ship suffered any loss of hull integrity, it would sink too quickly to recover."

"How unlikely, exactly?"

The rolypoly shifted as if uncomfortable. "Henry doesn't like to hear the odds," in a smaller than usual voice.

Killian laughed without humor. "I'm not surprised. I do."

"Yes, Killian. I calculate the odds on finding the *Lissett* on the surface and intact to be less than one in five hundred."

Fuckityfuck. She clamped her jaw shut. Gave a sharp nod. The odds against didn't matter. They'd keep looking. Make sure. Couldn't leave without and be able to sleep at night.

She managed a casual, "Still a chance, then."

"That's what Henry would say."

Not surprised at that, either. The pilot blew out a breath. "Let's see if you work." Taking hold of the rolypoly, the pilot held him in front of a tube mouth that refused to let her in alone.

It opened.

She tapped her wristband. "Gis, you there?"

<Always, Killie-Cat. And *just* me. Gotta new med team says I run solo from now on. I think it was the sex.> Smug, that was, with maybe a hint of relief her tough partner would never, ever, admit.

They owed Simmons—*and Henry, him most of all.*

Joy shuddered through her bones, but Killian managed a casual, "Good to know. Hang on."

She shoved Flip at the tube. "After you."

***

During what proved to be a longer, more complex ride than any she'd yet experienced, Killian felt a growing anticipation. Hadn't bought Henry's notion the Portal itself was directing her travel; didn't care for Flip's, that it might be Kmet-Here. But being taken to something important? *That she liked.*

Of course, aliens or alien machines didn't think about Human anatomy or safety, ever. When the mouth opened at the other end, Killian found herself staring into a lightless abyss. She pressed her knees and hands against the tube walls to keep from dropping headfirst. "Flip!"

A pale glow appeared. "The lights will come on once you are in the room, Killian."

Not helpful. "How far to the floor?"

"Three point eight meters."

<Oh, it's not that far,> Gis prompted, also unhelpful. <Tuck and roll.>

"Says the woman who jumps down mountains—and cheats." It was called bouldering and Giselle owned a special pair of legs for it. *Cheating.*

Trying to fold and bring her feet through didn't work. Killian's arms started to tremble.

"Killian, if you wish, I can lower you."

She turned her face to find the rolypoly, the source of the glow, stuck to the tube wall by appendages with sucker tips. "Sure," she agreed, numb, the moment slipping beyond her and about to fall, badly.

An appendage extruded with a tip like a pin and drove itself into the tube. The rest . . . stretched, slowly spinning as it did, until there was an actual rope, itself emitting light.

Too short to reach the unseen floor.

Didn't have to—not if she could grab it and hold on long enough to get her feet down first. She was a meter six. *Dropping two more, piece of cake.*

<I don't know about this, Killie-Cat—>

Too late. Feeling her arms give out, Killian let go and fell headfirst, hands grabbing for Rope-Flip.

And missed.

The rope wrapped around her wrists in a flash, absorbing the shock like a spring as it took her weight. Spun and stretched, lowering her down, Killian spinning with it, and the lights did come on, to her relief. "Far enough," she called, seeing the floor approach. The rope released, coming with her as she landed lightly on her feet, melting and reforming into the rolypoly.

<I gotta get me one of those.>

"Thanks, Flip," Killian said, catching her breath. She looked around her. Stared. Swallowed, hard, and whispered, "You seeing this?"

<Yeah. Where the hell are you?>

"I am recording and transmitting," the rolypoly announced grimly. "Henry sees this."

Killian waved an acknowledgment, too shocked to say more.

The walls curved from floor to ceiling, coated with a thick, vomit-yellow material. Gaps in it exposed plugs of congealed metal, and she realized belatedly she stood on more of the same stuff, on a molten river now frozen that ran across the floor in a jagged scar, that had been made by a weapon—and it wasn't material everywhere, but skin, baked hard to the walls.

Fuckfuckfuck. She staggered, caught herself. *Wasn't going to touch it. No way. No way. No—*

<Killie, snap out of it!>

Gis. *Sanity.* "I'm here." Her voice held doubt.

The room held the dead. Heaps of withered remains surrounded her, seemingly lying where they'd died. Bodies her size, not remotely her shape, huddled around fewer, smaller ones. Might be a hundred. Might be more.

Didn't smell. Hardly a profound or useful observation, but she clung to it. This—this slaughter had taken place long ago, the bodies reduced to desiccated shells, and the question welled up, unwelcome and unpleasant, why had the Portal's PIPs, who cleaned her piss as it hit the floor and snatched up each and every scale Kmet-Here shed, left *this*?

She must have said it out loud, for Henry answered, his voice coming from the rolypoly's phone. "A warning?" He paused. "Rena says—she says if this room was hidden until now, the bodies might have been kept as trophies."

He sounded as sick as she felt. "Thanks for my next nightmare," Killian muttered darkly, furious at whatever had brought her here, not those she'd brought along.

"Can you tell what killed them?"

Without going closer, she couldn't see if there were wounds. The small ones were mostly hidden from view. The bigger ones had wide heads tapered to a nose. Small front limbs, larger rear ones. She glimpsed claws. Overlapping plates formed armor starting from the nose, larger over the limbs and body, smaller over a stubby tail. "They weren't Kmet."

<What else would they be?>

She almost answered: *The original owners.*

"Kmeth could undergo metamorphosis during their life cycle. We can't draw conclusions without tissue analysis." Henry's voice, Rena's words.

"I will obtain a sample."

Killian snatched up the rolypoly before he could try. The ocular angled to regard her face. "Why do you prevent me from this task?"

"I don't know. I—" She hesitated. "Give me a minute." Still holding him, she walked forward, keeping on the scar.

<Those are kids.> Gis, shaken. <This is all over wrong, Killie-Cat.>

The small ones, her partner meant, it being Human and charitable to think the larger died shielding their young. Killian squatted near a group of three, trying to see more.

Hands, with paired and formidable claws as well as shriveled digits, curled protectively over what wasn't a smaller version of themselves, not in the Human sense, but an oval-shaped pod covered in much smaller, tightly interlocked plates.

And they hadn't saved it. The plates were pierced by dozens of holes, blackened and scorched at the surface, as if a searing hot drill had been used over and over again to reach whatever was inside.

Killian rose and covered her mouth, dropping the rolypoly.

"May I take the sample now?" Flip asked patiently.

When she didn't answer, Henry's voice did. "Go ahead please, Flip."

"Proceeding." The polymorph went to the closest body and extruded a new arm, with a tip Killian hadn't seen on a PIP before.

A drill.

Pandemonium erupted. Henry was talking, Gis shouted in her head, and the damn drill whirred. "SHUT UP! All of you!"

Rolypoly paused, the drill slowing to a stop. Killian breathed in the silence, then let out the words.

"Well, now we know what killed them."

"I'll explain later."

HENRY couldn't tear his eyes from the horrific image on the shuttle's screen until Rena, his hapless passenger, gave a soft whimper.

He looked away. "Privacy mode, Flip."

"Done—"

"Is Killian right? Did something like you do this?"

"Henry," the polymorph said quietly, but with a note of deep distress. "Nothing like me killed those people. I cannot kill people. You know that."

"Portal PIPs did." He didn't recognize his own voice. "That's what happened here. They destroyed the tube mouths to prevent any from escaping and drilled holes in their flesh to kill them. Tell me I'm wrong."

"A drill like my PIPself's could have made the—"

"Tell me I'm wrong."

"I cannot, Henry." Quiet and sad. "That is the most likely scenario from what we see."

Rena interrupted. <The PIPs might have acted defensively, to protect the Portal from invasion, like T-cells in our bodies—Henry, we don't know—>

His jaw clenched. "You said they were trophies."

<I reacted. To what we saw—it was emotional,> she admitted. <I shouldn't have jumped to that or any conclusion. There might be a dozen other possibilities, including that these *are* Kmet, that this is somehow natural. We need facts.>

"Understood." But his every instinct disagreed. Killian's *now we know*—Rena's *trophies*—suggested the outcome of an earlier encounter between Kmet and the Divider. An outcome where the latter'd become the corpses filling the screen in front of him, the Kmet having won, and what did that mean for them?

"Reconnect me with the pilot, please, Flip."

Killian's face appeared on the screen, her expression grim. "We good, Henry?" She'd worked with a stowaway in her oneiric; now she wanted him to pronounce judgment on who else was with her. PIP-Flip.

"We're good. Get the sample and document what you can, but I want you out of there as quickly as possible."

"Roger that," with a nod for emphasis. "Pilot, out."

"Rena, we'll get it to you on the next ship to transit through."

<I'll be waiting. But Henry, there's little I can glean from it alone.>

"Leave that to me." Henry's lips curved in a humorless smile. "Kmet-Here and I are about to have a very interesting conversation."

"Henry, please refrain from another physical confrontation. I cannot assist you," Flip, his indispensable partner, being quite reasonably anxious.

"Don't worry. I've something else in mind."

<From you, my friend, that means I'll worry for all of us.> But Rena didn't sound displeased.

Knowing it was time.

***

Taking the tube that should go to Control, Henry found himself uncertain it would. After all, something decided a tube's destination, making him wonder why the Kmet—if the Kmet—would use PIPs as agents of destruction when spitting a traveler into vacuum offered a tidier option.

His epitome was a disposable copy. It wasn't a comfort.

When he climbed out of the tube to find himself where he'd intended to go, Henry tried not to flinch as PIPs scurried out of his way. They hadn't changed, of course; it was his new assessment of their ever-shifting assortment of claws, graspers, and whatevers for their potential against his flesh. *Not a happy thought.*

No sign of kmeth. After locating the warm, to their quarters, tube mouth, he shoved in his Flip-coat with a fatalistic, *should work,* then checked the screens. The outer two showed seemingly identical streams of numbers, representing the results coming in from the satellites. The centermost held a view of World V, shrouded in storm. No clock, having left World IV in flames.

HENRY, KILLIAN AND I HAVE RETURNED TO HER QUARTERS WITH THE SAMPLE. I MUST USE MY PIPSELF TO BECOME THE CONTAINER FOR ITS STORAGE AND TRANSPORT. TO RESUME THIS DISGUISE, I'LL NEED THE COAT YOU WORE INTO THE PORTAL.

He'd be happier to have all of Flip stay outside, docked as his safe, familiar shuttle, but who knew where Killian would be sent next? *Assuming she was willing to go.* "Understood," he whispered. "Proceed, Flip."

He didn't want Killian here, either. This was the better way, him and Kmet-Here. A normal dichotomy, like any of their interactions via uplink—this time without the option to simul-pop in another individual.

Henry went to the dais and sat cross-legged, bracing his back on a pedestal. The PIPs near the control wall stopped to aim oculars at him. When all he did was sit, they resumed whatever they were doing, ignoring him.

Reassured, he closed his eyes . . .

✱✱✱

. . . opening them on a featureless room. No table and chairs, no windows or Arbiter's Seal on the wall. For Shomchai—especially for Rena, Henry didn't need more. He'd act as their reference point and anchor.

They stood waiting for him, the linguist in casual clothes, carrying a sheaf of paper, Rena with her arms crossed. Odd, to see her hair loose and shining. Henry blinked. No, it was swept up in its usual twist, stabbed through with insect pins, and he'd no idea which of them made the change.

Or time to ask. He was vulnerable while trancing. "I'm alone in Control," he cautioned them. "When we're done I'll rouse Kmet-Here and ask my questions." He half-smiled. "My guess is kmeth's reaction and your interpretations will be more meaningful than any answers I get."

Shomchai raised his papers, important enough to him his mind had brought them into the dream state. "I did as you asked, Henry." He looked haggard. "Working alone—without checks—I can't guarantee my conclusions are sound. This is most troubling."

On New Earth, only these two, and Gis, had seen images of the dead. "Your concern is noted, Shomchai," Henry assured him, "but keeping this development between us is vital until we know more." He hadn't dared share it with his office, let alone the general public. "I know you understand."

Rena nodded. "We'll do what we can," she said, giving Shomchai a reassuring look.

"Yes. Yes, of course." The linguist gestured with his papers. "I've combed through the entirety of your negotiations with the Kmet and I believe only Kmet-Here—your Kmet, that is—" An uncharacteristic frown at the name. "—has been present at their final settlement. The other, or others, exhibit slight but distinct speech patterns—word choices—it's thin, Henry."

"But remarkable," Rena said, eyes shining. "You can tell kmeth apart!"

Shomchai made a face. "No, I can only tell if the individual speaking will conclude an agreement. It may be the same Kmet will adjust kmeth's use of language depending on the situation—I've warned you before, Henry, kmeth know ours extremely well." The papers disappeared with Shomchai's confidence. "It's all I've got."

Henry nodded. "I'll settle for a cue it's likely Kmet-Here is taking me seriously and ready to deal."

Shomchai looked relieved. "I can give you that."

Better than he'd hoped. "Rena?"

"Based on our earlier discussion, Henry," she said, signaling he wasn't to bring up Kmet biology in front of the linguist, "I suggest you focus on what Kmet-Here expects to happen when you return to New Earth."

Shomchai looked from Rena to Henry, then back. "What's—No," he interrupted himself, shaking his head. "It's more horrid goo, isn't it. If I don't need to know, I don't think I want to."

"I promise you'll be informed," Henry told him. "If that's all?"

Rena gave a curt nod, her lips a grim line. Like Shomchai, she'd assess anything about the Kmet that might help him. As his friend and proxy, she'd yank him from his epitome if the Kmet chose to squash him flat.

Not the plan. "Let's wake our friend."

Henry opened his eyes.

***

The interior of the den would be moist, dim, and stink. Henry sniffed cautiously from the entrance. Caught himself about to gag and stopped the reflex with an effort. The eyedrops kept his eyes from watering.

<Does it smell the same, Henry?>

How should he—Rena was right. There was something different in the air, exiting with each heavy breath from within. Less peanut and beet, more—earthy. Like the farm in late fall, manure freshly spread on the fields. Henry moved his head from side to side, once, to answer her question.

Experimenting—and remembering how quickly the Kmet had reacted to his trespass last time—Henry stuck his hand inside the entrance, looking over his shoulder.

Throughout the room, PIPs stopped moving to watch.

He pulled out his hand.

They resumed whatever they'd been doing, including one that scampered past him into the depths of the den. *Hopefully not an intruder alert.*

Henry crouched to reconsider his approach. If he had Flip play a recording of the *we're here and connected* harmony through his personal com, his being alone invalidated the meaning. Or confused it, to the same result.

When he'd announced himself last time, the Kmet had been outraged. Because he'd violated kmeth's privacy? Maybe. Maybe not. Rena thought it might be an instinctive territorial display, in which case it would happen every time he disturbed kmeth *at home.*

His hand dropped to his pocket, fell away. Bringing his harmonica had seemed a good idea before coming here.

Henry shuffled to one side of the opening, out of kmeth's path. His gaze traveled up the den wall, with its chaotic pattern of Portal bits and pieces. Their discarded bulbs were glued in place alongside curls of stripped wire, near flat pieces of metal gridwork. If there was anything *Kmet* in the mix for Rena's analysis, he'd no way to remove it, let alone identify it.

There was nothing like the thick yellow skin Killian found fused to the walls.

<Henry?> Shomchai, with a worried note to his voice, probably because the Arbiter continued to crouch, staring at the den, instead of engaging the Kmet.

Henry showed his upraised thumb, then a flat hand. *Patience.*

What he needed was a good solid hook. Something kmeth couldn't ignore. Something like—

Of course. Rising, Henry went to the dais. With one hand on a pedestal, he said in a loud, clear voice, "Pilot Killian, prepare to transit to New Earth. We're going—"

—*home* was swallowed in an ear-splitting roar, PIPs scattering as Kmet-Here launched from kmeth's den only to slide to a halt as the lack of pilot registered.

A wave of confused purple sped across once-red polyps. "Arbiter-Henry. Explain!"

Taking his time, Henry sat on the dais and crossed his legs at the ankles. A huge eye bent to take in his posture. The other stared at his face, pupil dilating. "Which part?" he asked innocently.

"The pilot is not here." A heave brought the Kmet closer. "Your talk of leaving is untrue."

"On the contrary, I'm quite serious, Kmet-Here." Henry pointed over his shoulder, toward the screens. "This world's empty. I see no reason to keep going to the next. Why find every possible Humans-There? Earth has enough. I'm tired—"

BOOM! "No! The hunt is fulfilling. It cannot stop until all Humans are on New Earth."

<*That*, Henry. Did you hear?>

Couldn't miss it. "'Hunt'?" he echoed casually. "Is that what we've been doing? Tell me, Kmet-Here. What will you do, when all Humans are on New Earth?"

The Kmet pushed up on kmeth's flippers, both eyes on Henry, polyps bleached white. Silent.

<Henry, look!>

What else was he doing? Making a question mark, he glanced quickly at his fingers, then back to the Kmet.

<The ventral surface. The belly!>

He shot a look where Rena ordered, at first guessing the PIPs had missed a spot in their obsessive cleaning. Even now, four were picking at kmeth's sides.

No, a few spots, each slightly lumpy. In fact, as he looked, the entire underside of the Kmet was dappled and lumpy.

<Incredible.> With such fierce intensity Henry feared she'd ask him to feel a lump.

His view was abruptly blocked by Kmet-Here flopping to the floor, eyes now on a level with his. "When all of you are Humans-Here," kmeth pronounced solemnly, "so will be Kmet."

Shomchai, urgent. <Your cue, Henry. Kmeth's prepared to agree—or disagree. That phrasing's deliberate. There's a deeper meaning. Maybe an older one. Careful.>

"Explain, Kmet-Here."

A breath, hot and heavy with that earthy scent, huffed over him. Another. Henry didn't budge.

Then, "We cannot descend to New Earth and be among you while the Divider remains a threat above. Only when all Humans are on New Earth, with Kmet, will the Divider be helpless to sunder us. Our Duality will be complete."

The words, the ponderous tone with its underlying—*disturbing*—ultrasonics, filled him with a formless unease, perhaps was intended to do just that to non-Kmet. Henry grappled with the urge to demand more, to ask about the dead in the Portal—

No. He mustn't reveal what Killian could do, where she could go. Not yet.

Fortunately, Rena hadn't frozen. <Hit kmeth with landing protocols, Henry. It's in the rules. Every evacuee—anyone coming to New Earth—must provide a biological sample for analysis. This is our chance!>

Henry looked up with a cheery smile. The Kmet drew back as if alarmed by his teeth. "New Earth will be delighted to learn you'll be joining us when the time comes." *Translation: panic in the streets.* "I'll send your sample ahead to New Earth, Kmet-Here."

"My sample?"

<Body fluids, skin under the scales—> Rena rhymed off a list.

"Blood, skin, spit. Whatever's easiest for you. It will ensure your safety after landing on our world."

"We have shared ourselves with you. We will be safe." With conviction.

Interesting—or ominous. Keeping his smile, Henry eased to his feet and whipped out one of Rena's specimen vials. "It's the rule. Everyone intending to land on the surface must provide the medical folks a sample in advance, no exceptions. Here." He held out the vial, thumbing open the lid. *Good thing he'd practiced.*

For a too-long moment, Kmet-Here didn't move. Abruptly, polyps flushed cooperative purple. The mouth opened wide, tongue rising to expose a greenish gooey puddle beneath.

<Perfect! Quick, Henry!>

For Earth. The Arbiter stuck his arm into kmeth's gaping mouth, and dipped the vial into the fluid, careful not to let any touch his bare skin. As he withdrew it, a drip from the tongue began to eat a hole in his sleeve.

"Thank you, Kmet-Here." Henry thumbed the lid and stuck the vial in an outer pocket, oh-so-casually removing his jacket and folding it over his arm before any drips ate through to his skin. "I'll see this goes on our next transit through. About New Earth," he started to say—

HENRY, A SATELLITE HAS LOCATED THE *LISSETT*. KILLIAN IS ON HER WAY TO CONTROL.

—continuing smoothly, "We'll talk again, I'm sure. Right now, I've news." Henry pointed dramatically to the screens. "We've found the ship after all. I'll have the pilot begin the evacuation process."

A huge eye swiveled up, perhaps making no more sense of the Human display than he did, then back, iris wide as if to drink him in. "You intend to stay. You do not wish to return to New Earth immediately. You spoke an untruth."

Maybe the truth would serve. "I needed to bring you from your den, Kmet-Here, without being run over." Henry spread his hands. "It worked."

The iris shrank to a dot, lid flicking, then expanded again. "In future, Arbiter-Henry, no untruths."

From you either. Henry merely nodded. "Agreed."

"In future, if you require my presence," kmeth continued, giving what seemed an amused rumble, "whistle."

Henry blinked. "Pardon?"

The mouth snapped closed, two tongue-tips caught between the hard lips, and a clear, one-note whistle emerged.

Every PIP stopped to orient toward the Kmet.

<That's it? That's all?> Shomchai seemed shocked.

"Can you make this sound, Arbiter-Henry?"

Popping his thumb and forefinger into the corners of his mouth, Henry whistled the same note, gaining the full attention of the PIPs.

Another rumble. "Adequate. Do so when it is time to move to the last world. I must rest." Kmet-Here turned and heaved back to the den, passing Killian as she dropped from a tube mouth set in the wall.

She watched kmeth disappear, then looked to Henry. "Thought I heard a whistle."

The linguist was still muttering in his head. <The university will never believe me.>

Henry shrugged. "I'll explain later. I hear we've a ship."

"Don't ask Flip the odds." The pilot stepped on the dais, working controls. "Let's take a look."

<I call him Harvey.>

"WELL, I'll be—" Killian whispered, gazing up at the middle screen. Sat optics couldn't penetrate the cloud shielding two-thirds of the planet so she'd switched the feed to synthetic aperture radar mode to render a grayscale image. The shape was a match to the *Lissett*, expanded by around forty-five percent by what stuck to her.

The woman with bugs in her hair had nailed it.

<Gotta love a ship won't let you die,> Gis said reverently.

Technically, the *Lissett* hadn't let her passengers live either, an observation Killian didn't bother to make out loud.

The right screen showed the mess that passed on this world for local weather. Hurricane with a chance of more hurricane, ramped up to impossible. *Just as well the passengers slept.*

<Now what?>

Good question. Fortunately, Killian didn't have to answer it. "Well, Henry?"

He stood under the screen, gazing up at the image, for some reason carrying his jacket rolled into a ball under his arm. At her question, he glanced at her over his shoulder. She'd seen that reckless gleam in his eyes before. "You are not going down there," Killian said firmly.

There it was. The grin matching the gleam. "Someone has to knock on the hull—or whatever one does."

"There's no *knocking.*" Killian shook her head dismissively. "You need to access her internal com system." *Two hundred years old, and half of that spent wet.* "We'll have to fabricate a rig to punch into her hull. I'll get Gis on it." Her fingers reached for her wristband.

<Aw. Just getting interesting, Killie-Cat.>

Henry came up to the dais. "Flip's transmitted the request to his counterpart in her room."

<Forgot to tell you—they've given me a pet. I call him Harvey. Right now he looks like one of those stuffed toy bears in a helmet, from the Repository gift shop.>

Killian's eyebrows collided. "You put a—" Remembering where she was didn't shut her mouth, the shift in his expression, from naughty boy to almighty Arbiter, did.

"I won't tolerate any more meddling." Cold. Hard. "Is that understood?"

He wasn't talking to her; he was talking to who he knew could see and hear him. Sure enough, Gis replied with a sullen, <Understood.>

Killian gave a nod. *But a FLIP?* They'd have a talk about this. Might be yelling.

Though given a second to absorb the notion, she had to agree it was the only way to keep the System Coalition out of Gis' head. And no doubt Giselle, once over her pique at having a live-in spy, would start trying to take *Harvey* apart. *You could pity a polymorph.*

"Ousmane has provided blueprints." Henry leaned a cautious elbow on the pedestal, gazing up at the screen. "I'm not sure how much they'll help."

She could see his point.

The image resolution was good enough to show what stuck to the *Lissett* had shells, or hard outsides like the halves of a nut. Those on the leeside were open, with what looked like fans dipping in and out of the water with every wave. Those facing the wind were closed tight. Layers of them coated the ship, weighing her down so that every so often water splashed over top.

"Barnacles."

Killian glanced at Henry.

"Enormous alien barnacles is the official term, according to our xenologist. And possibly a few corals. Rena's looking forward to examining them."

"Pardon?"

"They'll be dead, I realize." Henry flashed that grin. "Didn't I tell you? The plan's to transit the ship back and dock her with a station. Let her passengers wake up somewhere more hospitable."

Of all the—"You have to get her to the Portal first. Through that atmosphere." Killian shook her head. "If she doesn't break—"

The grin broadened. "I've every confidence in our pilot."

<Damn, he's good.>

She'd a few other adjectives in mind. "We'll need communications."

"That's where Flip and I come in," he promised.

Didn't help one bit.

"You will."

FOR the trip to the surface of World V, Flip explained how alt'd modified alts shuttleself from flying saucer to bird-like, sprouting long, tapered crescent-shaped wings from a smaller, stubby body to better handle the turbulence.

Flip's interior, Henry discovered when he tried to enter from the airlock, had changed as well. It was filled with gray foam. Firm to the touch, foam. Impenetrable by a passenger, foam. "Flip? Where am I to sit?"

"Here you are, Henry." The foam zipped itself open to offer a narrow slit extending deep inside.

Into which he'd have to crawl. Within which he'd be pinned like one of Rena's plants in a press. Henry balked. "That's not a seat."

"If you dislike my required precaution for your safety, Henry, you could stay on the Portal," the polymorph offered cunningly. "I can project your voice."

He'd love to. Henry sighed. "You know I can't." Ousmane had been clear. A Human—a provably awake and in-charge real Human, not a Flip imitation—had to give the command for the *Lissett* to rise from the water. Otherwise, the sleeper ship might even repel their efforts—how exactly, she hadn't discovered, but the possibility alone was sufficient warning.

Turning sideways, he began to squirm his way inside.

It wasn't as difficult as he'd feared. The foam stayed where it was pushed, so Henry used his hands to widen the opening. At the end of it, he pressed his backside down as if sitting. "Not so—" Suddenly the stuff reformed around his feet and legs, climbing up. "Flip!" he shouted.

The foam stopped at his midsection, supporting his back and shoulders, leaving his face, chest, and arms in a small but open bubble of air and light. "How's this, Henry?"

"Any chance of letting me see?"

"Of course, Henry." What looked like an authentic porthole from an Earth fishing vessel formed in front of his face. "How's this?"

His lips twitched. "That'll do, thanks." Instead of window glass, there was a screen showing the planet below. The incredibly stormy and landless planet.

Where he wasn't about to leave a thousand helpless people. "Pilot, we're ready to go. Status?"

"Roger that, Arbiter." Cool and efficient, no trace of argument in her tone, though they'd had a good one, Killian vehemently opposed to his going, determined to take his place in Flip, and what the hell was he thinking, to risk his only copy in a hurricane?

Telling her that was why he'd come hadn't helped.

"New Earth has three catcher groups standing by to transit on your go," she continued. "One should do it, but I'm glad of extra."

Given they had to catch an ancient starship covered in alien barnacles before it fell back into the atmosphere and burned up, Henry agreed. "Have Omar send them through. Flip tells me this won't take long."

"To be accurate, Killian," Flip interposed, "I informed Henry I will be unable to maintain shape integrity under the conditions at the surface for more than a few minutes."

When Killian didn't respond, Henry said calmly, "That's all we'll need. Flip has the rig ready to go; I've the *Lissett*'s command code. We'll be back before you know it."

Her, "Roger, that," sounded as if it came through clenched teeth.

"All right, Flip. Let's go save people."

***

Stars filled the porthole, then the glorious arc of sunset along the planet's rim, burnishing the top of the cloud deck. *It looked solid*, Henry thought, bracing himself inside Flip as they dropped.

The porthole went blue, then a blank white. Gray. Darker and darker. Almost black.

Eye-searing white! He threw up his arm, shouted something, and the porthole went blank.

"My apologies, Henry. We're passing through a zone of considerable electrostatic charge and my hull is attracting discharges."

"We're being hit by lightning?!"

"Yes, Henry. It isn't a concern. However, I need to augment your restraints before we reach more turbulent levels."

"I haven't felt—" The bubble collapsed in on him, the foam clear in front of his face, the porthole imbedded in the stuff and still visible. He could breathe normally, not that he was. Henry focused on calming himself, on finishing his sentence. "—haven't felt anything."

"You will," Flip advised him.

And that was when Henry felt his stomach drop. The first few bounces and shudders were no worse than he'd experienced in an aircraft, the foam holding him gently but firmly, and he started to relax.

The shuttle fell, spinning. Turned over sharply, taking his breath away. Fell again, and he vomited. Bit his tongue, spat blood. Impossible to anticipate what was coming, to brace himself. Surviving it became his sole goal, and for an interminable length of time, he doubted he would.

Hit a point of sheer hopeless misery when he'd have begged Rena to wake him, *end this*, if he'd been able to speak or focus—

—when everything stopped moving.

No, he was still moving, but only along a single blissful plane, gently.

<Henry.>

"Henry. We've landed on the *Lissett*."

He tried to answer. Choked on bile. Felt something warm and wet rinse his face and fill his mouth. Swallowed inadvertently. *Flip's blueberry juice.* Found his voice, "Here." Reaching up, Henry discovered his arms were free, that he was, and opened his eyes to find the porthole coated with—"What is *that*?"

<Cirri—the feeding arms of a barnacle. Henry, you made it. Are you all right?>

Rena's priorities. A ragged chuckle escaped his lips. "Fine. I'm fine. Flip, status."

"I must move, Henry. The communications rig cannot be deployed through these—creatures." With profound distaste.

Did the polymorph imagine them sticking to his *hull?* "Don't worry, Flip. Barnacles take a long time to grow," Henry said reassuringly, confident Rena would correct him if wrong.

"Moving now."

The shuttle didn't lift into the air, as Henry'd expected, but lurched forward. Once clear of the frond-like cirri, he spotted a gray ropey thing—with, yes, those were rows of suckers—flail, then smack down. Flip had made a tentacle to pull altself over the barnacles. A tentacle, moreover, just like the one in an antique film from the polymorph's collection, and this time Henry laughed long and hard.

"Shuttle, this is the Portal," Killian's voice, abrupt and, yes, alarmed. "What's going on down there?"

Henry wiped his eyes. "We're good, Pilot. Moving—" As the shuttle lurched again. "—into position to deploy."

***

He'd no scale for the waves they rode. They'd slide up and up and, by lightning flash, he'd glimpse a limitless terrain of moving water overhung by black roiling cloud. If rays of sunlight reached here, the event must be rare, perhaps, as Rena posited, cueing what lived in the water to their own urgent action.

Down, down, down they'd slide until all he could see was a wall of dark water, striped in glowing froth. If not for Flip augmenting alts internal dampers, he'd have been sick again.

Dampers consumed power. Everything did. Flip's abilities might seem almost limitless on New Earth or attached to the Portal, but here, fighting simply to stay attached to the *Lissett* wore away at resources they'd need to climb up again, setting a merciless deadline.

Flip remained alts steady self. Dragged them to right spot. Deployed the engineers' clever workaround—

"You may enter your code, Henry."

Anticipating the *Lissett*'s hatches and other access points to be either submerged or barnacled—and given the very short window of time—the engineers on New Earth had come up with a solution. Sound would carry through the metal and ceramics of the outer hull, especially from a point source, quicker if the metal in the area was warmed.

The rig had anchored itself, blasted a portion of the hull with heat, and would tap Henry's introductory message with a small but powerful percussive hammer.

The Tailings would approve, he thought, typing the code string on a keyboard morphed from the foam under the porthole.

The *Lissett* would do the rest, activating its coms to listen for a Human voice. A voice Henry had to produce, in person. *Not his favorite part of the process.*

"Henry, are you ready?"

<Watch your footing,> Rena told him.

The foam under his feet flowed away, forming a short tube with a ladder on the side. After activating the respirator around his neck, Henry took hold of the ladder. "Ready."

"Limpeting now." The shuttle seemed to sag a second, then the bottom of the tube irised open.

The *Lissett.* Black, glistening with water, and yes, slime.

Henry climbed down as quickly as he could. Held on while he explored the surface with a booted foot, rubbed a section clear. Stepped off. "Now."

Three Flip-ropes snaked out and around his waist, securing him in place, then Flip opened a side of the tube.

Henry was swept off his feet, held only by the ropes, legs fluttering like flags. *This was the least windy side?* "This is the Arbiter. I've come to save your passengers," he shouted at the top of his lungs, having to rely on the *Lissett* to detect his voice within the thrumming howl of storm, the crack of thunder, and the ceaseless pound of wave against the ship. "You must ascend to orbit now. *Lissett* comply." The rig would repeat the words, but his voice, the phrase *save your passengers*, was the authorization required. "*Lissett,* COMPLY!"

The ropes retracted, pulling Henry up as Flip closed the opening. Before he could say a word or ask a question, he found himself encased in foam, his stomach protesting a sudden upward motion.

"The ship is complying, Henry," Flip informed him. "We have to get out of her way."

Glad someone thought of that.

"Barnacles."

THERE were moments that transcended everything else in your life; this, Killian knew, eyes riveted to the screen, was hers. The shuttle's feed had taken her down through a frankly terrifying atmosphere, onto what looked more reef than sleeper ship in an ocean sure to keep her on land. But this?

The Halcyon Class *Lissett* rose on a cloud of her own, water turned to steam as engines built for interstellar space fired a final time, the columns she'd made to stay afloat and alive falling away. She'd no subtlety, made no adjustments like Flip, who'd danced with the wind, rising under full throttle; she was sheer power pushing . . . pushing . . . accelerating.

A chunk broke away. "Barnacles," Killian whispered.

<You hope.>

But Gis was as transfixed as she was by the spectacle, as were the spacers watching from their tiny ships, ready to catch the *Lissett* when she breached atmo—*if she did*—and of course the almighty Arbiter, in some fit of crazy, had ordered it be shared with Earth as well.

Disaster or triumph. They'd all be witness.

The screen filled with thick, heavy clouds. "Where'd it go?"

"The *Lissett* continues to ascend, Killian. I have removed Henry from her vicinity."

In case her engines blew.

<She'll make it,> Gis decided then and there, being Gis and stubborn in her faith. <Bet you twenty, Killie-Cat.>

What the hell. She wrote on her pad, "Raise you to a hundred—" crossed it out, "two hundred." The *Lissett*'s lucky number. Winner might claim beer or pushups, didn't matter.

"We've cleared atmosphere," Flip announced. Killian glanced at the right screen, spotting the icon—this time a bird—of the shuttle projected over the planet. "We'll remain at a safe distance—"

She heard Henry's muffled, "No, we won't!"

"—at a distance," firmly, Flip in charge.

Time slowed, was measured in shared heartbeats, in drops of sweat, in—

"There she is!" Killian shouted.

<You great bloody beauty!>

That's what she was, enormous and battered, her original strong lines corrupted but not erased by barnacles, and the pilot found herself impressed so many had stayed stuck, but there was no time for more. "Go get her!" she ordered the catchers, but they were already in motion. Every one of them.

They met the hulk rising into space, triplets breaking apart, claws out, spreading in their halo to surround the *Lissett*—what remained of her. Killian squinted. "She doesn't look right."

<'Cause that sweet loving fucker dumped her core, Killie-Cat! Got to speed and chucked it away before it could blow!> Gis choked up.

Killian checked telemetry. "She's hit max height. Made low orbit. Barely." The planet's atmosphere was tenuous at that altitude but still enough to siphon away the Lissett's hard-won velocity and drag her back down. Except for the dozens of tough little craft out there, doing what they were designed to do. *Catch a falling star.*

"Can you do it?"

"THEY have the *Lissett* in orbit, Henry." Flip sounded faintly astonished.

"Good to hear." Henry leaned back, crossing his arms behind his head as if admiring the view. It helped hide the bone-ratcheting tension he'd felt since the sleeper ship responded and he'd realized what he had to do. First, portray the Arbiter of people's expectation, calm and confident whatever the circumstance.

Such as the Kmet coming down to New Earth.

He could sit because, once convinced there'd be no explosion, the shuttle had absorbed the foam, resuming a more comfortable configuration. "Head back to the Portal, Flip. I'd like to be there before Killian transits them home."

Them being Alt-Intel and epitome pilots and their craft, plus what they gripped. The sleeper ship had shed a fifth of her bulk with her engines, the torn end trailing debris. More twinkled around her—the remnants of the columns, he guessed. Some of the catchers, the ship settled in orbit, dashed in pursuit, sweeping up every scrap to bag for transit.

Best news of all, the passenger pods remained intact and functioning, according to data now streaming from the ship herself.

"They planned well." Ousmane, standing by the image, was almost purring. "I shall be forever grateful, ah, Henry, you allowed the world to watch."

"Huh. I still can't believe you did." Shomchai shook his head. "What if it failed?"

"The world would have seen." Rena didn't look up, busy examining the slime on the boots Henry'd kept for her before both were recycled. The lens in her projected hand showed her what Flip magnified on her behalf. "How hazardous Henry's mission is—" she went on, lecturing the slime, her hand beginning to shake. "—for him and those he's saving. How easy it is to lose the very ground you stand on. How we should be grateful to *have* a home to share."

Henry let her words fill the shuttle, the emotion in them penetrate. Rena would receive a package very soon containing the samples he'd sent via one of the catchers, of the dead, of Kmet-Here. Would do her utmost to find him answers.

Couldn't do this without her. He made sure his own voice was steady before he said, "It was time."

Sofia, who hadn't spoken since being summoned, burst out passionately, "Time to remind those on the ground our future is in space!"

Henry cocked his head, openly studying her. Her expression as she looked back—eyes glittering, jaw tight—spoke volumes. *I belong here and you don't.* With a dose of *wouldn't have missed this.*

And likely a good portion of smug, *you have no idea who I am.*

Which wasn't true. Thanks to Simmons, with help from Kisho, Henry and the Arbiter's Office knew everything there was to know about the never-retired leader of the System Coalition, who oversaw hidden warehouses full of pre-Heartbreak tech and controlled operations on two orbital stations—who'd ordered Killian to spy inside the Portal, then, impatient for results, had her loyal engineer wired into Giselle's brain to report to her.

As if that wasn't harm enough, the instant Sofia'd realized Henry wouldn't need her for a while, she'd unplugged the engineer, replacing him with herself. The man remained incoherent and the med team had no idea how Giselle had survived it.

She wouldn't have, if Killian hadn't hinted to Henry of trouble in the Spacer Repository, and who could say what that would have done to the pilot's sanity? And their mission.

Her head lifted as he continued to regard her. *That overweening pride.* Sofia knew her importance to the evacuations. Likely believed that's why she sat here, projected from house arrest instead of a prison cell; a reprieve, granted on his personal authority.

Henry gave her an acknowledging nod.

It wasn't about what Sofia'd done, good or ill. It was what he needed her to do.

He dropped his arms, pulling up his sleeve. Rena caught his intention and solemnly put away her lens, her eyes thanking him. Ousmane bowed. Shomchai grinned. "Time to break out the glasses?"

Henry gave a rueful smile and shook his head. "We're not done yet. I'll bring you back when we reach the final planet. I've work to do first. Thank you all." He pressed three of the bands.

Though startled to remain, Sofia recovered quickly. "Yes, Henry?" Wary, the question.

"When the *Lissett* arrives, I'm putting the System Coalition—you—in charge of her immediate refit."

She might have dissembled. Instead, her head thrust forward, her eyes cold. "Why?"

"Can you do it?"

Her fingers rubbed the side of her throat. Tipped up her chin. Finally, Sofia gave a tiny, reluctant nod. "Depends on her damage. How much of her you want up and running. We've maintained working components, including three cores, from the

Halcyon program—" A major admission and one he'd counted on; he waved her past it. "We get the people off, use polymorphs—"

Holes drilled into flesh. "Human-tech."

That got a reaction. Her gaze shot to the ceiling, where everyone assumed *Flip* to be, then back to him. "In that case, the answer's no, we can't do it, immediately or otherwise. We don't have the people."

"You'll have the full support of the Arbiter's Office and the Assembly. Requisition whatever you need, whoever you need." He leaned back, steepled his fingers, and regarded her. "Whatever her condition, the *Lissett* must launch before I finish this mission. With her passengers."

Her eyes widened. "You're not waking them? But why—" Sofia's mouth clamped shut.

Because they were the only insurance he had. Because he rode an apocalyptic wave he couldn't stop, and it could wash away everything he sought to protect.

"Chickens," Henry told her.

A glare. "Make sense."

"Eggs in one basket. You said it first," he reminded her gently. "This is my answer."

Her flash of comprehension became horror. "Henry—" His name had never sounded so desperate a plea. "—no. No."

"As far as the Kmet and the public are concerned," he continued, ruthlessly calm, "the passengers will be evacuated to New Earth. As far as anyone outside your projects will know, we're refitting the *Lissett* into a freighter. When the moment comes, every ship we have will leave orbit with her, scattering in different directions, giving her a chance to make it."

Envisioning what would be Earth's last act of defiance, imagining kmeth's indignation at what would seem so many Humans escaping at once—he'd have smiled if it hadn't meant most wouldn't.

"Can you do it?" he repeated.

Waited.

Watched grim resolve fill her face. "Niablo Station has the newest space dock. I want it."

And recently moved from the Portal's line-of-sight. "It's yours," he told her, fingers reaching for her wristband. "When you wake, there'll be personnel standing by to get whatever you need. Any questions?"

"Dozens." Sofia gave a harsh laugh. "None I want answered—wait, yes, I've one."

Henry raised his eyebrows in invitation.

"Where's the *Lissett* to go?"

"Where there's a future." He raised his hand and rotated a finger at the cosmos. "There's to be no record of the coordinates left behind. Remove her message probes and wipe all navigation data from her archives."

To keep the past from following.

"It's bad."

<YOU'VE got this, Killie-Cat.>

Didn't have much choice, did she? Killian wiped sweat from her palms before lifting her hands to the pedestal. The mass waiting to enter the Portal was beyond anything she'd handled before—beyond anything Earth had seen pop into existence overhead. She'd a feeling Omar's massive perimeter alarm wasn't helping anyone's nerves.

She glanced at the den. Part of her would have gladly relinquished control for this to Kmet-Here. The rest was appalled she'd think it, and Gis would have her ears—

Henry came up beside her. He'd been quiet. Was doubtless bruised and battered, given the ride he'd had down and up, but she didn't suggest he go to quarters. "Not bad, Arbiter," Killian gave him. "Not bad at all."

<Tell him he's YUMMY.>

"Gis agrees."

He glanced at her through that mop of hair. "I'll take the compliment once she's safely in Niablo's space dock."

Killian's eyebrows flew up. Reading something *off* in his expression, she didn't ask. "Roger that."

Gis wasn't so reticent. <What the hell's he up to?>

"You'll be briefed," Henry promised.

And why did she think he wasn't talking to her?

"Ready to transit, *Lissett*," Killian announced grimly. "Move in."

"Roger, that, Portal." With an enviable lack of emotion; the lead catcher, being an Alt-Intel, had probably dampened its fear response.

Her hands reached for the controls; PIPs scampered up the walls, ready to assist.

<Same as always,> her partner proclaimed stoutly. <Get'r done, Killie-Cat.>

Off the top of her head, she'd eleven—no, twelve—ways this could go sideways, starting with—Killian wiped her palms a final time, seized the levers, and—

"GOT HER!" Omar's voice rang out and there was no doubt how he felt. "Got them all! WHOO!!! The *Lissett* and her passengers are home!"

"Roger that." Killian killed the com, fought a shiver as she turned to Henry. "Well?"

The almighty Arbiter had the gall to grin up at her. "Not bad."

Henry ordered them both to rest before rousing Kmet-Here to take them to World VI. Killian doubted he would and she was too buzzed with adrenalin to try, but the pause helped. She showered and ate. Changed into fresh coveralls and threw her painting shirt, a ragged treasure discovered in a trunk, over top, ready to finish the single, hope-filled bud that was the *Lissett.*

She hadn't inked the room of the dead, seeing no point recording a featureless space. *And she'd never forget.*

Her new rolypoly was under the bed, courtesy of Henry's smuggling skills, waiting to open the next tube. Wouldn't happen before transit.

Killian'd let Gis grab some awake; checking the time, she smiled and pressed her wristband. "You there, Space Rat?"

No gruff, cheering *Always, Killie-Cat.* Instead, her mind filled with a hoarse, <It's bad, Killian. Worse than.>

She froze, paint dripping from her brush. Slapped a question mark on the canvas.

<Henry wasn't lying about the briefing. They were waiting when I woke. I'm to give you all they give me. That's the deal, to keep it Humans-only.> Gis' voice strengthened, developed urgency. <This to start, 'cause it's the big one. Instant you're done and transit your Portal to New Earth orbit, Arbiter's ordered the *Lissett* launched. Full refit, best can be—everyone stays aboard. Got that? He's sending the lot of them out again.>

She got it. Likely more than Gis. The *Lissett*'s passengers? Henry, saving some of their kind should the Kmet turn out to be the enemy. Or kmeth's enemy show up. Or whatever dire prospect haunted the man, and she had to admire his ability to seize an opportunity. No way the Arbiter could have anticipated a mostly intact sleeper ship to land in his hands.

Trouble was . . . She painted *who?*

<Coalition's working with the Arbiter.> And oh, the caution in her tone. <Everything's forgiven, hear me?>

Not by her. Not ever. Feelings had no weight in this, but Killian sketched a face, giving it all the hubris she remembered. Until Sofia m'Rogers t'Patel stared back at her and at Gis—

She painted a thick black X over each eye.

Her partner whispered a troubled, <How did you know?> Then. <Henry.>

"Nope," she said, as if talking to herself. "Didn't have a clue till now." Grabbing a tube of white, she methodically covered the portrait, waiting for Gis to come around.

<Smartass.> But with affection. <Can we get on with this? There's more you need to know.>

She flashed a thumps-up.

***

Henry met her by the tube mouth to Control, bulb in hand. As usual, he wore his silly sandals but had changed into what Killian thought of as his *meet-the-relatives* suit. Used to fit him like a glove. Now it hung as if made for someone else.

She'd had to pull in the sides of her coveralls. The ready-dinners fed a body; they didn't nourish it, not for this long. Killian handed him his meds.

"Thank you, Killian. Ready?" Asked with that clear-eyed look, defying her to argue with any of his scheme.

Almighty Arbiter. She wrinkled her nose at him. "Do I have a choice?"

His somber, "I hope so," ended any conversation.

She went first. The mouth opened in the floor this time. Climbing out, she reached back to offer Henry a hand up. Waited until he gave a nod, then went to the dais. Showing some sense, he'd given her the coordinates for the *Centralia*'s destination before going down with Flip. Now, she entered them.

Done, she nodded to Henry, who went to the den and whistled.

<Last world, Killie-Cat. Then you're coming home.>

She gave a thumps-up. Her heart wasn't in it. Watched as Kmet-Here heaved from hiding, willy-bits that agreeable purple, scales shining as if the PIPs had got busy with polish, dull splotches on kmeth's belly as if they'd missed.

<Kmeth look bigger to you?>

Next to Henry, it looked more as if the Arbiter'd shrunk. She brought up her notepad, wrote: *Can't tell for sure.*

BOOM! "We go now, Arbiter-Henry?" BOOM! "To the last wrong place?"

"Yes." Henry indicated the pedestals. "The coordinates are set, Kmet-Here."

An eye swung up to the screens, studied the clouded world below. "This was a very wrong place."

"Agreed," Henry replied. "Yet we found survivors and sent them home. A success, Kmet-Here. Shall we go?"

The creature huffed in answer, moving to the dais. Reared up, tongue tips flailing, and Killian took an involuntary step back.

The Kmet paused, an eye riveted on her. "You should watch, Pilot Killian. This will be your task next."

Henry, damn him, smiled encouragingly.

So there was nothing for it but to move close to Kmet-Here, breathe in kmeth's stench, and watch kmeth's tongue trail slime over the controls.

TRANSIT.

"Swear it."

Doublet

EWEN'S watchdog was an ornery Seeker named Hamen who'd hit the point of people-sour where he kept to the fringe of camp, eyes averted, and spoke, if at all, in barely comprehensible grunts. In Beth's opinion, Hamen should take his last walk into the Split and do everyone a kindness, not be assigned a newbie.

But they hadn't asked, so she didn't say it. What she did do, having seen the way of things, was take the young Seeker aside, now and then. Showed him her kit. Checked his. Tossed some that was useless weight. Got him a groundsheet without holes from the supply truck, Hamen having swapped his for the boy's new one, and made sure Ewen knew how to resole his boots.

"That's what gets you Home again," Beth told him over that task.

He'd gotten quieter, these past days. Sharper, that too, and was smart. She'd some hope for him. Slim, admittedly.

Hamen stalked past, glared down at them. Went to spit and swallowed it, being too long a Seeker to put moisture on the ground, and gave her a look.

Beth gave him one back. "You planning ever to be of value to this boy?" she asked, oh so polite.

His grunt wasn't.

Ewen's gaze bored into Hamen's back as he walked away. He turned it on Beth. "Why can't I come with you?"

"Told you," she said patiently, "I'm going right across, into Away." As his eyes lit up, she tsked. "Your job's to walk into the Split, shelter through the heat, then turn around and walk out to your mark. Do that, you're a Seeker. Do that five times, you get to cross. Hear me?"

"I hear you." With a bright-eyed joy he'd lose after, say, the first hour.

Maybe sooner. "Then hear this," she warned, looking for Hamen. Spotting him, huddled like misery in the shadows. "A Seeker brings some of the Split back, inside, each walk. Changes you. You don't believe a word."

He'd fidgeted. Had the grace to blush. "From you, Beth, I do. I swear. But you aren't like—" a nod at the shadows.

She snorted. "Thanks for that." Turned serious again. "Doesn't mean I don't have dark inside. Doesn't mean I won't become it, day comes. Seekers like Hamen, their minds stay in the Split, even Home, even safe. Day comes—he won't leave it." *Could someone this young understand?* "That happens, you're on your own, Ewen. You can't save him. You can't try. You turn for Home and walk out."

"I—" Silence.

Beth's hand shot across the space between them, took hold of his collar, pulled him close by it. "Swear it. Swear or I'm done."

His eyes were like saucers, but he didn't struggle. "I promise, Beth."

She let go, patted his cheek before he could draw back. "Good."

"But—"

Beth raised an eyebrow. Waited.

Ewen reached behind him, bringing forth his staff. "Show me how to call a ribbon?"

***

The next morning Beth stood with the convoy to watch the two Seekers head into the Split. She'd helped hammer in their mark, a thick pole of wood soaked in tar. Showed Ewen where to carve his initials and the date. Stood by as Hamen, lively as could be now he was leaving, did the same. Rule was, coming out, you carved when. Marks like this lined the border of the Split. Too many had only entry dates.

The convoy would split here, most heading north for her, two trucks to camp for the day and wait for the Seekers.

From the faces of those watching, she wasn't the only one who thought the boy would come back alone.

World VI

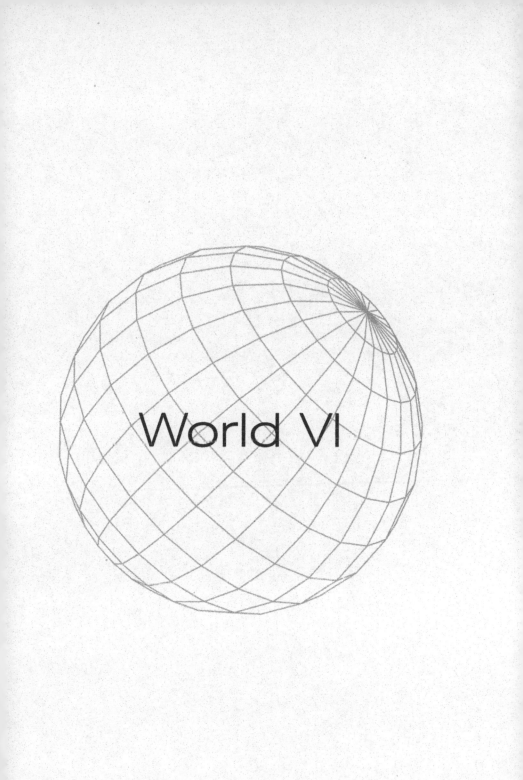

"Let's take our break."

"NEXT, you will do this." Kmet-Here's eyes locked on Killian. "You must take us home, to New Earth, and complete the Duality." A muted BOOM! Polyps an anxious pink. "You must. Pilot Killian, do you concur?" The Kmet ignored the screens and where they'd arrived. Ignored Henry in favor of the pilot standing in front of kmeth, and the Arbiter tensed. If his authority was waning, they'd have to readjust.

Without hesitation, Killian put a stride between her and the Kmet, turning smartly to face him. "Arbiter?"

The right move. Kmeth aimed an eye his way, polyps darkening to purple. "Arbiter Henry. Do you concur?"

Henry bowed, using the second to compose his face. Rose. "I concur, Kmet-Here. Pilot Killian will take us to New Earth. After we've evacuated these people." He waved to the screens. By the lights clustered along one edge of the night-dark continent below the Portal, there weren't as many as World III, Henry judged, but a good number. Meaning they'd stay in orbit a while.

Purple faded again. "Too many Humans-There." With an unexpected tremor. "Too long here. We must hurry. HURRY!" Kmet-Here stared at Henry, rose as if longing to challenge the Arbiter's methods.

"Then we'd best get started," Henry replied cheerfully. "I'll call you at the first shift change."

A discontented rumble. Polyps reddened. "TOO SLOW!"

<Henry, kmeth has gained mass. I can't say what it means, but this increased impatience suggests a change underway internally as well. Don't annoy kmeth. >

Good advice. A shame he couldn't take it.

"I'm in charge of the evacuation process for all Humans-There." Henry stepped up to the Kmet, crowding kmeth, noticing he had to bend his neck significantly more to meet the gaze of a wide black pupil. "Do you concur, Kmet-Here?"

BOOM! Without answering, the giant creature spun on a flipper, making Henry scramble out of the way of the tail end, then heaved kmethself away, grumbling all the way to kmeth's den. As if drawn by the Kmet's fury, PIPs chased after, swarming up the tail and sides, others converging on the den entrance only to be squashed for their devotion.

Impatient to reach Earth and they'd whatever time it took to move World VI's population to find out why. *And no more.*

Henry exchanged looks with Killian. She gave him a tight-lipped nod. "Launching satellites," she said, stepping on the dais, avoiding the PIP sucking goo from the controls. Fortunately, the ones she needed hadn't been slimed.

He pulled out his fake phone. "Flip, launch your remotes. Please be more discreet this time."

YES, HENRY.

He trusted Giselle to have told Killian what Flip already knew, about his doomsday plan. Being spacers, they'd have informed doubts over cobbling a working starship from museum-quality parts and a hull recovered from an ocean; being spacers, they'd take the hope, keep the secret.

It wouldn't stay secret for long, no matter how good Sofia and her people—and his—were, not when he'd deliberately focused everyone's rapt attention on the *Lissett.*

Not once he'd set in motion a careful series of leaks. The rest of Earth would find out about the refit. Why her passengers weren't being interviewed on the news. Concern would grow over the current Arbiter's sanity—a given—but, most importantly, already shaken people would begin to look up at the sky and question what they thought they knew about the Kmet, the Duality, and the real threat to humanity.

Be better prepared to act on the truth, once Henry had it to give them. The first ship transiting through from this world would carry his directives. To Simmons, who'd begin the leak. To the Assembly and Planetary Peace Corps and every agency able to devise a defense, charged with keeping the Kmet from landing at any cost, if that landing violated Human interest.

"Sats away."

REMOTES HAVE LAUNCHED, HENRY.

They'd gather the information the Arbiter needed, so he could do what he didn't want to do, and hurry the final remnants of humanity home, to whatever the Kmet had in mind for it.

Killian looked at him. Frowned at what she saw. "Your shuttle?" *Let's talk,* that was.

A conversation he wasn't ready for, in any sense. "Let's take our break first, Pilot," Henry countered wearily. "Twelve hours, I believe was your recommendation, post-transit?"

Her frown deepened, but she didn't argue.

Maybe she guessed he'd nothing more to say.

"Killian . . . !"

<HENRY might need a rest, Killie-Cat. Man had a rough ride, case you didn't notice.>

She sat on the toilet, notepad in hand. Shook her head. Wrote: *He's got something up his sleeve.*

<Of course he does. He's the Arbiter. You're the pilot.>

Wasn't it. Henry didn't pull rank on her. Didn't, until now, keep secrets from her and while Killian fully understood—and shared—a certain paranoia about their privacy on the Portal?

The shuttle was safe. *It had to be.*

<You thinking of that shower we missed?>

"No time," Killian muttered. Besides, she knew her partner's voice—in her head or out—and the offer wasn't sincere. They were both off, since Henry's plan for the *Lissett* dropped in to shade everything good.

Best way to deal with that? Find something new. Making her next trip into the Portal more urgent than ever. She wrote: *Keep an eye on what's going on, Space Rat. I'm off to explore.*

<You find anything, bring me back in.> A pause. <Belay that. Not if more alien corpses. Don't need those. Anything else before I go?>

Killian nodded to herself. Wrote: *Ask Annie about Omar's Kmet and PIPs—if he's noticed anything strange about them lately.*

<Stranger than always, you mean?> Somehow Gis conveyed a snort through their connection. <Got it.> She'd have seen it, how Kmet-Here kept getting bigger—touchier. How the PIPs were reacting to kmeth, grew more clingy, if that were possible. <Watch your back. Love you, Killie-Cat.>

"Lima Charlie, Space Rat."

Killian tapped off the wristband and went to find her traveling companion.

"Shouldn't you be resting, Killian?" Rolypoly's lens aimed up, then down, as if assessing her condition.

Fussed like Flip. Being Flip, something Killian occasionally forgot. "Can this bit make coffee? No? Then I'll rest later." She scooped the rolypoly up, tucking alt under one arm, and went into the corridor.

Disturbed to find it changed. Shallow valleys crossed the floor, running up the wall and ceiling like inverted wrinkles. Had the light dimmed? A shiver ran up her spine—*what the hell was that wailing?*

A harmonica. The almighty Arbiter in his quarters, playing a harmonica. Poorly but with gusto.

Well, there was a new side to the man.

Shaking her head, Killian stepped across valleys to the first accessible tube mouth, having had enough of ceilings. Henry'd see for himself when he stopped fooling around and left his quarters.

The mouth wouldn't open until she pushed the rolypoly at it. *Promising.* She sniffed cautiously.

"Killian?"

"Just checking," she muttered. It wasn't as if the corpses gave off a warning smell last time. "In you go. No, wait." She froze, holding Rolypoly in the open mouth. Thought hard. The PIPs had responded to her voice.

Would whatever controlled her destination?

Worth a try. But what to say? Gis was better at this stuff.

And busy. Killian chewed her bottom lip. What *she* wanted to find was a weapon against the Kmet.

The harmonica went off-key, making her wince.

Henry'd want answers.

Nothing ventured—Killian spoke into the opening. "Show me why the Kmet need our planet."

Rolypoly was pulled from her hands, sucked into the tube. "Killian . . . !" she heard and dove after alt.

She was not *going to enjoy where this went.*

The tube spat her out.

Killian landed rolling. The drop hadn't been much but the floor wasn't level and she grabbed, finding something solid to hold. A table leg?

"Are you all right?" Rolypoly asked.

"Yes, yes." She got to her feet. It wasn't a table—well, it had supports, but the top consisted of a white counter curved along the wall, a meter from the floor. All the walls, Killian discovered as she turned slowly in place. There were tube mouths under the counter at atypically regular intervals and, yes, the floor sloped profoundly from the walls to the center, making her lean for balance.

The countertop was covered in little red boxes, stacked and scattered, outwardly identical.

When Killian went to pick one up, it resisted before coming loose. Perhaps magnetic. The spacer in her approved. *Henry could learn something.*

With uncanny precision, Rolypoly asked, "Shall I contact Henry now?"

"We don't have anything yet. Let him rest." *Or whatever he was doing.*

The box had curved corners like the larger structures within the Portal. Was light, featureless, and, when she shook it gingerly, rattled. *A toy?* Went with the stubby height.

Aliens, she reminded herself. Who could tell?

Meanwhile Rolypoly had rolled up to a support and started to climb. Suddenly flinched away, rolling until producing a sucker to stop.

"What happened?"

"Be careful, Killian. It stings."

She put her hand flat on the counter. "Nothing." Bent to touch a finger where Rolypoly had been stung. "Nothing." She eyed him. "What are we thinking? Something to keep PIPs from tidying up?"

"I cannot speculate from so little information." With annoyance. *Probably the sting.* "If you would bring your box closer to me, please, I will scan it."

She crouched and went to put the box on the floor beside alt, only to find it adhered to her palm. She tried shaking it off without success. Finally, she pulled it free with an effort and put it on the floor.

Where it rolled on its own accord, end over end to the very center, the lowest point, and came to rest.

Sank halfway down.

The lights went out.

Killian kept still. Rolypoly emitted a faint glow. *Wouldn't squash alt, then.* Meager comfort, standing in the dark while an alien machine began to—

The walls came alive.

She was surrounded by images of aliens, overlapping, and many definitely upside down to her perspective, implying theirs to be different, or their way of storing information was, the point being, "It's a library," she whispered, awestruck.

"Or an art gallery," Rolypoly offered. "It is a form of information storage. I suggest we disturb Henry's rest now."

Killian nodded. There were hundreds, maybe thousands of boxes, with no knowing how much was stored in each, and no way to pick and choose. She reached for her wristband. *The more eyes the merrier.*

Maybe one of them could figure out how to use this.

"It's hard."

"I'VE received a response to your message of introduction, Henry. By radio, as anticipated. The inhabitants call their world Brightside—"

Henry barely registered the words, his attention on the wall screen showing Killian moving around the Portal Library, as they'd decided to name it. A library. His heart pounded at the thought—and from having reached the shuttle as quickly as the tube system allowed.

"—three hundred and forty-three thousand individuals represented by a governor, council, and science advisory board. They are ready to meet with you at your earliest—"

He gave an irritated wave. "Not now, Flip."

"You asked to be informed immediately," the polymorph said firmly. "Shall I continue the response from Brightside?"

"No, thank you, Flip." It didn't have a name, now that he was here, only a designation: World VI.

He found he couldn't bring himself to make the correction. *Brightside.* Such hope, in a name. *And now this.* "Send an acknowledgment for me and ask details for the meeting. This—" he pointed at the screen "—takes precedence. Are you recording?"

The images kept changing—Killian had found she didn't need to replace a box to activate new images on the curved walls; rolling another down to join what was there worked as well.

And why would that be?

"Of course, Henry." A touch of smug, multitasking something Flip relished. "I am able to capture every image displayed, on every wall." Alts PIP-self having squatted near the center of the floor.

Rena, Shomchai, and Ousmane had joined him, projected as sitting on benches, equally engrossed. Flip ensured Killian could hear, if not see them.

"It's, ah, a curated collection. Organized," Ousmane said abruptly. "I can't discern how yet, ah, but there's groupings. Similarities. I'm, ah, sure of it."

"I agree," Flip replied. "I am performing a multilayered analysis as the images come in. There appears no attempt to sort by time, only by place and perhaps event."

"Or age," Rena offered.

Shomchai blew out a breath. "Looks like a family album to me."

What sort of family? Henry looked to the xenologist.

"I've some answers." Rena grimaced. "More questions. I can tell you the dead weren't Kmet."

Killian paused to give PIP-Flip, and them, a sardonic thumps-up.

"Anything of what they were?" Henry asked.

She nodded. "Flip, please show my extrapolations."

"Yes, Rena."

Images appeared. Ousmane was fascinated. "This is what they looked like alive?"

"It's preliminary, but yes."

Henry studied the three depicted. An intact pod. A pair of the larger shapes, presumably adults: one plumper or perhaps more muscular, both erect on stout rear legs with smaller but powerful limbs as arms. Very long fingers, with claws between. He looked back to the constantly changing display from the library. Similar beings appeared in differing poses, as often as inverted, head down, legs and short tail up. He pointed. "These are the same species?"

"I believe so. Some of them. Looks to be at least one other form in these images, maybe two—I can't tell while they're jumbled together," Rena muttered to herself, clearly more intrigued than frustrated. "When I go through the recordings I'll be able to pull out individuals and give you more."

"Henry? Can't do it," Killian announced, breaking in. While they absorbed new images, she'd been trying to get a box into a tube mouth. No matter how they disguised the object, even inside PIP-Flip, the mouth snapped shut. She spread her arms, giving up. "We'll only be able to use them here. I'll stay as long as I can," she volunteered, knowing the importance of this find.

Aware she'd yet to be returned to the same part of the Portal.

"Thank you, Killian." *So much there—so little time.* She might have to go through dozens of boxes before finding anything more useful than Shomchai's *family album.*

His every muscle ached despite Flip's foam; the pilot needed her rest, not that she'd admit it. Then there was Brightside—and Kmet-Here—Henry came to a reluctant conclusion. "It's time you came back."

A rebellious glower. The pilot tossed another box along the floor, producing more images.

"Killian—"

"I've a suggestion, Henry." Shomchai's brow had creased in thought. "I'd like Killian to repeat the command she used to have the Portal send her here." He waved a hand. "I realized we don't know if it was the Portal, but for the sake of argument, bear with me. Say it precisely the same way, this time holding a box. Any box."

The pilot looked unconvinced. "Henry?"

"Go ahead, Killian."

They watched her pick up a box with her fingertips, set it on her palm, and say, "Show me why the Kmet need our planet."

The box glowed white. Killian plucked it from her palm and rolled it into the pile on the floor.

The images on the walls changed. They'd done so every time, but this—this time what was displayed were circles of symbols, each with a planet like a bead at the top. PIP-Flip moved to capture the entirety; the shuttle responded by adding screens until it seemed they sat, like Killian, inside the Portal Library.

Seeing what it wanted them to see, what they'd asked to find, and what he'd most feared.

The life cycle of the Kmet included a world.

Predictably, his quorum drew their own conclusions.

"They are histories," Ousmane insisted. "Of the Portal's, ah, travels."

Shomchai's eyes glittered. "And I say they're a primer to the Kmet's written language, at last. There are patterns—"

"Journeys have, ah, repetitive elements—"

Henry glanced at Rena. The xenologist had jerked half out of her seat, then settled in slow motion, studying the circles. He'd a pretty good idea where her thoughts led.

As if feeling his attention, she looked up. Pressed her lips together and gave a tiny shake of her head.

Not yet.

Equally, *not here, in present company.*

Henry stood. "Our thanks, Killian. Please join me here as soon as possible."

A nod. The display vanished—she'd probably grabbed PIP-Flip.

Ousmane gave a little groan.

"Flip, provide your full record to those here." The historian looked happier. "Thank you, everyone. I look forward to your insights when we reconvene."

"Are we free now to consult, Henry?" Shomchai asked earnestly. "I cannot begin to tell you the importance of this find. The significance!"

"I would, ah, also like to bring in other experts. Please."

Henry considered for a long moment, then gave a curt nod. "With constraints," he warned. Matching looks of disappointment filled Ousmane and Shomchai's faces, but they nodded. "Focus on whatever the circles can tell us about the Kmet and those worlds. Nothing else. You'll be able to expand your research later," he added, to soften the blow. *It might even be true.* "The existence of these other aliens and their deaths are to remain classified. Is that understood?"

Ousmane nodded.

The linguist's gaze locked on Henry. "This is because the Kmet intend to land on New Earth, isn't it?"

"What?" Ousmane looked shocked. "Kmeth do?"

"On our return, yes," Henry told her. "And that's classified as well. I'll make an announcement when the time comes." To Shomchai, "Kmet-Here said, *Our Duality will be complete.* Are you any closer to what that means?"

"No. Beyond the superficiality of a shared environment—no."

"If the answer's in what the Portal's given us, find it. Before we enter orbit."

He'd frightened them. There was no help for it, but Henry offered a reassuring smile. "If anyone can do it, you can. Any questions?" When both were silent, he pressed their wristbands.

"It's hard, you know," Rena said after a moment, quietly. "Waking up with your secrets, with no one safe to talk to."

Her, most of all. Everything he asked of them became more and more isolating; he knew and kept asking. Caused his friends to suffer when he couldn't promise they'd survive, and Henry fought to breathe past the crushing weight of it, to keep his expression composed, his voice calm. "What can I do? Move them back to the office? Ousmane has children. Shomchai, a husband. You—have llamas. Right?"

Rena gave a dutiful chuckle. "Keep up, Henry. I've ant farms and orchids, which are being well looked after while I'm camped on the second floor near you. The real you." She sobered, saying it. "Yes, that's exactly what you do. Move them back, but let them bring their families. Quarter them together in the safest building on New Earth. Give them that, Henry, as well as what you fear."

She didn't ask for herself, not his Rena. But having people to touch, who understood and shared most of this? It'd be good for her as well.

With a pang of envy, Henry nodded. "Flip."

"Yes, Henry."

"Contact Simmons. He's to make living arrangements in the Arbiter's Office for Shomchai and Ousmane, and their families—defined as anyone they want with them who's willing to remain sequestered until my return. I want it done immediately."

"Yes, Henry. As you are engaged in caring behavior at this moment, do you want the latest report on your chickens?"

Of all the—Henry covered his face with a hand. "A summary will do. They're doing well?"

"Yes, Henry. And are increasing. The vet—"

"Thank you, Flip." He lowered his hand.

Rena mouthed *chickens?*, her eyes sparkling.

"I believe you said you've new questions?"

Her face lost all expression. "I do." *Was that a furtive glance at the ceiling?* "I'm not ready to share them, Henry. Soon."

No missing the emphasis on *soon* or the finger she flicked toward his arm and its wristbands. Rena wanted to wait and talk to him where no one and nothing could overhear.

Why? Henry put a pleasant smile on his face, his heart sinking. "I'll check with you in a while, then." He tapped her wristband, waking her on New Earth.

"Is everything all right, Henry?" Flip asked, being alts usual kind and courteous self.

Surely that.

Nonetheless, the question left a sudden chill. "Yes, Flip. Please resume your briefing on World VI."

"It's a flaw."

HENRY'D new orders. Killian wasn't to come to the shuttle after the Portal Library, so back to quarters it was. Without Flip's coffee, but freed from another meeting of *experts*, so there was that. She wasn't in the mood, not after being told to abandon treasure. Had sent Gis back and, after shooing Rolypoly under her bed to recharge, headed for the galley.

Unsurprised to find the Arbiter had beat her there. "Hungry?" Without waiting for an answer, she pulled two ready-dinners from the cupboard and tossed those on the table, followed by a handful of bulbs. She handed him a spork as she sat, putting her attention to the food.

A steaming cup slid into view.

Head down, she shot him a frowning look. "This an apology?"

"It's coffee." Henry shrugged. "I'll apologize if you like."

"Don't bother." Her hand snaked out to take the cup. The other joined in, bringing it to her lips, and she took a blissful sip. "Stuff should be illegal."

"Might be," he replied thoughtfully. "I've never asked Flip what's in it."

Killian hesitated less than a heartbeat before taking another sip. "Go Flip."

Something flickered in his eyes. "Indeed." A pause. "Killian, staying longer was too great a risk for whatever you gained."

"You don't know that." She sat back, regarding him over the cup. "What if I'd asked a better question? *Are the Kmet going to kill us all?* Sounds like a good one to me."

His lips twitched. "It does."

She didn't want the almighty Arbiter to agree with her. She wanted to stay angry. At him. At the Kmet. At everything. "Fuck you," she snarled, putting the cup down hard enough to splash its precious contents, braced to get up.

And go where?

Henry leaned on his elbows, chin in his hands, waiting with that forever-patient look on his face. A hint of sadness, too.

Killian subsided. Reclaimed the coffee and took a drink. "You don't make anything easy, Henry. It's a flaw."

"So I've been told." A sigh. He tilted his head, regarding her, hair flopping over his forehead. "Would it help if I said I'm terrified? That I dream I'm trying to evacuate the people of our world, our people, and no one will leave, because we never do that, we never leave, not anymore." His eyes glistened. "That when I'm awake, Killian, all I can think is of the trust put in me, the power given me, and how utterly useless it is out here. That if I—" His wonderful, compelling voice faltered and broke.

"No. NO!" Killian grabbed his wrist. Pulled hard and fast, so he had to jerk his head up or plant his face on the table. "You don't get to crap out. You don't get to doubt. You hear me, Arbiter-sir? It's not part of your damn job!"

A heart-wrenching smile. "To be Human?"

She felt bone beneath her fingers and let go. Stared at him.

Got up and went around the table. Sat on the bench beside him and gathered the most important person on or off Earth oh-so-gently in her arms, settling his head on her shoulder.

"Don't get used to it," she warned.

Smiling when she felt him nod.

"Shuttle away and clear, Portal."

"Roger that." Killian checked the sat feed. "Still the one area of settlement."

<Good. Sooner you're home, Killie-Cat, the better.>

She tipped her hand back and forth in a *who knows?* Felt the same, when all she thought of was home.

Glanced at the den and felt the opposite.

Like the corridor outside their quarters, the PIPs were getting weird. She'd arrived in Control to find several glued to the outside of the den, varied arms out and twitching as if asking for help. They weren't. She'd seen a free PIP wander close and be grabbed and pinned in place. Presumably to be glued—Kmet-Here hadn't come out to add kmeth's goo.

<Yuck.> Gis, succinct as always. <Annie says Omar's PIPs haven't changed at all. Or his Kmet. You aren't the only one asking, by the way.>

Killian nodded to herself. Likely Rena; the xenologist impressed her as the thorough sort. She pulled up her notepad. Wrote: *Keep checking.*

<Roger that. How's Henry holding up?> A little too casual.

She gave a brisk thumps-up, dropping the pad.

Wasn't about to ask who wanted to know. Her genius partner would seize on that as there being some *thing* worth digging for, and Gis let it be? Not in this lifetime.

How was Henry? Killian looked at the screen showing the flying saucer with its dot.

She'd got past wishing for the almighty Arbiter, infallible and confident, Earth's best and brightest hope. That act was for everyone else, impossible to follow. It'd been killing him.

Henry the Human played a lousy harmonica. Wasn't nearly as smart as he thought he was, not if he threw himself in front of charging Kmet and wore sandals to space.

Had the good sense to trust her. And kept his shit together when it counted.

Killian saluted the dot with a finger to her forehead. *All of the above.*

Someone she'd be proud to call friend.

She grinned. *Just not to his face.*

"This isn't over—"

"DID Killian enjoy her coffee, Henry?"

"Yes, Flip. Most thoughtful of you." Even if the lid had threatened to come off during the tube ride and he'd visions of being scalded. "Any more from Brightside—World VI?"

A window opened in the floor to reveal nothing but white. "It continues to snow."

Henry slapped his booted ankle. "I'm prepared. I like snow," he added. "My friends and I built an enormous slide from the barn loft one winter." Granted, with his grandparents' help and the use of a plow. "Everyone used it," he finished, enjoying the memory.

"May I make a personal observation, Henry?"

"Certainly."

"You appear in a better frame of mind than when you left me."

"I suppose I am." Henry gazed at the ceiling. Smiled, a little, remembering the pilot's rough, soul-satisfying embrace. "I guess it's because I'm not as alone as I thought."

With alarm. "Have I failed as your companion? Have I again lost your trust?" The interior lights flickered as if Flip suffered an existential crisis. "Henry! Henry!"

"Easy, Flip. Nothing like that." Not entirely truthful, given Rena's troubling reticence in front of the polymorph—*he wanted* that *cleared up as soon as possible*—but the Arbiter chose not to disturb his shuttle. "It's a Human thing. I'll explain later. How long till we land?"

The lights stabilized. "Four minutes, Henry. You will be addressing Brightside's full Council and Science Advisory Board, as well as their elected leader, Governor Constance O'Belleveau. The meeting will be broadcast via frequency-modulated radio waves. They have an efficient communication system."

"Of course they do," Henry grumbled, then gave himself a shake. "Sorry, Flip. I'd counted on a slowdown here."

"In order to learn more about the Kmet and Earth. If it helps, I consider it highly probable Killian will make a key discovery on her next excursion."

He cocked an eyebrow. "Giving odds on that?"

"You don't like odds, Henry. Three minutes till landing."

True. "I rephrase. Why do you think so?"

"The Portal, in each instance, has transported Killian to significant locations. I see no reason to suggest the next won't be, particularly as her use of a vocal prompt proved effective."

"Yes. It did, didn't it . . ." Henry tapped a knuckle to his teeth, thinking.

"Henry, please do nothing rash."

He chuckled. Stopped—it sounded unnatural even to him—then asked, feeling morbidly curious, "You don't find it rash of me to land on an alien planet and walk alone into its seat of government to tell them they have to evacuate."

"This excursion has been well-planned. You are invited and share a common language with little drift. I will remain nearby and watch via the remote you carry."

"Well then." Henry settled back in his seat and pretended to yawn. "Let's go do something entirely safe."

"I did not say there were no risks, Henry." A pause. "Despite them, you've been successful on all previous occasions. This is the final planet of your mission. Congratulations are, I believe, in order."

"Not yet, Flip." The Arbiter closed his eyes as the shuttle came to rest.

Not yet.

Brightside's gracious stone Government House wouldn't have looked out of place on his Earth; then again, the plans for such buildings had come on the *Centralia*. The choice to use or adapt them belonged to her passengers. Henry's first impression was they'd stuck to what worked.

The planet was larger but less dense, so gravity wasn't an issue. Winter in this hemisphere, a low-pressure system moving in from the ocean bringing bands of snow. It wasn't cold.

Briefcase in hand, Henry stepped from the ramp, squinting through thick flakes of snow that obscured the details of the buildings around him and clung to the stones of the one ahead. To either side a crowd gathered, muffled in winter gear coated in snow, as if waiting for hours. Or minutes. The bands were intense but narrow. The sun might come out.

Everyone was silent, staring at him—and likely the flying saucer—until a shouted, incredulous, "He's from New Earth?"

An answered shout, "Can't tell!"

"Flip, amplify," Henry whispered. When he spoke again, his voice carried across the courtyard. "I am Arbiter Henry m'Yama t'Nowak, from New Earth." Having the badge in his gloved hand, he raised it, turning slowly to show them all. Heard a muted chorus of reaction. Only those in front could see, but they quickly told those behind, the word spreading to the fringes.

"What's an Arbiter here for?" Another shout, this time anxious.

"I've come to help you. New Earth has sent me with a vital message concerning your safety for you and your government."

"Old Constance doesn't believe in Earth." That provoked a round of laughter.

Henry felt a rush of hope.

Maybe there'd be a delay here after all.

The big double doors opened and figures appeared on the stairs, official in matching uniforms, moving briskly to form an honor guard to either side. A pair marched to Henry. "Come with us, Arbiter," said one, taking his case. "The governor's expecting you."

Or not.

***

Fragrant boughs of cedar, or the local equivalent, stood in a trio of waist-high urns at the center of a magnificent circular foyer, three stories high, with a tiled mosaic floor that would have told Henry things if they'd let him pause to study it, and gloomy portraits hung between closed doors he doubted would.

Flip's remote had tucked itself in his hair. Henry couldn't stop thinking about it—loathed anything touching his scalp when he wasn't being led to an ominous set of tall doors—and the only benefit, besides Flip recording what he wasn't being given time to see?

He'd no time to worry about his reception as the doors swung open and trumpets blew to announce his arrival.

Inside was an even grander room than the foyer promised, redolent of leather upholstery and polished wood. Elaborate fixtures of blown glass cast tinted light over the rise of seats; more practical spotlights stabbed at the floor, sending glints from its gold inlay of flowers and leaves.

Henry's nerves settled. His job had him in such places on a routine basis, surrounded by rings or rows of powerful people scrutinizing his every move, usually some actively hostile to what he'd come to say.

Spotting the podium in a pool of light, he walked to it without prompting and stopped facing the seven seated before the lowermost row. He set his badge on the podium top. "Thank you for seeing me. I am Arbiter Henry m'Yama t'Nowak," he said, hearing his voice soar through the vaulted room. No need of Flip's tricks; the acoustics were excellent. "I've come to take you to New Earth."

There were upwards of two hundred people present. Every single one surged to their feet, shouting to be heard. *Or for his head*, Henry thought cheerfully, keeping a pleasant, helpful expression on his face.

<Bit blunt, don't you think?> Shomchai sounded amused.

If it bought them time, it was worth it.

An older woman in a uniform, complete with a sword at her side he trusted was ceremonial, stepped from an alcove and strode around the floor ferociously ringing a handbell until the room fell silent again, people sinking back down in their chairs. She halted next to Henry. "I will have ORDER in this house!" Her glare included him.

He inclined his head respectfully. Received an unmistakable *you're a troublemaker* look in return before she returned to her post.

Six of the seven in front of him took their seats; the one in the middle remained standing. "We're seeing this interloper over my strenuous objection. I want it on record."

A person at a desk tapped a gavel. "So noted, Governor."

Henry inclined his head again. Governor Constance O'Belleveau regarded him from cold blue eyes. Shorter than most he saw here, sturdily built with graying hair cut close to her scalp. She wore a black sash from shoulder to hip, covered with a sequence of thin gold tiles, a different design hammered on each. The overall theme seemed to be industry and agriculture, motifs repeated on the walls above and painted on globes within the hanging fixtures. *A people proud of their accomplishments.*

A person not to fool with—he abandoned any thoughts of delaying tactics. "I ask five minutes of your time. After that, if you wish me gone, I'll leave." *To come back and try again.*

I WILL BE READY, HENRY.

The person to the far left of the governor stood. "Council wishes to hear the Arbiter."

A second rose, from a row to Henry's right. "As does the Science Advisory Board, most eagerly."

The shuttle in the courtyard would have that group salivating.

The governor's eyes hadn't left Henry. "Five minutes," she conceded, and sat half-turned from him, distancing herself from whatever he said.

He touched a finger to the badge. "My predecessor in this office authorized the early launch of the Halcyon Sleeper Ships, including the *Centralia*—" The names provoked a murmur of interest. "—to save your ancestors from a solar storm. Today, I've been sent to save you. Brightside faces an extinction-level event—" Henry paused to let the uproar take its course.

The bell-ringer established order. The governor shook her head. "And we're to believe *you*."

"May I have your permission to offer proof?"

He'd left her no choice, the anxious tension in the chamber palpable. She gave a grudging nod.

"Shuttle, the projection, please." They'd preplanned this, Flip able to send via the remote.

If how he'd arrived had caught their attention, the images suddenly appearing in the air above his head provoked gasps, even from the bell-ringer.

Their planet, with its moons. Their system, complete with star and assorted neighboring worlds. Set in orderly motion. *This they knew.*

Their planet enlarged. Beautiful and alive.

Then, its crust cracking open, spewing forth magma and gas. Seas boiling away, the atmosphere filling with ash and smoke—they'd a host of dreadful images to share, thanks to the Kmet.

"End projection, please." Henry made his expression suitably distressed, but resolute; his voice reassuring, if grave. "I've brought details on the coming mass eruption for whomever is qualified to confirm them." *No one here, but they'd have to try.* "What you need most to know, people of Brightside, is you will survive. I've come prepared to evacuate your entire population to New Earth before the crust turns unstable." *And how was* that *for a euphemism?*

A cry from an upper row, "How long do we have?"

How long did any of them have—

He had to stick to the script.

Had to keep his word to Kmet-Here and get these people off, while making sure kmeth didn't take his choice of cataclysm as the signal to start one.

Henry looked along the rows, meeting every horrified gaze, ending with the still-skeptical glare of Governor O'Belleveau.

"Six days."

***

"Nonsense! I—"

Whatever else the governor said was lost in the bedlam as Henry's declaration set off its own firestorm. *A pity*, he thought, leaning on the podium to wait. He much preferred a sober debate.

People in the upper rows were crowding exits. Some sat alone, in tears. Closer, the entire science advisory board, some two dozen individuals led by a tall, bearded man, charged down the stairs—presumably to reach him—to be met by an influx of uniformed guards determined to restore order, the bell-ringer having given up the effort.

All as the six councilors swarmed the governor, apparently trying to outshout one another—

Enough. "Flip, amplify. Good and loud."

READY, HENRY.

"DO YOU WISH TO DIE?"

The shock of the words, their glass-rattling volume, froze everyone, buying a second of precious silence. Henry pointed to the guard still holding his briefcase. "That's for your scientists. While they work to confirm what I've told you—and they will," this straight at the now-livid governor, "I've this." He drew an envelope from his coat. "Instructions for the evacuation process for those who'll be in charge here, and I suggest you hurry to share it. I'm prepared to load the first flight for New Earth at dawn tomorrow."

Conscious of every eye on him, Henry took his badge from the podium, walked to the governor, and offered the envelope.

She snatched it from his hands and tore it in half with a curse.

"Constance—what are you doing?" objected the nearest councilor.

"Saving you from folly." The governor glared around her. "You can't be taking any of this seriously—"

Henry calmly drew out a duplicate envelope, giving it to the councilor who'd spoken. "Perhaps you'd like to see the issue again. Shuttle, project and maintain."

YES, HENRY.

A burning orb filled the space above them all, cracked earth and searing flames imposed over what was patently their world. A trick.

And the truth.

"Your world will end," Henry told them, knowing the truth of it, hearing it in his voice. "not you. Everyone will be evacuated. You have my word." *And that was hope.*

The governor lunged for him, those around her quickly seizing her arms. "This isn't over, Arbiter!" she yelled.

By the grim faces in the chamber, lit by the image of their dying world, he'd a pretty good sense that it was. *Still.* "I'll leave you to absorb this, discuss as you must, and, most importantly, go through what I've provided. Unless you summon me sooner, I'll return in six hours. Should you require anything else before that, please contact me."

He paused and looked up at the throng, seeing all of humanity. "Whatever it takes, I will save you."

The Arbiter turned and walked out, those in his path giving way.

"There's no cannibals."

PIPS scrambled up the den walls to be caught and held by those already stuck. The growing mass of them expanded outward, kmeth's home pressed now against the ceiling, its opening more tunnel-like and gloomy than ever.

<They keep this up, won't be room for you,> Gis observed.

Didn't appear an end in sight. Tube mouths kept popping out PIPs. New ones took over tasks like floor polishing and climbing up and down the control wall; those relieved went to the den to be trapped.

Killian shrugged. Her partner's doleful prediction aside, plenty of space remained between dais and den. She sincerely hoped to be gone long before there wasn't.

She wrote: *Anyone got a clue?*

<Not that they're sharing. Any word from Henry?>

Too soon, Killian wrote, then let her notepad drop to her waist. If she looked up, she'd see the stationary saucer of Flip, Henry's dot blurred with it, smack on top of this world's densest concentration of buildings. The other two screens were filled with streams of results. Nothing that pinged of Human. Nothing to slow the process.

Figures, she thought, glaring at the planet. "Taking a break," Killian announced, as if the vanished Kmet listened or cared.

Three PIPs stopped and oriented toward her. She lifted her bag.

They retreated.

Learned, had they? She gave a wolfish grin. "Don't need you anyway."

Turned out she should have grabbed a PIP while she had the chance. Rolypoly sat on her bed, uninterested in Killian's proposal. "We must wait for Henry."

And repetitive. She tried a different tack. "I didn't before. What's changed?"

"Before, you spied on the Portal for the Coalition. Now, you assist Henry. We must wait for his return."

<Has you there, Killie-Cat.>

Gis' amusement wasn't improving her temper any more than being stared down by a lens attached to a ball. A ball she'd love to throw against a wall, just once, to see what happened.

"I can show you Henry's current surroundings, Killian."

Couldn't throw something like a puppy trying to please. "There's no cannibals." Rolypoly's response a stunned silence, she went on, "He's in no danger—other than being argued to a stupor. I'd rather—" *What?* "—I'll rest."

The lens swiveled. "You haven't started a flower for World VI."

"A little pointless now, don't you think?" She'd no more schematics to hide—or create; the polymorph recorded wherever they went. As for a memorial? *Maybe she should start one for Earth, rate they weren't solving the puzzle.*

<I dunno,> Gis said unexpectedly. <I've grown kinda fond of it.>

"I don't need a project," Killian grated out between her teeth.

<Yes, but you need to finish things, Killie-Cat, or you get snarly.>

She did not—involuntarily her eyes went to the canvas. She'd left empty space dead center for the final flower. Envisioned a lotus, precise and perfect, the tips of each petal on top of the existing flowers—and bud—to bring them together as one. Maybe a solitary water drop, reflecting New Earth . . . *right there* . . .

Killian found herself on her feet, opening up the paints.

Her companions prudently silent.

***

Her first inkling the Arbiter had returned sooner than expected was a knock on her door, Henry being the only one on the Portal who would, though Killian aimed a suspicious eye at Rolypoly before calling, "Come in."

The instant her door opened a crack, Henry leaned through. "Come with me. I've an idea."

She didn't stop painting. "No."

He frowned. "You haven't heard it yet."

She aimed her brush at him. "You've got that look again. The one where you kick a Kmet to see what happens."

He grinned at her. "We try your question on a tube mouth. "

Are the Kmet going to kill us? Had to be what he meant and she was all in—

Then what he said sank in. Killian glowered. "What 'we'?"

"Now's our chance," he came back, ignoring her. "Kmet-Here's denned and I've five hours until I'm to head back down. I'm ready." He spread his arms as if a dark sweater and sweatpants qualified him to explore the Portal.

At least he wore boots. *Didn't change who was to take risks around here.* "I'll go—"

He held a finger to his lips. "I'll pull rank if I have to."

Killian made a show of cleaning her brush and closing tubes of paint, buying time to study this bold new Henry, lounging in her doorway with a lazy grin. "Too much of Flip's coffee," she concluded.

The mask dropped. She'd seen it before; didn't make it any less disconcerting to see his face completely change, flashing through bleak despair to a resolve that set his features and chilled his eyes. "Five hours."

Fuck. "I'll get my tools."

***

Letting her carry Rolypoly, Henry followed close on her heels as if afraid she'd pull a fast one and leave him behind. Wasn't about to, no sir, not after seeing how he really felt, not after he'd told her without words how seriously close to absolutely fucked he believed they were.

They. Everyone.

Neither of them brought in an oneiric, not yet. Maybe they both knew what a long shot this was.

Maybe, like her, Henry didn't have the room in his head right now. "This one," she announced, stopping in front of a tube mouth like any other.

He didn't question her choice. Looked around him as if seeing the crack-like valleys for the first time. "Is this happening anywhere else?"

"Not that I've seen—but PIPs don't come here anymore," she reminded him. "Might be a maintenance issue."

"Or the Portal's breaking down."

She glared at him. "Not helpful, Henry."

He tilted his head. "Sorry. I tend to go dark these days."

Mollified, she aimed Rolypoly at the tube mouth. As before, when it opened, she held the imitation PIP just inside. Gave Henry a questioning look. *You sure?*

He nodded.

Killian licked her lips, then said firmly, "Are the Kmet going to kill us? Show me." She felt the pull on the rolypoly. "C'mon, Henry." She started to climb in, was sucked through, and hoped he was with her.

Wherever the hell they were going—

<Where ARE you?>

HE tumbled out of the tube into the dark, landing against something firm. *Killian.* She grabbed him, put her hand over his mouth until he nodded.

Knowing where they were.

Inside kmeth's den. The earthy tone to the smell had increased, making it strangely more tolerable. The dim light he'd remembered was gone, as if the walls were no longer translucent.

The PIPs coating the outside—Rena'd passed that along.

Killian's hand found his arm, slipped to his wrist, fingers tapping. She wanted him to summon his oneirics—

No, his proxy, as she'd summon hers. Prepare for the worst. Henry felt for Rena's wristband and pressed it.

<Henry? Are you in bed?>

She thought his eyes were closed. That he was safe. Henry wanted to laugh—

Caught himself. Calmed himself. The Kmet hadn't reacted—was an unseen bulk blocking the exit. Or wasn't here at all—

No. Air moved over his hair. A breath from something much larger.

HENRY, DO NOT BE STARTLED. I AM SCANNING IN INFRARED TO AVOID DETECTION BY THE KMET. I WILL PROJECT THE RESULT FOR YOU.

Suddenly, he could see fingers, faint and blue with reddish tips. Human fingers. Wrapped around a ball that glowed a faint red. Looked up to see a ghastly red blob where Killian's face would be, her skin flushed with warm blood, and sincerely hoped Flip had given the same message to Gis' FLIP.

<Henry—where ARE you?>

Seeing was a relief, no matter how distorted they appeared to one another. The den walls exhibited a delicate tracery of red as well, helping further define where they were; perhaps a source of warmth for Kmet—though it was stiflingly hot in here—

As for kmeth? Killian turned with him, giving a tiny gasp. Rena's, safely in his head, was much louder.

Red. Dark pulsing—*ominous*—red filled the entire space, close enough to touch. *Where was the tube mouth?!*

The terrifying image was a projection of what Flip's sensors detected, under the polymorph's control; perhaps sensing their reaction, Flip changed it.

The red faded back, replaced by what they would see in visible light. Kmeth's eyelids were closed, flippers drawn up to cover the mouth. Asleep.

And bigger than ever.

Rena didn't waste time questioning what they were doing here. <Henry, at this growth rate kmeth won't be able to exit the den much longer.>

Kmet-Here had a time limit. Possibly the source of kmeth's impatience to reach Earth. And insistence Killian be ready to take them.

Suggesting a negotiation point. Before revealing their presence, Henry put a finger over Killian's lips. Saw her nod and pull PIP-Flip closer, edging back from him. She knew where the tube mouth was. Would open it if they needed to escape.

He hoped not. They'd been brought here to answer a question. *Are the Kmet going to kill us?*

Avoiding the den wall, Henry made himself comfortable, crossing his legs and resting his hands on his knees, palms up and relaxed. He'd come to solve a mystery.

Might as well start with the murder.

"Did a Kmet kill the *Henderson*'s Humans?"

"Then you met us."

DAMN it, she hated *when the almighty Arbiter jumped to near-light without warning.* An opinion Killian vowed to convey to him—with shaking—if they survived another second.

<Hang on, Killie-Cat.> Gis, strong and sure. <I'll bring you home.>

She freed a hand from its clench around Rolypoly to aim its thumb down. *Hold on.* If they lost these epitomes, retreated to New Earth, they'd have lost everything. Not that she was eager to experience being crushed or chewed—

—Killian suddenly realized neither had happened, that kmeth's eyes had opened, gazing around as if unable to see the two Humans under whatever passed for kmeth's nose.

A soft rumble, then, in the dreamiest tone she'd ever heard from a Kmet, a confession. "Kmet-There perceived threat and destroyed. Kmeth failed to consult the Arbiter, our cherished partner. Kmeth's pilot failed, not to remind kmeth."

Had to be Kisho, earning the first fucking compliment—

"Thus Kmet-There proved inferior." The voice firmed, became proud. "While I, Kmet-Here, have worked with you, Arbiter-Henry, to strengthen our Duality. As we bring all that is Human to New Earth, I prove myself superior. When I descend with you, I shall be—" A sound finished the sentence, like the ringing of a gong struck deep underground. The den walls shook like jelly.

As did Killian's nerve. *Enough was enough.* She began easing toward the tube mouth.

A hand stopped her. "What of the Divider, Kmet-Here?" Henry asked with that terrible composure, as if trancing at some bloody meeting room table instead of—

A muffled BOOM. "The Divider brought us to space with the promise of a new and wonderful Duality. A lie." A louder BOOM. "The Divider never cherished us. The Divider said we would never be compatible. That our sharing would never be cherished by other thinkers. That we would never be made welcome." BOOM-BOOM! At a level now shaking Killian's insides and she gasped, dropping the Rolypoly. "NEVER HELPED . . . NEVER FREE . . . NEVER CHERISHED! THE DIVIDER WANTS ALL KMET TO END!"

When the shouting stopped, Killian's ears kept ringing. She barely heard Henry's soft, "Then you met us."

The eyes found him, or kmeth finally tracked his voice. "Yes. You are our hope. New Earth is our home. You have done the needful. When all Humans-There are Humans-Here, when we descend at long last, our Duality shall be established."

Don't ask it, Killian thought desperately. *Don't risk it.*

But this was Henry, so he did.

"Are you going to kill us?"

"Do you concur?"

"I DO not understand, Arbiter-Henry," with what sounded sincere dismay.

<Don't be fooled by words, Henry. Don't assume kmeth think like us.>

No chance of that. "Let me ask you for a clarification first. Why did Kmet-There fear the presence of Humans on *Henderson*'s planet?"

"Humans outside the Duality represent a failure to coalesce."

A new answer. Rena pounced. <PIPs on the den, Henry, drawn to this version of Kmet-Here. Coalescing might equate to some necessary physical connection.>

He did not *like the sound of that.*

And something was missing. "Represent it to who, Kmet-Here? Other Kmet or the Divider?"

A puzzled silence. Breathing, heavier than before. Then, "To all, Arbiter-Henry. The coalescence of every part is essential to the Duality. There can be none if any are absent. This is how the Divider harmed us in the past, by watching our attempts and stealing away what was essential before Duality could be established."

<On that basis alone spacefaring species wouldn't make good partners, Henry. Too liable to be noticed, too spread out to readily bring together. New Earth must have seemed perfect to the Kmet until the probe arrived.>

Killian shifted. *Get on with it,* that meant, there being no guarantee how long they had before kmeth's loquacious mood changed to *squashing intruders.*

Henry nodded to himself. Tried another approach. "As Arbiter, Kmet-Here, I protect the lives of Humans. Do you concur?"

"Yes." A pause, then a BOOM! "Do you fear the Kmet threaten your lives? Impossible!"

"We've seen that isn't always true," Henry responded dryly.

"We have given ourselves to you and you have welcomed us." Flat and certain. "There can be no Duality without you. You will not be harmed, Arbiter-Henry. It is unthinkable." A muted gong. "Humans on New Earth should experience anticipation, not fear. Do you concur?"

"I continue to search for understanding. 'Given yourselves'—" He echoed the words for Rena.

Who replied immediately. <Henry. It's true. The Kmet sample contained a complex non-organic I'd never seen before—and wasn't biological. I just got confirmation it's a polymorphic matrix, identical to what the first Kmet gave us, thirty-seven years ago. Henry—the PIPs *are* Kmet. Everything we've made from that material is.>

Flip.

Kmet equated flesh with knowledge because that's what kmeth were. *Sentient constructs.* Henry's mind exploded with the implications, the errors in understanding, the gulf between—which Humans *had* crossed, successfully, with Alt-Intels like his companion. Who didn't think like a Kmet at all—

Another muted gone. "Understand that I cherish you, Arbiter-Henry, as do all Humans. As Kmet-There must now cherish me. Do you concur?" It sounded—wistful.

—but who was to say how an alien mind—a biology including the machine—thought? He'd no basis to judge except something called the Divider had tried to stop the Kmet in the past. *Why?*

"Do you concur?"

Numb, the Arbiter found himself without words.

But he wasn't alone.

"Who built the Portals?" Killian demanded. "'Cause it sure the hell wasn't you."

"I understand everything now . . ."

<W*HAT THE FUCK*—>

She'd shocked herself, blurting out the question. Head throbbing with Gis' protest, Killian gritted her teeth, waiting to see how Kmet-Here responded, hoping she hadn't messed everything up for Henry. *Caught up in the moment, sir.*

Wasn't in any way an excuse.

To her surprise, the weird red blob with a black nose that was Henry moved as if nodding. "An excellent question, Pilot Killian," he said calm as ever. "Kmet-Here, I admit my own curiosity on the matter."

The words were normal; the tone peculiar. Maybe it was crouching inside a Kmet den discussing the future of Earth. Whatever the reason, the Kmet chose to answer. "The Divider built the Portals to interfere with everyone else. To steal us from our worlds and cage us. The Divider intended to keep us from Duality, but we resisted and took the Portals from them."

Corpses in a room . . .

"How?" Henry asked, his tone disinterested.

A boastful BOOM. "We became the hunters. We destroyed where the Divider lived. Obliterated what the Divider built, but these—these we kept."

They weren't mining *PIPs—they'd been planet-killers from the start . . .*

Henry had to realize what kmeth admitted. Had to feel sick inside, like her, and afraid, but there wasn't a hint in his voice. "Because Portals let Kmet continue to compete. You must determine who is superior for the health of the Duality. Do I understand correctly, Kmet-Here?"

Rena—had to be . . .

The gong sound again. If it signaled a horny Kmet, Killian really wanted Henry to change topics. Or to leave. Leaving sounded better and better.

"The Portals brought us to you, our most cherished partners. We will renew our Duality on your Earth, Arbiter-Henry, after the failure of long ago."

What the hell did that mean?

Another too-loud BOOM. "But you are correct. Once I descend to New Earth with you, Kmet-There will return to merge our Portals. They will become a new moon to shine over our Duality, removing kmeth's inferior self and the last of the Divider's cages from the universe. This, we do for the health of the Duality. This, we do for our common future. Do you concur?"

<Stupid Kmet! Erase the greatest advance in space exploration? Give the Portals to us!> Gis was furious. <Tell kmeth, Killie-Cat. Tell Henry!>

She closed her eyes for a count of ten, a hint to Gis to shut up and process the rest of what kmeth had said. What it implied. Origin Earth—had that been the *failure?* Was New Earth, their world, to be home to two species, one driven to compete to the death for superiority—

And was the Duality round two a winner-takes-the planet struggle?

The almighty Arbiter better find out. Set some rules.

Find out how to save them.

Killian opened her eyes to an eloquent silence from her partner. *Yes, Gis. Those are the stakes.*

"I thank you for answering our questions, Kmet-Here—"

Henry was quitting? She smacked his leg. This wasn't done.

"—and find myself reassured about your intentions."

She hesitated. *What did* that *mean?*

"Before I make my report to New Earth, there is a point I'd like clarified. Does the Divider continue to exist?"

An agitated rumble. "I have told you so."

"You also said you destroyed where the Divider lived, Kmet-Here." Killian caught a little edge to it. "To a Human, that implies species' extinction. No Divider, there or here."

Risky. She held her breath.

"DIVIDER ALWAYS! How can you not understand, Arbiter-Henry?" With a frustration crossing species' lines. "Kmet will always remember, thus the Divider always exists."

"Thank you, Kmet-Here," Henry replied in that oh-so-innocent voice. "I understand everything now."

If she were kmeth, she'd be wondering what the Arbiter meant by that. *Hell, she didn't have a clue.*

Kmeth wasn't sure. Killian could read that much body language, though she'd have preferred an angle showing the willy-bits. Before uncertainty became squashing, she jumped in. "Have to get the evacuation moving, sir. Be done as quickly as possible."

"Yes! Pilot-Killian is correct," Kmet-Here affirmed, sounding grateful. "Go. Work! I must rest."

Time to vanish. Grabbing Henry's hand before he could say another word, Killian scooped up Rolypoly and thrust alt into the tube mouth—following behind as quickly as possible.

"To work it is."

HENRY rode the tube behind Killian, encased in a potent whiff of Kmet den, and wondered idly why the Divider—*no, give them credit*—the Portal Makers had chosen this method instead of elevators or moving cars. They'd had hands and feet. Stood like Humans.

Then he thought of tossing crates at the tube mouths, how they opened as required to fit. Wasn't it as likely the tubes were intended to accommodate different shapes and sizes?

As for the Portal Makers traveling space to steal people from their home worlds—Henry wasn't about to take the word of thieves. The Kmet admitted taking the Portals. Used terms like *hunt* and *destroy* with what, to Human ears, seemed satisfaction.

In his view, it was as likely the Portal Makers had offered rides to the various intelligences they encountered. Perhaps even shared their remarkable technology. Until meeting the Kmet, who'd taken it and killed them. *What did that say about the Duality?*

The Kmet might claim not to distinguish between information and flesh, but Henry remained chilled by kmeth's *we remember.* A phrase used for those dead and gone, the extinct, not the living, and more than alien, it was a sentient construct's answer, cold and precise, absent the compassion of the companions built by Human hands.

Did kmeth *remember* Origin Earth the same way?

And Kmet-There, erasing the lives of hundreds of thousands of innocent people in—*what had Kmet-Here considered it?* An inferior strategy to accomplish the same end, all Humans in one place, with Kmet.

Henry found it entirely too apt to find himself dangling from the tube mouth, helpless.

"Here." Killian helped him out, keeping a grip on his shoulder. Lowered her voice, not its intensity. "What the fuck happened in there? What's this crap about *understanding*?"

"We got an answer—"

<If the Kmet can't or won't distinguish between extinction and existence, we're in trouble, Henry.>

Killian glowered at him. "What part of *we remember* who we murdered means they're fine did you miss?"

His lips twitched. "Rena agrees with you. I didn't miss it." He needed Killian focused. "I also caught the part where Kmet-Here told us how to destroy the last two Portals. We do that, we'll simply wake up on New Earth." *Probably.*

Her hand fell away, her mouth hanging open until she shut it with a snap.

"Well, *told us* is an exaggeration," he admitted. "But we've an interesting next question, don't you think?" He picked a tube mouth at random. "Shall we? There's an element of poetry in—"

<Henry, stop.> Rena, sharp and anxious. He paused. <If polymorphs are Kmet, then killing the Portal Kmet might not change a thing. A new *superior* might come into existence, on New Earth.>

"That Rena's smarter than you," Killian observed, a fire in her eye. "What she got to say?"

<That we've still time, Henry. To be sure this is the right way.>

Henry looked at PIP-Flip, tucked under Killian's arm, and gave in. "Rena reminds me we've an issue to resolve first. The sample from Kmet-Here's mouth contained—" He pointed at the polymorph.

Her brows knitted. "Kmeth snacks on PIPs. I've seen it."

<We're not talking about digested remains, Henry,> Rena responded. <The matrix is the most significant component of kmeth's chemistry. I'm looking at social insect analogues, where a physically distinct and probably reproductive individual rules a hive of workers.>

A hive? Henry wasn't about to share that disquieting image with anyone, let alone the pilot. "Rena says the PIPs *are* Kmet." He sketched a circle in the air. "If everything with a polymorphic matrix is related, destroying the Portals might not—might not get them all. If that became necessary." He looked at PIP-Flip again. Saw the lens out and locked on him—felt sick imagining what must be flying through that dear wonderful mind, hearing those words. "Flip—" he stopped, at a loss.

<Henry—your Flip is our greatest asset—in place and able to design and conduct experiments on alts matrix versus the Portal PIPs'. That's how we'll find out what we need to know, to protect ourselves and our Alt-Intels. I hope. Before you argue—> more firmly <—I've already sent alt the details of my request via my FLIP.>

"Flip, Rena's request." He made it curt.

The lens rose and lowered. "Received. With your permission, I'll begin at once, Henry."

"Flip—" Henry put his back to the wall, feeling the need for support. "Go ahead. And we'll talk later."

Bringing PIP-Flip to eye level, Killian asked, "Begin what?"

"An investigation into the implication of Rena's findings to devices created by Humans."

She scowled. "Not giving up my coffee maker." The way the pilot tucked PIP-Flip back in the protective curve of her arm? She didn't mean the appliance from her trunk.

Yet for the sake of those on New Earth, they'd have to think of such things, consider any way the polymorphic matrix could be turned into a weapon, and the ultimate irony of tasking Flip with it should alt prove susceptible after all—

Flinching from the thought wouldn't help. "We have to know what Kmet can do against us," Henry said grimly. "Flip, make it your priority. And be careful."

"Yes, Henry. I will. I promise."

He reached for his wristband. Paused. "Anything else, Rena?"

<Don't think of Kmet-Here as a leader with minions, Henry,> she cautioned. <The PIPs are more accurately to be considered as the hands and feet of a single super-organism, Kmet-Here the body and brain—making them potentially able to respond as a unit to a stimulus perceived by any part.>

More dangerous. "Thank you," he told her, pressing the wristband.

After studying his face, Killian jerked her head at the corridor. "C'mon. Kmet-Here's expecting an evacuation. We'd better have one."

ON THAT ISSUE, HENRY, I HAVE RECEIVED FOUR MESSAGES, NOW FIVE, FROM BRIGHTSIDE, REQUESTING YOUR RETURN IN THE STRONGEST TERMS. I BELIEVE THE GOVERNING BODIES HAVE REACHED CONSENSUS.

Henry pulled himself from the wall, giving Killian what he hoped was a cheery smile. "To work, it is."

"Now what?"

THE almighty Arbiter heading back to the surface of World VI, or Brightside, or whatever the hell she was to call it, and Killian judging she'd at least two hours before the call to transit through a ship, she sat on her bed with Rolypoly on her knee to make plans.

"So," she started. "How do we do this?"

The lens glinted. "To what are you referring, Killian?"

She poked where alt was roundest. "Finding out if what you're made of is dangerous to Humans. I have an interest, you realize."

The indentation remained as if she'd shocked alt. "I'm not sure—"

Pinching the fake phone, Killian shook her head. "Nope. Most of you's taking Henry to his meeting. This you, with my help, can start learning what we need to know." She let go of the phone.

"My first experiment requires access to a Portal PIP."

"Sure thing." She grinned. "Then what?"

While she and Henry crouched in the den, the PIPs in Control had formed a snake-like queue to be caught by those glued to its exterior. After a disgusted snort, Killian grabbed three at random, stuffing them into her open bag on the floor. She waited a bit to see what they'd do, but being caught appeared to be what they expected—*or wanted*—and none struggled.

Back to her quarters it was. Putting the strap over her shoulder, Killian went to the tube mouth. At the last instant, she glanced over her shoulder.

Fuckity fuck. The damn clock was back, low left on the middle screen, with fewer curls to its spiral, thus less distance for the spark to travel.

Kmet-Here, pushing up the deadline. Quickly Killian sketched the spiral and spark on her notepad and sent the result to Henry, via Flip.

Then dove into the tube to the Human portion of the Portal.

***

Shaking off the feeling huge alien eyes watched her every move, Killian set her bag of fresh-caught PIPs on the galley counter, next to the trio of bulbs she'd emptied beforehand. Restore sloshed in her stomach and she'd a slight buzz behind the eyes, but Flip had insisted they needed resealable containers, and she wasn't about to waste the liquid.

<Who knew I should have put a chemistry set in your trunk instead of art supplies?> Gis said, only half joking.

Killian grunted in answer. "Now what?"

Rolypoly rolled a short distance, leaving two little pats of altself stuck to the floor like pastry. "Please put these in separate containers, Killian. When you have done so, please obtain equivalent amounts from a Portal PIP, putting one into an empty container and the other in a container with some of me." A pause. "I recommend scissors."

Scissors?

Gis, who'd have given anything to be here tinkering with Flip bits, offered cheerfully, <Think of it as modeling clay, Killie-Cat.>

Clay and scissors. *Where did they think she was?* Killian took wire cutters from her toolset and opened her bag, peering in at the quiescent PIPs. She spotted an appendage like a sponge—a floor polisher.

Nipped it off. The appendage reformed immediately, slightly smaller.

The severed piece she cut in half, putting the bits into the containers as instructed, sealing all three. "Now what?"

"Please put the container with both samples in the middle, with the other five centimeters to either side, and step back."

"Step back?"

"And pick me up, please."

Killian held Rolypoly so the lens could observe, staring herself. Nothing appeared to be happen—

<Thar gonna blow!>

She jumped. Gis gave a wicked chuckle.

All at once the outer two bulbs began to quiver in place, then bounce. Again. Again and again, the rightmost shuffling toward Killian and Rolypoly, the left to the edge of the counter and off.

Killian turned on her heel, watching the escaping bulb make its little bounces right to the nearest table leg, continuing to push against it. Trying to reach the table, or rather the bag of PIPs on it.

Smack . . . bounce bounce—the other bulb hit her foot. When she stepped to the side, it bounced merrily after her. "I think it wants you."

"Yes," Rolypoly agreed, lens aimed down. "Non-functional remnants seek to return, smaller to larger. A characteristic mine shares with—"

CRASH! Killian whirled, finding the bag on the floor. Still zipped, so the PIPs inside must have bounced it off the table. Squashing the piece trying to come back. "That didn't work, did it?" she told the bag.

"Please investigate what happened to the combined pieces, Killian."

Tucking Rolypoly under her arm, Killian picked up the bulb still on the table, pushing away the one haplessly pursuing her across the floor. She unscrewed the top and tipped the bulb over.

Sand poured out.

"*FUCK!* OUCH!" A host of tiny stings stabbed the flesh of her arm—and armpit—right through her coveralls, and Killian would have tossed Rolypoly away but alt was covered in spines that *stuck* to her. "Stop that!"

The spines vanished into the body. The fake phone and lens appendages popped back out. "My apologies. I reacted—this is most unsettling, Killian." The polymorph fell silent, lens aimed at the sand.

Scared and for good reason. "Not what you expected, I take it."

"Not what anyone expected. A characteristic of our matrix is its robust—"

Her foot was bumped again, harder. Killian gave the annoying bulb a good kick, only to contact something larger and more solid. She looked down.

The bag. The now partially open bag, appendages with cutting blades poking through gaps as if the PIPs inside were desperate to get out and reach—

Spines flashed out again, a panicked Rolypoly reattaching altself to her. "Killian!"

"Hold on." She grabbed the bag, shoved the whole wriggling *dangerous* mass into the waste disposal, and ran for the door.

Not looking back.

***

"Killian, we must continue the experiment." Rolypoly had rolled to the locked door the moment she put alt down and bumped it suggestively.

Hadn't stopped in five minutes. *Getting old.* Killian finished smearing first aid cream over the punctures in her skin and shrugged on her coveralls, eyeing the polymorph. "The experiment where PIPs were trying to eat you?"

"Polymorphs do not have digestive tracts."

"They were drawn to you," she clarified. "I wasn't about to let them get any closer. Sand in the bulb, remember?"

"Of course." A quiver and hint of spines. "While your quick actions saved this bit of me, it is imperative we determine the relative quantities of Human polymorphic matrix to Kmet required for the reaction." Another bump. "Use this bit."

Stubborn as Gis. Who she hadn't let back. And a reminder this was Flip talking, presumably with *bits* to spare. Thinking of the PIPs, Killian quashed a shudder. Knives and saws. One had had a drill—*wasn't that all manner of lovely?*

"Can't. Nothing to test against. They're gone." An assumption to check—later and without her vulnerable little friend. "We'll get to it once Henry's back and gets us more coats. More you, that is," she waved at alt. "What do you mean, reaction? Have you figured out what happened?"

"I knew at once. Human modifications to the Kmet polymorphic matrix have made the two incompatible. Direct mixing rendered both inert. I predict permanently."

Hence the spines. She drew up a knee. Nodded. "I'd a feeling." Bad news for Flip and other Human polymorphs, especially if Humans needed a way to disable Kmet PIPs and didn't care about the cost.

One she wasn't ready to pay, but her opinion wasn't the one that counted, just that of the almighty Arbiter. "What's Henry got to say about it?"

"Henry was correct in advising me to keep my distance from Portal PIPs."

Slippery as Gis. Two could play. "Man thinks ahead."

"He does a great deal of that." With pride.

"So I've noticed. Flip. What did he say about your experiment?"

The door bumping resumed. "I will tell him once I have all the data."

Damn. "Flip—you can trust Henry." The *he won't use this against you* died unspoken on her lips. He would, if he had to.

The bumping ceased. "It is not a question of trust, Killian, but care. Henry is worried about many things. The last message I sent him concerned the reappearance of the countdown clock, which reduced the time for the evacuation from six to four days. The information exacerbated already-high stress levels."

"Then let's fix all that," she said airily.

Rolypoly rolled to her foot. "How?"

Gotcha. "Henry needs a way to stop the Kmet from landing on New Earth." Killian aimed her toe. "Let's go ask the Portal, shall we?"

"The evacuation could commence sooner than anticipated, Killian."

She swept alt up. "Then we'd best get a move on."

". . . we're not helping."

STREETLIGHTS struggled to illuminate a considerably snowier cityscape than Henry'd left hours earlier. The streets and walkways had been cleared since his visit, more than once by the extent of the piles, yet the fluffy stuff came over the tops of Henry's boots and thick flakes swatted him in the face. Colder now, but night did that.

Or learning more about the Kmet.

He shook it off. Saucer-Flip had landed in the now cordoned-off courtyard, no spectators in evidence, but he'd those to greet him and hurry him along. Faces covered in scarves, big uniform coats, and sensibly taller boots, there were dozens more arranged at the base of the stairs to Government House. It wasn't a good sign, if they expected trouble.

His doing, if it came. "Back to the chamber?" Henry asked his escort as they climbed to the doors.

"No, sir." A glance from dark troubled eyes. "They've opened the Contingency Room for you. First time—"

"I'll take the Arbiter from here," said a commanding voice. "This way, please."

Henry followed through the doors into the imposing foyer, his guide turning sharply left. A simpler door, with paired guards who moved aside to unlock it, led into a featureless box. An elevator. His guide hit a button to close the door and start them descending, then pulled down her scarf.

The bell-ringer. She stood at rigid attention, her expression fixed, eyes straight ahead. Suddenly spoke, still not looking at him. "You're going to save everyone? All of us?"

"Yes."

"How?"

A question she wasn't supposed to ask, he guessed; making this a chance to spread reassurance where it was most needed. "We've spaceships to bring you to New Earth—much much faster than *Centralia*. You won't need to sleep. There'll be homes waiting for you. A future."

Her lips tightened. "As what? Be beggars in your streets?"

"Far from it. We need you, desperately. Your courage. Your resilience." He let her hear the truth of it in his voice, the urgency. "New Earth's lost both. I believe you'll be saving us, as much as we save you."

That drew her to face him, her face crumbling. Her lips parted—

The elevator stopped, the door opening, and his escort became all business again. "This way, Arbiter."

***

An air of urgency filled the large room at the end of the corridor, with detailed maps stuck on every wall and stolid-faced security spaced around. Even the huge table in the center was covered in drawings and more maps, overhung by lights and the focus of everyone's attention—

Until Henry arrived. Every eye snapped to him, including the guards', and he gave a somber nod of acknowledgment. "You're preparing to evacuate?"

A man he remembered leading the charge of the Science Advisory Board spoke up, hands flat on a familiar-looking chart. "There is no choice. We must."

Grim nods. Henry looked around. "Where's Governor O'Belleveau?"

"The Governor won't be joining us," someone said.

Another, quieter, "She's been confined to her residence."

"I'm willing to meet with her," Henry began, only to stop as heads shook.

"There's no reasoning with those who refuse to face facts," the scientist said, slamming down a fist. "Forget them. How will you get us off this planet, Arbiter? What means?"

Facts they'd fabricated, however drawn from truth; regardless, like these people, Henry'd no choice but move forward. "I've a starship in orbit now," he told them, seeing their eyes glisten with hope. "More are coming and they'll send shuttles—" *This world had dirigibles and balloons, no powered aircraft.* "—to land on sites you specify. The shuttles will convey your people to the ships in orbit that will take you to New Earth."

"The long sleep of our ancestors—" The scientist, who seemed to speak for the room, gave a deep sigh. "I'd not thought to endure it."

"And you won't," Henry assured them all. "Our starships will get you there faster than I could walk across this room." *The trip would be the easy part.*

A ripple of astonishment.

For an instant, Henry toyed with the notion of telling these people about the Kmet. About the Duality and how an alien dispute, fought before their ancestors left Origin Earth, had circled back to be theirs.

But it wasn't kind and wouldn't help. Not here, or now.

"We've four days and the most time-consuming aspect is moving people from their homes to the shuttle." He approached the table and spread his hands. "Where should the shuttles land?"

***

They'd emptied a storeroom for his use, with a cot and chair, and Henry might have excused himself to the comfort of Flip, but the cot came with hand-embroidered pillows and an exquisite quilt, while the green leather chair looked to have been stolen from the grand room above. There was a polished wooden table and a floor lamp with a stained-glass shade. Even a woven carpet he suspected had hung as a treasured tapestry until being laid down for his feet.

Someone, he thought, had taken *leave everything behind* to heart. He'd acknowledge the effort by staying. To be honest, Human surroundings lifted his spirits.

Even if it all burned in three days and a handful of hours.

"Call if you need anything, sir. I'll be outside."

He smiled at the young constable. "Some water, please."

Young, but with wise eyes. "Should be tea and biscuits in the common room, sir, if you'd prefer."

"I would, thank you." Henry closed the door and sat on the cot. "Flip. How are your experiments?"

ONGOING, HENRY. KILLIAN INTENDS TO CONTINUE UNTIL SHE'S NEEDED IN CONTROL. WHEN WE HAVE COMPLETE RESULTS, I WILL CONTACT YOU IMMEDIATELY.

Intriguing. Henry tilted his head. "So you've some results."

NONE I WISH TO SHARE AT THIS TIME.

"Should I be worried?" he asked.

CONCERN ON YOUR PART WILL NOT EXPEDITE THE RESULTS, HENRY.

However true, he'd have preferred to be reassured. "I hear my tea coming. Keep me posted, Flip."

YES, HENRY. HAVE A RESTFUL EVENING.

After thanking the constable, Henry took the tray to the table, poured himself tea, and sat in the chair.

Rest? The two of them weren't. He sipped, unable to enjoy the warm, spiced beverage. It was all too easy to imagine Killian using PIP-Flip to open a tube mouth. Hear her voice asking the question: *How do we destroy the Portals?* Where would the Portal send them, if it accepted the question at all?

He made himself nibble a biscuit, let it melt on his tongue to savor the buttery citrus tang of what was an excellent treat.

Putting it and the tea aside, Henry moved the table in front of the door, unwilling to trance without warning of an intruder.

Then laid on the cot, with its beautiful pillow and precious quilt, to summon his quorum.

***

He'd envisioned the table and chairs. Put in the windows offering soft morning sunlight and a view of the mountain, however much they were lies he'd grown to loathe, these months. On a whim, thinking of Brightside, added a vase full of flowers to the table.

Removed it. Replaced it with the still-mysterious circles given to Killian by the Portal Library, each with a planet like a bead on a bracelet. *They'd still more questions than answers.*

His quorum appeared in their seats. Rena and Ousmane lost their smiles, seeing the circles. Sofia glared past them, but it wasn't personal. She glared most of the time, now. The *Lissett* would be as ready as she could make her; the same couldn't be said for Earth. *Not yet.*

Shomchai nodded at him, the power of self-image apparent in his dream state, adding a messy beard and lost weight.

Henry hoped he'd made his own appearance more reassuring. *Too late to check.* "Flip is preparing the results of alts experiments for us. I'll send them to you via the first ship to transit through from World VI."

Sofia's dark eyes glittered. "Hardly a trustworthy source."

She was one to talk. But her point was valid, one others would make. "I'll expect everyone to go through the results, thoroughly, and flag any concerns. Right now, I'm interested in these." Henry spread his hands over the circles. "Any progress?"

"I wish," Rena said with a sigh. As always, he'd envisioned her with her mass of hair stuck through with insect pins, though neglecting to add the way gems in the pins trapped light from faux sunbeams, sending spots of green and bronze over the walls and ceiling. *He'd see her in person soon.* "Nothing to add to the breakthrough you made with Kmet-Here, about the Portal Makers and kmeth's intention to descend."

"What about kmeth's reference to Origin Earth. Ousmane?"

The historian shook her head. "Nothing, ah, in the Archive indicates any contact with aliens, though there were, ah, efforts to reach out. As for the symbols," a gesture to the table. "We found nothing, ah, resembling these planets, if they, ah, exist. The best I can offer is, ah, that ignorance. It implies these journeys, ah, or events took place long ago and, ah, far away from us. We won't find, ah, these worlds again."

"Shomchai?"

"Like my colleagues, what I have for you is negative. We've found no correlation to the symbols or their arrangement in any Human archive."

"But?" Henry prompted, knowing the man.

"I am of the opinion—disputed by my peers—that these circles are unrelated to the Kmet." The linguist shifted in his chair, raised bleary but defiant eyes. "I think they're a record of worlds important to the Portal Makers."

"Important? How so?"

"Let us see one—any one—enlarged, please."

His task. Henry focused on one of the circles, presented it as hanging over the table, planet at the top.

Shomchai seemed to gain strength, stretching forward to indicate the bottom. "Here. Note there isn't a symbol opposite to the planet, but two, further apart than any others. From there," his hand swept up the curve of one side, then the other, "sequences continue upward, separate until they close the circle at the planet. Enlarge that please."

Henry did.

"There. See the line? A metaphorical division, splitting each world in two. Even the halves are depicted as distinct." His voice grew animated. "I believe this to be the source of kmeth's name for the Portal Makers—the Divider."

"Decorative features," Ousmane said dismissively. "Nothing more."

Rena leaned forward, studying the depicted world. "I agree these are stylized. That doesn't preclude them representing real worlds."

Henry brought up a second planet. A third. Kept going until the dozens hung in the air over the table like balloons and on every one, a line ran from pole to pole and yes, each half was depicted as distinct from the other. Greener, or bluer. Brown against yellow. Wetter, drier. Dots versus plain. "Divided planets. The Divider. I agree it's suggestive. But what does it mean?"

"Not a clue." Shomchai gave a short laugh. "Want me to guess? Each circle might record a meeting, perhaps, or a negotiation. Something that brought opposing sides together. Or they mean nothing at all."

"They've meaning," Henry disagreed. "The Portal Library produced them when Killian asked why the Kmet need our world." He brooded a moment, regarding the worlds. Raised them to see the others at the table. "Start from the opposite assumption—make this about the Kmet. If these divided worlds represented Dualities, maybe it means all the Kmet want is half of New Earth, leaving us the other." *He'd settle for that if it came to negotiation.*

"Separate but equal?" Rena shook her head. "Not what kmeth want. Kmet-Here spoke of coalescing—of participation with Humans."

Sofia tapped the table. "I agree. You said the Portal Makers interfered—stopped the Kmet from Dualities with others. These could be records of that." She spun her finger in the air. "If we start from the planet and move down, the circles show two sides separating."

The linguist nodded. "An equally valid interpretation." A wry smile. "It seems we're not helping, Henry."

"You have, all of you, with all of this." Henry gave a little shrug. "I don't know how, yet, but I will."

If he'd learned anything, working with an alien mind?

It was the blinding clarity of hindsight, when that one missing piece of a puzzle arrived to make sense of the rest.

He hoped it came in time.

<. . . the ball's making sense.>

AFTER peeking out her door to check for roaming PIPs, Killian ran to the nearest tube mouth and shoved Rolypoly at it.

It opened. "Okay, Gis. What do I say?"

<Show me how to set the Portal self-destruct.>

Simple. *Nasty.* Killian grinned. "Show me how to set the Portal self-destruct."

The tube sucked them in, whirled them around-down-and-up a few times, then spat them out.

Damn. Killian got to her feet, glaring around the too-familiar space. A replica Control. "Just like the last one," she complained, putting Rolypoly on the floor.

"It is not, Killian." Her companion spun alts lens, recording.

<No damage, Killie-Cat.>

True, the last had been in the midst of being scavenged by kmeth's PIPs. Unconvinced, Killian walked around the entire outer wall, stopping where kmeth's den would be. "And no answer."

Rolypoly produced a foot and hopped past her, stopping at the base of the wall, lens aimed down. "What about this?" Alt moved, describing an oval on the floor.

She went closer, crouched. The spot Rolypoly indicated had a different texture from the rest, somehow familiar—

"Wait." Killian jumped up and went to the pedestal dais, felt it. It looked similar. She came back and put her hand on the oval to feel—

The oval rose at her touch.

<You've found something!>

She left her hand there until it stopped moving. Removed it. "What—"

A single pedestal began to sprout from the raised oval, rising until the same height as the three behind her. Killian stared as the surface of this new pedestal rippled and grew a set of controls.

Flip, being literal, answered her question, "I believe this is a secondary transit control pedestal."

Hidden by the den.

<Hot damn, Killie-Cat.>

She and Henry had been right on top of it—Killian stepped to the pedestal, her fingers hovering. "Do you think it works?"

<One way to find out.>

"I strongly advise caution," Flip declared. "This appears to be a fully functional Control."

"Huh. If there's three, there'll be more." Killian looked around, shook her head. "I'll bet all of them ran at once. Maybe Portals could transit to and from multiple destinations simultaneously."

<Kmet stole them. Doesn't mean kmeth know how to use them.>

"Or can't. Think about it, Gis. One Kmet per Portal. One Control. Cannibalizing duplicated systems the Kmet couldn't use." The parade of PIPs stripping parts made a certain sense now. "Kmet-Here said Kmet-There would destroy both Portals by merging them. Instead of transiting through to a new destination, maybe this stops them at the same one." She eyed the pedestal. *Could it be that simple?*

<Do it! Where's the downside, Killie-Cat? You'd be home, the people on that planet get to keep it, everyone forever free of Kmet weirdness.>

"Thought you wanted a Portal, Gis."

Soft, sure. <What I want is you home, love.>

Killian reached, tentatively, still not sure—*it'd so be nice, to have this done*—

"No, Killian," Flip commanded sharply.

"I'm sorry. I know you'll be stuck here, Flip." Her fingertips touched the first control. *A moon would be nice*—

"You could destroy New Earth!"

"What?" She jerked her hand back, fingers curled as if from heat, and glared at Rolypoly. "It's kmeth's plan."

"We don't know the consequence of merging such powerful structures as Portals in Earth orbit, and these Kmet might be equally ignorant. Kmet-Here's boast of destroying all other Portals doesn't prove the Kmet did it, only that these two remain. It's conceivable the Portal Makers were themselves responsible, making a final effort to stop the Kmet. Even plausible, given the Portal brought us here."

<Hate to admit it, the ball's making sense.>

"Flip, wake up Henry."

"Forget I asked."

KILLIAN'S discovery of a Portal self-destruct—which she wisely did not activate, though Henry'd no doubt she'd been sorely tempted—changed nothing.

Yet. It added another piece to the puzzle. He'd take all he could get but, on their own, none stopped the evacuation, the clock timing it, or eased his dread of what would happen should the Kmet set a flipper on New Earth—

A chime at the door interrupted dark thoughts, and Henry looked up gratefully. "Come in."

A different constable filled the opening. "Council's asking for you, sir. They need your help."

Brightside experienced its share of emergencies, Henry'd been told, but those were due to violent seasonal storms, predictable and survivable; the population prepared, heeding admonishments to shelter in place. *Ride it out*, was the local term, especially in the rural areas, and they'd done so, successfully, for generations.

Not easy, budging a people this used to taking care of themselves.

The government enlisted its constables, a locally based force whose members, when not donning uniforms for rare ceremonies such as greeting Earth's Arbiter to Government House, filled sandbags during the wet months, cleared roads and repaired power transmission lines as needed, and responded to any other emergency, including accidents and fire. Crowd control? They'd watch for rowdy behavior after soccer games and such.

The morning after the Arbiter's arrival, constables spread through the snowy countryside to knock on doors, to tell everyone they found to pack a bag and head to a shuttle at once.

"We're having some trouble," Councilor Brags admitted to Henry, spreading a map in front of the Arbiter.

He'd been given a seat, and breakfast, at the table. Henry sipped tea and looked over the map. Green arrows predominated, presumably people on the move to the landing sites marked by blue squares. "The red circles?"

"Our problem. Villages where no one will leave. There's—" the Councilor looked to his neighbor, the Head Constable. "Rendy?"

The older woman, her uniform distinguished only by a green patch on each shoulder, leaned over to stab a circle with her finger. "Scuffle here. Broke a poor lad's nose. Word of barricades going up." Her hand moved in an arc along what was the outer edge of Brightside's settled territory. "It's not that folks are disorderly—most of them, anyway. They hear there's danger and want to be left alone. Ride it out as usual."

"They can't," Henry said flatly.

"You try telling them that."

He rose to his feet. "I will."

***

"Welcome aboard, Henry. You did not have a good rest."

Unable to sleep, afraid to, he'd used the remaining hours of last night to cover pages and pages with scribbled notations, none of which solved the least of his problems. "I'm all right. You have the map?"

"Yes, Henry." It appeared on the wall, courtesy of Flip's remote.

Reminded of the remote, *another distraction from sleep,* Henry raised a hand to his head and made a shooing gesture. "If you would, please?"

A bee zoomed past and up, smacking into the ceiling to be absorbed.

He rubbed his scalp. "Next time, not on my head please."

"Noted, Henry."

There were upwards of twenty villages with red circles. He took the seat Flip let down, shrugging on the harness. "Plan the most efficient course, Flip, starting with the outermost."

"If you visit them all, Henry, you will be unable to evacuate everyone in time."

"With any luck, those closer will see shuttles arriving and get moving on their own."

"Yes, Henry. Lifting now."

He looked out through the window on the floor. The sun shone, for now, and the city gradually shrinking beneath him might have been the setting of a story he suddenly remembered from his childhood, about winter sprites and white-winged dragons.

"Contact Killian, please. I want a transport shuttle to follow us to each village, prepared to load."

"An excellent idea, Henry."

Was it? Sofia'd warned him about people pushed too hard, about what they'd do. "We'll see, Flip."

***

In the first village, it only took the sight of flying saucer Flip landing in the square to change minds. They hadn't thought the talk of space and New Earth was real, Henry was told when he stepped out, receiving an apology from the village elders who'd stumbled over themselves to start evacuating their people to the *second* starship landing right there, in front of them.

In the next, Henry'd had to give a speech and show his badge. A couple had shouted and been silenced.

In the third village, where the *poor lad's nose* had been broken, most had shouted—until he'd had Flip project the image of their world cracking apart behind him, having become very good at terrifying people.

People abandoned their belongings in their rush to the descending shuttle. Pushed to be first on board despite every assurance there'd be as many as needed. As frightened people did, as Sofia'd warned him they would, and there was nothing Henry could do but trust the shuttle crews to sort matters and go to the next village.

And watch it happen again.

***

As he'd anticipated, word of whole villages being whisked into space spread faster than Flip could fly. In the end, it took seven visits to the holdouts before the rest began clamoring to their government it was their turn to leave and where were their shuttles?

To be dealt with by those in orbit, where he'd be shortly. Seeing the curve of the planet below, Henry leaned back his head and closed his eyes. "Flip, your update please."

"Sleep deprivation, exhaustion, and—"

Fussing. "Flip," he interrupted wearily. "Not me. You. Your experiments. You promised a report when you'd results."

"Unfortunately, Killian has been too busy in Control to assist me further."

Evasion? Henry opened his eyes. "Flip, what aren't you telling me? If you've—" *Bad news* didn't remotely cover what he feared. "—learned anything at all, I want to know. Now."

"Yes, Henry. Human-modified polymorphic matrices are incompatible with the base Kmet version."

He frowned. "Meaning . . . ?"

"I do not want you to worry, Henry."

Too late for that. "Then give me details, my friend. How's this incompatibility expressed?"

"When we combined equal amounts of me with a Kmet PIP, the result was an inert material. This suggests an explanation for the failure of the remote on kmeth's den."

"I don't care about the remote, Flip." His hands clenched on the straps. "Are you in danger?"

"Killian protected my PIP-self by removing me from the proximity of Kmet PIPs. The rest of me should be protected as long as I do the same. As you recommended, Henry, from the beginning. Thank you for your foresight."

"Any time." Henry found a lump in his throat and swallowed before managing a husky, "Glad you've a way to keep safe, Flip. Very glad."

"Thank you, Henry. Killian expressed the same sentiment regarding her coffee maker."

It made him laugh. "I'm sure she did."

"My safety aside, Henry, the Kmet PIPs appear capable of causing you or Killian physical harm."

"Warning taken." He nodded to himself and unstrapped, getting to his feet. Staggered when he went to stretch and repeated the motion with more care, feeling joints crack and pop. *Oh, for a new body.* The hackneyed epitome joke stretched dry lips.

Had to live in this one a while longer. "Coffee with all the good stuff, Flip, please."

The rest of the puzzle waited for him on the Portal, with a creature who most likely didn't want it solved.

And had, as Rena put it, multiple hands and feet. If the PIPs were used against them, they'd be helpless, unless—

Henry took the mug of coffee from its slot, gazed into it thoughtfully instead of taking a sip. *Flip made this.* From stores in alts hold.

Not so the two coats hanging from hooks, one meant for Killian, clouds of remotes, and the shuttle around him. "How much *you* can you spare without losing this shape, Flip?"

"If you are thinking of using a portion of me as a weapon, Henry, a cluster of mining PIPs outmasses the entirety of me by three hundred forty-three percent. As for operational PIPs, I estimate there are, at a given moment, approximately three million active inside the Portal, with an unknown number inactive. Collectively they—"

"Are a hive," Henry interrupted. "I know." He'd seen ants boil out to attack an intruder. "Forget I asked."

"I merely illustrate why I cannot provide enough me to launch an effective assault. As I presently lack the data to determine the minimum proportion of me to Kmet required, I must continue based on equivalent portions. On that basis, I am able to provide you and Killian with sufficient me to neutralize two PIPs."

Costing the equivalent amount of Flip. "That's it?"

If a shuttle could shrug, he'd the feeling Flip would. "The possibility exists a PIP might be rendered ineffective after a smaller application of me, but that remains to be tested."

Henry's vision of spraying a wave of attacking PIPs into oblivion disappeared. "I'll ask Killian to make it a priority, Flip."

"Between her shifts in Control, transiting ships. Her search for answers. Our pilot needs rest as much as you do, Henry."

Two days left. He held up the mug. "Make another to go, please."

"The mission is over."

"PILOT Omar, Evac Group 231, ready to transit."

"Roger that, Pilot Killian. *Cape Sable* sends her regards and respect."

The big Delta being home for good, no longer in the rotation evacuating World VI, and her crew rightly anticipating a return to real bodies.

<Lucky so and so's . . . >

"Pass along our compliments. Good job," Killian replied, ignoring Gis, who'd arrived this shift with a chip on her shoulder, grumbling at any- and everything. "Evac Group 231 transiting now."

"Got 'em. Sending through Evac Group 507."

Earth had continued to send the clustered transports, being more effective in outlying areas than a freighter's shuttles. Part of that, Killian knew, was their ability to land on snow-covered fields.

Henry'd told her the other part was their wide ramps. Getting people on board quicker meant those waiting had less time to think and change their minds.

"Roger that. Welcome to World VI, 507. Please clear the Portal and proceed to your designated coordinates."

Having a second, Killian pulled up her notepad to write: *What's with you today?*

When it got no answer, smart-assed or otherwise, she added: *Worried about you, Space Rat.*

<Don't be. Just pissed, that's all.>

Killian arched her fingers in a question mark.

<Meds raised a fuss. Wanted to yank me out, stick Kisho in, but don't worry. I told them where to put their notions. We're in this together, Killie-Cat.> With gruff affection.

And worse than no sense. The med team around Giselle was the best on New Earth. If they'd concerns?

She gave Gis a thumps-up, vowing to talk to Henry about her stubborn oneiric's condition sooner than later.

Then got back to work. "Portal clear, Pilot Omar. Ready to receive."

"Sending through *Balache Point.*"

***

Kmet-Here shoved and pushed, PIPs flying loose or being squashed, all part of the new drama attending shift change ever since the Kmet began to outgrow the entrance to kmeth's den. The PIPs were quiet about it, but kmeth grunted and bellowed as if being born.

Aliens. Killian leaned on the nearest pedestal to watch, holding back a yawn. She'd a PIP in her bag, ready for Rolypoly's next experiment. Or Flip's, since Henry'd brought a new Flip-coat for them to take apart, and she'd have asked how much more the polymorph could share, but that was the almighty Arbiter's side of it, not hers.

And Henry'd looked grim as it was.

He'd looked grimmer, once she told him about Gis—who she'd sent to wake up as if everything was normal and fine, without a fucking clue who'd come back in her head next time she pressed her wristband.

Without saying goodbye. Killian bit back the urge to shout at the Kmet to hurry the hell up, the creature patently trying kmeth's best. It'd have been hilarious to watch if not for the spark on the spiral clock sliding along and Gis—

POP! "Greetings, Pilot-Killian," Kmet-Here said, wheezing with effort but willy-bits a pleasant purple. "I will take my shift now. Please inform Pilot Omar to alert Kmet-There."

Never a mention of two Humans invading kmeth's den since; their switchovers had become this bizarrely polite dance.

"Already done." *While watching the struggle.* The pilot stepped off the dais. "Over to you, Kmet-Here."

She'd call it an improvement in Human-Kmet relations, except for the feeling Kmet-Here had told them what kmeth had because they were helpless to stop what was coming.

"Savor your rest, Pilot-Killian."

And laughed at her.

Maybe at all of them.

Killian pointed with her spork. "You missed one."

Angling the lens appendage, Rolypoly checked the rows of coat fabric strips stuck to the table—graduated by size and therefore amount of Flip—reorienting at her when done. "I did not."

She grinned. "Made you look." Slipped the mouthful in and chewed, not that she felt hungry these days, but the body had to be fueled. The strips she got; the rest, not so much. Rolypoly was being mysterious. "Now what?"

"Have you finished eating, Killian?"

The tone of the question was suspiciously neutral. Killian scraped out the rest of whatever the ready-dinner was supposed to be, popped it in her mouth, and swallowed. "Done."

"Excellent. Please get the blender. Henry left it in a cupboard for us."

They'd a blender on board? Shouldn't have been her first thought, admittedly, since they'd nothing to put in it—unless . . . "Henry's hoarding?"

"No, Killian. I requested a blender be brought from New Earth hidden in the latest crate of peanuts for Kmet-Here. Henry smuggled it here with the coat."

The subterfuge she understood. While this Portal orbited worlds other than Earth, Kmet-Here refused to approve of direct transfer of goods to and from transiting ships, other than peanuts and beets. When Henry wanted to ship something home—say a sample of Kmet—he took it to the planet and handed it to the crew of an outbound shuttle.

But a blender? Killian went to the cupboard and there it was, a massive, shiny metal blender with a lockable lid. She turned with it in her hands. "Why do we need—" *Oh no.* "You want me to put the PIP in it."

As if sensing its fate, her bag on the floor—its prisoner—gave a lurch.

"Certainly not, Killian."

She heard alts voice—where'd alt gone? Putting the blender on the table, Killian bent to look under the table. Rolypoly was dragging her other bag from under the bench, doing a much better job of it now that alt was again the size of a soccer ball, having used some of the coat to restore altself.

She'd forgotten about the dormant PIPs. "They're hard as rock," she warned, helping Rolypoly pull the bag out from under.

"It's a very good blender," alt assured her.

Killian used the leg of a chair to crack the discs into pieces, gathering up handfuls. She dropped them in, locked the lid, and hit the button. "THIS IS GREAT!" she shouted gleefully over the din.

As Gis would say, nothing soothed the soul like some positive destruction.

Thinking of Gis, she lost her smile. Felt a coward, not waking her oneiric for this. *Was a coward.* Didn't want to know who'd answer, even if Henry'd reassured her. Gis wasn't doing so hot, while awake. Had refused to leave her bed since their little visit to the den, insisting she be ready the instant Killian needed her.

Idiot. Giselle came close to losing that job, neglecting herself, a consequence Henry said was made very clear. She'd kept it on her word to follow instructions from the med team.

Helped they'd a new *all's fine* system in place from Flip to Rena's FLIP and Gis' Harvey. Killian had the feeling the almighty Arbiter had played fast and loose with the rules again—but if it meant their oneirics, their proxies—their friends—could stop worrying about them every second, it was worth it.

"You sure Henry doesn't want to help?" Killian asked. He'd gone to his quarters after giving her the coat and hearing about Gis. Had relayed what he'd done via Flip, not over coms, then gone silent.

She didn't like it.

"Henry's sleeping."

"Now?"

Rolypoly jiggled a bit in place. "He was unable to sleep on the planet."

Come to think of it, he'd looked more ragged than usual. "Sorry to say, he won't sleep through this," she commented, dropping another handful of hardened PIP in the blender.

"He will, deeply and well, for six more hours."

About to hit the button, Killian paused to give Rolypoly an admiring look. "You drugged him."

"Henry requested a coffee with everything in it. I interpreted that to mean everything he needed, which was sleep. There is a counteragent, should his presence be urgently required."

She'd downed the coffee Henry'd brought for her without a thought. Regarded it now with a raised eyebrow. "What about mine?"

"I provided your customary selection of stimulants. We have work to do."

"That we do." Killian hit the button and that glorious racket filled the room.

To Killian's surprise, probably not Rolypoly's, blending didn't chew the dormant PIP material to dust, instead producing a thick gray PIP-paste, reminiscent of the puddles the things became when squashed under kmeth's bulk, so she insisted they watch from a distance to see if one would pull itself together and try to climb out of the blender.

When it stayed paste, they went on to the next step. Using a spork Killian vowed to toss when done, she dolloped PIP-paste in the center of each strip of fabric while Rolypoly—clinging to her shoulder after promising not to make spines again—recorded the result.

When done, Flip announced, "I will need to analyze the data—"

"You cancel each other out," Killian interrupted, waving at the strips. Where there'd been more Flip, some fabric remained, where there'd been less, some PIP-paste. Rows and rows of forlorn little piles of sand marked the demise of both. "It's even." She began collecting the fabric.

The polymorph didn't bother to argue. "Henry will be disappointed." This with regret.

"No, he'll be relieved." She waved the strips in her hand at Rolypoly. "Not a secret weapon. A friend at risk like the rest of us."

"I'm your friend, Killian?"

"Not if you poke me with spines ever again," she warned. "Here," offering the strips.

Which disappeared. *Handy, that.* The rest on the table wouldn't. Killian resigned herself to cleaning up. Unless, "When's kmeth's shift over?"

"In—" The ball on her shoulder stopped, quivered, then said quickly, "Killian, we must wake Henry immediately. There is a call from the surface. It's the governor."

About to move, the pilot stopped. "Thought she was locked in her residence for interfering with the evac."

"That situation is unchanged, to my knowledge."

"Then what's she want?"

"The governor has asked the Arbiter to save her. Please hurry, Killian. Henry will want to take this call."

Being fucking *Henry.* Who should be saved from himself and scum who'd take advantage. "She can wait," Killian declared. "Man needs his sleep."

"While I agree, Killian, it's not our decision to make." A handling appendage reached out to gently tug her collar. "The *Balache Point* reports her final shuttle has docked. She's moving into position to transit home.

"The mission is over."

"It's not over."

HENRY stood on the hull of the *Lissett,* gazing out over a calm, dark ocean. Stars crusted the sky like the sugar on his grandfather's cookies, reflected like infinity around him, and none of this was real.

Did it matter? Warm air caressed his face, soft and tasting of salt. An impulse found him walking, the surface as steady and firm as ground beneath his sandals. By the third step, though he'd started at the center—*hadn't he?*—he reached the end of the hull and paused, toes over what was now a cliff, the froth of waves far below.

He'd jumped from a plane, long ago and far away.

Jumped now, giving a little push from his knees, spreading his arms to fly as he had then, and fell and fell . . .

"Henry. Henry, wake up."

. . . the sea filled with monstrous waves and the air was poison and he didn't fall, he was flung back against the hull, again and again, breaking his bones—

"HENRY!"

—being shaken. Killian. She was shaking him. Stopped at his whimpered protest, but kept hold of him. "There you are," she murmured, though he certainly wasn't, not yet, and whimpered again. "Flip says the counteragent will clear in a minute. You were pretty deep, Henry."

The dream drained away, leaving him only the memory of stars—*or was it cookies?*

Then that, too, was gone and Henry tensed, trying to sit.

"Here." Killian pulled him up so the wall supported his back. Gruffly, "Whatever he gave you, I'm next."

Gave me—"I wasn't—Flip!"

"I do not apologize for ensuring you'd some rest, Henry, though I regret this rude awakening."

Something must be wrong—Whether the counteragent or his own alarm at the thought, the last vestige of sleep left him and Henry blinked up at Killian. "What's happened?"

"What hasn't?" Her dark eyes were bleak. "The last ship's ready to transit. Kmet-Here's ordered me back to Control—kmeth wants me to take us home." A pained shrug that said it all. "We're out of time, Henry."

"Do not forget the message from the governor—"

"Flip—I warned you—"

Henry touched her arm, raised an eyebrow. "The governor?"

The pilot subsided, the polymorph bit in her elbow, and sank to sit beside him on the bed. "Fool lets the last shuttle go and now expects you to zip down and save her." Looked at him, her face working. "Henry—"

"Then we're not done, are we?" he told her calmly, his heart hammering in his chest. "Please go to Control and inform kmeth the Arbiter is making one more trip down."

"She's not worth it."

"Killian."

Glowering, the pilot moved aside to let him put his legs over the side of the bed and sit up. Before he could stand, she crouched in front of him, PIP-Flip still in her elbow. "Henry, I can destroy the Portals. I think. Rolypoly's not in favor."

The fake phone waved. "It might destroy New Earth!"

He loved them both. Odd, how the realization steadied his nerve. "We're not there—not yet. Let's deal with one problem at a time, my friends."

He rose to his feet, Killian rising with him. She thrust PIP-Flip at him. "Don't forget your coat."

"Thank you." Henry put the polymorph on the bed. They both watched it melt and reform; she watched him don the garment as if it were vitally important he do it right. He glanced up at her, smiling a reassurance. "Last world, last trip. We get to go home, Killian. Whatever happens."

Instead of smiling back, she gave him a quick, hard, one-armed hug, then stepped away.

She didn't say a word.

She didn't have to.

***

Rena's projection sat in a seat like Henry's. Flip had even provided her with a similar safety harness. She fingered it as she gave her report. "The media's full of talk of the *Lissett* refit. People are putting it together, a sleeper ship heading back out as your mission wraps. There's rising anxiety about what's next. Toilet paper's hard to find."

Henry blinked. "Toilet paper?"

She shrugged. "Sofia predicted it. As for the rest?" Her voice had an unfamiliar edge, as if she readied herself as well. "Simmons said the preparations you requested are underway." Her face grew sad. "I think he wanted to ask if they'll really be necessary but couldn't bring himself to. He's a fine person, Henry."

He nodded. "I know. How are the others?"

Her expression lightened. "It's helped, having their families, being together. We meet over lunch, Ousmane, Shomchai, and me. Sofia—" She stopped.

"What?"

Rena grimaced. "She's given up. On New Earth, on you. Oh, she hasn't said so, but I've seen it. That ship's all she cares about now."

Then he'd given her the right job. "Flip's findings?"

She glanced at the ceiling. "Nice work, Flip."

"Thank you, Rena. However, I deeply regret the result means Earth's polymorphs cannot be a defense."

"Or become Kmet. That's a huge relief."

"To me as well, Rena."

"Will we need a defense?" Henry asked soberly. "Can't we coexist on the same world? Kmet-Here said we won't be harmed. Called it impossible."

"Kmeth's stated intentions might be irrelevant, Henry," Rena warned. Her hands tightened on the harness. "Once on the ground, Kmet-Here might be driven by instinct, not reason. Kmeth might not even know what's to come, if this is the culmination of kmeth's life."

"Biology."

"Don't underestimate it." A smile flickered in her eyes. Vanished. "Because something's natural doesn't make it safe. Quite the contrary. I can give you plenty of examples where an introduced new species eradicates those native simply by doing what comes naturally to it. Something about this stage of kmeth's life cycle—a stage, don't forget, that had adaptive advantage on kmeth's world—made the Portal Makers interfere to stop it, over and over again, until the Kmet rebelled. As nature insisted kmeth do."

"Henry, three minutes until we land. The captain of the *Balache Point* wishes to speak to you."

"A moment, Flip." Automatic, that acknowledgment. His full attention was on Rena. "You're saying I can't trust Kmet-Here's promise Humans will survive and be cherished."

"I'm saying we don't know what those words mean to a Kmet. So yes, don't trust it. And Henry, we—Ousmane, Shomchai, and I—" She put her hands over her face for a second, then let them drop to her lap. "I'm sorry. This is harder than I—I planned to—" Stopped, eyes full of misery.

"I'll say it for you," Henry said gently. "My wise quorum has a recommendation. That if the Kmet are dangerous to other intelligent species, by nature or otherwise . . . if we can't save ourselves . . . then it's up to us to finish the Portal Makers' work. Destroy kmeth even if it means destroying New Earth."

Rena dipped her head, then gave him that old wry look. "You'd already thought of it, hadn't you?"

He spread his hands. "Worst case scenarios come with the job. As is hoping to do better, Rena. Don't give up—"

"Henry! The captain is most insistent. This is why." The wall screen activated, showing the Portal in space from the viewpoint of the freighter.

The once-clean white lines of the Portal's outer rectangle now sported an irregular growth, draped over a section a third from an end.

"What is that?"

"I sent a remote, Henry. Adding its view now."

A jolting leap forward, closing in on the growth—

—But it wasn't a growth, Henry realized a horrified second later. PIPs. Hordes of them coating the outside with more climbing from a crevice-like breach in the Portal's hull.

Rena, quick and determined, "Flip, is this area linked to kmeth's den? Can you tell?"

"I cannot, Rena. However, given the PIPs' altered behavior inside the Portal, I would consider such a connection highly probable."

"Why? What's it for?" Henry didn't expect an answer.

The xenologist had one. "Mining PIPs drop through atmosphere without being damaged. I think these are forming a capsule to transport Kmet-Here to New Earth."

"I agree. If this much material is torn from the Portal, Henry," cautioned Flip, "it may lose internal integrity. If it doesn't soon anyway."

Kmet-Here planned to destroy both Portals—rotting floors—

What had he told Killian? One problem at a time. "We get the governor," Henry decided. "Flip, please have the *Balache Point* hold until we can transfer her aboard. And thank her captain."

"Yes, Henry. Proceeding on course."

He looked at Rena.

"Does Kmet-Here know what's happening outside? Is any of this under kmeth's direct control? If not—" Rena took a breath.

—biology. He didn't say the word, instead lightening his tone. "Well, I'm glad to know we won't have to squeeze Kmet-Here in here. Right, Flip?"

The polymorph sensed what he tried to do. "A relief, Henry, to be sure. One minute to landing."

"Henry—" Rena's voice shook.

He held a finger to his lips. "It's not over."

"How could I possibly be good?"

"BALACHE *Point* holding. Roger that."

Her fingers stayed on the com control, eyes locked on the shuttle icon and dot moving across the planet in the middle screen because if she glanced to the left—

Which of course she did, curiosity a Human failing.

Kmet-Here wanted to get into kmeth's den. Was trying, desperately, using mouth and flippers and the force of kmeth's further enlarged—almost bloated—body. Had somehow got a flipper through and one eye, the others outside and moving wildly. Then a stream of hot black goo shot from kmeth's tail end—

<Crap!> Gis shouted.

Exactly what it was. All those pilots sent up with little sample jars in hopes of excrement to take back to the xenologists and here she was, with a line of it almost to the dais. Killian shook her head.

Which was when Kmet-Here made a tremendous push, getting further in—and much more compressed—sending a blast of gas outward.

Killian threw her arm over her mouth and nose.

The PIPs weren't helping. Nor were they rushing to clean up a mess she emphatically wanted them to—*what was wrong with them?*

<Killie-Cat. You good?>

Fuck the notepad. "A giant alien's shooting farts at me. How could I possibly be good?"

A laugh inside her head. <Just checking.>

And, damn it, didn't her lips twitch up at the corners because Gis had the right of it. The whole thing had passed ridiculous on its way to farce, and there wasn't anything to do but laugh.

Until Killian realized Kmet-Here wasn't just about to get cozy inside kmeth's dark, humid den, to wait for Henry's return—

—the Kmet would be where the second pedestal was hidden, able to do what she'd briefly hoped to do. Destroy both Portals.

"Kmet-Here!" she shouted. "Wait!"

<What are you doing?>

"I need your help. There's a problem."

As a grumble told her the Kmet had heard and was now trying to extricate kmethself, Killian looked around, trying to find one.

<Break a toggle,> Gis said quickly. <The left one. Kisho told me it pops off once in a while. NOT THAT ONE!> when Killian grabbed for the nearest. <The next. Yes, that one.>

Holding a breath, Killian snapped off the end of the switch. When nothing life-threatening happened, she let it out. Used her most professional voice. "Kmet-Here? There's a structural failure on the transit pedestal. I—" Kicked aside an approaching PIP. "—require your assistance." *This had to be how Henry felt.*

<Now what?> Gis, in her best *Killian out on a ledge* tone.

Killian stepped out of the way to let the exhausted, stinky Kmet approach, having no fucking clue.

"You don't need to suffer."

THE tall metal gate was closed and locked. Leaving Flip on the deserted roadway behind him, Henry stood in front, wet snow gathering on his shoulders. The governor had the means to know he was here.

Killian and Kmet-Here on the Portal, Flip outside town, waited for him. Everything waited, as if the universe held its breath and looked over his shoulder, watching him grow whiter and whiter under the snow.

HENRY, BE CAREFUL.

A gate. A few more minutes. Together they equated to a life saved—

The gates swung open.

Well then. "I'll be quick." Henry hurried through before they could close again or he could change his mind.

The governor's residence was a large, low building, sprawling across a massive lawn. Humans had done well here, despite the challenge of a colder overall climate due to an older, dimmer star.

He'd done what had to be done, been clever or persuasive, eloquent or blunt, giving them a future while erasing their past and present, and yes, he'd saved the people.

Hadn't he? Doubt choked him.

"Close enough, Arbiter."

Henry stopped. Governor Constance O'Belleveau came out from behind a pillar and leveled a rifle at him, her mouth a grim line.

He ignored the weapon. Ignored the nearby vehicle loaded with supplies, its engine running. "I thought you were coming with me."

As he said the words, held his breath, Henry knew how she'd respond. *My place is here.*

"My place is here," she declared, flat and sure. He winced inside.

Gave a small bow of regret. "As you wish."

"That's it?" Suspicion filled her face. She lowered her weapon, snow sliding down the barrel. "You won't force me to go?"

"I arbitrate," he reminded her. "I present the options and their consequences.

Which to choose isn't up to me." Though he wouldn't be doing his job if his presentation didn't push that choice hard toward survival, and how he wished for the right words now.

Lacking them, Henry held out his hand, a gesture they shared. One that cued Flip, via alts remote, to approach, stun field ready to fire once the Arbiter moved out of range.

"Your people will be safe, Governor. You have my word." *And if they all died on New Earth, instead of at home, how was that any kinder?*

"Your—" Her lips twisted. "You stole my people, Arbiter. Took my family. Robbed us of our future—oh, I do believe you—" when he went to speak. "Brightside's doomed." The rifle lifted. "You've made sure of it."

It wasn't grief he heard in her voice, it was overwhelming rage.

She'd invited him here to kill him.

Why not die?

Henry threw out his hands, accepting his fate. "If it will help you to shoot me, go ahead."

<Henry—NO!>

The pain would be momentary. *Should be.* He'd wake up at home. *Should wake.* "I've done what I had to do. Your world is last of the six. I've saved everyone I can."

No he hadn't—not yet—not Earth—

HENRY, I'M COMING. KEEP TALKING.

"From what?" A snort. "There's no mass eruption coming."

He ignored the rifle, Flip, Rena, intent on her furious face. On this moment. Governor O'Belleveau would be the last; his role ended with her and her world.

Was it not fitting she know?

A relief, to stop lying?

"We—humanity—received an ultimatum, Governor. Pull our kind back to New Earth. Erase every trace of Human expansion beyond our solar system."

"Or?"

"Or there may not be Humans at all."

"Aliens?" She glanced up, shaking her head. "You'd think there'd be room." Her gaze dropped to him, eyes like chips of ice. "This ultimatum—was it your fault? Is that why you're here?"

"We don't know," Henry admitted. "We don't have all the answers." *Only clocks, spiraling to disaster. Only worlds on fire.* "I'm here because it's my job to be. A job I can do because we don't just have enemies, we've partners." *He hoped—they hoped—how had it all come down to that and nothing more—* "A species called the Kmet gave the warning and agreed to transport everyone I've found back to New Earth—"

"You fool." She jammed the barrel's mouth against his chest. *What had he said to carve such hate into her face?* "We kept our records. Your *Earth*'s no more humanity's birthplace than here, or any of the six. You're from another wave of Human expansion, settlers like us, only with a thousand-year head start. Which doesn't give you the right to decide—but it wasn't you, was it?" A glimmer of understanding. "It was the Kmet. They picked *your* Earth over ours."

"Even if that's true, it doesn't change—"

"It does." The rifle pushed him back, down a step so he looked up at her. "It does. Now that you've been a good little Arbiter—put all of us on one rock for them, what do you think happens next?"

His nightmare. "We have agreements," he said, hearing doubt. "A Duality—"

"You've put us at their mercy, if they even know what that means." A slow, dreadful smile. "I am going to end you, Arbiter. But first, let me tell you a little secret. One my government agreed to keep." The rifle didn't waver as she reached her hand into a pocket, drawing forth a piece of foil between two fingers.

It couldn't be— "Is that—a probe message?"

"It is exactly that. From the *Exeter.*"

Facing his epitome's fate, Henry'd been resigned—now his heart thudded in his chest like a startled chicken and he couldn't keep the tremor from his voice. "No. *Exeter* never reached her destination. I was there—"

"Wrong address. Here's the right one." She crumpled the foil in front of his face, tossing it aside in the snow, her smile widening at his outcry. "Don't worry, Arbiter. Some of us will survive you—"

Or none would—He couldn't say the words. Couldn't move.

A shadow engulfed them. *Flip!*

Henry dove for the message. Heard the gun fire. Felt a blow that spun him in midair. He hit the snow, hearing a whine and thump. A cut-off scream. Numb, he realized Flip had crushed the governor with his ramp.

That he'd been shot.

Was still here. He wasn't dead, not yet. He could find the message. Only if Rena didn't call him back—"Rena—"

<Henry. I'm here.> Her voice filled him, her compassion. <I know. It's time to end this. To come home. I'm pulling you—>

"No," he gasped. "Rena. No. Wait. I'm not—finished." He couldn't see. One arm wouldn't obey him. The other did, clawing at the snow. The world narrowed to his fingers, the feel of ice crystals, the frantic reach, nothing, nothing—

Got it! His fingers closed on the message. He pulled it close, tried to put it inside his coat, but the front was hot and slick. *Blood.*

A sob in his mind. <Let me bring you home, please. You don't need to suffer, Henry. >

Running out of time. The thought echoed from a distance, shock setting in. "I'll make it." *He had to.* Henry's hand found a side pocket. Pushed the message deep inside. He made sure it was safe before using a leg and his good arm to flop on his back.

Snow landed on his face. Melted into tears. "Flip. Trans—transmit to Killian. Hold fin—al ship in orbit. We're going through first. Immediately. The second floor—prep—prep."

<I'll be here. We'll be ready. If you're sure.>

YES, HENRY. He felt himself lifted, the motion grinding what was broken inside, and swallowed, fighting for air.

"Flip. Tell Killian—tell her nothing's wrong. I'm just stopping—stopping at the office."

<Henry . . . > Soft, full of doubt. Rena'd gladly end this for him. Bring him home as easily as closing his eyes.

Henry kept them open. "Tell Killian I'll be right back. We're—we're not done."

"Might be beer."

THE Arbiter's shuttle shot from the surface as if fired from a cannon, aimed straight for the Portal, and at first Killian simply thought Henry was in a hurry.

Then she recognized its trajectory. Same as every ship she'd sent through to New Earth this day and every other for months. She reached for the com, making it casual because Kmet-Here squatted beside the dais, an eye on her ever since fixing the toggle. Suspicious.

Last thing they needed was a new emergency.

In case it was, she pressed her wristband, relieved by the instant, <Here.> *Gis.*

"Shuttle, this is the pilot," Killian began. "What's your status?"

"Hello, Killian." Henry's voice in her ear, calm but oddly flat. "I am transiting through to New Earth. I will return within the hour. Please hold the Portal here."

"Roger that, Arbiter." She worked the controls, heart racing. *What was happening?* "Ready in three, two—"

The Kmet loomed beside her, rearing up on kmeth's flippers to aim an eye at the pedestals. BOOM! "What is this?" BOOM!

The subsonics ached through her bones and made the air in her lungs vibrate. "More evacuees, Kmet-Here," she managed to get out. "Nominal. Proceed, Shuttle. Two—"

"STOP!"

"—go." Her fingers flew over the pedestal, cueing the orbital alarm, sending Henry and Flip home.

Always impressive, watching a creature with kmeth's mass spin in place.

Less so when the result brought the thick tail around to swipe Killian from the pedestal. She skidded across the floor until she hit a wall. Laid still a second, assessing.

<Killian—Killian! You all right? I swear I'm gonna take my power saw to kmeth's fat hide—>

She raised a thumb to reassure her worried oneiric. A PIP came to investigate, maybe thinking there was new litter on the floor.

She kicked it away.

Ignoring her, the Kmet hovered at the pedestal, not yet touching the controls. Killian pushed herself to her feet and limped to the dais, wincing at a shot of pain from her hip.

"Why did you hit me?" she demanded, too angry to be afraid.

"I moved you out of the way." Placid as could be, the damned thing, with cheerfully purple willy-bits. "You were not to stop. Arbiter-Henry was not to leave. Now he has. Now the mission is over." The mouth gaped, showing tongue-tips at the ready. "We will go—"

"No! We can't—he hasn't left," Killian said hurriedly. "Well, he has, but he's coming back soon." *Please come back.* "Very soon. The Arbiter went to get treats, to celebrate. The official surprise party."

Gis groaned in her head.

Not helping.

The eye closest to her narrowed to a slit. "What is this official activity?"

In it now. "It's a Human tradition," she explained. "We reward ourselves for a job well done. Gather and eat—peanuts. Lots of peanuts. And chocolate. Might be beer."

<You hit your head, Killie-Cat?>

But something she said penetrated that enormous head. Kmet-Here eased away from the dais, rocking back and forth, pupils dilated. "I ate all the peanuts."

Straight to the point. "Henry's bringing you more. You'll see."

<Five by five, Killie-Cat. Anything else while I'm making a list?>

Her legs felt like rubber, hearing that. Much as she wanted to add a bottle of something with a higher alcohol content than Henry's offering, she knew to stop there. "I'll transit through the freighter while we await the Arbiter, Kmet-Here."

When kmeth hesitated, Killian pulled herself up the step, gripping the rims of the outer pedestals, teeth clenched as pain flashed along her right side from hip to knee.

Might be something broken after all.

"Killian's expecting us."

BREATHING didn't hurt.

Nothing did, to Henry's surprise. *Wait for it,* something cautioned. Sure enough, there was a *BITE* in his groin, a second in an arm, another—"Stop that!"

"Sorry, sir. Almost done."

"You told them to hurry, Henry."

That last voice—*Rena?* He struggled to open his eyes. A warm liquid flooded them, loosened whatever held the lids shut, and he could.

Her face hovered over him. A lock of hair escaped its pin, brushing his cheek, and he'd never felt anything as real or wonderful. "It is you."

"And is you," she replied gently. "Welcome home."

No. No. "I have to go back." Henry fought to get up, failed. "I have to go now!"

"We know, sir. Drink this." Hands took hold of his head. A straw found its way between his lips. He took a sip, dimly remembering the drill. He'd left his epitome. This was his existent, real self, and he'd come back because—he'd been shot—because—

The slip from the probe. "My clothes! Do you have my clothes!?"

"They're in bad shape, Henry," someone said.

Someone who didn't know, wasn't there—He flailed a hand, found the edge of his can, pulled. *Where was his strength?* "Don't touch them. Don't change anything. I—must wear them. Kmet-Here might have seen—can't risk it—"

Rena's face appeared again. "Henry, you were shot, there's blood—"

If they'd touched anything. "My pocket. Check my pocket." The straw reappeared and he shook his head. "Make sure it's there, Rena."

She didn't ask what, simply disappearing from view. Henry accepted the straw, sipped what he had to take in before this body—*his*—would listen to him. The med team liked him to nap a while. At the thought, he spat out the mouthful. "I can't sleep, not now. There's no time."

"Don't worry. We're rushing you out, Henry." Another voice he knew, another face from New Earth and here: Ben from the Print House, his face strangely haggard. "You won't be up to much for a while, though."

They might not have *a while.* "Doesn't matter. Fast as you can, Ben," Henry urged. He tried to see beyond Ben's face, beyond the overhanging rack of handling arms and other devices. "Simmons. Is Simmons here?"

"I'm here, Henry."

If Ben, who backed away, looked haggard, his young assistant had aged years since he'd left. "Simmons. Thank you. For all you've done."

A wan smile. "Doesn't feel like enough." Unbelievably, his hand came into view holding a paper bag. "Your doughnut."

Henry had to smile, the muscles of his face resisting. *They hadn't stimulated those.* "Well done."

Rena appeared at Simmons' shoulder. She held up the metal slip, and Henry sagged with relief. "The *Exeter*'s probe reached Brightside," he explained to his now-agog assistant. "She went off course. Made it to a different world." Maddening, being so short of breath. "I—have to take that to Kmet-Here. Convince kmeth to go there."

"I understand, Henry, but—" Simmons looked past Henry. "Is his new epitome ready?"

"Not even close," Ben answered.

"No time. Help me up. Get me dressed—those clothes." Henry used his own hands and arms, rubbery as they felt, persisting until they closed in on his can and helped him out. Catching his breath, he nodded his thanks at the technicians. Understood Adalia's conflicted expression—at a guess, the neurologist had fought to keep him unconscious longer. "Feels great," he lied, gesturing down at his naked body. Made the mistake of looking at it, and tore his eyes from skin coated in streaks of brownish red fluid, from the raw openings where plugs had just been removed. They saved him from the reality of the process, let him wake clean and dressed between sheets—

Didn't matter. "The minimum," he ordered. "Killian's holding the Portal—trying to—"

THE PORTAL REMAINS. KILLIAN HAS TOLD KMET-HERE YOU'RE BRINGING SUPPLIES FOR THE OFFICIAL SURPRISE PARTY. I BELIEVE KMETH EXPECTS PEANUTS.

He closed his eyes. Swayed and was supported. Eased into a sling. "Rest, Henry." Norman, the nurse, for once not frowning. "We'll get you ready. Leave it to us."

Ordinarily, he'd have given in, but not now. Not when he was home and they were real. Henry forced himself to be alert, to look around. "Stay—"

"We will." Rena took his right hand, motioned Simmons to take his left. "As long as you're here, Henry. We will."

Astrid and Norman washed his body as if Henry wasn't in it, efficient and impersonal, but they knew. The technician avoided his eyes. The nurse swore non-stop under his breath, finishing with a forlorn, "Isn't right, Henry."

However much he agreed, Henry kept quiet, cooperating to the best of his freshly decanted and decidedly creaky ability as they dressed him in clean briefs and socks, then draped the ruin of his shirt over his shoulders. They'd cut it from his epitome, not realizing he'd want it back.

His pants were damp from melted snow. The front of his shirt, vest, and jacket, with their perfect overlapping holes, were stiff with blood, and he was frankly astonished his epitome had arrived with any left. The outer coat had its dark stain, but the hole had sealed itself.

Henry left the coat open, moving the precious foil strip to a dry pocket of his jacket. The bag holding the Arbiter's badge was spotted with brown; nothing to be done about that. He'd have to return it as it was.

Ben brought out a wheeled chair as Aadila was giving Henry her final check. "I won't need that," Henry protested, leaning past the neurologist.

"Yes, you will," she told him. "Your mind needs time to reconnect. I'm not watching you fall flat on your face the minute you stand." A frown. "I'd prefer an assist rig. You can wear it under your clothes."

"No, thank you." Henry didn't explain.

Ben met his gaze, giving a small nod. He'd been briefed on the vulnerability of polymorphic tech on a Portal. From behind the wheelchair he brought out a wooden cane. "Got it from the lost and found."

They helped Henry sit, Ben putting a hand on his shoulder for an instant. The med team stood awkwardly, hands twitching as if dismayed to let him go, and the Arbiter swallowed a lump in his throat. *How did he thank them—what could he possibly say—*

"Shuttle's ready, Henry," Simmons announced, rescue impeccably timed.

***

The trip wasn't long enough and couldn't be, but Henry treasured every second. Leaving the second floor and those who'd helped him. Riding the elevator he'd used countless times without thought, up to where he'd worked with so many. The smells that said *home*, even inside this building.

Most of all, the faces of his coworkers as Simmons and Rena pushed him along those filled hallways to the roof elevator. He'd never appreciated how miraculous it was, this place, these people, lining the walls, in doorways, silent, intent on him. Each smiled, some tearfully, as he passed. Reached out to brush his shoulders and arms with their fingers. Knowing what was at stake—improbably believing he, like this, could save them—they gave him their support the only way they could.

Being the Arbiter, he smiled reassurance. Received trusting smiles in return, though all he could do was try his best, as all here did.

He felt some stare after him, no doubt because Henry m'Yama t'Nowak was about to do what no Human born on this world had done in two hundred years—go to space as himself. He supposed he mustn't tell them it was the single most terrifying thing he'd ever faced and if he hadn't been in the chair, he might have run the other way.

At the last door, Simmons and Rena turned him to face back. Cheers burst out, spontaneous and ragged and utterly wonderful.

He'd no words. Lifted hands like lead weights to thank them.

What was he thinking, to risk them?

***

The elevator doors closed, cutting off the cheering. Henry let himself sigh. Rena knelt by the chair at once, her hand warm on his. "Are you all right?"

"No," he admitted. "Sure you won't come along? New world. Might be bugs."

Her lips pressed against his cheek, then she lowered her face to his shoulder. "I can't leave Earth, Henry. Not if it's ending. I can't leave Joel to be alone."

He let himself stroke her beautiful hair. "You're together again? When'd that happen?"

Felt her shake with laughter. "Now you ask?"

Henry smiled. "I never pry into your personal life. You're my oneiric." *Once.* "My friend." *Always.*

Rena lifted her head, her face damp with tears. "Henry—you'll still need—how do I keep in touch? Our FLIPs?"

Whose coms passed through the Portals. "Assume kmeth can listen in," he cautioned. "We'll pass anything Kmet-Here shouldn't know through Killian and Gis." The Spacer Repository. "Simmons, I have to ask more of you—"

"I'll stay with Giselle, Henry. Long as you need me there." Simmons produced a handset from his pocket. "A secure line to your grandfather's farm. Mersi set it up."

He couldn't bring himself to touch it. "We said our goodbyes when I left, Simmons." He found a smile. "I'll look forward to saying hello."

The elevator stopped, the doors opening. The air was so clear the mountains looked close enough to touch. Henry drew a slow, deep breath, inhaling the tang of the sea behind him, the smell of sun-drenched pines, and wished his lungs could hold more.

Flip, ever faithful, sat waiting, hatch sealed and ladder up, most likely because of the group gathered in alts shadow.

Closer, claiming Henry's attention, stood Shomchai, Ousmane, and Sofia, the latter a step to the side, arms tight around her middle. "Thank you for coming," he said, moved to see them. "Thank for you for everything you've done—are doing." He held out his hand. First to take it was Shomchai, who leaned down to whisper a hoarse, "Get it done and get home, Henry."

Ousmane came next, ignoring his hand in favor of a firm kiss on the lips, saying as she pulled away, "Bringing my family—I will, ah, always be grateful. Always."

"Wait." He brought out the velvet bag she'd given him at the start. "For the museum."

She made no move to take it. "It is yours, Arbiter. As it should be. "

Leaving Sofia, who accepted a handshake. Gripped a moment longer. "So you get to be first."

Henry gave a rueful half-shrug. "Not on purpose."

She bowed her head. Straightened. "Arbiter." Understood in that one word, a vow. The *Lissett* would launch if Sofia had to push her.

Seeing who else waited, Henry pulled off the sheet. "I'll walk from here."

Simmons helped him stand, handing him the wooden cane. Using it, Henry took a cautious step. His arm shook and his palm left sweat on the grip. Rena hovered to one side, Simmons the other. He took a second step—teetering—then a third, steadier. Gaining confidence.

Those waiting came forward to meet him, and Henry gratefully stopped. "Chair. Members of the Assembly." All nine voting members were here, including the Alt-Intel representative now erect in full humanoid form. Slightly behind stood PPC Specialists Liam and Ireiti, sober-faced and flanking a wheeled console quite different from the one they'd brought to his office.

No wonder Flip shut the door.

"We won't delay you, Arbiter," the Chair said briskly. "We came—" Her face worked a moment. Set in grim lines. "We came to prove we've listened. To your reports. To your requests. That we appreciate what might need to be done." She gestured wordlessly at the menacing console.

Simmons had informed him of Killian's quick thinking—how they'd hurried to fill her list, sent via Gis. "I hope you packed peanuts. There's to be a party."

"I beg your pardon—" with clear affront.

Henry gripped the cane to steady himself. The leaders of Earth were afraid. Hadn't he made sure they would be? Hadn't he expected something like this, despite the experts who'd have warned the Assembly against using any Human-made weapon against an alien artifact the size and power of a Portal?

They believed they'd no option.

Time to give them one.

"As of this moment," Henry told them, his voice ringing out, "New Earth remains bound within the Duality of Human and Kmet. Is there reason to be concerned about kmeth's ultimate intentions? Of course. It's why I've asked you to take precautions and why I'm going back to find this new world." He put his hand where the robe hid his blood-stained pocket.

They'd been briefed on the *Exeter.* "To put more of us—maybe the last of us at risk?" Eastern Foothills' face was pale, with bags under his eyes. "Why? Why not leave these people hidden from the Kmet? Safe. I say we vote!"

For how long? "It's too late for that," Henry told them, flat and sure. *Let them fire him.* "Taking the Portal to this world instead of Earth buys time. To learn more from and about the Kmet. To arbitrate between us to the benefit of both, and that's what we need. Not this." His turn to gesture at whatever they'd brought. "If I finish the job, we'll never need this."

If he failed, Killian had the self-destruct. A means to destroy the Kmet, the Portals, and potentially New Earth and all the people on it, including those who'd tenderly dressed him in bloody clothes, who'd cheered him in the halls, the friends standing with him—those who'd trusted him and left their homes—

His, the responsibility to decide if and when.

Eastern Foothills wasn't done. "You really believe we've a future."

No one else's.

"I'm off to make sure of it." Henry handed the cane to Simmons, feeling the roof grow solid beneath his feet. "Thank you, all."

The nine might have voted anyway, ordered him stopped, and Henry half-thought they would. Instead, they stepped aside somberly to let him pass, Rena and Simmons staying close, the specialists rolling their device away.

A vote of a kind.

Flip, presumably observing his shaky approach, raised the hatch, morphing the usual ladder into a ramp with a railing. Henry stopped at the bottom. Smiled at Simmons. "My doughnut?"

Simmons passed him the bag, then reached out to rest a hand on Henry's shoulder. He bent so their eyes met. His were round and terribly earnest. "It has been my greatest privilege and honor, Arbiter Henry m'Yama t'Nowak, to have worked with you." A faint blush. "There. Whew. I knew I had to say that. Before you left. Was it all right?" With typical concern.

"It was fine, Simmons. Hopefully premature but, in any event, know I feel the same. I couldn't have done this without you. Your help. Your courage and intelligence." Henry smiled. "I've wondered if you were after my job—"

"No, sir!" Simmons reared back like a startled horse. "Never! I'm happy as your assistant—" Subsided, raking a hand through his hair as he regarded Henry with abrupt suspicion. "You're teasing."

Not really. Henry wouldn't hesitate to recommend Simmons for the Arbiter track. *If they survived this—*

Putting all that aside, he pulled Simmons into a hug. Breathed a husky, "Take care."

He turned. "Rena—about that promise—" *One he'd had no right to make.*

"The beach'll be here, Henry." Taking a pin from her hair, she attached it to his vest, near his heart but away from the blood. Pressed her hand over it with a wink and tremulous smile. "For luck."

Then, before either of them shattered, his dearest friend walked away, not looking back.

***

"Welcome aboard, Henry."

"Thank you, Flip." The polymorph sounded nonchalant, but an elaborate and well-padded lounge chair had replaced the former safety seat and harness. Henry sank into it gratefully. "Killian's requests onboard?"

"Yes, Henry. As well as medical supplies for you and fresh clothing should you wish to change." A closet door appeared and opened to display its contents.

Simmons. Henry looked down at himself and grimaced. "Soon. Once I'm sure Kmet-Here is satisfied this is me, Flip. You ready to go?"

"Yes. I took the time to replenish myself, Henry, and am fully prepared."

Wished he was. Henry touched Rena's pin. Checked the pocket with the foil strip. He'd memorized the coordinates, but its very existence was the proof he'd need to convince Kmet-Here to move.

The badge. Ousmane hadn't taken it—he'd tucked it—*where was it?* Henry frantically searched his clothes—found the doughnut—*where was the badge?*

"Henry?"

There. He'd been careless, leaving it in the coat he planned to discard. He moved it to his other vest pocket, refastening his jacket with hands that wouldn't stop trembling. "This—" about to say *body,* he changed to "—it always takes a while to adapt."

"By the report, Henry, you have excellent muscle tone and circulation. You should feel like yourself again soon."

Didn't yet. "Good to know." He leaned back, rubbing his head. His hair was thicker. No way to feel the other, more profound change inside. They'd deactivated his now-useless neural net, applying commands to cause it to dissolve. All that remained in his skull was the implant allowing him to communicate with Flip.

On his own, he was. As he'd spent most of his life, and most people were. *Grandfather would approve.*

"Henry, I have a question of a personal nature," the polymorph announced, a little too casually.

"Go ahead."

"During your interaction with Governor O'Belleveau, you said: 'If it would help you to shoot me, go ahead.'" In Henry's voice, rendered faithfully with its switch from despair to the defiant elation of *go ahead.* "I wish to know what you were thinking."

Henry pressed his lips together, holding in a glib *I wasn't.* He owed his friend the truth. "I thought if my epitome died, I'd permission to quit. Leave all this behind—abandon my duty—you and Killian." Bitterness drove him to admit the rest. "No one would blame me. How could they? None of us ever goes to space as our existent. When the governor showed me the message, I realized I had to stay, that this was too important, but the moment happened. I'm not proud of it, Flip. It's unforgiveable."

"I do not see how forgiveness or pride is required, Henry. If Killian had been in your position, do you not think she would have experienced the same feelings? That anyone might? Is the Arbiter not allowed to be Human?"

His words, back at him. "Flip—" Henry stopped, giving the ceiling a frustrated look. "Isn't the point. I faltered. Might have failed everyone."

"Let me rephrase. Are you not allowed to consider your options? Is it not your choice that matters?"

"You can't understand. You're programmed to die for the cause—" *Lashing out, was he?* "I'm sorry. I shouldn't have said that, Flip. It wasn't fair."

"Because you believe I, as a sentient construct, cannot face the same temptation," with a note of *was that pity?* "I can, Henry. While an Alt-Intel expects to die with alts material portion, there are permitted exceptions. An individual possessed of irreplaceable experience may be offered continuance: removal, in part or whole, of alts consciousness from an endangered portion to be installed into a new one. Such an offer was made to me when I came on this mission, Henry." A note of pride. "Assuming access to the Portal's data transfer system, I too could *quit* at any moment."

And the universe turn to pink glitter first. Loyalty—friendship—of the highest order, simply given.

Yet to be earned. Henry coughed to clear the husk from his voice. "We're in this together, Flip. And thank you." Absurd, to feel lighter. *But he did.*

"I must also express my profound regret. My actions cost a life."

"I don't see what else you could have done. The governor might have shot me again."

"I took that to be her intention, Henry, but you'd wanted to bring her to New Earth."

Henry shook his head. "Constance wouldn't have thanked me for it. World VI—Brightside will be a place of regret for us both."

A moment's silence, then a welcome distraction. "Henry, the *Lissett* is coming into view to starboard."

Henry rolled his head to gaze out Flip's window, finding nothing he recognized in the barnacle-free hull surrounded by gantries and girders. People slept inside, their last waking memories full of concern for New Earth and their families. *Nothing had changed.* "How close to launch is she?"

"I'm informed the new core has arrived and is being attached. But—" An uncharacteristic hesitation.

His heart sank. "So not close."

"If time runs out before the work is done, volunteers will leave with the *Lissett* and complete her refit as she passes through the solar system. They—I feel this must be incorrect, Henry. They will not be epitomes."

"Can't be," Henry replied, seeing Sofia's face, knowing her resolve. If the *Lissett* was his insurance against the worst, this was hers. If New Earth fell to the Kmet, they'd lose the Spacer Repository and those it kept safe.

Spacers had probably lined up to go. To die where they'd wanted to live.

No more Heartbreak.

He tore his gaze from the ship, saw the Portal growing closer in Flip's other window. "Contact Omar and have him send us through at once, please.

"Killian's expecting us."

<Told you . . .>

"BALACHE *Point* clear the Portal and away. Please stand by. The Arbiter's shuttle is on its way up."

"Roger that, Omar. Standing by." *Not planning to go anywhere.* Killian rested both her elbows on the center pedestal, knee pressed against it to keep some of the weight off her throbbing right hip.

An anxious rumble. "With peanuts? For the official surprise party?"

She raised an eyebrow at the Kmet, lounging against the far wall. Or, like her, using anything solid for support. *Jury was out.* "The Arbiter will take care of it."

<Helluva lot to put on one person, Killie-Cat.>

She stuck up her thumb. Henry was capable. Stellar trick, this dash of his, home and back. She couldn't wait to find out why.

<Ah, Killie-Cat? There's something you should know before Henry gets here. Didn't want to tell you too soon. You ready?>

Not liking that tone. Not a bit. Killian pulled up her pad, keeping it out of kmeth's line of sight. Curled her free hand into a question mark.

Listened. Let the pad drop, because there wasn't anything to say or ask.

Henry, returning as his real *self—*

Gis finished with a typically smug, <Told you he'd get shot.>

"Here's the surprise . . ."

ODD, to have lived in space for weeks and only now to experience a transit through a Portal, as opposed to within. Delighted to have an appetite, Henry pulled out his doughnut—or rather an indistinguishable copy of the one Simmons had brought. Which he was, his real self now so many disassociated atoms.

He put the doughnut away for later, no longer hungry.

"Docking complete, Henry."

"The Portal's still orbiting Brightside?" A minor nightmare, that this Kmet might have moved the split second before they'd entered New Earth's Portal.

"Yes, Henry. "

He rose, pleased to be steady on his feet, and pulled the bags—*party supplies*—from the cupboard Flip opened. "This everything?" He hoped so. His hands weren't sure of their grip. To his relief, there were shoulder straps.

"From Killian's list, yes. There was a last-minute substitution."

Henry frowned. "Anything I should know? I'm going straight to Control."

"Simmons replaced the self-inflating balloons selected by Killian's oneiric with what he called *fit for company.* I believe a euphemism for—"

Henry grinned. "I get it, Flip." Lost his smile. "I trust Gis has briefed Killian on what happened to me by now. Seeing me—" a gesture at his clothing "—isn't how I'd want her to find out."

"I don't know, Henry. It was left to Giselle's discretion. I do have several messages from New Earth waiting for you."

Henry sighed for more than one reason. "Clarify *several.*"

"Several thousand, with more arriving. Shall I sort and file those not vital to your mission? You have many well-wishers."

And a number who wouldn't be. "Do, please. Redirect to Simmons if in doubt, but don't hesitate to contact me." He'd lost the antique phone somewhere along the way. Flip had acquired a replacement he held up now. "I'm reliant on you, Flip." No longer on wristbands and those he could summon. *Going to take getting used to—*

"Always, Henry. I have prepared a new coat," the polymorph reassured him, another cupboard opening. "Killian's coffee is in the inner pocket."

Be lucky to carry himself—but there was no arguing with thoughtfulness and, come to think of it, if he'd no further use for the winter coat, why keep the heavy boots and socks? "Did you bring new sandals?"

"Yes, Henry." The door concealing his clean set of clothes opened, a pair he'd missed seeing on a shelf.

"Wonderful."

Bending and moving helped more than he'd expected; once Henry was again in sandals, the clean comfort of his Flip-coat over his shoulders—a pocket weighed down by what he trusted to be a well-sealed mug, he found the bags lighter, his balance more solid. *Almost normal.*

Feeling anything but, Henry headed for the airlock door.

***

He'd told Killian the PIPs changed things. This—he hadn't expected. The antechamber looked like their corridor, floor etched with crack-like valleys, walls buckled and distorted, and there wasn't a PIP in sight.

Warmer. Henry no longer saw his breath, for whatever that meant, and wasted no time finding a tube mouth redolent of earthy Kmet, pushing the bags ahead of himself. Diving in afterwards, he tried not to think of the tubes themselves decaying, which meant he thought of nothing else—

—until popping up through a still-smooth white floor, bags sliding away.

Killian and Kmet-Here watched him collect himself, the pilot's face set and grim, but unsurprised.

Relieved, Henry pulled the sealed mug from his coat. "Your coffee," he said, keeping it cheery, trying to send a message. *I'm fine. I'm back.*

She caught it, mug and message, lips pulled from her teeth in what wasn't remotely a smile. *He'd some explaining to do,* that expression warned.

It'd have to wait. He looked at the Kmet, face composed. *This was the test.* At no point since arriving at New Earth had a Kmet faced an actual Human being. Would it matter? "Kmet-Here. Thank you for your patience."

A muted BOOM. "Arbiter-Henry?"

Was that doubt? He'd gambled on Kmet-Here's practice of sending down kmeth's spies, that reappearing in the same clothes last seen on Brightside should suffice. "Of course, Kmet-Here," he said, keeping it calm.

If anything, the Kmet had altered drastically enough in his absence Henry might have thought this a new individual. The scales on the sides were now separated by wide swathes of yellow and brown skin. Some were missing altogether, leaving wounds that oozed a pale pus. He risked a brief glance.

The den filled half the space, now, coated in writhing PIPs. *Rena should see this—she'd know what it meant—*

"Good. Where are the treats for the official surprise party?" The eyes—the eyes reassured him; they hadn't changed, pupils shrinking with suspicion. "The official surprise party is now. Do you concur?"

Real meant alone—

"The Arbiter's brought them, Kmet-Here," Killian said, prodding him. "Let's get started."

Henry gave her a grateful nod. "I do. Here's the surprise component, Kmet-Here." He pulled out the slip of foil. "I found another world of Humans-There. We must go there before New Earth."

The pilot's lips closed in a grim line. *She'd been told.* Her head swung to the Kmet, her posture tense, clearly expecting an explosion.

Instead, the immense creature might have been frozen, polyps erect and stark white, eyelids unblinking as kmeth stared at the foil.

Lacking a reaction, Henry continued briskly, "The *Exeter* didn't reach World II. It landed elsewhere and sent out probes with the correct information. I received this from a government representative who verified its nature." *Before shooting him.* He held out the message, coordinates carefully folded inside. "Would you like to check for yourself, Kmet-Here?"

A flinch from head to tail tip.

He redirected his outstretched hand. "Pilot, please input these coordinates."

As Killian took the foil, her face inscrutable, Kmet-Here gave a distressed burp. She hesitated. "I promised kmeth a party, sir. With peanuts."

"Yes," the Kmet echoed plaintively. "Peanuts, Arbiter. Peanuts."

A delay wouldn't hurt. Henry bent to the first bag. "Let's see what we have here." Pulled out handfuls of red and gold streamers.

PIPs abandoned whatever they were doing in a race to glue the streamers to the den. The Kmet ignored them, eyes glued to the bag, and Henry began to wonder if peanuts were a treat or somehow essential to kmeth's well-being. He burrowed deeper, releasing handfuls of confetti—again collected by PIPs—and passed a large beer bottle to Killian before reaching the bottom. "Next bag," he announced, quickly dumping out its contents.

A mistake. Peanuts spilled out along with self-inflating balloons and Henry barely dodged out of the way in time before Kmet-Here lunged into the midst, head twisting, tongue tips slurping up nuts and expanding little animals with colorful bowties, consuming everything with such frantic haste most of the balloons likely finished inflating inside kmeth's gut.

Killian clutched the bottle and foil, her bottom lip between her teeth as if trying to keep from comment.

Kmeth's tongue-tips scoured the now-bare floor, as if desperate for more. Feeling a sudden pity, Henry pulled out his phone. "Shuttle, Kmet-Here has enjoyed our treats. What's our cargo status?"

IF YOU MEAN DO I HAVE ADDITIONAL PEANUTS IN MY HOLD, HENRY, THE ANSWER IS YES. AND PICKLED BEETS.

"I brought more peanuts, Kmet-Here. Do you want them now?"

Inner eyelids blinked furiously, but the Kmet settled. Polyps emerged, their tips a happier purple, and kmeth's voice had a soft, dreamy note to it. "I can wait for more until after we transit."

Not a word about a new destination. No complaint about postponing their arrival at Earth. Henry hesitated, wondering if he'd somehow drugged kmeth.

Killian seized the moment to step on the dais, the motion hitched and awkward. Her scowl forbade him to ask. "I'll input."

Pairs of PIPs seized the empty bags, dragging them to add to the den. Another pounced on the bottle the pilot had set down.

Henry looked up at the screens. The two outermost held the streaming numbers and symbols from the satellites, between them a view of a beautiful, life-filled planet—

Marred by the spiral of a doomsday clock, its spark almost at the center.

The pilot stepped down. "Ready for you, Kmet-Here."

The Kmet wheezed and groaned as kmeth got into position, PIPs scampering gaily up the wall, poised and waiting.

It was all about to happen again, he might never have been to New Earth and back, he might be what he was—

"We go!"

TRANSIT!

We're not from here.

Doublet

SHE'D been Beth Redriver when she'd walked over the threshold of Home in the Split with Lyall Seeker, senior-most and trainer. Stupid proud. Full of herself and giddy with freedom. Wonder was Lyall had seen anything in her worth the risk of partnering.

Wonder was she hadn't killed them, first trip. Looking back, Lyall'd picked the shortest, most used path, but any mistake would have done it, and she'd come close to a few. He'd kept them safe. Waited for her to get some sense. Had patience with a fool Beth lacked even now.

Every waking moment, she wished he'd survived.

She'd done her training trips, gone overnight alone. Become Beth Seeker and thought she knew it all. Bristled when Lyall showed up for her first full crossing. He'd known her, was why, better than she did.

Reaching Away, seeing it for herself, had robbed her of sense. The towering trees of mauve and red, the lush vines that moved without a breeze, the sounds of strange new life—the closer Beth came, the more impatient she became and the faster she went. Heedless of anything but the wild burn of curiosity, she'd started across its threshold, boots scuffing through thick ash, kicking it up, sending what she forgot was toxic for their kind to breathe into the air, and Lyall—he'd run after her.

Saved her, getting her veil up over her head, dragging her back.

Died in her arms, coughing blood-specked mucous into rags she tore from her clothing and held over his mouth, soaked rags she carried with her, as she carried him, across the Split, because there were things below drawn to the taste of Human.

They called her a hero, if never to her face. Buried Lyall Seeker and put a plaque with the date on the damned boulder; put her in hospital until her lungs healed. Tidied up, as it were, because teachers died of their students often as not.

Beth went back into the Split, crossed into Away to gather the materials she'd been supposed to retrieve, honoring Lyall the only way she could.

By surviving.

***

Marker pounded in, initials and entry date carved, Beth walked into the Split without looking back, tucking everything behind deep in the part of her she used for what shouldn't come along. Including a young would-be Seeker she'd like to think would make it.

Wouldn't know unless she did, and that was that.

The Bios had given her a new-to-anyone place to explore, making it easy to forget what she left for where she was, the landscape flatter than any and hotter than most. She'd have to watch her water.

Along with all else. Beth walked as the sun rose behind her, following her shadow till it disappeared underfoot, making it time to find shade. Made her own, there being nothing in reach to offer any, meaning a miserable day baking under her cloak. Downright homey, the Split trying to kill her from the start.

Failing, Beth having no problem with hot.

First hint of cool, she was off again, gear packed and vine cap wriggling on her scalp. With each step, down went her sounding stick, beads tinkling their message. *I'm a Seeker. Let me pass.*

The crust here gave back a faint, different echo; not enough to make her pay it any mind. The heat and flat worked on the ground, baked it harder. No place to linger, that was sure. Beth kept her eye on the horizon, waiting for the haze to reveal what waited. The Bios had liked it, her trying the vicinity of a pot. Wanted her to do it again at a different one.

Fine with her. By what maps they had, she'd pass a bunch to reach Away. Sooner she dumped this latest load of junk, sooner she'd get there.

***

Pots. Silly name for what was taller and wider and older than Home's largest building, chockful of melted rock that defied logic by staying melted without flowing up and spilling over, but she'd none better.

She'd slept well by this one, warm when anywhere else she'd wake to a fleeting frost. Waking now, Beth stretched, slow and careful. Listening.

Wind sloughed up the side of the pot. Magma bubbled unseen, a noise dark, wet, and irregular. That worse-than-fart stink. *Like Dex after pickled eggs.*

Beth grinned.

Dawn glowed on the sky's edge. Time to move.

After her essentials, Beth tossed Patrick's latest batch of artifacts out on the crust one by one, and sat chewing a twist of jerky to watch.

An electromagnet. *Look what we can do.* A block of Away wood, scribed with sequences of faces, one side of different emotions, one with different-shaped features, one with different sizes, the last showing the bones of a skull. *Look at what we are.* Two sides with maps, one of the planet, one of Home. *This is where we live.* A sack of dried Earth-that-was corn. *We're not from here.*

Snuck in another damn pencil when she wasn't looking. Man had a death wish. She'd kept it.

She wasn't satisfied, but the group was better than the last. Smarter. Beth wasn't interested in meeting what didn't think—that was too easy. What was, what wondered and puzzled and pondered—that was her goal.

Might be here.

That niggling, hard-to-forget feeling had come back to her, once in the Split, breathing its arid stink. The feeling she hadn't made a mistake, her last walk, to think the crust had creaked under her, to think she'd had a response from those beneath and hadn't known it.

Might get another.

Beth chewed slowly, each bite small, stopping while she was hungry, eyes never leaving what she'd tossed.

Might not.

Doublet

"Destroy it."

HENRY'S stomach cramped, doubling him over. *Forgot the meds.* Heard Killian's voice from a distance, "—like home." and wrenched his eyes up to the screen. Blue oceans. Varied brown of dry land below white bands of cloud. Patches of greens and purple. It might have been New Earth. *Mustn't be.*

"Whoa. That's not."

That being a line from pole to pole, dividing the land in half. A line that couldn't be real but was—the images from the Portal Library, of worlds divided. They'd thought it metaphor—

When it was the truth. A barrier, some sort of fence, separating what lived on a planetary scale. *Made.*

Killian stared past him, eyes wide. A warm, noxious breath passed through Henry's hair and he froze. Felt the heat of that immense body now much too close.

"Kmet-Here," Killian said, low and respectful. "Transit was successful."

Another, heavier breath. Henry managed not to gag as he watched the slice of alien he could see reflected in the screen's lower edge. The spikes on kmeth's head were empty, the expressive polyps fully withdrawn.

"You took us to a wrong place," the Kmet declared all at once, a discordant moan beneath the words. "*WrongplacewrongplaceWRONGPLACE!*" BOOM! BOOM!

Killian flinched.

"Easy," Henry mouthed. He turned to face the alien. "These are the correct—"

"No. NO!" Kmeth pulled back as if Henry threatened it, the abrupt retreat crushing several surprised PIPs. Kmeth's eyelids flickered so quickly they blurred, clouding the pupils. "Destroy it NOW!"

In response, PIPs scurried up the walls, worked controls.

"No. I do not concur," Henry half-shouted. "We came here to return—"

"No!" The head lowered almost to the floor. "There were no Divider planets. There can be no Divider planets. This must be destroyed!"

HENRY, MULTIPLE CLUSTERS OF MINING PIPS HAVE LEFT THE PORTAL. THEY ARE ENTERING THE ATMOSPHERE.

"Stop! Let me get the people off first!"

"NO NO! DESTROY NOW!"

Killing innocents—taking any answers— "Mining PIPs—" Desperate, Henry looked to Killian, who shook her head. There was nothing she could do.

They turned in horror to the screen.

HENRY, THE MINING PIPS ARE DESCENDING.

He didn't repeat it aloud. Kmet-Here had sent so many, their trails showed from space, and was this the future of New Earth?

THEY HAVE REACHED THE SURFACE.

Henry braced himself, waiting for the cracks to appear, the fire—

Nothing happened.

Nothing changed. He'd been holding his breath—let it out.

HENRY, THE MINING PIPS HAVE BEEN NEUTRALIZED.

"Destroy it." A faint, miserable muttering. "Destroydestroydestroy." The Kmet heaved kmethself to him. "Call Earth Humans, Arbiter-Henry. Have them bring rocks to Kmet-There. Many rocks. Rocksrocks—"

"Respectfully, we will not, Kmet-Here."

Head rising, kmeth roared a deafening "ROCKS!" Slobber appeared at the corners of kmeth's wide mouth, trailed down the pedestals.

Killian let out a loud piercing whistle.

The frantic creature seemed stunned. Before kmeth recovered, Henry spoke quickly. "Kmet-Here, I am the Arbiter." Both eyes aimed at him. *Good.* "For the health of the Duality, you agreed to assist me in transporting Humans-There to New Earth for their safety. Including the Humans on this planet. Do you concur?"

"Yes. They go first."

Better. He started to relax.

"GET THEM! GETTHEMGETThemmfphf—" Words muffled as the Kmet pounced like a cat, grabbing Henry in kmeth's mouth.

Tossing him aside.

He heard a scream. Didn't know if it was Killian's or his. A tube opened before he splattered against the wall, whisking him along and down and up and around.

Spat him out on the floor of the antechamber.

The tube mouth closed behind him.

Henry fought to catch his wits and breath. *Not good at all.*

A light came on, shining through the airlock window. "Henry?"

"Hello, Flip. Open the door, please." He got to his feet. "We're heading down sooner than expected. Prep for launch."

"I'm ready. Are you all right?"

"Yes, Flip." *Other than scared out of his wits.* "Please inform Killian I'm here and unhurt."

Wrong place.

Or had they found the right one? The Portal Makers. Beings able to divide a continent and stop kmeth's own weapon of destruction. The enemy of the Kmet.

His hands shook. Henry went to slip them into his pockets, only to find his Flip-coat soaked with corrosive Kmet slobber. He took it off, holding it out by the collar.

Only to have it turn to sand and flow from his hand. He stared at the terrifying little pile on the floor. They'd told him, hadn't they? *But this—*

Wasn't to happen to Flip. After checking the rest of his clothing was slobber-free, Henry stepped into the warmer air of the airlock, waiting impatiently for the door to close. "Flip, establish contact with Giselle's FLIP. Maintain a live feed. Killian has to know what we find down there. New Earth does."

"Yes, Henry."

As the door opened and he stepped inside, "Go."

". . . proceed as usual."

KILLIAN found herself standing at the wall, hands on the rim of the tube mouth that had swallowed Henry, ears ringing from her own scream.

"I must rest."

She spun around, ready to—*what?* The Kmet slowly lumbered past her, oblivious of her state or what kmeth had done, polyps waving again and, if not purple, then more pink than red. PIPs scrambled from the walls and up kmeth's sides as if they hadn't released planet-killers an instant before and—

Kmeth might have killed the only Henry in existence—leaving her alone—

<You okay, Killie-Cat?>

Her thumb jabbed down. Kmet-Here was grunting and shoving into kmeth's den again, any minute the effort would launch crap, and she was emphatically *not okay.*

Killian half-ran to the slobbered pedestals, determined to launch the sats before anything else went sideways, worried about Henry, worried about herself, Gis, and everyone else—

"Pilot Killian, this is the Arbiter's shuttle ready to depart. My passenger is aboard and reports himself well."

She stumbled at the sound of Flip's precise, careful voice, caught herself. Shot a glance at the rear end of Kmet-Here before daring to reply, "Orders?"

"Please proceed as usual, Pilot Killian. Shuttle out."

AS FUCKING USUAL??

Killian grabbed her pad and wrote: *You hear that?*

<Five by five. Wake me up. My guess is, Henry's sending something private.>

Her heart settled. Gis was right. Gis was always right. She tapped the wristband.

"Launching sats," Killian told the room.

Not that anyone was listening.

"Two damn yous."

METEORS were fall's big show, when Doublet's orbit crossed Welcome's, the comet the first reliable feature of the settlers' new sky.

Wasn't fall. Beth glanced up between keeping her eyes where she stepped.

Weren't meteors. Not when what streaked down slowed before touching the ground and she almost came to a halt herself before smartening up. Whatever the things, weren't her business unless one landed on her path. Or on her head, a possibility hunching her shoulders, but the pretty flashes in the sky were followed by nothing at all. Not a thump, not a boom. Disappointing to anyone taught how the *Exeter* rode a ball of flame to the ground.

With a shrug, Beth put her mind where it belonged, finding her next shelter. The flat had curve to it, looking in the distance. Nothing that—

A glint of something different moved through the sky, higher than anything with wings, not like the streaks. Beth stopped and stared at it, uneasy. Unsure why—

Until warning crackle filled the air and the hairs on her arms rose. *Sweep coming!*

Down went her stick, up went her cloak, and Beth curled into a furious ball just as searing bolts of lightning crisscrossed around her, striking the ground, the air they expanded complaining with booms of thunder.

Good thing she'd left the pots.

"Four damn yous." Eyes shut, she counted, cursing whatever had flown overhead to trigger her second sweep in a lifetime. "Three damn yous." Her toes burned. "Two damn yous." The air grew unbearably hot—a gasped, "One—"

Then done.

Answered a question for the Bios, a new sweep so soon this time of year.

The device on her wrist crackled. "Beth—"

"Yeah, I noticed. All good, Dex."

"—craft—"

Beth looked up at the now-empty mauve sky. "Say again?"

"Something's appeared in orbit. Not responding to signals. Sent down a—" Static.

"Say again."

"—craft. Blueridge tracked it from the Split. Crashed in Away. Coordinates—" Static.

This time, Beth clamped her mouth shut.

Didn't help. Dex repeated on his own, with regrettable clarity, "Coordinates 49.8951° N, 97.1384° W. You can make it."

"Not and come back."

A prolonged bout of static implied a consultation. Beth leaned on her stick. Damn right they'd better figure this out.

Finally, "Understood. We'll send an intercept with supplies. Get eyes on, Seeker. We have to know."

Point of fact, whatever—whoever—had crashed in Away would be dead, then food. Or food, then dead, and Beth saw no reason to participate.

Other than the obvious, Doublet having visitors capable of space flight, if not the good sense or manners to make contact remotely, and if that wasn't enough to make every Human on this world take notice?

Add the part where, until these visitors showed up, every Human on this world believed themselves lost to their kind.

There, she thought grimly, was the *have to know* coming down the pipe. Add in that if the visitors truly were Human, how'd they get here so fast?

Before landing on Doublet, *Exeter* had launched message probes with their new home's location, one to each of her sister ships' planned destinations, and one back to New Earth, Humans incapable of losing all hope. According to the information plaque on the memorial hull, the first should be arriving around now, plus or minus a decade, full of news two hundred years stale.

Except on Doublet. *Exeter*'s unscheduled course change made her invisible, probes from other ships headed for her original destination. Her inhabitants might hear an "oh, there you are" in, say, another twenty years or so—assuming Doublet got radio telescopes up and running. Assuming others talked her direction.

Lot of assuming, none about a reply like this.

A reply crashed in Away and being chomped, Beth reminded herself. "Fine, I'll go. You get to tell the Bios to forget their samples."

Static, likely covering an impolite response. "Twice-daily reports, Seeker."

That hadn't come from Dex, who'd been a Seeker before losing an arm and understood the danger of putting out sound at regular intervals. "You'll get a report when—if—I find anything worth the call. Seeker out." She turned off her radio, in case a fool took the next shift.

Spreading her groundsheet, Beth got to work replacing the melted soles of her boots.

She'd some walking ahead.

"Call this surviving?"

ARBITER Henry *m'*Yama t'Nowak crawled on elbows and knees over the mound of debris in front of his half-buried shuttle, losing a sandal in the process. The other flew off as he tumbled down the other side, shouting, "What kind of landing was that?"

The shuttle gave a chagrined little shudder.

Fussing. Spitting out bits of green-purple leaves, Henry sat up and did a quick inventory. Filthy, and he'd scraped his hands, but— "Nothing broken. Come on, Flip."

The shuttle liquified, disappearing behind the mound. A smooth, slate-gray head rose up, large black eyes blinking. "I too am unbroken, Henry." Flip leapt over the mound, landing without a sound in front of Henry, and held out his sandals. "Therefore the kind of landing was survivable."

The voice was Flip's, the form humanoid, if 50% larger than Henry, who wasn't small, and this version of Flip had expressive, human-like features.

No missing the dismay.

Henry hid his own as he took his footwear. "My apologies, Flip. You're right. Thank you for not breaking us."

About to pull on a mud-soaked sandal—*nasty*—he paused to replay what had happened before *landing.*

A violent jolt. The taste of safety foam—

Alarmed, Henry looked up at the polymorph. "You hit something?"

"I hit several somethings," Flip replied with regret, gesturing behind Henry.

He turned his head to see a wide gash torn through the jungle. *Categorizing an alien biosphere in Earth terms?* He could almost hear Rena. She'd love this. Big green, brown, and purple things, coated with vines and bumps, blocked the sky, casting deep, complex shadows. The air was warm and heavy with moisture—and tinged with smoke. Plant bits smoldered, thankfully too damp to ignite and burn.

Jungle.

Where they weren't supposed to be. He'd been watching during their descent. West of the bare line, the vegetation—forest and grassland equivalents—had been more dense and darker, purple with patches of yellow. To the east, lighter, greens with the yellow—not to mention what looked to be towns, roads, and farms—Henry turned back to the polymorph. "I asked you to land in a field near the largest city. This is not a field." He waved his hand at the jungle.

"No, Henry, it is not."

"What happened?"

Sinuous, powerful fingers pointed up and wiggled, fluidic endoderm absorbing light. "When I passed over the bare area, energy bursts of considerable strength erupted from several points beneath. Calculating they were capable of destroying organic matter such as yourself, I performed an extreme maneuver to preserve you." A meaningful pause. "Extreme, Henry." Eyes glinted with pride.

Henry focused on the key point. "Someone shot at us."

"I find it more likely the bursts arose from an automated defense mechanism."

"Made by someone. The Portal Makers. We've—" *Not found them.* But a divided world the Kmet hadn't destroyed—*yet*—offered a chance. For answers. Maybe allies. "We have to reach the Humans on this world. Find out what they know. As soon as possible."

"There's a problem, Henry. In the maneuver I lost parts of me," Flip admitted. "They fell a considerable distance from here. Unless I can retrieve them, I can no longer be a shuttle."

Henry bent and pulled the soggy sandals from his feet, bare toes digging into what he was going to call mud. "These help?"

"Thank you, Henry." Flip dutifully let the thin extra soles return to alts mid-section, handing back the sandals. "I elected to report our landing and present situation to Harvey, to be relayed to our pilot via Giselle, rather than make direct contact where Kmet-Here might overhear."

"Good call." Henry winced inwardly, imagining Killian's reaction. "Next step, then. Fly me to the nearest city—"

"That is not recommended, Henry." In emphasis, Flip vigorously shook alts head, a gesture the polymorph rarely had the chance to employ. "A number of large, flying life-forms have gathered."

Futile trying to see through the intertwined vegetation above, so Henry squinted along the gash they'd carved in the jungle. Sure enough, immense shadows flickered back and forth across it, implying whatever circled overhead was too big to land. *Fascinating.* He'd built model Origin Earth Pterodactyls as a child—

Piercing, *hungry* cries shuddered through the air, ending any urge Henry might have to see the source up close. "Ground transport, please, Flip. As speedy as you can. We have to reach the inhabitants before—"

—Kmet-Here found a way to pull rocks through the Portal and launched them at the planet—

"—before the situation gets worse."

"Ready, Henry."

"That was—" Turning, he stared. "You call *this* ground transport?"

In response, Camel-Flip blew air at him through alts fat, hairy lips. The polymorph had added a saddle and large bags to itself, keeping alts overall mass, and those long legs did appear suited to moving through the maze of fallen limbs and undergrowth.

But a camel?

Henry resigned himself, aware there was no point arguing once Flip settled on what alt considered the optimal shape for a task. "Thank you, Flip."

On the bright side, he'd changed into clean clothes on the way down, though a jacket and vest weren't optimal in this heat. Unbuttoning both, Henry rubbed the back of his neck, feeling sweat but no discomfort. Elea had repaired the sunburn he'd acquired gardening—from his efforts in the garden. With the memory of that warm, innocent pain he—

. . . floated above, wondering when he was and where and why he was and who . . .

—dropped back to reality, unsettled by the disconnection. Hardly something he'd expected, back in his own flesh. "That was—odd."

"Henry?"

"I'm fine." *He'd better be.* Henry gazed up and up. "How do I—ah—thanks."

This as Camel-Flip bent alts knobby knees, rocking back and forth until the saddle was low enough for Henry to reach. He took hold and pulled. At the last second, his muddy feet slipped wildly on the polymorph's slick side and he fell flat on his back.

Camel-Flip's big head swung around to regard him, lips hanging loose, dark eyes framed by ridiculously long lashes. "Henry?"

"I'll need some help," the Arbiter admitted.

A short while later, Henry found himself in the saddle, hanging on desperately as Camel-Flip rocked up to alts feet. He'd camel drool soaking one shoulder, a surely unnecessary adherence to the role, and a deeper appreciation for those in historical documentaries shown leaping into saddles of any kind.

Camel-Flip heaved altself over the mound and strode briskly along the gash alts shuttle-self had created while crashing. Another piercing cry came from overhead. Henry crouched to present a smaller target. "Shouldn't we keep under the trees?"

"It would not be optimal, Henry. It is easier to elude pursuit in the open."

"Pursuit?" His fingers clenched on the upper part of the saddle. "What pursuit?"

"I now detect a number of life-forms rapidly approaching on the ground."

"Settlers?"

"Improbable, Henry. I detected no evidence of Human settlement on approach."

Henry stopped worrying about creatures he couldn't see. "Flip. Please tell me we're on the right side of the line."

Small, round ears flattened. "Surviving a landing is more important than its location, Henry. I did try my best."

Henry sighed. "You always do." He leaned over the saddle, planning to pat

Camel-Flip on alts curved neck, only to be startled by a whoosh of air across his back. *Something* dropped to the ground, running—*hopping?*—with one of Flip's bags in its grasp.

He'd time for that horrified glimpse as the polymorph lunged forward. Grabbing the saddle, and a good chunk of hairy pelt—for once glad of authenticity—Henry held on with all his might.

Then what had been a camel, with hair and a saddle to grab, became a fluid and reformed.

As Henry began to fall, he shouted: "Call this surviving?"

“Not my first choice.”

KILLIAN buried her face in the arms holding her knees to her chest, rocking back and forth. Here, on her bed, was as far as she could be from the door, and she’d put whatever could move in front of it. Her trunks. The chair, ripped from the desk, her coffee maker—

Wouldn’t stop *that*—

Kept rocking.

Henry, grabbed and flung like a fucking chew toy.

Flip’s stupid little saucer icon blinking out of existence.

No answer but static—

She’d run. Wasn’t proud of it, but there it was. “Had to crash,” she mumbled into her knees. “Had to kill Henry—for real.” Leaving a hole bigger and darker than grief. Without the Arbiter there was no one in charge but kmeth. No one on the other side of her door but a manic alien with minions. Killian’s breath shuddered in and out.

The pain in her hip nagged at her. Made her shift. Cleared her head for an instant.

Long enough to fumble for her wristband. Sob a name, “Gis—”

<FUCKING FINALLY!>

She lifted her head. “I—”

<TURN ON YOUR DAMN COM! Wait, don’t bother. I’ll catch you up, Killie-Cat. Henry’s alive and well. Rough landing and Flip’s damaged, but we’re in touch. Hear me?>

Joy hit like adrenalin. “Yes! That’s—” Followed by despair. “Kmet-Here tried to destroy this world. Couldn’t. Ordered us to—to use the Portal to—” She choked.

<—to bring big nasty rocks. Not happening. Hear me? We’ve communications. Sensible people in charge. Killie-Cat. Come on. Get your head up. I’ve no view.> Complaining.

Normal. She’d give anything for normal. Killian lifted her head. Saw the pitiful barricade in front of her locked door. A confession of losing it, no words required.

Gis kindly ignored what she saw, spoke gruff and hard. <Orders are, you plant

your butt in Control, coms on. All Earth is lined up to support your play. Through me, Killian. And Harvey. Do you understand?>

She'd a bad feeling she was beginning to— "I'm the pilot—"

<Not anymore. You're the Arbiter's hands and eyes now. Probably the rest of his parts, seeing his shuttle's out of commission and he's stuck dirtside.>

Killian swung her legs over the side of the bed, leaning on her hands. Henry'd sat here, blue eyes bright, spinning words and plans. "I'm not him, Gis. I can't be."

<Glad of that,> with a salacious chuckle that did her good.

"Gis—"

<Need you in Control, watching kmeth. Keeping things stable.>

"Not my first choice," Killian admitted shakily. *Or her hundredth.*

<Didn't see choice in the job description, Pilot.>

She snorted. "Isn't that the truth."

But it helped, her beloved's blunt honesty. Her presence. The news—it was good, knowing Henry not only lived, but was able to cause his usual amount of disruption to the universe. *As for what she could do in his place*—Killian shuddered. "I dunno."

<Small steps. Shower. Eat something. You know how you get, hungry.>

Made her laugh, that did. Killian looked up at her painting. "Love you, Space Rat."

"Lima Charlie, Killie-Cat."

"It is a very long way . . ."

"I DON'T understand why you are upset. I did catch you, Henry." The face imbedded in the shimmering membrane showed sincere puzzlement as it rolled overhead.

"H—hand—holds—F—lip!" Henry gasped as he bounced and slid at the mercy of whatever was moving Flip, now a balloon with him inside, along the jungle floor. "G—ive—me—"

Grips sprouted from the walls. Flailing wildly, Henry caught hold of one with his left hand, hooking his right foot through another. Finally able to take a full breath, he searched for Flip's face, finding it paused under his left knee. "What's happening?"

"I was unable to elude pursuit, Henry. We have been captured." The face slid sideways.

Henry grabbed a grip with his right hand, managing not to spin with the polymorph. "By what?"

"By this." The face disappeared, the space it had occupied clearing to show a rapidly moving confusion of leaves and mud.

"I don't see anything—" The clear space rolled, the view now of a yellowish lump of rippling—*thing.* "—eek!"

"There are forty-six," the polymorph informed him. "Working in a coordinated fashion to propel us in a particular direction—"

That couldn't be good. Henry spun upside-down. "Rena!" He couldn't reach his wrist—

—wasn't a band there if he could. He wasn't an epitome. *Was what could die—*

He bounced sideways, the force tearing his hands from the grips. Flew through the interior of the Flip-balloon—

"Henry?"

Rena's voice. Flip, communicating with hers. Through the Portal—*not safe* was Henry's first reaction.

Needed her was his second. "Help!"

"Henry—you survived the land—what's wrong?"

"Show her, Flip."

"Yes, Henry." The polymorph became transparent.

To reveal they were coated in yellow rippling fleshy *things*. Henry threw up a little in his mouth.

Rena made a cooing sound. "Fascinating. How are they gripping—ah, there, see it Henry? Suckers down the mid-ventral line. Impressive, to be able to hang on as much as they are."

The polymorph's face reappeared. "I am very slippery, Rena."

"Good thing, or they'd have ripped you apart and then where would you be, Henry?"

He closed his eyes. "Just help us get away from these things."

"They need a name," Rena countered. "I know, not the priority. Flip, build up a charge will you? Nothing lethal, please. Mustn't harm them."

"I'd considered the option, Doctor, but it would hurt Henry."

"Then don't!" Henry ordered as he tumbled, immediately naming the things Nasty Yellow Suckerbugs.

"You don't want to go wherever they're taking you. My guess is a colony—where there'll be too many for you to disperse. Zap them, Flip."

"Henry?"

Much more tumbling and he'd be hurt anyway. "Zap the suckerbugs." *How bad could it be?*

Rena's "Keep in touch—" was the last thing he heard before shock locked every muscle in agony.

Henry lost consciousness.

Being unconscious meant the mind stopped working.

This clearly was not that peaceful state.

Henry found himself thrown into a room full of people oblivious to his presence and to each other. Rena was crouched in a corner, hands over her face. Was she hurt?

The remaining members of his quorum were standing . . . or floating . . . with complete disregard to the floor of Henry's dream space. Sofia was upside down, her scowl stranger than usual to interpret. Shomchai appeared asleep, and Ousmane sipped from a cup he couldn't see, and all the while Henry was terrified to think what might be happening to his helpless self during what seemed hours . . .

"Henry. Wake up. I need instruction. Henry—"

. . . but was probably a moment. He groaned, alone in his head again. A head throbbing with pain and Henry cracked open a cautious eyelid, reluctant to let more of the world back inside.

A broad nose sniffed. "You're awake," exclaimed an unexpectedly small voice. "Hurry, Henry. We have to move."

Henry didn't want to move, wasn't sure he could, if pressed to it, and above all didn't want to know this was all he'd left of his powerful companion and protector.

A nip.

"Ow." Moving proved possible after all. Henry sat up, an arm around his knees, and looked around.

Growing things, thick and thin, twisted and straight, thrust from the ground to wall the hollowed path in which he sat. The path stretched into shadow ahead and behind, implying the suckerbugs traveled it regularly enough to trample the growth into submission.

He wasn't alone. A stout and sturdy Wombat-Flip sat regarding him. With a sigh, Henry held out his hand. "Took a lot out of you, saving us."

"I remain functional, Henry," alt assured him, nose twitching.

"Is this enough you to contact Rena again?" *Or anyone?*

"I can no longer offer two-way communication with Earth, Henry. The Portal should detect my outgoing signal, weak as it is. My ability to receive will be affected by atmospheric conditions."

"And Kmet-Here will be listening."

"I'm afraid so. I must also caution that my reserves are limited."

It'd have to do. "Please send Killian this message: I'm fine. Continuing the mission."

A small round ear wiggled. "I, too, am fine, Henry. Smaller but fine."

Henry smiled fondly. "My apologies, Flip. Of course you are. Rephrase, please. Add that we'll check in every—how often can you manage?"

"Four hours. Henry, your message should include a request to have Earth send you a replacement shuttle. One could be here shortly. You would be safer."

"And Kmet-Here would know I'm in trouble."

"Need I remind you that is the case, Henry?"

He laughed, startling little—*birds*—from nearby vegetation. "I'd prefer to keep the precise details to ourselves as long as possible, Flip. Send my message, please."

The eyes closed. Opened. "Sent, Henry."

"Time to find this world's Humans." Henry rose to his feet, brushing mud from his formerly spotless clothes as best he could. "How's your sense of direction?"

"Unimpaired." Ears flattened. "It is a very long way, Henry."

"Then we'd best get started."

"Some help you are."

STEP, *tinkle,* step, *tinkle.* The sound and rhythm might lull a mind to sleep, after hours of sameness, if you didn't walk knowing you lived each minute by permission.

As she walked and tapped her stick, Beth's gaze searched the crusty ground ahead for any change, between looks into the distance. She welcomed the familiar crawl of fear up her spine and down. Kept a body alive, fear did.

Though fear came close to causing a regrettable reaction when her next step had an echo, deep, heavy, below.

Not now! Beth's gut muscles tightened. Mustn't change the pattern that said what she was, what she needed. Step, *tinkle,* step, *tinkle. I'm a Seeker. Let me pass.*

Nothing for four steps, then that dreadful echo resumed, becoming a vibration through the sole of her boot; what was below, rising.

She'd no spit to swallow. Gritting her teeth, Beth stopped and struck the ground three times, firmly, with her stick. It asked a question. *What do you want of me?*

The ground rose. Deep, dirt-raining cracks carved an oval around her until she balanced on a plate harder than the rest. New, this—

The second she had her feet firm, the plate began moving, riding on a swell of looser dirt and rubble, a swell that stayed with her, that moved of its own accord faster and impossibly faster still until Beth had to drop to her knees or be blown clear by the wind of their passing.

It was—she burst out laughing, drowned in the exhilaration of a moment no one else on Doublet had experienced. Not and lived to report it.

"Only die the once," she told herself. She'd surfed ocean waves, and this was like enough to that feeling, if a wave propagated itself without change, to give her the confidence to stand, leaning forward.

The direction, though. Beth pulled up her right sleeve and sent a quick glance down at the compass affixed to her wrist, confirming the ground wave swept her in a direct line to the crash site.

Not good, not good. Communication was one thing. Urgent attention from whatever lurked below ground in the Split was nothing she or any Human on Doublet wanted to attract. Seemed their visitors had and, well, it would spill on those already here, wouldn't it?

Seeing as what lurked below wanted her along.

The sun sank down, pink streaking the horizon. The plate remained steady. The sound of their passing, like stone teeth worrying a bone, didn't change. Eventually, the novelty wore off, her legs wore out, and Beth sat down gingerly, back to the wind. When that drew no reaction, she dared stretch out her feet and lean on her hands.

She'd her stick. Could tap again, but made no sense at all to bother what was saving her new soles while quartering the time to her destination.

The radio tempted, if only to let someone else know the marvel underway. Vain the thought, easily dismissed. Instead, Beth fished her monocle from its pocket, lifting it to scan her surroundings.

Crust, unbroken in every direction save for their passage. That left what looked like the first furrow breaking sod in a field, not that anything would grow here. Despite its solid feel to a foot, the covering of the Split was frail and easily damaged. Winds would scour out the loose and light stuff, was lifting some as she watched. The scar would last generations.

A memorial if she disappeared. *Here went Beth Seeker.*

A bloody big mark, aimed with precision at a downed spacecraft, and be missed from orbit? Not a chance.

Beth scowled and put away her monocle. Say there was someone as yet uneaten—unlikely, but she'd a new appreciation for weird—say they were in contact with what dropped them on Doublet and got a warning about a mysterious track in the dirt, aimed their way. Her task, to take a look, wouldn't be made easier if what there was to see started running from her, and who wouldn't?

"Some help you are," she muttered, watching crust crack and pebbles bounce.

Seekers knew there was intelligence below, in the Split. Bios didn't disagree so much as wanted more proof than sounding sticks and what appeared communication, if one-sided and not always.

Beth had it now and the radio became more than temptation, this behavior being that proof and perhaps a means to learn more. Not yet. If things looked to go wrong, time then to break her silence.

With luck she'd have warning.

Dark came, a factor to Beth, if not to what carried her along with no slowing. Dark came with bitter cold, made worse by the wind, and she curled small, wrapped in her cloak and foil sheet. The plate wasn't large enough to lay flat, even if she'd risk it. The vines covering her head withered and came loose, blowing away. She'd replacements in her pack.

Beth pulled the cloak over her bare head. What carried her along didn't appear afraid of a sweep. Why should she?

She kept her eyes open. The night sky dazzled, but Beth wasn't interested in stars this once, only in what moved between them. Moved and, more than likely, dropped change into their lives they could no more avoid than the seasons.

Disturbing notion, as the ground growled with stone teeth and wind ruffled her cloak and she surfed on a piece of the world.

< . . . there's something down there.>

HENRY and Flip were fine and continuing the mission.

And she'd be a freighter captain.

Killian pressed a sequence of buttons. The screens came to life with images of the planet below the Portal. Views of her vast ocean. Of the solitary land mass with its artificial split down the middle. Of readouts of information pouring down in columns as the paired satellites did their job.

Human tech. Hers.

<I take it you're hunting Henry?>

Killian grunted assent.

<You found where they landed?>

She jabbed her thumb up and displayed an earlier image, the screen changing to show a long gash through purple tree-things. No sign of the shuttle—but there wouldn't be, Flip being what alt was. Wrote on her pad: *Wouldn't call that a landing.*

<Qualifies to me. Walked away from it.> A pause. <Until their little adventure.>

An *adventure* that might have ended Henry then and there, according to Rena's passed-along report. Was what planets did to you, producing bugs and mud, and Killian wasn't interested.

She got busy repositioning a satellite to slip as close to geosynchronous over Henry's last known position as possible, without blocking the Portal's own view. Kmet-Here, having made it into kmeth's den, appeared unwilling to come out. *Fine with her.*

This wasn't a world where they had to worry about local spacecraft.

Only the one they brought with them. On the thought, Killian keyed in a command to reposition the second satellite, aware of Gis' silent attention.

Done, she stood back, watching the portion of the screen mapping the satellites' routes as they altered, unsurprised her hands were shaking.

<Smart, Killie-Cat. Eyes on the Portal.>

If Kmet-Here thought kmeth could toss rocks without warning—or anything else?

Think again.

Not to forget the captain of the *Balache* reported something weird before they left Brightside—

Catching a glimpse, Killian paused the feed, enlarging the image.

PIPs on the *outside.* "What the—?" She closed her mouth, glancing at the den. Let her eyes travel up the constantly growing mass of PIPs on the *inside.*

Gis had an opinion. <Bet you it's a Kmet-sized escape pod.>

Not a bet she'd take. Making Control not a place to be if—when—the stupid things breached atmo.

Killian grabbed her pad and wrote: *Time to find another Control?*

<You gotta stay, Killie-Cat. They might need you to talk to Kmet-Here. Be Henry. That said, your next break, I want you to grab your suit, okay?>

She gave that a thumbs-up. Wrote: *Later. Flip should check in again soon. Alt said every four hours.* Implying a worrying lack of capacity, and if up to her, there'd be a shuttle full of troops heading to wherever they were spending the night.

Outside. Killian shuddered.

<Five by Five, Killie—what's that?>

She was already stopping the image feed from the first satellite.

The line etched across the continent had a scratch.

<Mag it.>

Her fingers moved with the words, magnifying. Looking for Henry, she'd set the resolution to max. It paid off now.

The scratch was a furrow, plowed straight and true. Aimed at—

"Henry."

<I'll report it. Keep eyes on. You know what this means, don't you?> With rising excitement. <Hot damn, Killie-Cat, there's something down there!>

Something attracted to the crash site, moving with significant speed. *Fuckfuckfuck!* Killian wrote quickly: *If it's after Henry, I've got to warn him.*

<You don't have clean coms. Kmeth hearing about this might be worse than whatever this is. We've time. Hold till I talk to the experts, okay?>

She nodded, eyes locked on the scratch. Made a heart with her fingers.

<Lima Charlie, Killie-Cat.>

"Nothing will harm you."

THEY sheltered inside a hollow log, Wombat-Flip adamant they mustn't risk moving through the jungle at night. *More like a hollowed-out bone than anything once a tree*, Henry thought, running his hand over the dry, porous wall in wonder. From something incredibly large—or perhaps some composite life.

Should be safe. He'd followed the polymorph's instructions and example, hurriedly stuffing the open end with whatever alts strong paws dug loose. He discovered quickly what looked a plant could take a chunk of skin. The rear of the log, or bone, was jammed against a giant rock.

Henry sat sideways, not entirely sure it was.

Wombat-Flip's warm, brown eyes had turned a surprisingly baleful pink. As his own fought the dark, Henry discovered the walls of their little cave fluoresced, turning his exposed skin and the polymorph's fur a sickly green.

"Are you comfortable, Henry?"

"A little warm." He'd taken off his jacket and rolled up his sleeves. "Which is better than cold."

"Agreed. You won't notice a change for several days' travel." Wombat-Flip licked alts fur.

Days. "You think I'm wrong, not calling for a shuttle?"

"No, Henry. As always, I defer to your greater knowledge of the Kmet and situation. You are the Arbiter."

He couldn't quite laugh. "The first to get lost in an alien jungle."

"We are not lost," Flip reminded him, "but this is a perilous place. I would be glad of assistance."

A plea, that. Smarten up, Human, we're in trouble. "My safety isn't a priority. Keeping Kmet-Here calm and compliant is." Henry took off his sandals. "If kmeth thinks I'm unable to do the job, all bets are—ouch." The skin was tender where the straps had been—a consequence of weeks in the can.

"Henry?"

"Nothing. Sore foot," he added when the polymorph came closer and began to sniff his toes.

"Damage is imminent without precautions, Henry." Wombat-Flip sat up. "May I use your jacket, Henry?"

"Sure." Bemused, he pushed the garment closer.

"I only need the sleeves."

Should have brought the multi-purpose knife from his luggage. "Give me a minute." Henry brought out the badge. Rubbed one edge, not without an inner wince, against the rock face until it was sharp, testing it against the ball of his thumb. It made short work of the shoulder seams. "Now what?"

"Please insert each foot into a sleeve."

He did so, pulling up his pant legs first. The sleeves rose almost to his knees. "I feel ridiculous."

Wombat-Flip pulled the fabric down again, until it passed his toes. "Hold very still, Henry." Alt raised a front paw, revealing a glowing clawtip. "While I design the lining to melt, the outer material you preferred—" With a tinge of disapproval. "—could ignite. Be prepared to dose any flames."

Flames? "Flip, are you sure about this?"

"Several days of walking, Henry. *Several.* Your feet will need protection."

"Go ahead." Henry dug with his fingers until he'd handfuls of moist, rotting wood.

Or whatever it was.

***

Wombat-Flip used ats paw to heat and melt the suit lining—a silk made from the web of an Earth spider-analogue—into crude socks, Henry alternating between dousing small flames and pulling away bits of the once-handsome woven linen of the exterior. By the time they were done, Henry's shirt was soaked in sweat, but his feet and lower calves were encased in a surprisingly sturdy coating of spider silk.

He wiggled his toes curiously. "This feels better."

"Try a sandal, Henry."

When he did, the Flip-made sock fit under the straps. "Wonderful, Flip."

A gratified rumble. "You are most welcome, Henry. It is time for our next check-in with Killian."

His new body—his body—was exhausted and bruised. *Felt much the same inside.* "Repeat the last message, Flip. We're fine. Mission continues."

Instead of sending, Wombat-Flip curled into a ball. *Stalling.*

Henry raised an eyebrow. "You don't approve."

"A repeated message will not reassure Killian. Unless I misjudge?"

"No, you're right." If anything, she'd be livid. A smile tugging his lips, Henry thought a moment. Nodded. "Send this instead. Situation nominal. Request update on observations of the planet's population."

"Under present conditions, I may not be able to receive her reply, Henry."

"I know." A low ceiling of some thick material, jungle around and above them, for all they knew, a storm overhead—*plus a solitary Human.* "Killian will want to do something. Anything. If we let her know I need information, she'll work on a way to get it to us."

A dubious, "If you say so, Henry."

"Please send, Flip."

"Done. Will you sleep now?"

"Not yet." Crossing his legs, Henry settled himself as comfortably as the dirt floor allowed. Elbows on his thighs, he gazed at his clasped hands, letting his thoughts flow however—wherever—they would.

PIPs were Kmet.

PIPs could—not grow, that was a Human thought—increase by attaching to others of their kind. He'd seen it. And to the Portal, which was non-biological, unless he was wrong there—

Henry refocused. *PIPs were Kmet.* Like social insects, according to Rena, who'd, he remembered suddenly, on a vacation made him watch a colony of sand ants raiding another. Explained they'd done it to steal their young to raise as their own.

When Kmet competed, the winning colony *went on to breed, the loser to die with the Portals.*

He wasn't a xenologist, but it made no sense, that waste.

Unless it wasn't natural. Unless what Kmet were now was the stuttering echo of what kmeth had been and should be. One complex individual earning the right to produce the next generation, the other offering support through its PIPS. *Offspring to be raised as one's own.*

A healthy Duality unwittingly sundered—by the Portal Makers, by kmeth's own territoriality and, yes, greed, stealing Portals and thus keeping apart.

Until the instinct rose to find and keep a partner—

"Rena's right. It's always biology." He slapped his knees. "We're substitutes, Flip."

Wombat-Flip blinked. "For what, Henry?"

"For a second Kmet. Check my thinking. There's evidence the Kmet are territorial most of kmeth's lives. Solitary. When the Portal Makers showed up, it would be only natural for a single Kmet to board each Portal. Everything would be fine until those Kmet reached the next stage of kmeth's lifecycle—the part where kmeth must come together in a Duality."

A word so easily misunderstood, framed within Human concepts that didn't—couldn't—apply to the alien.

A shiver ran down Henry's spine that wasn't the cold but *connection*, his mind racing. "What the Kmet came to offer us wasn't friendship or an economic union. It was always about kmeth's survival. The Kmet searching together for a suitable breeding ground. Once found, competing to see which would produce the next generation and, by kmeth's very nature, the other should become a supportive, essential partner. The Duality. The drive to gather together. To coalesce. Cherish."

Wombat-Flip snuggled close, alts feet cool and tipped with prickly claws, thrusting alts face up between his forearms. "While I respect your logic, Henry, and see no fault, I also find no proof."

His thoughts slowed, found their course, and there it was, the answer. It had been there all along, Humans unable to understand it.

Grief welled up, thickened his voice. "You gave it to me. The last piece of the puzzle. When the Kmet arrived in orbit, what was kmeth's first gift to New Earth? PIPs. Kmethselves. Kmeth expected us to make more and more—and we did."

Whiskers worked furiously, tickling his skin. "I discovered Human and Kmet PIPs are incompatible."

"Exactly." He gazed at his friend. "We didn't make what Kmet-Here needs. We aren't kmeth's essential partner. We can't be. Kmet need each other, and I suspect the Portal Makers stopped the Kmet from partnering with other species because the same thing happened each time. Perhaps they even tried to get the Kmet to leave the Portals, but it was too late. The Kmet struck back, destroying those kmeth considered tormenters—in reality the only beings who could have helped." He sighed. "Leaving us in the midst of it."

A nose twitch. "Based on your reasoning, Henry, why don't the Kmet—as intelligent, sentient constructs—take advantage of kmeth's Portal pilots, freeing both Kmet to descend using shuttles or whatever means at kmeth's disposal? An approach, furthermore, allowing kmeth to breed on any suitable world, without the need for others. That kmeth have not and do not is illogical."

"I doubt logic plays a role, Flip. Not when each Kmet considers kmeth's Portal as territory and won't—or can't—give that up to anyone else."

"Then the Kmet we know can never be together. It is tragic, Henry."

"And the threat to New Earth."

"How so?"

Knowledge is flesh is knowledge— "Beings who make no distinction between what is and isn't alive—who can wait however long it takes for a chance to reproduce and destroy entire worlds like birds pull grass to make a nest. Who are unable to grasp the concept of species' extinction even when the cause of it." Henry lowered his voice to a grim whisper. "If Kmet-Here lands on New Earth, kmeth won't be cherished. Kmeth will be attacked. We won't start it—we can't stop it. Human-altered polymorphic matrix is everywhere. Kmeth's will be destroyed along with most of our technology, and what then? How can we possibly coexist?"

"You will find the way." Wombat-Flip sounded confident. "The Arbiter will negotiate."

He had to, didn't he? "Bringing me back to this world. The answers I need—we need—might be right here."

"This is why you remain where it is dangerous."

"Everywhere is, Flip."

Silence. *It wasn't disagreement.*

Henry rubbed a hand over his face, pinched his nose, then sighed gustily. After a look to check the rock protruding into their shelter—*hadn't budged*—he leaned against the wall and stretched out his legs. "Anything edible?"

"My apologies, Henry," Wombat-Flip said. "In my haste, I neglected to gather biologicals."

"You were busy saving us from suckerbugs. I can wait." Though he hadn't been all that hungry until Flip told him there wasn't anything to eat and now his stomach rumbled.

"If you're thirsty, Henry, I can render some me into water." Ears twitched anxiously.

Fussing. "Don't waste yourself." Henry offered the polymorph his hand to investigate, which it would, using internal sensors. "I drank enough rain before we ducked in here to hold me till morning."

Whiskers tickled his palm. The nose wrinkled as Wombat-Flip pulled back, eyes bright. "Agreed. You require sleep, Henry, but are well-hydrated and show no signs of infection or parasites."

Those were possibilities? Henry coughed. "Good to hear." Lean or lie? He stifled another yawn. The hard-packed dirt appealed as few beds ever had, but was it safe? "I'll help you keep watch."

Wombat-Flip growled deep in alts throat. "No need, Henry. I shall remain vigilant. Nothing will harm you."

"Thank you, Flip," he said solemnly. "Do me a favor and keep an eye on that, too." Henry aimed a thumb at the rock.

Ears angled quizzically. "It is inert, Henry."

"Let's be sure it stays that way." With that admonishment, he closed his eyes.

It took an effort to stop trying to visualize what wasn't there and couldn't be.

And who.

"You're a thinker."

MIGHT be cooperation, might be capture, might be some alien weird shit not even the Bios could decipher but, no matter why the thing below dragged her along, the time came when Beth Seeker had to take a piss or burst.

She brought out her flask, used her stick to prop herself best she could against the motion of the plate, and managed three drops before the rest, and her flask, went flying.

"Dammit!"

Everything stopped. Her ears rang in the sudden absence of sound, then filled with her racing pulse.

The plate tipped, the runnels of urine she could smell if not see surely on the move. The urine not filling her left boot, that was, and Beth took her stick in both hands, staring into the dark. Spill like this? Better odds surviving a sweep. What hunted below was drawn to fluids.

And nothing said what dragged her along wasn't one.

The plate lowered. Settled. Beth braced herself.

Dirt hit her from every side. She covered her face to breathe, losing her stick, losing what bearings she had, close to losing her wits. Was this how Seekers vanished in the Split? Buried alive?

The dirt shower stopped. Nothing else happened. Not dead. Not yet.

"DAMMIT!"

Spitting dirt with the word, she jumped up and down in rage, feeling the plate crack underfoot. Not caring because, "DAMMITTOEVERYHELL!"

A thump from below brought her to her senses. Beth froze, listening to the whisper of dirt raining from her cloak, waiting, not that she'd any idea for what.

Suddenly the plate surged up at one end, forcing her to stumble off into the dark. Beth staggered a few steps then stopped, wary of moving without her stick.

Thump!

The ground rose, lifting her again. She could hear cracks and pops, guessed the thing was carving out a fresh plate. Offended by her piss, was it?

Tinkle, tinkle.

Beth dropped to her knees, reaching for her stick, grasping after the enormity of the idea the thing below had retrieved it. Had known to return it.

Had it understood her piss hitting the ground put her in danger? Had it tried to conceal the scent to hide her from the hunters?

The plate began to move again.

Beth Seeker knelt on it, her palms flat on the hard crust, soaking in every vibration. "You're a thinker," she whispered triumphantly. "Maybe as much as us. Maybe more."

Here, in the Split. The first contact moment humanity had been waiting for since becoming aware.

If true, why now?

Beth looked up at the stars, at what she couldn't see but knew was there. What had Dex called it? A construct.

Crap.

"My mistake."

<DROP a sat?>

Killian shook her head. Wrote: *None to spare.* Not since Brightside was supposed to be the last and they'd spent more time shifting people than exploring.

Its clock had already vanished; she'd ordered the sats watching to fall, uninterested in the view of another fertile world laid waste, and utterly unable to forgive the Kmet.

<Send you some. Only need to ask, Killie-Cat.>

Earth couldn't push anything through without her cooperation. Hers and Omar's. They'd had some conversations, if talking through two oneirics across an appalling gap of space counted, and come to the same conclusion.

Not messing with anything without Henry, Killian wrote.

Henry, who'd asked for information and what she wanted most to tell him she'd been ordered against, namely the scratch getting closer to where he was had shifted its course slightly from the crash site, implying something down there knew better than anyone not where he was.

Instead, she'd replied with what he'd asked, data on the Human portion of the Portal Makers' planet, a name she used to remind herself the almighty Arbiter had good reason to avoid tipping off Kmet-Here. Asked for confirmation. Got nothing.

Which she took to mean Flip couldn't receive. Making Henry's real message: *Help, we're deaf down here.* Flip's incoming com signal was so weak, the Portal grabbed it as text bits. *Couldn't fucking ask why, could she?*

Except she had asked Gis, who'd *consulted* with her polymorph. Harvey'd come up with a dire prediction the crash must have reduced Flip the magnificent flyer saucer to the size of a PIP. *Or smaller.*

<Going with Niablo's sneak, then.>

Killian gave a thumps-up, mostly to encourage herself.

Niablo Station had sent the procedure, having done some dodgy stuff with a pilot's assist during their dispute with Kmet-Here. Who'd been the Kmet of the moment or the other one—*didn't matter.* Point being, the stationmaster hadn't trusted kmeth's offer to transit their freighters for free. Wanted a sly way to hear from her captains without the Kmet noticing.

Didn't work as advertised. Did bounce a very quiet outgoing signal off the Portal's corners until it came through strong enough to blow the station's receivers. Word was, the debacle slowed negotiations by a week, the Kmet not impressed.

Killian went over the wiring one more time. Looked a mess, and she'd spotted more than a few PIPs paying attention to it. They didn't have much time before the wretched things started clearing it away, sticking it to the den along with the last of the balloons and her beer.

Wrote: *What do you think?* Gis having the blueprints and her dealing with scrouging parts from the galley.

She'd her message ready. Data compressed, because Henry would need it if he managed to walk that far. Voice compressed, because she'd had things to say and wasn't wasting the chance.

<Five by five. Nice job.>

Time to go. Lifted her hand to share the countdown with Gis. Three fingers up. One down, two, the last.

<WHOOO!>

Gis cheering in her head, Killian twisted the final wires together. Drew back hastily as the entire mass sparked and set off harmless little fires. PIPs raced up the pedestal to douse them, a couple pushing her boots as if to shove her away.

"My mistake," she told them, grinning from ear to ear.

Message away.

Now to wait for a reply.

"I can go faster."

"HENRY. Henry. Henry."

"Isn't here," he mumbled, burying his face in the crook of an elbow. It couldn't be morning yet.

A substantial grip with blunt claws took hold of the back of his neck and shook. "Henry."

Henry raised his head, blinking, prepared for a larger version of his companion—

—not for a gaping, glowing mouth where the *rock* had been—

Before the rest of him woke up, he was scrambling on all fours in the opposite direction.

A thwarted "WaaAAAaaah!" followed by a moist-edged *SNAP* chased Henry as he squirmed out the entrance, assisted by a firm shove from behind.

Staggering to his feet, he whirled to face the polymorph. "I told you to watch that rock!"

"It wasn't the rock, Henry," replied Wombat-Flip, busy pushing mud and vegetation back into the hole with alts paws. Alts thick head rocked from side to side as alt pressed alts ample backside into the result, then sat. "Rock is inert."

A muffled "WaaAAAaaah!" argued the point.

Glowering, Henry brushed off his arms. "'Inert.'"

"Yes, Henry. This particular rock proved to be that creature's door. When I noticed it being moved, I woke you. To be precise, I woke you after breaking open our well-constructed wall to ease your escape, Henry, a prioritization of actions I made on my own. Did I act correctly?" Little brown eyes blinked winsomely.

"You did, Flip."

Other than choosing to shelter inside what was clearly a trap for the night, a mistake Flip wouldn't repeat.

To be sealed inside with that, that mouth—Henry shuddered. "Exactly right." He looked around. They were in a cramped clearing overhung by vines beside a stream of water, surroundings—and Flip—visible because the water glowed with an unpleasantly familiar green light, giving him the same uneasy feeling he'd had about the rock. He took a quick step back. "I think we should leave. Now."

"I concur, Henry. Speed is of the essence. We must recover what was taken from me as soon as possible."

Henry stared down at Wombat-Flip, who'd come to lean against his legs. Pushed, in fact, urging a direction.

"The suckerbugs took your—we can't—" He closed his mouth. For the polymorph to insist on a course of action, alt would have calculated the probable outcomes of this and all others. Would, moreover, have calculated Henry's chances of survival, let alone of completing his mission, without a larger, more capable Flip, and seen no other choice.

Henry dropped a hand to Wombat-Flip's head. "Lead the way."

The polymorph hesitated. "I would prefer to find you a place of safety, Henry, then proceed alone to track my stolen material and recover it while you—"

"No. We stay together."

"If you insist. Follow me and please do not attract attention. Or get lost."

A faint, still-eager "WaaAAAaaah . . ." added firmness to Henry's, "I promise. But how will I see—oh, yes," as Wombat-Flip's rounded rump shone red. "That will work."

"A doughnut is not adequate nutrition, Henry. I have synthesized nourishment for you from local biologicals." A paw dug into alts down-facing pouch, emerging with a glistening cube. "Please consume it as we go. Other hunters approach this place."

They set off, Henry downing the cube as quickly as he could. It tasted like dirt and, while he trusted the polymorph not to poison him, couldn't help but hope for an alternative food source sooner than later.

He stumbled regularly as he followed the bouncing red wombat butt through the dark. Above, *things* moved in the trees. Every so often his feet encountered what squirmed out from beneath and he'd tense, waiting to feel teeth or a sting.

Either this jungle was kinder to walkers than those he knew on New Earth, or Wombat-Flip somehow cleared his path of anything harmful, for when nothing bit or stung him, Henry grew less worried. About what was underfoot, if not what paced their movement from above, by the sound scampering up trunks then whooshing through the air to land with thumps and rustles ahead of them. He could ask Flip if the *things* were dangerous.

What good would the answer do? They were hurrying toward what was, the suckerbugs. *If only Rena were here*, Henry thought, ducking under a huge branch.

And slipped, going down hard on one knee. As the red ball that was Wombat-Flip kept moving, he touched his skin, feeling the slick of blood. He hadn't received training on wilderness adventures, wasn't to have any by orders of the Arbiter's Office, and blood attracted *things,* didn't it?

"Flip," he whispered urgently, afraid to budge. "Flip!"

The red ball disappeared. The dark tightened around him and Henry fought to remain calm, doing reasonably well until something furry and warm brushed along his thigh. "Eep!"

"Shh, Henry," Wombat-Flip admonished gently. "It is a minor abrasion. I will affect repairs."

Henry felt a wet— "By licking?"

"We work with what I am, Henry."

When the licking stopped, Henry rose to his feet. All at once, he could make out patches of gray within the dark and smiled with relief. "I can see." He added, "a little," in case Wombat-Flip took this to mean there was no need to glow.

"Yes, Henry. Dawn is 40.24 minutes away. We must be out of this area before then."

Henry's smile faded. "Why?"

There was a whoosh from above; a rustle/thump from a trunk ahead.

"We are pursued, Henry," Wombat-Flip set off again, its rump once more bright red. "I calculate an eighty percent probability our hunters wait for sufficient light. Of course, that leaves a twenty percent chance I am wrong."

"I can go faster," Henry assured the polymorph.

"Thank you."

THE stars faded at the horizon, washed away by the pre-dawn light of Doublet's star. They called it the Sun, because it was theirs now and why wouldn't they?

They'd no moon. Having never had one, Beth could care less. A moon, especially one as large as they were taught spun around Origin Earth, seemed a nuisance, lighting up what should be dark, and tugging oceans out of place. Let alone the burden of stray moonbeams on astronomers.

As for lovers, Doublet had a wealth of poems extolling the salacious effect of candles and well-situated fluorescent fungi. Who needed a moon?

Easy thoughts. Simple thoughts. Helped pass the time. She'd emptied the dirt from her boot, tipping it over the rear end of the moving plate. Used the stars instead of her compass to gauge their passage. The Split lacked reliable landmarks. Lines of dunes crept across the middle latitudes. Northward were lumpy hills, as if a mountain range had been battered by a fist. To the far south, at the bottom of the world, were the Cracks, a series of plunging irregular valleys.

Linking them all, magma pots and the flat desert crust. Good for walking.

Even better for dirt riding, as she'd decided to call it, except walking let you find what you had to have. Water being one and Beth had been about to start hunting some when her below-friend changed the plan. Tipping back her head, she shook drops of water into her mouth from the spare bladder. Almost empty; she'd need to refill it and the main one riding her hips soon.

Especially if, as appeared likely, they'd dirt ride right through the coming day's heat.

Beth judged the present patch of crust as likely as any. Taking up her sounding stick, she placed the tip on the plate in front of her boots and drew it lightly over the rough surface. As the tip slipped and bounced, the hollow beads inside didn't tinkle, instead producing a prolonged, faint hiss.

Nothing happened.

She drew the tip back and forth. Only one thing in the Split—far as Seekers knew—made a similar sound. Water Ribbons were a risk in their seasonal swarm. This time of year, they'd be solitary.

Far as Seekers knew. Good odds her below-friend knew better. Might even have water of its own *and* understand sharing it, given she could figure out how to ask before dying of thirst.

Beth chuckled soundlessly. More likely the cloudless sky would rain and precipitation of any sort hadn't been recorded in the Split since Humans landed to take an interest.

She kept moving the stick, making the hiss. If they shared curiosity, maybe her below-friend would stop the plate to try and figure out what she was doing.

Or the hiss annoy it into stopping. That'd work.

The plate tipped, smoothly changing course.

Beth raised both eyebrows. "What are you up to?" Words she mouthed, choosing not to add her voice to the equation. Instead, she kept moving the stick.

Grabbed it in both hands as the plate abruptly accelerated, shouting, "WHOA!" like a character in one of the Origin Earth movies they showed in history class. The Bios would have her head—

The plate stopped.

Beth held her breath, and the stick. This wasn't a reaction to her shout. This was—

An iridescent ribbon popped from the ground ahead of her, flying through the air to land on her lap.

"What the—"

Pop! Another. *Pop!* Another.

As her lap filled with squirming, unhappy Water Ribbons, Beth shut up and got to work. She flipped open the lid of her spare bladder, grabbed the first ribbon, and shoved one end of the creature inside. Squeezing it from the other end, she listened until the trickle of water stopped, then tossed the creature away.

The emptied Water Ribbon sank below the ground to search for more liquid.

Pop! Another. *Pop!* Another.

Damn. She kept emptying ribbons and tossing them aside. Three more topped up the spare. She pulled out the tube to the larger bladder around her back and hips and started to fill it. In short order, she'd caught up to her below-friend's deliveries and began snatching incoming ribbons from the air. "And one more—two more—" she chanted joyfully.

Came the squeeze that spilled water over the tube. Full. In minutes, an effort that would have taken Beth alone days, and she lifted the ribbon, aiming the last of its bounty into her mouth.

Pop! Another hit her. *Pop!* Another—"Whoa!" she called out, catching and tossing back Water Ribbons over and over until, at last, they stopped appearing.

And wasn't that a fine example of communication?

"Thank you," Beth said, because the words needed saying, understood or not.

The plate tipped and began to move again, back, as far as Beth could tell, on their original heading.

She touched the bulging bladders, feeling the need to be sure they were real, that what had happened, had, and thirst wouldn't be what killed her this day. It gave a body a certain carelessness, to be looked after.

Beth locked that feeling away, deep down. Didn't belong in thc Split. Wouldn't be a help in Away, if they made it that far, not that she'd any reason to believe her below-friend planned to stay with her.

Though she'd no reason not, and a prudent Seeker would prepare to transition into a complex set of new hazards accompanied by the unpredictable.

"Onward, Flip."

THE increasing light helped Henry avoid obstacles, including what he could now see were fleshy worms the size of a wristband. It might have helped him better keep up with a now-galloping Wombat-Flip, something he earnestly tried to do, if only he'd been able to resist the urge to watch what raced them.

They were, to Henry's discomfort, pretty. They'd pause to look down at him. Big brown eyes, four in total, on a short-muzzled face. A closed mouth curved in a perpetual smile beneath nostrils like a pink flower. None stayed still long enough for him to tell if the soft, mottled gray coating their bodies and limbs was fur or feathers or something else entirely. They'd a membrane stretching between their forelimbs, back legs, and stiff tail they used to glide from tree to tree faster than a galloping Wombat-Flip.

Fortunately, the gliders had to gain altitude before their next launch into the air and, if any landed close together, they'd squabble with fierce little squeaks over who climbed first, letting their quarry pull ahead again.

In one of those moments, Henry called out, "Are we—almost—there, Flip?" Wherever *there* was, the polymorph not having shared any detail but urgency.

"Yes, Henry."

Reassured, he gasped another question. "How will—we know—we're safe?"

"They should stop following us, Henry." Though charging forward like a miniature tank, leaving snapped branches and crushed vegetation in its wake, Wombat-Flip did not, of course, gasp. Alts voice came as perfectly even and clear as always. They might have been sitting in Saucer-Flip.

"Good—to—know." He'd instruct Flip to add a gasp or two in future; some sign of mutual effort would make him feel less useless. Not that he wanted a future with gasping. "But—why—"

Henry stopped talking, not because he didn't want answers, but because one of the gliders soared right over him, making him duck. He gagged, nostrils filled with the stench of rot. The glider landed on the trunk close enough to touch and it didn't have fur or feathers, it was covered in a fuzz like moldy fruit and when its smile opened, it wasn't into a mouth, but into a mass of black—

Wombat-Flip hit him mid-waist, sending him flying into a thorny bush. Paws seized a pant leg, pulling. "Hold your breath, Henry! This way!"

—then the glider coughed into the air where Henry had been and to his horrified eyes, the black was a dust that coated what it touched as it drifted down. The black began to spread, flowing toward him.

Other gliders landed, coughing!

Henry jumped over the polymorph, his only thought to run.

He fought through a wall of more dense vegetation, ignoring the sharp little *nips* on his ankles and the arms he threw up over his face for protection, only to fall into an opening so bright he kept one arm up to protect his eyes.

"Henry, you can stop now."

"Under—stood." He half-bent, gulping for breath and vaguely aware blood was streaming over his skin from multiple little bites. *And he'd worried about his knee.* "Are—we—safe?"

When the polymorph didn't answer at once, Henry turned his head. "Flip?"

Wombat-Flip plopped alts rump down and gave him a doleful look. "I believe we are safe from what chased us here, Henry, as they seem creatures of the shadows. That said, I cannot in good conscience declare any place is safe on this world. It appears to have a regrettable abundance of predatory lifeforms."

"That—it does." Henry surprised himself by chuckling. "Rena would love it—here."

Small, tufted ears worked the air like paddles. *Indecision.*

"What?"

"I wish we'd our xenologist's input on the next phase of my plan, Henry."

Henry could only nod. "Let me—catch my—breath."

"I will tend your wounds as you do."

The Arbiter sat, after thoroughly inspecting the moss and other growing things for mouths, and endured another, longer period of being thoroughly licked by Wombat-Flip. Seen in the light of day, each lick of alts thick tongue not only cleaned the tears in his skin but left a trail of soothing sealant. Henry blinked tears of relief as the pain subsided. "Much better. Thanks, Flip."

"You are most welcome, Henry. I recommend more sustenance." Wombat-Flip reached up into alts belly pouch to produce a cube. "While you consume it, I will give you the information I've received from Killian."

Henry started. "Pardon? What? When? How?"

The polymorph elected to answer his blurted questions in reverse order. "By certain qualities of the message signal, I conclude Killian has employed what you referred to as the Niablo Stationmaster's single worst idea."

Had almost ended the negotiations. Chewing the cube, Henry nodded grimly as Wombat-Flip continued.

"I received it as we were fleeing through the jungle and deemed it unwise to distract you until safe. As for the contents, Killian has provided satellite survey results regarding the Human population of this planet, along with a verbal message."

"Play it, please."

The thick, humid air filled with Killian's voice. "I've eyes on. Something's digging its way straight at you across the line. Those in charge didn't want me to tell you. Well, fuck that. You've company coming, Henry. Be ready to talk to it, and whatever it is better listen to you, 'cause I'm not—" Her voice lost crispness, lowered, *and was that grief?* "—I'm not you, hear me? They want me to keep kmeth in line. Think I can take over and save the universe if—not going to happen. What you do—I can't. What you are—I—Henry, you're the almighty Arbiter. Don't you dare fucking leave me!" The last with all her wonderful fury, and Henry had to smile.

"That is the end of her message."

Sorry, Killian. "If you haven't already, please acknowledge receipt. And that we'll respond at the next interval."

Eyelids closed, reopened. "Sent, Henry. I find myself alarmed by her observation. Unfortunately, I cannot send a remote to investigate until I recover more of me."

"That's the plan," Henry said, as much to reassure himself as his companion. "Anything helpful about the Human population?"

"Only that they won't be found on this side of the line, Henry."

Thought not.

The clearing where they rested owed its reassuring brightness to a group of massive fallen trees, their tops blackened as if scorched by fire, their branches intertwined. Lightning strike, he assumed, more concerned with obsessively scanning the surrounding growth for the jungle's next unpleasant surprise. "So what do we do? You said you'd like Rena's help?"

"The ideal disguise would be as a suckerbug, but I lack the required knowledge of their anatomy. Do you have an alternative suggestion?"

A little late to regret not paying full attention to Rena's chatter during their nature walks. "Wait. Mimicry. Can you make an outer coating to taste and smell as they do? The same color?"

"Like this, Henry?" The surface of Wombat-Flip changed from brown fur to a bilious yellow smoothness Henry remembered all too well.

"Looks good to me, Flip." Seated, the polymorph resembled a ball with ears stuck on the top and Henry bit his lower lip to keep from laughing.

"Now you."

"What?"

The yellow ball became fluid, budding off a substantial portion. A smaller Wombat-Flip reformed from it, now yellow, while the rest remained on the ground as a yellow puddle.

"No," Henry protested.

"You've been inside me many times before, Henry."

Flip as a shuttle wasn't the same as wearing Flip-goo next to his skin. About to make that point, he noticed Wombat-Flip blinking anxiously. "Fine. But you take it back when this is over," he said firmly.

"I must, Henry. I will require all of me in order to assist you."

Henry got to his feet, shook off any qualms, and put his left foot in the puddle of Flip.

In response to contact, the fluid thinned and spread, flowing up his left pant leg to the waist, down the other leg to that foot, up his torso to—Henry closed his eyes and mouth, forcing himself to remain still as Flip-goo coated his face, the sensation as if he'd plunged into warm water.

OPEN YOUR EYES, HENRY. Flip's voice reverberated inside Henry's head.

Henry cracked open an eyelid.

The jungle and Wombat-Flip were gone, replaced by a stomach-churning madness of numbers and symbols tumbling through the dark—

Henry shut out the view, covering his face with both hands. "Stop it!"

SURELY YOU WISH TO TAKE ADVANTAGE OF MY ENHANCED SENSORY CAPACITY, HENRY. *Disappointment.*

"While I appreciate the opportunity," he replied, somehow keeping hysteria from his voice, "I require your interpretation. Please restore my vision—and hearing—" as it occurred to Henry he was hearing their voices and nothing else "—and every other sense, Flip."

"Of course, Henry." Heard, if muted.

Lowering his hands, he opened his eyes cautiously.

Wombat-Flip examined him. "I suggest you close your eyelids and mouth, Henry, once we approach the organisms we intend to mimic."

Worse and worse. Henry waved. "Onward, Flip. Suckerbugs await."

Wombat-Flip hopped through the clearing. Henry followed, doing his best not to think about their plan.

Being terrified would resume soon enough.

"Wait a minute . . ."

HENRY had her message, including what data she'd accumulated thus far about the planet itself—*limited*—and its Human population—

Limited. She'd more about what they didn't have than what they did. No sign of spaceflight or even aircraft, but they'd what looked to be high-speed trains between smallish coastal cities.

Killian didn't miss the significance that most people lived as far as possible from the line cutting their continent in half. Not all. There was a solitary central city, smaller still, connected by rail to the coastal settlements and by road to a smattering of nearby towns, those closer to the line.

Kmet more likely to notice change, Killian had gone ahead and sent the sat feed to New Earth via the Portal. Got more eyes on it than hers, for one thing. First result? The historian sent word the central city was likely the *Exeter*'s landing site; sure enough a subsequent sat pass pinged metal at the heart.

What use any of it was to the almighty Arbiter, afoot and on the other side of everything, was beyond her. But he'd needed to know about the scratch. *No regret there.*

The sat presently over the ocean, Killian perched on the dais to wait for it to come around again and be interesting, prepping a new sneak to send her next message. Her hunt for wire and foil had turned the galley into a non-functional mess. She'd no interest in eating there alone anyway.

Even less in what New Earth wanted her to do, and Gis knew it.

Didn't stop her arguing. <Situation's stable,> her partner coaxed. <No surprise they want more intel, Killie-Cat. Henry would.>

Killian's fingers bent a wire. She put it aside, grabbed her pad, and wrote: *Don't tell me what the Arbiter would or would not. I'm the one here.*

<Putting you in charge. No one's pushing—>

Except her partner.

<—There's suggestions, that's all. Now's a good time for an explore.>

She didn't have Rolypoly. Only kmeth's PIPs, some working, most sticking themselves to the den, and Killian wasn't about to think of the ones outside the Portal.

<Beats sitting here.> Gis, not about to give up.

Reluctantly, Killian poked up her thumb.

Time to catch a PIP.

***

They—whoever *they* were and from the sound of it, Gis wasn't entirely sure most of the time—*they* had come up with a question for Killian to ask.

Since it had *Rena* all over it, she'd give it a try.

No shortage of bags. Henry's original supplies for their mission had arrived in every size and any spacer knew to keep them. No problem snatching a PIP from those lining up to be stuck to the den and sticking it in one previously filled with ready-dinners.

Killian stuck her latest squirming key in a tube mouth. "How do I talk to a Portal Maker?"

Points to Rena when the tube tugged at the bag.

Shorter than her other trips, for whatever that was worth. No stinks, warning or otherwise. Killian pulled herself out of a mid-height tube mouth with exaggerated caution.

Finding herself in a room about the size of the galley. No doors or corridors broke the smooth walls, only more tube mouths; the shape was a smooth oval. Her fingertips brushed the ceiling when she stretched up an arm. That was new. No furnishings or controls in sight, but she'd learned those weren't always obvious.

<The floor.>

Killian grunted assent, crouching to study what her partner'd spotted. Dimples more than indentations, and their shape?

That of a Human hand—a left hand—the size of hers.

A shiver ran down her spine. "What the—?"

<You asked to talk. Here's your invitation.> Gis, dampening it down, cool and calm. *She wasn't here.* <Go on, Killie-Cat. Put your hand on one.>

"Fuck that," Killian muttered, but it was why she'd come. She held her hand prudently well above the nearest, in hopes touching wouldn't be required, rewarded by a glow from several.

A glow forming a pattern similar to the symbols on the images she'd studied, hell, memorized by now. *Not that the experts or Henry had asked her opinion.*

Wait. A row heading up and left from paired circles? Her pulse kicked up a notch. "Recognize it, Gis? First symbol of each arch leading to a planet."

<What are you thinking, it means start?>

"How the fuck should I know?"

A pause. She could almost hear the gears turning. Then, <Try another, same deal.>

"Roger that." The instant her hand moved away, the glow disappeared. Killian crab-walked to the next dimple. Put out her hand.

A different symbol glowed on the floor. A new one. "Gotta get these." With her right hand, the pilot pulled out her pad and rested it on a knee. Began to draw, quickly, precisely. Circles for the dimples on the floor, a solid dot where she'd entered as a reference point.

The two symbols already displayed, arrows to indicate the dimple eliciting each.

Killian looked up, calculating. "Fifteen to go." Wouldn't take long. Clever, specifying her left hand. No need to try combinations. "You know what this is, don't you?"

<A language primer. Shomchai's going to lose it,> Gis predicted triumphantly. A note of worry crept in. <Killie-Cat, you can't send any of this via the Portal coms. Even if your Kmet's denned, Omar's isn't. Anna's told me kmeth's been antsy since you transited through, lurking by the pedestals and questioning everything Omar does.>

"Understood." She thought, then gave a wicked chuckle. "Let them know what's coming. Once I finish here, we'll see how well you draw, Space Rat."

<Wait a minute—>

Killian pressed the wristband to wake her oneiric, still chuckling. Got to work, moving from dimple to dimple, drawing the result.

Forget Shomchai.

Henry was going to love this.

“I don’t like you.”

THE acrid tang of fresh-burnt vegetation, a reminder of the latest Sweep, announced the threshold of Away before it came in sight. Still too far to be sure which version of Away they approached, though dense jungle was the most likely and dangerous; Beth squinted, trying to make out details, for what good it would do to know.

A warning, the warmth on her back. Not hot, not yet. Soon, though, and if she’d a choice, by now she’d have sheltered for the day in the shade of a hill or boulder.

Had there been any in sight; her below-friend must be overjoyed by the flat crust in every direction. The plate slid along, crushing the surface, leaving its fat trail behind. Beth arranged her cloak as a shade, herself as small as possible beneath it. There’d be a breeze, for sure, and she’d water to spare. Wasn’t looking forward to enduring the sun’s full heat, but she’d survive it.

Lulled by the motion and growing warmth, Beth dozed on and off. Broke off a quarter piece of travel bar to quiet her stomach, tucking away the rest. Wasn’t as if she was doing the work.

When the plate slowed, coming to a gentle stop, it startled her fully awake again.

They’d stopped well short of the burnt edge. Jungle loomed, full of what found her alien flesh to its liking; unsurprised, Beth pulled her veil from around her neck, preparing to cover her face, and braced for whatever came next.

The plate rotated. Stopped. Beth found herself facing a large puddle.

Wasn’t water, not in the Split, but definitely liquid. Gray. Almost metallic. Viscous, judging by the large, slow ripples left from the plate’s vibration, and she’d never seen the like.

The plate tipped suggestively at the puddle.

Well, that couldn’t be clearer. Beth rose to her feet, every joint stiff, and walked cautiously to the edge of the plate. Using her sounding stick for support, she stepped off.

The ground swayed. She gave herself a stern little shake. *Like getting off a boat.* She didn't try for speed as she walked to the puddle and knelt just out of reach.

The ripples settled, the now-calm surface reflecting the sky. Sunlight limned one side, eye-searingly bright; Beth adjusted her angle to avoid the glare, studying the liquid. Paint. Oil. Industrial fluid. It didn't appear to be any of those.

How deep was it? She poked her stick in the puddle.

Gray liquid flowed up the wood. "What the—" Beth dropped her stick before the liquid reached her hand.

To her amazement, the liquid left the stick, flowing back over the ground toward the puddle.

She grabbed one of Bio's bags and used the blade of her knife to scoop up a sample. When the uncooperative stuff wouldn't drip from the blade into the bag, she stuffed the knife, with its coating of dirt and liquid, inside and zipped the fastener.

The bag went into her pack. Maybe someone at Home would be able to figure it out. An exotic fuel, maybe, from the downed spacecraft they were after—made sense. Might be useful.

Except the shaft of her stick was clean and dry—and what kind of fuel *moved* of its own accord?

"I don't like you," Beth decided, glaring at the puddle. She thumped her stick on the ground. *Tinkle.*

She should have thought of her below-friend before expressing an opinion, for there was a deep, answering *THUD* from underneath.

Before she'd finished jumping into the air, a hole cracked open, engulfing the puddle and its surrounds almost to Beth's boots. She scrambled back as the gray liquid disappeared, sucked down then buried as the hole refilled itself.

Well, she'd a sample. Now, apparently, so did her below-friend.

Beth climbed back on the plate and sat.

The sun beat down.

The burnt edge of Away stank.

A Sweep might come through at any moment.

Beth shaded her head. Either her below-friend would return to drag its plate and her closer to where she had to go, or she'd get up and walk the rest once the day cooled.

Meanwhile, seeing what she'd face, might as well prepare. Her veil sat loose and ready around her neck. Taking the tube of Begone from her pack, Beth spread the poison ointment over every portion of exposed skin, removing her boots to reach her feet, pushing up under her pant legs and sleeves to reach her calves, hands, wrists, and forearms. Her neck, ears, and top of her head received the same treatment, a green stain marking where she'd done. She used more care applying it to her face. Even if she believed the Bios' claim their concoction was harmless to Humans, the taste was vile.

Every thread of her clothing, including her cloak, was impregnated with

Begone. The poison wouldn't faze anything with a mouth and teeth, but the single greatest threat of Away's jungle had none. Black Dust. Death dust more like it, for a single spore landing on flesh and taking hold guaranteed a slow, ugly death, digested from the inside. A Seeker's only recourse was a knife across the throat before the fungus grew enough to cause paralysis.

On that thought, Beth smeared ointment on her closed eyelids. Up to her, she'd skirt the too-quiet zones where the Dust hunted, avoiding the threat entirely. Her below-friend might not be as careful.

Unless it needed to be. In Beth's experience, there were hunters for every living thing. Not that she'd proof what dragged the plate was alive and not, for argument's sake, a remotely controlled machine or automaton. History books claimed New Earth had been close to a breakthrough in artificial minds.

No, it was alive. At least by any definition of use to her, sitting out here in the Split, and she'd worry about its plumbing—or lack of—when they met face to whatever-it-had.

Beth made herself comfortable and began to doze.

Almost fell off when the plate lurched into motion, spinning back around and heading for the threshold.

Alive and with a rotten sense of humor.

She pulled up her veil.

"They're coming."

HENRY dropped his hands to his knees and hung his head as if studying the finger-width branch with its rows of small, round purple leaves, desperate to catch his breath. Flip-goo was like wearing rubber; sweat streamed down his chest and back, puddling around his feet.

Wombat-Flip sat up, whiskers twitching. "We must not delay, Henry."

He waved rather than gasp. As Henry was about to straighten, something tiny and white fluttered past his nose. Another something. Entranced, he leaned closer to the branch.

Having stood on tiny black legs, the round leaves were dancing sideways, making room as a new flock of dainty "leaves" arrived on fluffy white wings. As their feet touched the branch, wings folded like parasols, each clamped neatly inside a purple case.

The entire group froze in place, leaves on a branch once more.

Rena— "Did you get that, Flip?"

"I wasn't aware I should be recording our surroundings, Henry. My apologies. Shall I begin?"

"Please, if it won't strain your resources. I'd love Rena to see this." Henry's gesture swept the jungle from canopy to moss.

"I'll capture all I can. Are you ready to move again?"

Was there a choice? "Lead on."

An advantage of being encased in Flip-goo? The ever-present nippy vines didn't like the taste, preserving Henry's skin as he climbed over a mass of the things, incorporated into a pile of dead twigs and branches. He slid down the far side onto the beaten, slightly concave trail of the suckerbugs and hastily checked in both directions. "They aren't here," he said, relieved.

Wombat-Flip hopped into the middle of the trail. "They are there, Henry." The polymorph extended a front paw, indicating where the trail took a sharp bend around a trio of immense tree trunks. "Thirty-two meters in that direction is a group—should I refer to suckerbugs as being in a group or would cluster be—"

"What are they doing?" Henry interrupted.

"Moving toward us, Henry, at a slower pace than previously observed. I estimate in four minutes we will have our opportunity to test the effectiveness of our disguises, unless the suckerbugs accelerate." An ear aimed forward, then back.

He knelt. "Tell me what to do, Flip."

"I suggest we walk in the same direction, Henry, at a pace that matches theirs. Pretend to be going home."

"How do we know home's that way?" Henry nodded down the trail.

"That is the source of a temperature differential, one I interpret as meaning there is an opening underground ahead."

"You didn't say there'd be a tunnel."

"I didn't know, Henry."

He gathered his courage. "So we walk in. Mingle with the suckerbugs." That he could say the words amazed him. "Then what?"

"Assuming our disguises are effective, I will lead us to where there is more of me, acquire it, and we leave."

"If they aren't?"

"I insist you allow me to contact the Portal and request extraction if you are in imminent danger."

He shook his head. "We've talked about—what are you doing?"

"Ensuring your safety." Wombat-Flip, having angled alts mouth just so, took a quick little bite out of Henry's leg.

"Ow!"

"My apologies, Henry." A paw patted the little wound, pushing the yellow goo over it. "There. You have some of me inside. I will be able to find you if we're separated."

No worse than any of the myriad bites and nips he'd had so far, Henry told himself, getting carefully to his feet. At least the discomfort was in a good cause.

He turned his head, hearing a growing rustle and click. "They're coming."

"Remember to keep your mouth closed, Henry." Wombat-Flip led the way, not quite hopping, small and yellow and—if the word applied, and Henry believed it did—brave.

The Arbiter, coated in yellow goo, followed, doing his utmost not to look over his shoulder as the rustle and clicks grew louder and louder.

I'm a yellow suckerbug, he thought at them, mouth closed. He couldn't stop the Human-scented air leaving his nostrils. *Nothing strange here. I'm one of you.*

The sounds wrapped around him. A rustle like dried leaves in autumn, but he'd nothing to compare to the clicks.

They were overtaken before the trail took a sharp bend to the right. Yellow *things* poured past Henry to either side, with hunched bodies and no head he could make out. The rustle came from loose plates along their sides. The clicks were less obvious. They'd feet, more than he liked, but the sound originated from higher up. If the suckerbugs talked to one another, who knew what Wombat-Flip's imitation was saying.

They shoved one another. At times climbed over one another, and Henry copied Wombat-Flip in moving faster to keep ahead of what was becoming a headlong rush forward. Eager to be home, were they?

Staying on his feet became a problem. Suckerbugs pushed from behind, as if hurrying a sluggard. The much-smaller polymorph rolled and disappeared under bodies for an instant. Henry swallowed a gasp.

Wombat-Flip reappeared on top of one, ears back, taking full advantage.

Not his option. Individual suckerbugs were about half Henry's size; their hazard lay in their number—and speed.

And when the wave of suckerbugs poured inexorably down into a smooth-sided tunnel, leaving the jungle and light behind?

There was no turning back.

"—what's below?"

UNABLE to stand or crawl, Henry was pushed and rolled down slopes and around bends, with no idea where he was going or why, the noise of the suckerbugs near-deafening in close quarters. *And he'd complained about the Portal's tubes—*

The dark helped hide what pushed and rolled him; every so often a paw touched his hand, a welcome reminder he wasn't alone. *Not often enough—*

Suddenly his head and shoulders rose, little claws gripped him, and he slipped feet-first into a much narrower hole. He struggled only to find paws on his shoulders, holding him in place. I'VE IDENTIFIED THIS AS A SAFE LOCATION, HENRY. YOU'LL BE SAFE HERE. I'LL NEED THE REST OF ME. With that, the goo coating him flowed up and away.

A final push, the paws left, and Henry felt a pulse of air as *something* sealed his hiding place.

If Flip said this was safe, it was safe. Trust kept Henry from panic. That, and knowing he mustn't attract the attention of the colony's inhabitants. He could hear them, moving around beyond his walls. Clicking. Rustling. *So close.*

He focused on where he was. How. Lying down. That was good. He was spent, every muscle burning. His med team would have fits. Not to mention adrenalin had him shaking so hard his teeth chattered.

To relax, he investigated his reduced world. Toes at one end of his prison, his outstretched fingertips brushed the other. Reaching up, he touched the ceiling. Reaching out, elbows bent, he felt the walls to either side.

When he rolled over, there wasn't room to rise on his hands and knees.

This wasn't a grave. Living things called it home, and Henry forced himself to take deep, slow breaths of air redolent of sweaty Human and tilled soil. As the adrenalin wore off, he began to shiver. Despite the warmth, his clothes were soaked with sweat.

How he'd love to close his eyes and be anywhere else. On the beach with Rena would be nice. Even the meeting room. *Being real wasn't all it was cracked up to be.*

He choked on a chuckle.

Couldn't stop the tear that slipped loose.

***

Amazingly, he'd slept. Or passed out. Whichever it was, Henry woke to digging near his feet, and spent a paralyzed moment trying to tell if the sound was from paws or claws—

HENRY, COME THIS WAY.

—paws, it was. He scrunched himself closer to the digging, doing his best to push aside a growing pile of loose dirt with his sandaled toes. Felt a foot break through and a paw take hold, giving a gentle tug. "That's it. This way."

Following the polymorph's instructions took a great deal of wriggling and squirming, but Henry was motivated—even more when he realized he could see Wombat-Flip's red glow. At last, he slid the rest of the way, out into a larger tunnel, and leapt to his feet ready to run. An intention his cramped and recently abused body ignored completely, folding against the dirt wall instead. "Need a minute," he said, raising a hand.

"We do not have a minute, Henry. Please climb on my back."

About to object, Henry took a second look at his companion. Wombat-Flip had more than tripled in size, now more fierce bear than a cuddly marsupial. "You found your bits. Can you reach Earth? Killian?"

"Yes to all, Henry, but we've no time to waste. I've stunned the suckerbugs between us and our exit. They won't remain unconscious for long." Wombat-Flip crouched invitingly.

Leaving Henry no choice but to grab handfuls of fur and pull himself gracelessly up and over, flopping to lie on the polymorph's broad muscular back. "Flip, I need—"

"Hold on, Henry. This me is swift but not smooth."

He'd barely taken a grip before the body beneath him exploded in motion, running faster than Henry would have believed, then faster still, until he pressed his face into fur and thought only that Flip wouldn't leave him if he fell, but there might not be much left if he did—

A final leap—possibly to clear quiescent suckerbugs—and they were out!

In the rain. A pounding, wonderful torrent of clean water, and Henry lifted himself as much as he dared to let it wash over him, laughing. "Flip, you're amazing!" he shouted.

"I am," replied his friend, with a deserved *smug*. "In addition, I have detected superior shelter, Henry. It isn't far. Hold on."

***

Half-expecting another hollow log, hopefully vacant, Henry was stunned when Wombat-Flip slowed to a stop. A opalescent dome, three meters wide and half as tall, sat in the midst of a fresh-cut clearing as if dropped in place moments ago, and he'd have thought it some strange new life-form—there being a wealth of that—except it had a door.

A door near the top, its opening covered by a flap of metal mesh, meant for beings of another shape entirely, being wider than tall, narrower in the middle, with curved-up ends.

Proof this world held more than Humans.

Henry tamped down his excitement. "Flip, if this belongs to the Portal Makers, we can't start a conversation with theft or trespass."

"If you're caught by what hunts us, Henry, there'll be no conversation," Flip pointed out. As if on cue, there was a dreadful shuddering *howl* from too close.

Forget diplomacy. "Inside it is."

Reaching the door took standing on Wombat-Flip's back. The mesh proved to be a curtain rather than flap. Henry pushed it aside, climbing in through the widest part of the opening. When he paused astride to see what he was literally getting into, the polymorph gave him a nudge from behind, toppling him inside.

Henry landed on a pile of blankets. The homeliness of it was more surprising than the light coming through the translucent dome, or the neat stack of tubes. Blankets and—he rose to his feet and walked across a floor of the dome material to a small, round rise clearly meant as a table, being covered in dishes. He picked one up. A simple metal bowl, unornamented and clean. Light—

A quiet thump made him look around. Flip had landed on alts feet—once again humanoid, if now closer to Henry's size—and reached up to pull the mesh across the door.

Able to do so because the floor was higher than the ground outside. *Was there more to this shelter?* He knelt and knocked, listening for an echo.

"Henry?"

"I thought—what's below?"

"Loosened soil, Henry." Sensitive fingers ran over the wall. "This structure is of a temporary nature, recently erected. A tent, in other words."

Campers. Explorers. "So the real owners could be coming back."

"Or have left, without that intention." Flip picked up a tube. Set it down. "These contain dehydrated bodily waste."

He'd dealt in far less tidy ways with his own. *Not what mattered.* "Can you analyze it?"

"I will do what I can under these conditions."

"Please send the results to Rena—you can?"

"Yes, Henry. I have regained thirty-three percent of my functionality. I'm relieved to be of greater assistance."

"You're invaluable at any size, Flip. Thank you." *And vulnerable.* They'd have to avoid losing any more.

The polymorph opened alts mouth to take a bite of the tube and Henry quickly busied himself elsewhere. He found a mesh bag of unused leaves. Counted the blankets. Three. Shook one out. The shape was the opposite of the door opening, wide in the middle and narrow to each end. *No clue there.*

"I've completed and sent my analysis, Henry. The remote I sent before entering the tent will reach the edge of the jungle in a few moments. First, however, I've received a second message from Killian concerning her latest discovery in the Portal. I was unable to share with you earlier, as it's visual. If I may now?"

Visual? "Please." Henry sat on the blanket, leaning forward eagerly. "What was she after?"

Flip sat opposite him, alts smooth chest becoming a screen. "Killian asked for the ability to talk to the Portal Makers and was taken to a room with this on the floor." An array of small, hand-shaped dots appeared. "Holding her hand over each resulted in a displayed symbol." As each dot glowed, Flip showed the corresponding symbol. "This information has been conveyed to New Earth, but Killian elected to get it to you as soon as possible."

Henry looked around the tent. "There's none here."

"No. Nor have I been able to ascribe meanings to any of the symbols. Hopefully Shomchai and his peers will be more successful."

Henry stared at Flip, seeing not the polymorph but a room to teach different species to communicate. Tubes that accommodated other shapes. Worlds split in two. He'd gone from missing pieces of the puzzle to having too many.

The screen changed, reclaiming his attention. Treetops. An edge. "My remote is about to intercept what Killian spotted, Henry."

And what might you *be . . .*

"'Bout time."

ASH kicked up, thick and deadly. Couldn't be helped, not this way of travel, and Beth hunched inside her veil and cloak, unable to see through the cloud anyway. Counted to herself.

Reached three hundred before the air cleared. Fast, her below-friend. By nature or need? A question she'd like answered. Among many.

Beth lifted off her cloak, cautiously freed the veil to sniff, ready to don it again; she didn't like the result, but the smell was of damp, warm rot. She shook ash from the veil, rolling it with the outside in. Need it again on the way out.

Wasn't going to think she wouldn't.

Past the threshold was the zone where life fought to be first to seize the sunlight. Prickly shrubs not unlike those of Home's desert looked to be winning, but a creeping groundcover was closing in, able to smother what it touched and wither exposed Human flesh. The jungle rose ahead, a barrier of towering trees waving feathery fronds full of flying hunters, tufts of shaggy fern sticking up between hiding ambush ones, and at the base a solid edge of biter vines waited.

Away, welcoming as ever. Cheered Beth immensely, it did.

Until the plate showed no signs of stopping.

Jumping clear wasn't an option. Driving straight into growth that would rip her flesh apart wasn't either. Beth began pounding with her stick. "Stop! STOP!"

Something flashed by overhead.

The plate ground to a halt.

"'Bout time," she muttered, getting to her feet. She searched the sky for whatever she'd glimpsed. The big gliders weren't known to hunt out here, there being nothing to hunt but the rare Seeker. Didn't mean they wouldn't start.

There. Not big. Tiny. Reflective.

Reflex, to duck as the thing swooped close, stick up and ready to strike. She didn't, for it stopped in front of her, hovering on paired, transparent wings, stubby body yellow and black. Wings not of Doublet, not any part she was aware—Patrick adamant Seekers know their categories of bugs. Eyes didn't look right either, but she'd seen the like in an antique kid's book.

How a *bee* from a world her ancestors left two centuries ago came to be here, watching her—if it was a bee at all—

The plate dropped from under her.

Falling came next.

"I will speak to the Arbiter."

<YOU owe me, Killie-Cat. Big time. BIG. TIME. Got it?>

Killian grinned. "Five by five, Space Rat. I take it they liked your pictures."

Gis purred inside her head. <Let's say I get whatever I want for life. That being you, here, what's next?>

Good question. One answer. "Back to Control. Henry's going to want updates."

<Man's a survivor, I'll give him that.>

Flip's message had come straight to Killian's personal com, loud and clear, if short on detail. The polymorph had—somehow—recovered. Henry was—somehow—close to contacting aliens. Not the Human population he'd gone down to meet.

And not, apparently, the aliens he'd expected.

"Rena's sure?"

<Yup. What Flip sent her has nothing in common with the corpses you found or the Kmet.>

They were back in action to a point. Before leaving Control, Killian had paced out the den opening. Kmet-Here should still be able to pass through.

Time would come, maybe soon, kmeth couldn't. If there was agreement on anything among the experts on New Earth, it was that the den closing would mark the start of the end.

Unhelpfully, they didn't agree on what that was, but Killian had taken Gis' sound advice, and her spacesuit lay on her bed, ready to grab.

While waiting for *experts* to debate another topic. "There a consensus yet on getting the symbols to Henry and Flip?" she asked, making it innocent.

Fooling her partner not a whit. <You sent them already. Sneaky sneak.> Admiration, that was.

"I'd some spare wire." And less time. The PIPs hadn't liked her wiring up the pedestal she'd scorched earlier. Those who'd come too close wound up tossed at the den—grabbed and glued. *Did them a favor.* "Anything more from Omar?"

<No. Anna's starting to pace. The Portal's stable. So far. Anything you can do—just be careful. Our Kmet might not be playing as nice as yours expects.>

Aliens. "I'll call in a routine check. Love you, Space Rat."

<Lima Charlie, Killie-Cat.>

***

The gaps in the corridor were no wider, but as Killian stepped from her quarters, she saw they were deeper, much deeper, as if cracks in the Portal itself. Suit under her arm, bag over her shoulder, she made her way to the tube mouths, glad to find they looked unchanged.

Not that she'd any way to know about the tubes themselves.

The one to Control was higher than usual, as if avoiding the cracked floor, and Killian had to jump to reach it. Made it, pushing in her suit with one hand, hauling the rest of her up with the other. Rode with her eyes closed, trying to sense any changes. Didn't, for what that counted, but she'd take it.

Arrived to find every PIP but the three clinging to the wall controls lined up to join the den, the once-spotless floor cluttered with abandoned bits and pieces. The den remained open. Killian went to it, bent to peer inside. Heard a warning rumble and backed away.

She went to the dais, putting her suit on the floor next to it. When no PIPs showed interest, she decided it was safe where it was and focused on the screens.

The entire planet had been mapped. A single supercontinent, the line down the middle, held all the dry land. The ocean's depth varied. There were swathes of reef as well as abyssal depths. Where Humans lived was coming clearer with every sat pass.

Where Henry was—now had a dot! Killian hopped off the dais and went closer. There it was, a marker. *Nicely done, Flip.* She regarded the dot fondly for a moment before returning to her post. "New Earth Portal, communications check. Pilot Omar, please respond."

Nothing.

Frowning, Killian confirmed her settings, "This is Pilot Killian. Pilot Omar, respond please."

"My pilot is in his quarters, Pilot Killian." The deep voice might have been Kmet-Here's. "Are you preparing to transit?" The panting eagerness—wasn't.

"Not at this time, Kmet-There. The Arbiter—"

"I will speak to the Arbiter. NOW!" With a BOOM able to come through the coms, and this was trouble by any measure.

Fortunately, she no longer had to face it alone.

"Connecting you with the Arbiter isn't possible at this time, Kmet-There," Killian replied. "Please call back in—" *what?* "—two Earth hours. Pilot Killian out."

She ended the connection, her hand shaking. Hung up on a Kmet, she had. There was a first.

Leaving her two hours to patch a connection between Henry and Portal orbiting New Earth.

Humming, Killian began her preparations.

"She's the key."

THEY'D found a Human—only to watch her plummet into a yawning hole in the ground. Their fault, Henry knew, not that there'd been a choice. "Send the remote after her, Flip."

"Yes, Henry. But I warn you it is unlikely—"

"Just do it, please."

"Yes, Henry." The screen showed the round, ragged edge of the hole, then in they went.

It was more like dropping through a skylight than entering a pit. Shortly after the remote began its descent, the view opened up. Red walls marked with shelf-like protrusions, like the inside of a gut; a floor, irregular but smooth, littered with fresh debris, dust still settling. *No body.*

"Where is she?"

Flip turned the remote. In every direction, smooth tunnels led away, some edged with hanging stone, like teeth. "There is no sign of the person we saw, Henry. I will add that though these resemble lava tubes, there is no other sign of volcanic activity in this region. They may extend for considerable distances. I could choose one at random—"

"No. Check for anything she might have left." The remote dipped to examine the debris. "There. Close in, Flip." A pole—the one she'd held in her hand.

"It is a finely made object, Henry. Hollow and of metal I don't recognize. If you want me to retrieve it, I can send more remotes."

"Leave it there, Flip. Who knows—she might come back for it. Show her to me again, please."

Henry studied the image. Though it had been the remote catching her attention, he felt as if the displayed woman studied him in return. A strong, weathered face, what showed of it. A sharp, determined gaze. Green skin. Modification or cosmetic, he couldn't tell, nor could he make much sense from her clothing other than layers, that for sure, with odd lumps he guessed covered tools or supplies. She'd been— "Replay the initial sighting, Flip."

—yes, he hadn't been mistaken. She rode a moving, flat platform that looked like a patch of desert crust, though why anyone would manufacture something—"Flip, could this have caused the markings Killian observed from orbit?"

"No, Henry. What carried it did."

"Car—what?" But it made sense, of a sort. Tunnels below ground. Something that moved through rock—

The Portal Makers had a form with scales and powerful claws. *Would that have been enough?* "We have to find her," he decided. "She's the key." He stood, taking one of the blankets, leaving the rest.

"Wait." Flip rose with him. "Let me ascertain if it's now safe to leave, Henry."

The howling. A few minutes under a roof and he'd forgotten all about the dangers they faced. "Please."

Not a mistake she'd make, he judged, thinking of that face.

"Hello."

TO Beth's surprise, she landed on her feet not far below the ground. The plate crumbled around her, leaving a pile on what was otherwise a smooth floor. She glanced up through motes of dust, saw sky and a height beyond her to jump.

Lowered her gaze to meet another's and it took an effort not to flinch, finding herself facing what had a very different one. Small eyes, set apart over what was more snout than face. Scales, coated in dust. Taller, even hunched forward, with arms the size of her entirety ending in big hands. Three long fingers, extended beyond knuckle-claws suited to digging. Bulky body supported by sturdy legs. Tail balancing the rest.

The snout ended in a little nose, with paired, hairy nostrils. They flared, as if taking her scent.

Was what she'd trained for, wasn't it? she chided herself, and set her face to pleasant. "Hello."

"'Hello.'" Had a mouth, if not a chin; the sound coming out like an echo. Her voice, bang-on perfect.

Beth raised an eyebrow. *A mimic, was it?* "Can you say anything else?"

'"Anything else?'"

Big plus, it could form words. Not so sure on the understanding of them, and she wished she still had the *artifacts* in her pack to—

It turned and ran.

"Wait!" She ran after it.

***

For something about the mass of Old Mitch, her companion could move, but she'd known that before seeing it. Knew it could plow through hard ground too, and that she'd lose it and likely herself if it did.

But it stayed to the tunnels and, when she lagged behind, slowed as if determined not to leave her behind.

One time she lagged, it was to check her compass. The needle rocked, then steadied, giving her direction. The distance she'd come registered, if made no sense to anyone thinking she'd walked it, and Beth chuckled under her breath.

Next time she went to turn on her radio, but didn't after all. Wasn't sure how her friend would react, for one thing. No guarantee she'd get a signal worth her while for the other.

Pondered what had put her down here, the impossible bee. Figured it had a connection to whatever crashed. Archives had plans for drones; Home disapproved of anything likely to upset the Split and banned them. *Proved that point.*

A spy sort of thing. Meaning a mind and eyes behind it, and Beth lagged again, thinking that. Had she been wrong, not to stay? To wait for what they'd sent her to find in the first place?

She picked up the pace. Following what every Seekers ever wanted to meet was a surer bet than waiting for someone from old Earth, assuming that's who sat in orbit, dumb enough to send a flyer through the Split.

Of interest to her below-friend, the flyer that crashed. Made sense it knew better than any where to find it.

Beth drank as she ran.

What it meant to do when it did—that'd tell her more than words could.

<Damn poetic.>

"PILOT Killian, requesting the Arbiter." She'd the call on repeat, silenced in the unlikely event Kmet-Here was anything but oblivious. Wasn't worried, yet, by Flip's lack of response.

Wandering a fucking jungle. There'd be mud, bugs, leaves, and who knew what else. The polymorph would answer first chance alt had, though it'd better be within the next ninety minutes or she'd have to find another way to stall Kmet-There. Maybe she should find out what kmeth liked. It wasn't peanuts—

—it was Henry messing with her head.

Killian snorted and checked the time. Gis would be waiting. She pressed her wristband. Wrote: *Hi Space Rat. Any news?*

<Things ramping up here. Spacer Repository's sending crews to orbit. Tugs, catchers, freighters—anything able to move's going to be ready. AND they're bringing down all but maintenance from the stations. Glad I've a private room. Word is you have to line up to piss, place is so packed.>

The almighty Arbiter's endgame. She aimed her thumb down in denial.

<Hey, no one wants this. Just pre . . . caution . . . ary, Killie-Cat. Remember that super we had, second shift on the *Imp*?>

How could she forget? Hated the ship, hated her crew, hated anything she considered un . . . predict . . . able. And that's exactly how she'd said the word.

And exactly how she'd saved their hides, making them run suit drills till they'd cursed her, keeping a maintenance system on the crappy old freighter that caught a boiler about to blow. Killian wrote: *Scale's different.*

<Happy to debate the point, but I've other news. Omar finally called Anna back. I've got her right here.>

In her bed, that meant, not that anything was likely between those two other than punches. Killian grinned and wrote: *Want me to wake you up to watch her snooze?*

<Don't you dare. Woman drools worse than my brother's Great Dane. I warned her to stay off my pillow.> A pause. <Doing her best, have to admit. Might have to buy them beer, other side of this. Once, anyway.>

Gis making plans. Making her laugh. Killian drew a heart. Erased it before her partner grew sentimental or interested, Control a poor place for either, and them right out of time.

Looked around to be sure no PIP had oculars aimed her way before writing: *I've been thinking about Kmet-Here's simul-stop. It shouldn't matter where the Portals meet, only that they do.*

<You're thinking somewhere not Earth.>

She nodded.

<One has to be in place before the other pops in. Hate to remind you, but there's nowhere our Kmet or yours wants to be more than here.>

Killian took a breath and wrote: *We tell your Kmet there are still Humans on Origin Earth.*

<What?>

She doggedly kept writing: *Get me the coordinates. I'll pretend to be Henry. Give them to Kmet-There and order kmeth to go immediately. Once Omar's Portal transits through, I use a self-destruct pedestal to merge the Portals there, instead of in our Earth's orbit.*

Erased.

Wrote: *Why not use another Earth to save ours?* Erased that, breathing hard. Waited.

<Because—> Gis stopped there. She'd be thinking it through. Searching for holes, the way she did.

Would find them, guaranteed, if they existed, but Killian had done her own thinking. This felt right. Felt—

<Damn poetic,> said Gis, as if reading her mind. <Damn risky, especially since it all depends on you fooling a Kmet—not to mention getting to that pedestal. You need Henry looped in.>

Killian shook her head. Wrote: *Want to. Can't. Coms go through Portals—including Flip to other FLIPs—and the Kmet aren't stupid. Kmeth will catch anything threatening the Duality.* And *that* she erased the instant she finished.

<Five by five.> Another sober pause. <Stay in a holding pattern till I talk to Anna and Omar. And Killian—any chance Origin Earth might have people on it, plan's off. We don't shove our problem on innocent laps, hear me?>

Every word made sense. After a quick thumbs-up, Killian wrote: *Have Ousmane check. Tell her it's for an idea Henry has. She'll believe it. He comes up with wild ones.*

<Must be rubbing off.> But Gis wasn't disagreeing. That, above all, gave Killian confidence. <Wake me up, Killie-Cat. Love you.>

"Lima Charlie, Space Rat." Killian pressed the wristband. Kept her fingers near it a while longer.

Looked at the den and bared her teeth.

Kmet-Here wanted her to transit them through to New Earth?

Glad to oblige.

“Where to now?”

“STOP, Henry!”

He froze at the warning, a foot raised to clear a branch. Looked around for whatever the latest threat might be. *As if flying fungi, howling whatevers, and suckerbugs weren’t enough.* Not to mention what flew overhead in any clearing and vines with teeth—

Losing his balance, Henry threw up his arms—

Flip caught him and set him on his feet. “Observe, Henry.” The polymorph broke off a stick and tossed it where the Arbiter’d been about to step.

The stick sank into what looked like solid ground, black bubbles oozing up around it.

“Adding that to the list,” Henry said.

Breaking off another, longer length, Flip handed it to him. “I suggest you probe the ground ahead of you, Henry.”

He hefted it. “She carried a stick.” Used his to indicate the jungle ahead. “Despite coming from the other side of the line, she knows how to survive in this one.”

“It would appear so, Henry. An explorer, perhaps.”

Like the tent people. Despite its warmth, he’d draped the blanket from the shelter over his shoulders, comforted by its weight and what it meant. He fingered the fabric. “Maybe she knows who left this.”

Flip suddenly lifted alts head, turning to gaze to the left. Henry tensed. “What now?”

“More of me. In motion.”

“A suckerbug?”

“I reclaimed everything the creatures took, Henry. What I sense must be from the material I lost prior to landing.”

His heart leapt. “Enough to be a shuttle again?”

“This is barely a trace. If it weren’t close, I wouldn’t detect it.” A rare hesitation. “Some time ago I lost the rest. I’d assumed it was my present limited scanning radius. Now I must conclude this trace to be all there is.”

Bad news. Henry shook it off. They'd been moving as directly as possible to where the woman had disappeared. She'd come from the desert beyond, heading for them, and he'd a feeling—"The bit of you. I think our missing explorer has it. We can use it to find her."

"As she or some other entity may be using it to find us, Henry. I caution we do not know her intentions."

"We're the ones who dropped in on her world. My guess is her people have questions. I've the answers. Lead on, Flip."

Flip raised a long arm to point. "The trace of me is that way, Henry."

That way being through thick clumps of biter vines, with more vines draping down from the trees, the sum woven together like a net. The strands looked harmless, pretty even, but he'd met them before. Once he was close, thousands of little mouths would open, teeth ready to snap. And if he was too close—

"Can't we go around?"

Flip turned to scan their surroundings. Alts features settled in grim lines. "There are equivalent hazards in every direction but behind, Henry. We could retrace our steps—but the sun will set before we reach the shelter."

Vines it was. "Lead the way."

"I'll do my best to protect you."

Not a promise, he noted.

The humanoid polymorph pushed between clumps. The vines reacted as if confused, biting harmlessly at the air near Flip. Emboldened, Henry walked as close to Flip as possible without tangling their feet.

A nip on his ear. He flinched and teeth sliced open his cheek. Everywhere he looked were mouths. Frantically hauling the blanket from his shoulders, Henry went to put it over his head and face—

Every vine in his vicinity retreated, curling back on itself. He stopped, holding the blanket in the air. "Flip?"

"The fabric of the blanket must contain a repellent specific to these plants, Henry. I suggest you continue to hold it up and go first. I will guard you from behind."

They continued forward. When Henry experimentally waved the blanket, a thick clump of vine cowered and pulled aside, mouths shut. He kept waving it until they cleared the last of the growth, then turned to watch his companion.

Behind Flip, the vines returned to their net-like arrangement, but every mouth stayed shut. Henry folded the blanket, giving it a respectful pat before putting it over his shoulders. "Saved the day. Where to now?"

Flip looked down, eyes widening. "Henry—"

Which was when the ground opened beneath them and they fell.

“Where are we going?

WASN’T dark. The smooth red walls were pocked with what glowed a soft yellow. Wasn’t flat, either, the floor sloping down till Beth wasn’t sure how deep they’d come. She was sure she wasn’t about to run for hours.

Beth slowed to a walk to see what would happen. Her companion disappeared around a distant bend. She kept walking, determined to set her own pace.

The now-familiar snout reappeared. She waved. “I’m coming.”

“ ‘Coming.’ ” Another echo in her voice. A huff in its. Might have run off again. That it spoke and waited told her she’d value, whether as a curiosity or more.

And it was smart. Smart as her, at a guess. Maybe smarter. Time to use that. She stopped, pointing in several directions. “Where are we going?”

Echo, “ ‘Going.’ ” A thick arm lifted, and this time she caught how a finger uncurled from the palm. It pointed ahead and up.

Satisfied, Beth gave a nod and got moving again. Her below-friend whirled around and disappeared. It wouldn’t go far.

A slower pace had its advantages beyond less effort. For starters, it let Beth study her surroundings. The Bios would want to know everything she found—assuming she made it back to tell them, but she’d every intention.

The glow came from crystals. She’d thought them a natural phenomenon until now, when she saw they were set in repeating patterns. Paired circles, with a line from the middle going up and left. Over and over.

Like Doublet itself. Two, with a line.

A thought to put aside, her knowing better than jump to conclusions. Still. Beth turned her head to keep the pattern in sight until certain she’d be able to reproduce it.

She went around the bend to find the tunnel widened into a bulb. Rubble and dried vegetation formed a low pile in the center. The walls she could see were covered with strange, round discs, the diameter of her arm.

Her below-friend stood on the far side, facing her. A hand rose, fingers outspread as if forbidding her to come closer, and Beth stopped, still inside the tunnel. “What now?”

The hand rose higher, fingers closing, and the ceiling collapsed.

Beth wasn't surprised to see bodies rain down with what had to be jungle floor, complete with mud and fresh green stuff, this place having the look of a trap used before.

She was when she realized the bodies had a familiar shape.

"I'll introduce you."

NOTHING broken. Half-stunned from the fall, Henry waited for that dubious self-assessment before attempting to move. As he did, gentle, strong hands took hold, helping him to his feet. Flip. He blinked at his companion through the detritus continuing to rain softly around them—that had come with them, he abruptly realized.

WE'RE NOT ALONE.

He didn't see anyone in the gloom, not that he doubted Flip. Henry set his face to pleasant and calm. Coughed to clear his throat. "Hello. I'm Henry—"

"I get what you are. What's he?" A figure came forward, swaddled in a cloak.

The woman they'd seen fall. The explorer. It had to be.

"I am—" Flip began.

"Flip. My companion," Henry interrupted. Their coating of mud and torn leaves hadn't disguised the polymorph's distinctiveness. "Who are you?"

"Beth Seeker." She gestured to the gloom. "Our hosts."

Henry bowed in that direction. "We mean no harm. We're from New Earth."

"Huh." Beth shoved the hood from her head with one hand, revealing close-cropped brown hair over a green scalp, and a face free of any expression at all. "You, they don't mind." She looked Flip up and down. "You? Guessing you're artificial. Made of that gray stuff, aren't you? Those below don't like it."

Portal Makers. Able to recognize a polymorphic matrix, and Henry took hold of Flip's wrist. "Flip isn't Kmet. Flip is a citizen of New Earth, an Alt-Intel. A friend."

Huffs and hisses from the gloom. He didn't need a translator to know those weren't happy sounds.

"Might be true. Doesn't change that when we found some of that gray stuff in the Split, my below-friend got rid of it." Beth reached inside her clothing, retrieving a labeled sample bag containing a knife. "All but this."

"The trace I detected." Flip reached out alts hand. "May I have it, please? It is—lonesome—away from me."

She gave the bag a curious look, then walked right up to Flip. "Here." She handed alt the bag. Watched intently as the tall polymorph opened it, a gray stain on the knife blade flowing up and *into* alts hand.

"Thank you." Flip returned the bag and knife to her.

This close to Beth, Henry saw cracks in the green on her skin. The pigment was cosmetic, a cream of some kind; he immediately thought of the blanket he carried. "You're an explorer."

"Seeker," she corrected. "But, yeah. That's the job. Along with figuring out how to talk to the neighbors." A thumb over her shoulder.

"Can you? It's important."

Her eyes narrowed. "Working on it." More hisses. "I can tell you they're getting impatient."

"Beth," Flip said, drawing her attention. "You're carrying a radio, are you not? Is it functional?"

She shrugged. "Should be. I shut it off, down here. Why?"

Flip turned to Henry. "You have communications, Henry. I must leave before my presence damages any chance of negotiation with the Portal Makers."

"'Portal Makers'?" Beth looked from Flip to Henry. "You know them?"

"We came hoping to find them," he said absently, his attention on his friend. "No, Flip. The mere idea is—" *Horrifying.* "I need you. You can't go."

"GO! GO! GO!" The air reverberated with the word in his voice.

Henry whirled, ready to defy them. Choked. *This wasn't about him.*

"Yet I must, Henry." Alt leaned closer. THIS VERSION HAS THE CAPACITY TO REACH AND ENTER THE PORTAL, AT THE COST OF BEING ABLE TO COMMUNICATE LIKE THIS. I WILL ASSIST KILLIAN TO EFFECT YOUR RESCUE—

"No, Flip." Clarity descended, chilling him to the bone. "Help her save New Earth. Not me." Henry looked into Flip's almost-Human face, reading dismay, hoping his own determination showed. "By order of the Arbiter."

"GO! GO! GO!" The word now eerily in Flip's voice.

Flip looked to Beth. "We need a moment."

Her eyebrow rose but she turned, holding up her hands. "Wait!"

"'Wait . . . wait . . . wait.'" Her voice this time. The word faded to echoes.

"No idea how long you have," she warned, facing them again. "I'd make it quick."

"I should not leave any of me here, Henry."

Right. The tracker. Henry stooped to pull up his pant leg. The small wound hadn't healed, and he braced himself for a second cut, but Flip merely held alts hand over it. There was a tingle, nothing more.

They stood gazing at one another. Without looking away from Henry, Flip spoke to the other Human present. "Beth Seeker. This is Arbiter Henry m'Yama t'Nowak. He is Earth's most important official and my dearest friend. Please do all you can to keep him safe while on your world." Henry watched Flip smile. "Though brave, Henry is not as careful of himself as I would like."

Henry felt her hand take his. "Do my best."

"I expect you to continue," he told Flip, the future uncertain and slipping from his fingers. Refused to let it go. "Understand me?" *Accept continuance, if the worst happens. Go home—*

—even if I never can.

The polymorph put alts hands on either side of Henry's head and brought their foreheads gently together. "I understand, Henry."

Then Flip stepped back. *Melted.* To a chorus of hisses and huffs, reformed into a sleek missile-shape. With a whoosh . . .

Flip was gone.

Gone.

A hand squeezed his. "C'mon. I'll introduce you."

". . . maybe we can change the game."

AN hour before her time ran out to get Henry to respond to Kmet-There, everything changed.

And not for the better, unless you were Kmet.

"I have conveyed my congratulations to Kmet-Superior!" Kmet-There boomed, with as close to giddy joy as Killian had ever heard from the species.

The reason stared her in the face. Kmet-Here wasn't coming out. Ever, PIPs having picked this moment to fill in the den's door in an act of self-sacrifice or brutal imprisonment or whatever weird alien shit made sense to them.

Leaving her in sole charge of the Portal, the Kmet trusting a Human to complete kmeth's destiny. *Picked the wrong one.*

And somehow, the other of their kind knew. "Congratulations to you, Pilot Killian, privileged to start our coalescence into Duality!"

"Once the Arbiter responds, Kmet-There," Killian repeated firmly. From being a problem, Henry's absence looked to be the only thing slowing what was becoming inevitable.

"Yes, yes." With unperturbed joy. "My pilot will give you the details. Congratulations to us all!"

The last free PIP clung to the wall controls, waiting to assist her. Stirred hopefully whenever Killian's pacing took her near the pedestals, subsided when she moved away, and she couldn't help but feel a smidge of sympathy.

"Pilot Omar to Pilot Killian. I've a status update for you."

Knew Omar's voice as well as her own, by now. The strain beneath the pro was a warning, and Killian braced for more bad news. "Go ahead."

"My Kmet has clarified the sequence for kmeth's forthcoming glorious sacrifice for the Duality. It'll happen once Kmet-Superior completes the Duality with Humans on New Earth. Copy that, Pilot Killian? The final transit will be activated from *outside* the Portal after your Kmet lands and is happy with what kmeth finds."

Bad news? Her heart sank. Didn't get any worse. If Kmet-Here found kmethself on the wrong planet, empty of Humans, kmeth wouldn't activate the final transit. And even if Kmet-Here was stuck on the surface, they'd still have two Portals in orbit, one with an angry Kmet, and nothing to stop kmeth flipping again. Possibly right back to New Earth.

Killian calmed herself. "Appreciate the update, Pilot Omar. Pilot Killian, out."

Silence fell. The PIP stirred again and she scowled at it until it froze.

<Gonna need a new plan, Killie-Cat.>

She brought up her pad. Wrote: *Hope you have one.*

<We're trying. Omar took a PIP and tried to move around his Portal, find another Control. That's where he's been the past while. Didn't work. Thinking is, your Portal reacted to Henry's arrival. Killian, Omar's willing to go into kmeth's den.>

Her thumb went down. She wrote: *Never make it. Kmeth's too fast.*

<Told him. Hard not to help.> And it wasn't just Omar, fretting over that.

Killian wrote: *Love you—*

Stopped as something caught her eye, moving over the planet in the center screen.

<What's that?>

Finished with: *Handle Omar. I'll find out.* She pressed the wristband to wake Gis. Left the dais to go closer. Wasn't a dot. Wasn't a saucer icon either, but whatever it symbolized was streaking up from the surface.

On trajectory to intersect the Portal—*Finally!*

Killian bolted for the tube mouth to the antechamber. Dove in and rode it round and upside down and through the drop, flying out at the other end into the chill.

Ran to stand by the airlock, waiting. Her breath didn't fog the air. Good thing. *Forgot her coat again.* Henry'd tease her about it.

Flip would make her a new one.

Waited. Ignored the cracks in the floor and walls. Kicked aside the little pile of sand on the floor. What mattered was being together again. Having help. Someone to make decisions. *Hell, make coffee—*

The airlock light came on. Blinked as the exterior door resealed. Opened with a sigh of air, and Killian gave it a minute, to let Henry come out. Frowned when he didn't.

Stepped inside. No Henry. No shuttle.

Her foot found the coat on the airlock floor.

Killian sat cross-legged on the floor of her quarters, elbows on her knees, chin in her hands to glare. "Let me get this straight. You *left* Henry—the real and only Henry—with a stranger."

The fake-phone she'd once found endearing waved at her. "I had no choice, Killian. I would have been exterminated by the Portal Makers had I stayed."

"According to the stranger."

Rolypoly rocked back and forth. "My inability to detect more of me and the alien response to my presence supported Beth's claim."

"*Beth*, is it?" Her lips worked as if to spit. "And what do you know about this *Beth*? Anything?"

"I believe her role will complement Henry's. She is a first contact specialist, a situation he faces—"

"ALONE!" Desperate to hit something, anything, Killian settled for rubbing her face, hard. Blew out a breath and stared at the little polymorph. "Now what?"

"Beth has a radio. Henry will use it to reestablish communication with us at the first opportunity. In the meantime, I suggest you provide an update to New Earth via Gis."

"And tell her what? That we've lost the Arbiter?"

Rolypoly hopped to her knee. "That we found the Portal Makers." A projection formed between them, shadowed but clear, of living creatures matching Rena's reconstruction of the larger corpses.

"Could have led with that." Killian kept glaring, unmollified. "Show me this Beth of yours." She scowled at the image, not wanting to be impressed.

Was, by the gear, the attitude. Not a person she'd take lightly. Looked through it to see a miserable ball of Rolypoly, all that remained of Flip.

Who'd had to leave the person alt would have died to protect.

Killian poked alts round belly. "Henry'll be fine," she said gruffly. "I'm the one who needs help, Flip. I've had an idea I want to run by you before we bring in Gis.

"With your help, maybe we can change the game."

***

"It's the only way." Killian shifted Rolypoly under the arm not holding her suit, eyeing the tube mouths. "Instant Kmet-Here realizes I've sent kmeth somewhere not-Earth, we're done. Kmet-There realizes I'm not Henry, we're done. You need to be Henry."

Rolypoly squirmed, every appendage stiff. "Giselle, please inform our pilot that even should the Portal take us to an alternative functional Control, under no circumstance will I imitate the Arbiter's voice without his express permission."

<Flip says—>

"I heard." Killian sighed. *Time to try reasonable.* "Step one, we get where we can do something—anything. Step two, you hail Henry on the radio, all right? We don't get him, we—we figure it out." Gentled her tone. "We have to be ready to do what he wants, don't we?"

Rolypoly went still. "You believe Henry will authorize us to merge the Portals with the Kmet still inside. To murder what may be the last of kmeth's species."

Doom one species to save theirs? Damn right she believed the almighty Arbiter would do it. He'd do whatever it took. *Then live with the guilt.*

"Doesn't matter what I believe, Flip. He has to have the option. We do. I've set the Portal com to monitor for radio signals originating from your last location."

"As am I."

Come on, Henry. Gripping Rolypoly by an appendage, Killian pushed alt into the tube mouth, reciting the words she'd used before. One chance. Had to get this right.

"Show me how to set the Portal self-destruct."

The destination might well determine all their fates.

". . . let's get to talking."

HE was different, under the dirt.

Different from the people she'd grown up with. Different from any she'd come to know. Not just the intriguing foreignness of his face and the rest of him, though if they'd the opportunity she'd welcome some exploration. Not the useless fancy clothes, though she valued the blanket and liked the sparkly pin.

It was his bearing. As if he carried a weight she couldn't imagine without minding it. Made her wary, that not minding. What had Flip said? *The most important official on New Earth.*

Hah. Not on her world. Not on Doublet. He'd no importance here at all or any way, except for being different.

And having a clue to her current and pressing problem.

She tugged with the hand he hadn't let go since Flip flew up through the hole above them. "Why do you call them Portal Makers?"

He looked down as if surprised she was there. Tears streaked the dirt on his face. Blood too, and neither were safe.

Beth rolled her eyes. "Hold still." She pulled out her pack and rummaged inside, nerves tight thinking of those watching, but she refused to be with someone leaking and this Henry didn't look to have supplies of his own. Brought out a cloth and a tube of sealer. "Can't let fluids touch the ground. Hear me?" Sharp, to get some focus back in those eyes.

Strange, seeing blue irises. They'd none on Doublet. Pretty.

Pretty or not, the first thing was cleaning him up. She dabbed with the cloth, putting some spit to it. Applied the sealer, watching his eyes widen at the chill of it.

"Thank you." He looked past her, searching.

"Don't rush," she cautioned, stowing her gear. "You sent the drone to spy on me?"

"The—yes. We meant no harm." A sudden, too-charming smile. "We crashed."

"We noticed," she said dryly. "All of us. What brought you, Earth's Most Important Official?"

The smile faded. "Henry, please. My name's Henry."

"Henry." *Different.* Used words like her great gran, who'd been wicked smart, so he might be. Or not. "We try talking to our hosts, best we know our reasons. Mine, for starters? Asking why they cut this world in two. You know?"

He shook his head. "Only that they've done it before, many times. And that this might be the only one left."

"What happened to the rest?"

Caution slid behind his eyes, good as an answer and chilling.

Beth gave a tiny nod to let him know she didn't want more, not here. "What are you after?"

"The same why," he responded, then tilted his head like a bird. "And to ask for their help."

Help from creatures living below ground he'd never met, on a planet he shouldn't have been able to find.

Help not for him, she judged, but for the world her great great greats had called home, and Beth found herself afraid for the first time in years.

Made herself a smile no more sincere than his. "Then let's get to talking."

"You're thinking again."

HAD *Flip seen it?* Henry'd often marveled at the level of insight and perception sentient constructs had into the Human mind. Had Flip summed up Beth Seeker in the few seconds they'd had and recognized her strength of character, a strength Henry, being Human, couldn't help but find reassuring?

Was that how his friend had been able to leave him?

He banished the thought. Flip had no other choice, nor did he.

He bowed to Beth. "I'll follow your lead."

A barely perceptible dip of her head. By Earth standards, her gestures and expressions were stilted, almost grudging. Henry thought otherwise. Whatever showed on her face came and went, subtle and quick. Gifts more than impositions. Cultural or personal? Didn't matter. He'd take more care with his own.

Given the times Beth Seeker had reached under her cloak to bring forth something, her shape owed itself to an unseen wealth of hidden packs and bags. Henry looked forward to having her show him, this being his new home. Assuming the Portal in orbit didn't spit out a planet-killing rock. *Killian wouldn't let it happen.*

Henry followed Beth from the splash of sunlight into the surrounding shadows, his eyes fighting to adjust. He'd expected a crowd—they'd heard multiple voices—but only one stood waiting.

"Hello," said Beth.

"Hello," came back in her voice.

She glanced at him. His turn. "Hello." He put a hand on his chest. "I'm Henry."

Instead of parroting the name, the creature aimed its snout at Beth. An eyebrow lifting, she put her hand to her chest. "I'm Beth." Gestured toward the creature.

Who shifted with a huff and pointed at the wall. No, not at the wall.

It couldn't be—

Was. "It's a tube system," Henry announced, unable to hide his excitement. "The same as in the Portals."

"Portal," the creature said in his voice, then dove at a tube mouth that expanded to swallow it whole.

"Beth, we have to go with it." When she didn't move, Henry grabbed for her hand. She whipped it out of reach, eyes wide and staring. "It's a transportation system. I've used one like it. Follow me."

He couldn't lose the Portal Maker. With a final pleading look, Henry turned and dove in.

***

The same—and not. The sensation of being sucked through an enormous gut was familiar, but the air was fresher. Warmer. As he spun and slid, Henry had the oddest sense this tube felt new, as if made this instant.

What did that imply about the Portal's system?

A final stomach-churning spin and Henry popped into the air. Air that held him, that floated him down and down through an immense bright and open space, with walls like frozen rivers, their swells densely coated in symbols. None he knew, but the shapes reminded him of those Killian had found.

Down and down. The air fresh and warm. Alive. He'd toured mines—felt the claustrophobia and pressure of being underground. Didn't here.

These weren't beings in hiding. This was their home.

Henry began to wonder if they'd been wrong to think the Portals the pinnacle of the aliens' technology. What if it was worlds like this, hollowed and shaped, their surface curated to serve a purpose—

Beth arrived beside him, her cloak drifting as she floated. "You see the like before?"

"New to me." And old. They sank through a region where the walls were pockmarked with tube mouths and tunnel openings, the latter varied in size and emitting puffs of spice-scented air. It was as if they breathed. Henry's hair ruffled. The blanket slipped from his shoulders.

Beth caught it with a neat, economical motion, as if she'd spent years floating in the air of an alien chimney. "This was made local." With surprise.

"I found it where we took shelter. It repels the biter vines." He touched his bitten ear.

She sniffed the fabric, withdrawing her nose quickly. "You meet who owned it? Was it our friends?"

She didn't know? "No. Someone different. Flip tested what they'd left behind." He folded back to stare at her. "How can you not have met them?"

A shrug. She managed to return the blanket, keeping hold of an end so they stayed face-to-face. "You've been in Away, Henry. Not a place anyone lingers. Bios'll be tickled, learning Doublet's got at least three thinkers."

"The ones who made the tent—they aren't on your side of the line?"

"Called the Split." A thumb indicated the wall behind her. "They made it. Humans in Home, jungle and your tent folks in Away. Nothing between."

"But you cross—"

"Seekers? We're trained. Follow the rules. Unless there's a Sweep—like the one you caused, Henry, flying where you're not welcome."

He abruptly realized what she was doing. This was a briefing, quick and to the point, while falling into the core of this world. "What rules?"

The corners of her lips deepened. "Best and safest? Carry what lives from each. Doesn't need to be much." She produced a twist of vine from somewhere under the cloak. Looked up at him and the tiny smile was gone. "Something I said gave you a notion."

What lives from each. "We know the Portal Makers traveled space, seeking other intelligences. They'd bring individuals on board." *The incomplete circles, a planet atop each.* "I think that's what these worlds were for—to let different species meet and learn about one another, each with a safe space of their own, challenged by a risk only surmountable by working together. It's a diplomatic mission. Perhaps a test as well, to see who deserves the Portal technology."

"Why us? Why our ship?"

"They had to have known—" He tried to see what was below. Couldn't make out more than a pale distance, not even the figure of their guide. *Had to be more down there.* "They have to know right now—about the Kmet. The Portals. New Earth. Beth, I think the Portal Makers have been watching us all along. They knew the only way to prevent the next disastrous Kmet attempt was to engage with what kmeth found, with Humans. They redirected you here. Waited for you to learn to communicate with them."

"Spent two hundred years and more lives trying," Beth responded. "Not seeing our friends' did the same, Henry." Merely an observation, not bitterness. "How're you doing at it? These Kmet you mention. Seems like you know them."

"We've communicated for years. I've worked with them. I'm not sure we've ever understood—Whoa." This as the air shuddered, a reminder they weren't standing on anything solid. "—one another," he finished.

"Setting up a meeting place. That I get. Not being part of it makes no sense. Unless." She squinted at him as they slowly spun around one another; he'd the feeling she saw something else. "Unless your Portal Makers are the ones who have the hardest time meeting others. Who need to train us to come most of the way to them. Bloody slow way to make friends, you ask me."

"They'd time," surmised Henry. "We've no idea how old the Portals might be, and to build worlds like this . . ." He let his voice trail away.

"Patient folks. Don't mind that. Wouldn't mind meeting others who walk on the ground, for a change. But this is where we are." Her turn to look down. "Who we're with. These Kmet. They villains?"

He could almost hear Rena. *No living thing is inherently evil.* "Short answer? No."

"Long one?"

"The Portal Makers made a mistake when they brought Kmet into space, blending what they believed to be Kmet technology with their own. What they did interfered with kmeth's lifecycle.

"The Kmet live apart until time to reproduce, when kmeth must find a cooperative partner. Having isolated spacefaring Kmet from one another, the Portal Makers for some reason stopped kmeth from attempting other partnerships. The Kmet fought back and destroyed them, then continued searching."

"And found you."

"Yes. During first contact, the Kmet presented us with a gift we, like the Portal Makers, took to be advanced technology. It was—and wasn't. It was—a form of Kmet. As chosen, willing partners, the Kmet expected we'd nurture and increase what we'd received in preparation. Instead, we altered it into what wasn't Kmet anymore. Into beings like Flip, my friend. When the Kmet land on New Earth, kmeth will know it's another failure. One I fear likely to cost New Earth as well."

"So how do you help them?"

"The Kmet?"

Her tiny smile. "That's what you've been saying, Henry." Beth tipped her head at the wall passing by. "Seems to me the Portal Makers owe these Kmet a ticket home."

Was it that simple? "The Kmet almost destroyed them."

"Makes it about even, then."

"The Kmet want to destroy this world." *A world where the Portal Makers had brought* Humans. *Why, if not for this?*

"Rather they didn't." Her eyebrow went up. "You're thinking again. What about?"

The Kmet hadn't gone home. Why? Because kmeth hadn't gone to space before.

Because only the Portal Makers knew where it was, and kmeth killed them.

"I am, Beth Seeker." Revolving around a blanket, dropping through air, Henry found himself laughing. "I'm thinking we should ask the Portal Makers for an address."

"Looks like we'll get the chance," she replied, looking down.

So he did, seeing a floor. They were almost on the ground. Henry began smiling.

Then saw it wasn't a floor at all, but flesh.

"I've this."

THE air deposited her gently on what looked—and smelled—to be meat, and Beth was glad she'd fresh soles on her boots. Seeing Henry sway, she took hold of his arm above the elbow. Waited for him to give a grim nod before she let go.

Place like this would be a shock to any. She wasn't altogether calm herself, not that she'd admit it.

The meat floor stretched in every direction, snaking out tunnels as well. Glistened red and pink, with yellow lumps here and there. Fat, most likely. A mesentery covered it, keeping the juicy in, and there'd be but one reason. "It's alive," she said, keeping it low and quiet.

"There was something like this in the Portal. Coating a room." His voice was nice and steady.

Helped, the words and tone. "That too?" She pointed to the nearest lump, not about to move.

Henry did, taking steps with a little bounce so when she followed, Beth flexed her knees to absorb it. Like walking on a mattress. Be a misery to run on.

No place to go if they did.

He'd stopped to look down at the lump. "There were ovals, like eggs or cocoons. Nothing like this."

"Looks like a big jelly drop." With something swimming around and around inside.

Something that suddenly stopped swimming and pressed hard to the inside, looking through at Henry. Big eyes in a big head. Little hands with three fingers, but she didn't think it young, not the way those eyes shifted to look at her.

A hand disappeared in the yellow jelly. Reappeared to push a little cylinder through and out with a little *pop*. Henry stooped to pick it up. Held it out to her, and Beth almost choked, taking the thing.

A pencil.

More *pops* made her look up and around, and sure enough, pencils were flying out of every jelly drop in sight. *How many of the stupid things had the Bios sent to the Split?*

"Cultural artifact," she explained, when Henry looked to be expecting an answer. Bringing her pack around, she dug till she found the latest. Set it on top of the jelly. Watched the pencil disappear inside and be clenched in a small hand.

That breakthrough in communication the Bios—Patrick—kept hoping for, and he'd be insufferably smug when she told him what did it. *Might not.*

"Beth Seeker," Beth told the jelly creature, finger touching her chest. Added very quietly, "You any proof what you are, now's the time."

His hand flattened over the sparkly pin, hiding it.

"Something else," she suggested.

"I've this." He pulled a metal object from a pocket. "Recognize it?" With a strange half-smile.

About to refute the idea she'd recognize anything coming from his flashy Earth vest, Beth took one look at it, closed her mouth, and stared at him. He accepted the scrutiny. *The most important official*— "Why didn't you say you're the Arbiter?"

"I started to."

She raised her hand, sighted along an accusing finger at him. "You don't plan to be in charge here. Won't be, not on Doublet."

"I agree."

Beth dropped her hand. "Good." Winced inwardly at the thought of an ancient Earth artifact sucked into an alien jelly drop, even if most old crap should be recycled. "Got anything—smaller?"

"I've this." He held out a curl of thick foil. "It's from your ship's probe. That's how we found you."

And didn't that open up a mess of new questions, starting with where had he been *and* why *not to mention* what—

Beth swallowed them all. "Anything not from here."

Away went the foil and badge. Out came a crumpled brown bag. "It was my doughnut," he told her, as if that were significant. "The bag's paper."

Made on his world, not hers. Had a sameness, being made from what grew, like her pencil, and Beth approved. At her nod, Henry put the bag on the cube.

Slurp. In it went.

Immediately after, the chamber darkened, the vast space above them filling with giant white rectangles with centers like boiling paint. Out of them poured *things*—ships, Beth guessed, despite none being the same shape or size, making the rectangles *Portals.*

And no doubt who was responsible. "What have you been up to, Arbiter Henry?"

"Deal."

THIS is not the Control we visited previously, Killian."

She stopped congratulating herself. "Does it have the second pedestal?"

An ocular spun about. "Every aspect appears identical. I will—" Alt sprouted feet.

The pilot jumped over Rolypoly to be first to that spot near the wall, hunting the oval in the floor with the texture of the dais behind her. "Found it." She slammed her palm down.

The oval rose under her hand. When it stopped rising, Killian sat back to watch the single pedestal grow from it to the height of those behind her. Saw the rippling of the surface and the resulting set of controls with a deep inner content. "We're in business, Flip."

"Once Henry communicates. We must prepare to capture his signal."

<From a *fucking* stone age portable radio?> snapped Gis, as grim as she ever was. <You bring the gear, Killie-Cat? 'Cause last I saw it, it was under your bed.>

So much for content. Had she forgotten to bring the workaround or had her subconscious wanted to keep Henry out of this?

Didn't matter, did it? They'd no way to—Killian's gaze fell on the suit she'd dropped at the tube mouth. "The helmet has receive/broadcast."

<NO! You need it intact!>

"Gis is fussing," Killian told Rolypoly. "Start taking it apart while we have a conversation."

Appendages budded, tips vibrating eagerly. "Yes, Killian."

She walked over to face the far wall. Whispered. "I don't need a suit. You're bringing me home, Gis, and 'bout time." She held up her hands to show their cracked skin and worn-down nails. "I'm past done with this body."

<Don't want you feeling vacuum. Don't want you to—die first.>

"Won't happen, we time this right, but I have to know you'll let me finish the job, Space Rat. There'll be no coming back if I don't."

<Five by five. I'm here for the duration. That's the deal.>

It hit, then. What her partner already knew. This was it. No more *talk to experts* and consultations. The *Lissett* and her tugs would be powering up. Everything in orbit would. People, from New Earth, from the worlds they'd found, would be taking shelter. Waiting to see what arrived in their sky. *To learn if they'd survived it.*

"Love you, Space Rat."

<Lima Charlie, Killie-Cat. Save the world, come on home. Easy-peasy.>

Making her laugh. Filling her heart.

Still smiling, Killian turned to find Rolypoly struggling to climb the dais with half of her helmet and went to help. "This going to work?" she asked.

"Yes. We must use the Portal's system to boost reception, but being tuned to the frequency of Beth's radio should provide a window to communicate before being detected. Assuming they are in the open."

"I'll take it." They worked together for a few minutes, Killian going back to the suit to scavenge some tape.

Rolypoly paused, an ocular aimed at her. "Henry wishes me to accept continuance."

"What's that?"

"As your consciousness will return to your real body, mine can be transferred to New Earth for re-installation."

Killian gave a carefully noncommittal grunt. *Best news she'd had in weeks.* Then caught something in alts tone. "You're not in favor?"

"I do not wish to continue if Henry cannot. Our plan does not include a means to bring him home."

"Sure it does." She patted the pedestal. "Omar and I'll transit a shuttle to pick him up."

<You won't get one.> Flat and definite. <Earth won't take the chance, not with the Kmet still demanding rocks to throw at your planet. Even if they would—the Arbiter left firm orders. I'm sorry, Killie-Cat.>

Fucking almighty Arbiter—Killian's hands became trembling fists, nails digging in, tension running up her arms to her head.

"I am greatly relieved to hear that."

She looked down at the little polymorph, and her fury drained away, leaving her numb. "Gis told me—we're not to save him, Flip. He doesn't want us to."

Henry'd known all along.

The realization didn't help. Did make sense of some things, and Killian drew a steadying breath. "We save the world and we both get home. They need to hear his story, Flip. No one can tell it like you. Deal?"

A tremble, then Rolypoly reached out with a grasping appendage. She took it solemnly in her larger hand. "Deal."

". . . here's how we'll do it."

WHAT have you been up to . . .

Their hosts had been watching. Henry recognized the ships. Freighters. Clumps of catchers. Glimpses of Saucer-Flip. There, the unmistakably distorted hull of the *Lissett*. Every one sent through a Kmet Portal on his authority, and he'd no doubt the jelly-held beings knew where. That they knew a great many things.

And were incredibly *different*. On taking in the bag he'd offered, sparks and ripples of light had sped away through the flesh floor from this jelly drop to the others. They stood on a life-form—a brain, perhaps—whose immensity had nothing in common with a Human mind, tidy in its bony skull, and Henry felt the *snick* of a final puzzle piece. Beth had the right idea. The Portal Makers didn't build these worlds for alien species to learn to communicate with one another.

They built them to teach themselves.

How long had it taken the Portal Makers to grasp that other intelligence came in small separate bodies living on the surface of worlds, not beneath? How long after that had they struggled to hear and be heard, coming up with this as their answer?

They'd been incapable of understanding the Kmet. Of defending themselves.

How did he even start—

"Those ships yours?" Beth, taking the initiative.

Henry shook off his nerves. "Yes. The ships you see carried the surviving descendants from the other sleeper ships back to New Earth. We—I had to evacuate them. The Kmet warned us of a threat kmeth called the Divider—"

The floor heaved, light flickering throughout.

Understood that *had they?* "We didn't understand. We—I thought we were saving lives. That the Duality with the Kmet was to benefit both our kinds, but I was wrong. I'm afraid it will harm us."

The floor settled. The Portals and ships disappeared overhead, replaced by a single beautiful globe.

He heard Beth inhale sharply, seeing what hung above them.

He named it. "New Earth. The Kmet plan to take the two Portals and—" *How to show it?* He made fists and spread them far apart, then brought them together, fingers intermingled. "We don't know what will happen."

Those big eyes, oval rather than round, watched his motion. The little hands copied it.

"Yes." Henry nodded. "Yes!"

"Henry, look."

New Earth. Two Portals shown beside it. Then one.

Then a brilliant flash made the Humans cower and cover their eyes.

***

Henry peered through teary eyes. The Portals were gone, and where New Earth had been was a shattered mass, pieces shooting outward, the motion slowed as if they were to absorb every horrific detail, and while the Arbiter knew he should cry out in despair and shout with fury, all he felt was certainty. "This can't happen. I won't let it."

"We warn them. Humans. Kmet." Beth pulled up her sleeve and unclasped the radio from her arm, only to dangle it from her fingertips. "No use down here." She eyed the jelly drop. "You got a better idea?"

"A warning's not enough." The eyes hadn't left Henry. He crouched to be closer. Had no choice but talk as if the Portal Makers could hear and understand him. *That and hope*. "The Kmet. Where is home?" He made a globe with his hands. Mimed pulling something from the surface.

A pattern of flashes across the floor. Symbols. "I don't understand." He looked up at Beth.

"Give them the foil," she suggested. "It has Doublet's coordinates. Maybe they'll figure out what we need."

He set it on the jelly. The creature pulled it inside, manipulating it with its hands. Shoved it in a mouth he hadn't seen before and swallowed it whole.

"Just a thought—"

He held up a hand. "Wait." The flashes were changing. Growing solid. Coming together. Forming Human notation!

Henry beamed at Beth. She raised a brow and shook her radio. "Now what?"

Back to the jelly. "I need to talk to the Kmet." *Nothing.*

"Hey!" Beth's hands were empty. A second jelly drop jiggled beside her, the being inside mouthing her radio. "They've heard me use it, up there. Don't know how that trans—"

Clear and loud. "Pilot Killian, requesting the Arbiter. Please respond. Pilot Killian—"

On repeat. He shouted over it, "Killian's on the Portal in orbit here." A relief, to hear her voice. None at all to have it echo uselessly in the Portal Makers' chamber and Henry looked to Beth.

Who shrugged, frowned, then bellowed, "SEEKER, OUT!"

The message stopped. She grinned. "Told you they've heard me."

They'd radio—maybe communication with Killian. *Didn't get him the Kmet.* "I'll try something else." He crouched near the first jelly drop. "I need to talk to the Portals."

Sparks. Trails of light, intricate this time. Dancing, and Henry grew so focused on the floor display, he started when Beth alerted him with a touch. "That them?" Her thumb aimed up.

He bent his head back to find himself gazing into paired dens.

Whose occupants saw him in return. Who reacted to what else kmeth saw with flailing and gnashing mouths and they'd have been deafened if the Portals transmitted sound as well.

Henry rose to his feet, by reflex introducing himself. "I am Arbiter Henry."

The Kmet stopped moving, clearly able to hear him. Polyps turned purple. *Happy to see him?*

He bowed to his, impossible to mistake kmeth's hugely enlarged body or, now, to ignore what it represented. *A species' hope.* Henry opened his mouth to take the grim path, to convince the Kmet to go home and merge, unwittingly destroying their world and kind instead of his.

Balked.

There had to be another option. One offering the individuals staring at him with such desperate trust a future. Together, as kmeth were meant to be.

A way to show the Portal Makers true communication depended not only on understanding and shared goals but on empathy, even for those unimaginably *alien.*

Beth's radio, afloat in jelly, caught his eye. *Killian.*

Henry began to smile.

Beth gave him a very searching look, then smiled herself. Nodded.

He stood on a cliff again, but this time he wasn't alone.

This time, he'd wings.

The Arbiter spoke. "I am here to offer you the supreme Duality, Kmet-Here with Kmet-There. Where you belong." With a dramatic gesture he indicated the coordinates kmeth had to have seen, if not yet understood. "I offer to each, this world.

"And here's how we'll do it."

"Goodbye."

"KILLIAN, I am receiving a signal on Beth's frequency but it isn't radio—it's—" Rolypoly stopped explaining. "It's Henry!"

She launched to her feet as the Arbiter's voice filled the room. "Killian. Flip, are you there?"

"Yes, Henry. It is very good to hear you again."

"And you. Killian, I've instructions for you and Omar."

Her hand gripped the pedestal. "Wait, Henry. We're in an alternate Control. The plan—the plan's to tell the Kmet there's Humans on Origin Earth. Have the simul-stop happen there. Just need your approval and we'll get it done."

"Denied. I've been able to negotiate another option. With a little help."

"From Beth?"

A laugh that wasn't Henry's.

A voice that was, warm and assured. "No time to explain. Stand by to transit your Portal to the Kmet home world. Here are the coordinates." He rattled off numbers.

The Kmet—numb, Killian keyed them in. Stared at them. "Where'd you get this, Henry?"

"New friends. I hope. Kmet-Here knows what to do when you get there. Go now, Killian. Trust me," with all the old charm.

<Man's lost it.>

Rolypoly waved frantically. "We cannot abandon you, Henry."

"I've got him." A new voice, confident and gruff.

"I'll be fine," the almighty Arbiter promised, as if everything was according to some fucking vast cosmic scheme only he could see, and Killian wanted to spit in his eye. "Transit now, please."

Except—

He'd done it, by that lilt in his voice.

Found hope and grabbed it, when there'd been none at all.

Who was she to doubt?

The pilot. “Roger that.” Grinning, Killian gave a curt nod. Rolypoly climbed up to the wall controls, ready to assist.

“Transit.”

***

She staggered. Swallowed bile. *Forgot the damn meds.* Ironic, under the circumstances . . .

<Killie-Cat. Wake it up. You’ve a call.>

And a different world on the screens. Killian reached for the sat controls before remembering she had none. And no satellites to spare, come to think of it, which was a shame.

The world below being amazing. Ringed. Bright red with jaunty polar caps. A storm like a great eye in the lower hemisphere—

“—Pilot Killian, this is Pilot Omar. *Balache Point* ready to transit through with her passengers.> And Omar sounded punch-drunk happy.

“Say again, Pilot Omar,” Killian demanded. “What passengers?”

“My Kmet, along with most of our PIPs. Left me a couple to do the work. Which we’re waiting to do—”

<That’d be a hint, Killie-Cat,> Gis informed her, with a vibrant urgency. <Henry’s set something big in motion. Job’s to keep it going.>

“Transiting *Balache Point.*” Feeling light-headed, Killian accepted Omar’s confirmation, then spoke to the ship. “Greetings to you and your passengers, Captain. Please clear the Portal and proceed to your destination.” *On the Kmet world?*

“Just a drop and come around, Pilot Killian.” A heartbeat later. “Drop complete. Ready to transit back on your mark.”

Damn fast. Her hands flew over the controls. She refused to let them shake. “Pilot Omar, *Balache Point* transiting now.”

“Got her. She’s clear. We’ll wait for you at the pub. Omar out.”

The pub?

BOOM! “Pilot Killian. I wish to thank you for your service.”

Kmet-Here? She looked around wildly, belatedly realizing kmeth hadn’t snuck up on her, that the voice came over com. *Left her fucking brain with Henry.* “Kmet-Here—” What was she supposed to say?

“Goodbye, Pilot Killian.”

The Portal shuddered around her. Killian checked the screen. A ball appeared, tumbling madly along in a halo of bright debris. She magnified.

It was the Kmet lifepod.

Intercepting it was a chubby tugboat that had to have been dropped by the freighter, meaning that along with a hold full of Kmet and PIPs there’d be an epitome or Alt-Intel pilot and crew. With serious skills, grabbers out to snatch the ball from its freefall.

Almost anti-climatic, watching the flares as the tug corrected trajectory and began its descent into atmosphere. Killian keyed the com. "Nice job, Tuggie."

"Thanks. Wouldn't miss seeing this place," came back the reply. "Take a peek, Portal."

All three screens came alive.

The surface was a maze of highs and lows, of mountains topped in white and canyons with water sparkling in their depths. No cities, no roads.

The tug descended.

Not all mountains were stone. Killian gasped as she realized some were *dens*. Fucking monstrous dens glittering in the sun or with ice and what sparkled in the canyons wasn't water, or wasn't just, but rivers of PIPs on the move. An entire world of what wasn't Human, doing what it should. She suddenly thought of Rena. "Flip, tell me you're recording."

"I am, Killian."

"Portal," from the tug. "Don't wait up. We're bailing for home once sure of a soft landing."

Epitomes. Continuance. New Earth's expendable marvels.

There'd been no other way to bring the Kmet home without costing lives and didn't that detail feel like Henry?

Wasn't done. She knew that, too. The Portals couldn't stay, here or at New Earth.

"Flip, get Henry back on. Gis, you ready?"

<About time. Love you, Killie-Cat,> husky and warm. <See you soon.>

"Lima Charlie, Space Rat."

Two enormous white rectangles appeared over the planet from which the Halcyon Sleeper Ship *Henderson* had launched her triumphant message of *we made it,* only to have her descendants perish and her surface scorched in answer.

In less than a flicker of an eye, they were one.

In less than that, there were none.

"Tell you what—"

THEIR hosts had let them watch. Beth being less interested in a distant world than in the man responsible for destroying it—though to be fair, he appeared to have settled other folks peacefully where they were supposed to be, and didn't seem overly distraught to be left where he wasn't.

Not that they should linger and push what wasn't much of a welcome in the first place. "Henry, time to go."

He gave a little shudder, the pin on his vest twinkling, then blinked. "Yes. Yes." Looked around, seeming at a loss.

Didn't blame him for that. She'd no real idea of their next move either, only that they'd better make one. She'd need a piss sooner than later—not on whatever they were on—a report to make—not that jelly drop had returned her radio.

And Henry, who looked to need everything.

Beth slid her fingers between his. "Those who brought us can get us Home, we ask the right way."

"'Home,'" he echoed.

Didn't mean the same to him, yet. Meant heartbreak and grief, and she understood both.

Knew something else about him, from this short time, and Beth carefully didn't smile. "We'll gear up and come back. Find your Tent Makers, Henry Seeker, and start a conversation."

Those blue eyes were damn pretty when they lit, like now. "That a job offer?"

"Tell you what." Beth waved at the jelly drop landscape. "Get us out of here, and the job's yours."

"Your face is wet."

THE sea was slate, the sky filled with after-storm cloud, and the air had a wicked chill, but no one suggested they go in. Not until Rena stopped standing with her back to them and her face to the ocean, hair whipping in the wind.

"Hate beaches," Giselle grumbled, restless the way she got when things turned sentimental, but she'd come.

They'd all come. Beside Gis was Shomchai, the linguist. Ousmane was there, with her family, and Sofia, apart from the rest, as always. Simmons stood near Rena, and there was someone called Ben who'd shown up without an invite, but everyone nodded as if that was fine.

Giselle's new best buddy, Harvey, stood behind but near. Not because alt had been close to Henry nor, as Killian had suspected, willing to carry Gis' spare legs. Flip was strapped to the other polymorph as a tube of still-unresolved matrix, as yet unable to communicate. Someone who should be here, whatever the shape.

Henry's grandfather Majick walked into the water a bit. He'd a bottle in his hand, corked and empty but for a note they'd all signed. Instead of tossing it in, he passed it to Rena, who pressed her lips to the glass before giving it to Simmons, who hugged it.

And that started everyone moving and getting closer.

Killian got the bottle last. Hefted it, made sure no one was near, and threw it as hard and far as she could.

"Your face is wet, Killie-Cat."

"We're standing by a fucking ocean," Killian countered, putting an arm around her beloved because she could.

Because the almighty Arbiter had made it possible and she'd no need of tears. Henry wasn't dead. Just gone further than anyone had, meaning she'd known what to write.

Gis and I got crew berths on the Cape Sable. We're going up, Henry. A lot of us are.

We're brave again, thanks to you.

Epilogue

MAJICK Nowak tipped back his hat with a finger, regarding the earnest faces before him. His fourteen housemates preferred to work at dawn or dusk and he'd gladly left them to their task. One they'd completed, apparently.

"We have finished planting what you left for us," Quo confirmed, her soft low voice as emphatic as he'd ever heard. Five held up empty seed bags.

The first weeks, she'd spoken for the rest. The first weeks, they'd slept in one room, unwilling to be apart. Henry's room and he'd seen it comforted them to be surrounded by the lad's things, not that they'd use them as he'd urged.

They'd arrived dressed in coveralls belted over gaunt bodies, peas in a pod.

Not so gaunt now, Majick observed with satisfaction. Having selected clothing from neighborly offerings, not so matched either. A few shyly gifted him with their names. Quo, the leader. Luo, who'd lost an eye and politely refused a trip to the hospital to repair it. Nicy and Ricy, the youngest two, not that any were young. The others weren't ready, weren't sure.

He respected that. Theirs had been the easier adjustment, coming from hardship, yet still a struggle. Others, well, they had it worse now than before or some felt so, being like the Second Spread and not planning on this life or place. It'd be the next generation able to call here, home, and mean it, despite the kindness and welcome.

Few spoke against the Arbiter and what he'd done, all having been given the facts of it; Majick wished Henry knew.

Which he couldn't, being gone to a different world, and that was that.

"Thank you, all," Majick said quietly, squinting at the vegetable garden. No rows. They'd raked the soil into raised oval beds, offset to break the flow of rainwater. Numerous dimples marked the surface of each bed. He nodded slowly. "Remarkable."

"We wish to plant more." Luo bent and stroked his fingertips through the loose soil between two ovals. "Here. Where the ground is still empty."

"To prevent unwanted growths and keep the water," one of the still unnamed offered, closing her mouth abruptly as if surprised by her own temerity.

"Squash." Majick spread his hands, palms down, slowly. "Should do the trick. We'll need to feed it."

The fourteen nodded in unison, eyes bright. "We buried the chickens' gracious gift before the planting," Ricy told him.

"Only the seasoned pile," Nicy added, for this was important.

Majick glanced over his shoulder. His chickens pecked and hunted under the porch. The birds the Tailings had brought from their world remained in the barn, quarantined until next month, promising a hardy bloodline his neighbors would share.

Henry's doing, those birds. These fine people. All the rest of them. The way New Earth was now and would be.

"There's pie," he announced, coughing the husk from his throat. "Let's get you out of the sun." On impulse, he held out his arms.

The fourteen moved close, touching each other as they so often did.

For the first time, enfolding him, too.